Ace Books by Steve Perry

The Matador Trilogy

THE MAN WHO NEVER MISSED
MATADORA
THE MACHIAVELLI INTERFACE

THE 97TH STEP

STEVE PERRY

THE 97th STEP

ACE BOOKS, NEW YORK

This book is an Ace
original edition, and
has never been previously
published.

THE 97TH STEP

An Ace Book/published by arrangement with
the author

PRINTING HISTORY
Ace edition/December 1989

ISBN: 0-441-58105-6

Ace Books are published by The Berkley Publishing Group,
200 Madison Avenue, New York, New York 10016.
The name "ACE" and the "A" logo are trademarks
belonging to Charter Communications, Inc.
PRINTED IN THE UNITED STATES OF AMERICA

10 9 8 7 6 5 4 3 2 1

For Dianne, yet again;
and for Uncle Jay the Fly, and Cheryl;
Aunt Judy; Mike and Connie;
and sometimes Kid Ford,
in Brusly, Louisiana, 1972.

ACKNOWLEDGMENTS

This book required more than I could possibly have managed on my own. Not so much the facts as the heart; not so much the words as the deeds. Here are some of the names of those who helped, with heart and deeds: Dianne, Dal, and Stephani Perry; Michael Reaves; Brynne Stephens; Meg Fremaux; Vincent Kohler; Mike Byers; and Ronald L. Johnston, wherever he is these days. And one more I've never gotten altogether straight—Greg Ellison. Thanks for the input, folks.

Part One
The Seeker Asleep

Since love and fear can hardly exist together, it is far safer to be feared than loved.

—MACHIAVELLI

ONE

THE SLAVER WAS about to buy trouble, though he didn't know it yet.

It was a spacers' pub, set in the run-down port section of Chiisai Tomadachi, the wheelworld that orbited the planet Tomadachi, in the Shin System. The stale air was thick with flickstick smoke and its smell of burned cashews, and the lighting was cycled to dim, giving enough illumination to see but hiding the shabbiness of the painted and scratched aluminum walls. The place thrummed with an undercurrent of tough talk and menace, but it was outlaw swagger, and not the force-backed brute power of the Confed—the upper castes would hardly demean themselves by coming to a scum hole like this for recreation.

At a small expanded-aluminum mesh table against one wall, two men sat drinking ale. Ashanti Khahil Stoll was a big man, pushing two meters, sheathed overall in a thick layer of fat. He wore a plain gray orthoskin coverall that struggled to contain his bulk, and he looked relatively harmless compared to many of the men and mues in the pub.

His companion, also dressed in plain gray orthoskins, was something else. He was called Ferret, and he had a cold look about him that seemed anything but harmless. In his early thirties, he was perhaps three decades younger than Stoll. Ferret viewed the scene through hard green eyes, and while his face and hands were pale, neither looked soft. In a room full of dangerous men, these two were harder than most, and those who knew the biz but didn't know Ferret and Stoll stayed away from their table. Mean dogs know how to avoid meaner ones.

Near the exit, the slaver stood glaring at his thrall.

Ferret stared at the slaver, then sipped at his ale. Slavery was illegal, of course, but none of the pub's patrons was apt to worry about law, save how best to break it and profit. Were the local cools or the Confed military to implode-bomb this place, the serious crime rate for five light-years would drop dramatically. Ferret was merely a thief and smuggler like his friend Stoll, but there were others who dealt in worse crimes. Some who made slavers look like saints, dark dancers on the fringe of the fringe.

The slaver's voice rose as he used it to cut at the thin boy who stood with his head bowed under the abuse.

Over the years, Ferret had learned to mind his own business, sometimes the hard way, and this was none of it.

None of his business at all, until the strap appeared.

The slaver, a bulky human mue with the look of a heavy-gravity childhood, produced the strap from a belt pouch. It looked like *hebi*-skin in the dim light, soft and pliable, but pebbled and rough like shark or ray hide, and it would be heavier than it appeared, were that the case. The big mue meant to work on his thrall with the strap, that much was obvious, and nobody in the pub was likely to stand in his way. Why should they? Might draw attention, and who knew what that might bring?

Ferret's grip tightened on the plastic ale stein; tendons raised on the back of his hand.

Stoll must have caught the movement, subtle as it was. He said, "Easy, lad. There's no profit to be made for the risk here."

Ferret looked at his friend, and nodded. He relaxed his hold on the stein. "You're right, Shanti." He struggled to calm the tension he felt. The slaver mue was big and obviously violent, and there was no way to tell how good he was. Ferret had learned not to judge from appearances. He'd studied close combat for more than a year with Elvin Dindabe, who'd been rated a Top Player in the Musashi Flex before he'd retired. Some men could kill you without raising their heartbeats, and they looked like nothing. It was not his business, no, he wasn't some kind of cosmic do-gooder, you got started on that and there was no end to it. But there was that strap—

The slaver's mistake was in timing. At that precise instant, he flicked the supple snakeskin strap up and snapped it at the cowering boy. The *pop*! of the leather as the tip slapped against the boy's shoulder reached Ferret then, and all logic, self-interest and thoughts of minding his own business fled before a fifteen-year-old memory. Against that power, all else was blown away like pollen in a windstorm. The past reached out and claimed him.

Ferret stood, muscles flexing into fighting mode.

Across the table, Stoll sighed. "Go," he said, sounding disgusted. "I'll watch your back."

Ferret spared him a glance as he started for the slaver. From his belt, Stoll pulled a focused-beam hand wand, quickly moving it under the table, out of sight.

"—Worthless dung-whelp!" the slaver said, using his wrist to clear the strap over his shoulder for another lash. "You'll learn to move when I say move!" One of the slaver's table-mates nodded. The slaver saw this, and he grinned. Now it was a show, something to entertain his friends. He wiggled the strap and his smile increased.

The slaver must have caught Ferret's motion peripherally, for he turned slightly to look at the approaching man. Softly, he said, "You got a problem, flo'man?"

Ferret managed to keep his anger at a low simmer. He glanced at the strap and said, "That. Better you shouldn't use it on the boy."

The slaver's smile never wavered. This must have happened to him before, somebody sticking his nose in where it didn't belong. Ferret knew that the mue wasn't afraid of what he saw: an average-sized pale human, no weapons visible, jamming his face into the slaver's business without call. The smell of burned cashews increased suddenly, now it seemed almost overwhelming, a hot stink that lay over Ferret like the sudden quiet the confrontation had brought to the pub. Men, women, humans and mues looked on, dogs watching to see if what went down was bark or bite.

The slaver said, "Oh? And what would you have me do with

it, Reverend?" He flicked his wrist, and sent a spiral wave down the length of the strap. A practiced move.

"Put it away."

"I got a better idea—how about I put it *here*!" With that, the slaver snapped the short whip up and over, and brought it down on Ferret's face.

Or, rather, where Ferret's face had just been. By the time the strap whistled over the mue's shoulder, Ferret was already moving. He V-stepped in, jerked his left hand back in a counterbalance, and drove his right fist into the mue's solar plexus, hard. The contact was solid, a rubbery give to the muscular flesh, and the force of it stung the plexus of nerve tissue enough so that the slaver's face froze in shock. He wouldn't be able to breathe for half a minute.

Ferret's mind fled. For the next six seconds, rage ruled him completely. He did not see his fists and boots as they battered the stunned slaver, who tried vainly to draw breath. Five, eight, twelve strikes—hands, elbows, knees, heels—fast, and harder than would have seemed possible from a man his size. The thuds seemed distant, the feel of flesh and bone under his blows unreal. The slaver tried to cover, but every time he moved his hands and arms to one spot, he revealed another. Ferret worked with trained instinct, choosing his targets for maximum damage. Three seconds. Four. Five—

The mue, big and strong as he was, took it for six seconds before he fell, only semiconscious. He would live, but he was damaged enough to need a few days in a medical kiosk. Had he not fallen, Ferret would have kept pounding until he exhausted himself, and that would have been no small time.

Still in the red haze, Ferret bent and snatched up the strap. Behind him, one of the slaver's party stood, reaching for a bottle to smash Ferret.

The strap seemed to coil around his hands on its own. When it was wrapped tightly, leaving only a few centimeters slack, Ferret screamed. The strap tightened and became like the string of some instrument. The leather cut into his flesh. There was a sharp *hum*! as the strap stretched, found its breaking point, and snapped, a dull, almost wet pop. It did not seem possible that a man could do such a thing—*hebi* was much too strong for that. Much too strong.

Behind him, the slaver's friend put the bottle back onto the table, and licked suddenly dry lips.

"A good idea, friend," Stoll said.

Ferret turned, to see the fat man standing nearby, pointing the hand wand loosely in the direction of the slaver's table.

Stoll said, "You done?"

Ferret nodded, feeling the adrenaline ebb. "Almost." He turned to the slave. "Go," he said. "You have a few minutes. Find a cool or hit the lanes, whatever your bent." Ferret glanced at the slaver on the dirty pub floor. "It's the only chance you're likely to get, you copy? If you stay with him, he'll probably kill you for this."

The boy nodded dumbly. He knew. He darted for the door. Ferret watched him go. Maybe he could figure a way off the wheelworld. The Confed kept a tight fist wrapped around galactic transportation, but there were ways, there were always ways, if you had stads, or if you knew the game. Or he could go to the cools. Locally, they were mostly honest, and if the slaver hadn't bought a pet in the shop, maybe the boy had a chance in that direction. It didn't matter so much to Ferret what the boy did, his concern had been less for the slave than for the way the slaver had gone after him. He had bought the boy a chance; what he did with it was his own worry.

Ferret had forgotten about the strap he still held. He glanced at it, now in two pieces. He tossed them at the slaver. The mue made no sign he saw or felt the broken strap when the sections of it hit him.

"We'll be going now," Stoll said. It came out as an announcement, as if he were a king informing his subjects of some major policy. He waved the wand in an offhand gesture. Some of the patrons flinched when the weapon's stubby barrel tracked past them. A blast from a hand wand was good for a very nasty headache when one awoke from the primary effect, itself not in the least pleasant.

"The drinks are okay, but stay away from the food in this place," Stoll said.

Ferret felt the urge to laugh, but he was still too wired to let it out. Stoll's comment could not have made any sense to anyone else, unless they happened to know the fat man was a gourmand of the most exotic rank, and what he said would have been of little use, unless they trusted his taste.

• • •

Outside the pub, Stoll tucked the wand out of sight. He glanced at Ferret, whose face was still flushed with the remains of his rage. "What was that all about?"

Ferret shook his head. "An old disk. Something that happened a long time ago."

Stoll nodded, but said nothing. The two men walked away from the pub in the general direction of the port where their ship, the *Don't Look Back*, was berthed.

Ferret said, "I'll tell you about it someday."

Stoll nodded again.

Fifteen years, Ferret thought, and it all came back as if it were only yesterday. So many light- and real-time years away, and still as clear as bottled air. Like the hand of God on his shoulder, he knew he would never be able to shake it, not if he lived to be a thousand. He did not want the memory, but it lay ever there. The strap had brought it back.

That goddamned strap.

TWO _____

HIS FATHER HAD been waiting with the strap when Mwili finally got home.

The boy's belly went hard and fluttery at the sight, and his bowels clenched against the remembered pain.

Not the strap. Not tonight. Not after today.

Full dark had fallen across the dusty land of Cibule, bringing with it the night's harder chill. Overhead, the Three Moons played their winter's variation on the High Right Triangle, shedding their pale blue, pink and silvery white lights over Cibule, itself a moon, and the largest of Kalk's four satellites. Kalk was below the horizon this week, and its cloudy surface was invisible from the cold farm lands of the Eastern Hemisphere. The rancid stink of the seed crop battled with the dry odor of dust, and the air's stench was worse for the combination. Mwili had grown up with these scents, and yet, every time he left and came back, it was as if he'd inhaled them for the first time. They never smelled any better.

At sixteen terran-standard years, Mwili Kalamu was work-strong and sturdy, if not tall, and within two centimeters and four kilos of his father's height and weight. He could fight back and maybe even win, but that would be a mistake—Mafuta had both God and the Law on his side, as he pointed out endlessly, and on Cibule, one was the same as the other. Mwili's bare hands were cold, and the warmth of his body leaked out through half a dozen worn spots on his heavy work gi and baggy cotton twill pants. Fortunately, his boots were of cast dotic plastic, and proof against the low temperatures. He had collected and sold tourist rock, saving every demistad for seven months to buy those boots, and had been whipped for the sins of Desire and Pride when he'd brought them home. Since they were custom-made, his mother had finally prevailed upon his father to allow him to wear them. They couldn't be returned, after all, and waste-not-want-not might not be a Holy Rule, but it was a farmer's creed, right enough.

Despite the evening's hard chill, Mwili wiped muddy sweat from his forehead with the back of one deeply tanned hand. Work-sweat, some, but mostly from fear. Unlike most of the settlers on this moon, his ancestors had been of terran Germanic/Nordic stock, and his natural skin color was pale, his eyes green, like his mother's. Eyes that now fed a message to his brain it plainly did not wish to accept, given the fight-or-flight reactions that brain was producing.

There, his father, dangling the strap.

When he was within two meters of the man, he stopped, and waited for Mafuta to speak. He was the elder, and such was his right.

"You are late," his father said. He twitched the broad leather strap. The end raised a small dust cloud where it touched the ground. The dust seemed to sparkle in the house's big exterior HT lamps. Mwili saw the curtain move at the kitchen window. That would be his mother, watching, even though she would have been ordered not to.

Mwili had a valid reason, for once, but he held his tongue. Valid or not, his father was just looking for a reason to swing the strap, and speaking before being given leave was as good an excuse as any. He merely nodded. True. He *was* late. He could not argue that.

His father said, "You were due back from the supply station four hours ago."

Again, Mwili nodded. His father would always state the obvious, as if he were certain God Himself hung on every word, checking it for accuracy.

"Jesu knows how much I have tried to do his work with you, boy." The man shook his head. "And no matter how much I pray, you are always found wanting. I cannot understand why He trials me this way. I have been a faithful servant, I observe the Holy Rules, and yet you task me at every turn.''

Mafuta spared the heavens a glance, as if expecting a direct reproach from God for his complaints. He was quick to qualify them. ''But it is not for man to understand the ways of God. A man must accept his lot and strive for perfection in spite of it. Such is the Rule.''

Mwili nodded tiredly. ''Such is the Rule,'' he echoed softly. Failure to speak that would gain him a glare and a fast slash from the whistling strap. It seemed like everything brought the strap. It was one of his earliest memories, and a constant part of his daily life. His mates all suffered under the heavy hands and belts of their parents, but that made bearing it no easier. None of them seemed to get it as often as he did.

''Why, son, are you tardy this night?''

Finally. ''The flitter broke down, Baba. The coil burned out again.''

His father stared at him, not speaking.

It was all Mwili could do to stand there at attention, waiting for his father to make his decision. The Jesu-damned flitter, old when Mwili was born, was a bucket of junk. He had re-wound the burned coil twice already, the last time only a week past. It had taken half a day on the shop lathe, and his father had begrudged him both the time and the copper for the wire. The flitter needed a new coil, it needed a new inducer, and it needed at least four new repellor grids. If prayer had any validity, then that must be what was holding the flitter together, because Mwili prayed every time he cranked the rattletrap up. Taking the ancient craft on the fly was an invitation to accident, and a broken head or worse. This time, fortunately, he'd only been half a meter up and cruising slowly when the engine shut off. He'd raised dust and a few bruises, but both he and the flitter had survived fairly undamaged otherwise.

''Where did this happen?'' his father finally said.

''At Three Rocks.''

Mafuta looked in that general direction, but Mwili knew that even if his father wore spookeyes and scopes, he'd never be able to see the flitter. It was twenty-six kilometers to the rocks. Twenty-six dusty kilometers and four weary hours on foot, by way of the only road leading to their farm. A more boring stretch of land could hardly be devised; God must have put his mind to it, and only He knew why.

"Did you leave the road? Strain the engine?"

"No, Baba. I went straight to the post and came straight home."

"Why did you not return to the post and call me?"

Mwili sighed. It was nearly twenty klicks from the rocks to the supply post. He would have saved all of an hour on the call, and *still* had to walk home—the supply warden didn't give anything away for free, and Mafuta Kalamu would never have agreed to pay for his son to *ride* home, not in ten times ten thousand years. That would have been sixty-five kilometers he would have had to walk, and that made no sense at all. But he wouldn't say that to his father. Instead, he said, "I thought it would be better to come home. The distance is nearly the same, and I could get started quicker on the repairs."

"You brought the coil?"

Mwili reached into his gi and pulled the coil out. It was the size of a drink can, wrapped in a greasy rag. "Yes, sir."

Grudgingly, Mafuta said, "That was good." But the faint praise vanished as he suddenly came to the point that Mwili had feared the most: "But—what of the supplies? You just *left* them there?"

Mwili took a deep breath and allowed it to escape quietly. Why, no, father, he thought, I packed all three hundred kilos of food, seedlings, chemicals and electronics into my back pocket and carried them home! Of course I left them there!

Aloud, the boy said, "I hid them."

"You hid them? Where?"

"Behind the center of the Three Rocks. Under a tarp, covered with dirt. They won't be visible unless you are looking for them—"

"And you think anybody who sees an abandoned flitter won't look around, fool?"

"Baba, what else was I to do?" Careful! That was dangerously close to the sin of Impertinence.

But the smaller sin was lost in the larger for his father. "Three months' worth of supplies! The seedlings will likely freeze! And there are dust dogs who prowl the rocks!"

There was nothing more Mwili could say. The last dust dog seen within a hundred klicks had been spotted more than five years past, and moving away, at that. The tarp and dirt would probably protect the seedlings. And the chances of anybody passing along that stretch of road for the next week were slimmer than Mwili's pet ferret.

The hard-faced man raised the strap. "You should have stayed with the supplies, to protect them against thieves or animals! I would have come looking for you, in a day or two. But no, you wanted the comfort of a soft bed, the warmth of a fire, over our precious supplies! Kneel!"

Mwili dropped to his knees, landing harder for his exhaustion. He leaned forward, bending at the waist, hunching his back. He heard the whistle of the thick leather just before he felt the slap and burn below his shoulders. He did not cry out, for he had long since learned that only made his father more angry at him for being weak.

"Pray!" His father's voice was a roar. "Pray for your sins, boy!"

Mwili prayed, but could his father hear his thoughts, he would have swung the strap harder. He prayed for a lightning bolt to strike his father. For the earth to open and swallow him, for—

The second stroke landed, overlapping the first only slightly. His father was an expert with the strap, God knew he had enough practice! The burn spread.

How can you allow this, God? How can the God of the Biblioscript, who is supposedly just and merciful, allow me to be whipped for something that wasn't my fault? Where is the Justice in that? The Mercy of Heavenly Love?

The third lash smacked into him, farther down his back. That one hurt more, there was a bruise there from the flitter's rough landing. The whippings themselves left no permanent marks—his father had made the strap wide enough to spread the pain without cutting the skin—but they did hurt. Although lately, it was not so much the pain as the unfairness of it. He would have replaced the damned coil, had it been up to him! But no—!

"Beg the Lord's forgiveness, son! Change your sinning ways!"

Crouched under the flailing strap in the cold light of the exterior lamps, Mwili prayed. Take him now, God. Take him and take this whole fucking planet!

His only answer was the whistling of the strap, and the dust it raised from his jacket when it landed.

His mother sat on the worn form-chair, pretending to read from the Holy Script when Mwili walked past her toward his room. The worn and old electronic reader on her lap hummed constantly, and squeaked each time she pushed the cheap mechanical button to advance the text on the small screen. She spared him a quick glance when he passed, then stared back down at the dim and flickery gray screen of the reader, lest her husband see her offering any kind of sympathy to her son. As an adult, she was not subject to the strap, but an hour's lecture on one Rule or another was not uncommon. Himself, Mwili preferred the strap to the preaching.

The boy did not speak. Later, when Mafuta was asleep, she might visit the fresher, and risk a side trip to his room, for a quick word or affectionate touch with her son. Only then.

In his room, Mwili knew he was too tired to wait for his mother's possible visit. The trip to town, loading the supplies, then unloading and walking from Three Rocks had been enough to exhaust him. Fifteen from the strap had finished the job completely. He was bone-weary, and in his misery, could only think of one thing: he had to get out. Somehow, he had to get away from his father, from Cibule, from the Svare System altogether. There were twenty-two other explored star systems out there, somewhere, fifty-odd inhabited worlds, and scores of wheelworlds. The Confed took a heavy tax from every planet to push Bender ships out to explore yet more systems and worlds. Among all that, there had to be places better than here. There had to be.

It had been on his mind for months now, hazy and ill-defined. His studies on the holoproj net had shown him that life was different elsewhere. He was a good student, he enjoyed the learning time, time he did not have to face his father and the ever-present farm work. There were other ways to live, and his resolve to find them crystalized as he lay on the narrow cot, face down to avoid pressure on his sore back.

That it was impossible meant little to him. He was too young to ship with the Confed military yet, though they would draft him in a few years; nobody would hire a boy his age for any kind of legitimate work offworld; and he had all of nineteen

stads to his name. That was less than half as much needed just
to buy an *application* for a ticket to anywhere offplanet. Yet,
there had to be a way. He *had* to find it. Otherwise, his future
was grim. Another four years of beatings, then he would be a
"man." Until then, he'd still be in thrall to his father, and he'd
continue to work the dusty shamba fields, trying to keep the
stubby *wembe* plants alive through the quakes, dry spells and
the cold. Then, he could look forward to his impress into the
military.

Four years. Until then, his only other choice was to run off.
Onplanet, he might lie about his age, and maybe get a job as
a contract laborer on somebody else's farm. Or as a flunky to
some merchant in Choo Mji—the worn, plastic-prefab Toilet
Town. Until Mafuta came to fetch him back, which would happen in short order. And every minute of every day, God would
ride on his shoulder, unseen but weighing upon him like an
overcoat of lead. How much interest God took in Cibule might
be open to argument on another world, but not here; the inhabitants were certain of their place in God's hierarchy—at the
top.

Mwili managed to drag himself up from the canvas cot. He
took the two steps necessary to cross the width of his room to
where his ferret prowled the inside of his own cage. The boy
slid the mesh door up and put his hand inside. Nyota scurried
up the boy's wrist and arm, to perch on his shoulder. He chittered excitedly, knowing the night's hunt was about to begin.

Mwili managed a small smile. He scratched the spot at the
base of the creature's shoulders near the recall caster. The smell
of the animal's musk was high. The boy caught the thin creature gently in his hand and brought him around so that he could
stare into Nyota's face.

"I think I understand how you must feel," Mwili said.

With his other hand, the boy pinched the pressure release
on the recall caster. The button-sized unit popped away from
the ferret's back. Were he to release the little hunter now, there
would be no way to make him return after his night of mous-
ing. Mwili stared at the little electronic caller for a moment,
before walking to the window. He touched a control, and the
triple-paned thermoplast grated as it slid over its warped track.
Cold air rushed into the small room and enveloped both boy
and ferret in its frigid arms.

"Go," he said gently. "Go and make a meal of some fat shamba rodent stealing the grain. Do it whenever you wish from now on. Be free." He put the ferret upon the sill, and it was but a heartbeat before the creature scurried down the outer wall and ran into the darkness. It did not look back.

Before he closed the window, Mwili held the caster like a marble and thumbed it into the darkness after the ferret. There would be no call to return at the next dawn, nor any dawn thereafter. Mwili had always treated the ferret well, loving it as much as he knew how to love anything. Or anybody. But he had proscribed its life by keeping it caged, just as his own life was limited. It would not do to leave his friend imprisoned while he escaped. Not after he'd finally realized the kinship.

He stared into the darkness, and for the first time in years, he felt tears form and begin to stream down his face. He closed the window before they could freeze on his cheeks. Farewell, little brother. Farewell.

It was midmorning before he had the coil rewound yet again. He trudged to the south field, where his father worked the dying soil with the old tractor. The vehicle was even older than the flitter, hardly more than a repellor plate with antique ultrasonic diggers and cutters. Amidst the cloud of dust, his father looked like a statue riding the tractor, both man and machine covered with the powdery earth, a red-brown hue, a single biomechanical unit.

He waited while his father finished the row, then brought the tractor to idle near where Mwili stood.

"Yes?"

"I have finished the coil, Baba."

"Took you long enough."

"I'll go to repair the flitter now."

"Be quick about it."

Mwili hesitated. There was no chance, but he might as well ask. "Could I take the tractor? It would save three hours—"

"No. I will not slack my work so that you may ride in comfort! Meditate upon your sins as you walk. Gain humility from prayer. Such is the Rule."

The strap was inside, out of his father's reach, and even if it had not been, Mwili could not have brought himself to echo the religious refrain. He was leaving, forever, and whatever he said now would be his last words to his father, whether the man knew it or not. Instead, he said, "Good-bye, Baba." With that, he turned and started walking away. He would miss his mother, but it would not come as a surprise to her. She knew. She had known for some time, he was sure of that. At night, or when his father was away, he heard it in her voice. He might have offered to take her with him but it was her choice to remain. She could have left years ago, and had not. She had her own destiny, and she had made her decision, based on things she would not explain to her son. Of his leaving, she knew, and he knew that she knew. There was no need to speak of it. Faced with her tears, he was not certain of his resolve, so he thought to avoid them altogether.

Behind him, his father might have considered calling him back, might have thought to chastise him, but he did not. Instead, the only sound was the whine as the tractor's old repellors cycled back online, and blew clouds of dust into the cold morning sky. Mwili marched away, passing the house where he'd lived his entire life. His eyes were dry, and he felt less regret leaving his home than he had for the loss of his ferret.

He did not look back, and thus did not see the tiny form of that ferret, scratching at the window of Mwili's room, patiently waiting to be admitted back into his cage.

THREE _____

"AUTHORIZATION CODE."

The Confed operator's voice was cold, and it was not a question but an order. Give the improper response, and you'd be in shit to the eyebrows, and fast. Do something really stupid, like try to manually bail out, and the wheelworld's antiship guns would fry you faster than you could blink. Coming and going was at the Confed's order, period.

Ferret punched a button, and his com computer fed a binary number series into the outgoing data. The numbers were legit, but the ship had no right to them. Such counterfeits were expensive, but part of the biz, figured in on every trip. High Confederation officials couldn't be bought easily, but the lower echelons supplemented their pay with graft; one of the many side benefits of being one of the Chosen.

There came a wait as the controller's computer digested and checked out Ferret's code.

"*Don't Look*, you are cleared for sling out."

"Copy, Chiisai Control," Ferret said into the com. "I am locked into sling."

"Stand by," the tech said. "Six seconds to commence. Five . . . four . . ."

Ferret glanced at Stoll, who looked to be asleep in his form chair. This was all automatic; Control would put them into an orbit that would avoid the lumbering boxcars dropping into the planet's gravity well; after that, he would fire up the ship and take over until they reached Bender distance.

"—two . . . one . . . and . . . launch," the tech said.

Ferret felt the soft hand of sling acceleration press him against the form chair as Chiisai Tomadachi spat the *Don't Look Back* into the vacuum outside its metal walls.

His viewscreens lit, and the photomutable gel cameras fore and aft showed deep ahead and the wheelworld behind as the ship left the city's embrace. He was glad to be away. There had been violence in his life—a smuggler and thief had to count that as part of the business, like it or not—but the incident in the bar had dismayed him. Not so much for what he had done, but for his loss of control. The slaver was scum, and he would recover from his injuries; likely that his stock-in-trade—people—fared far worse most of the time. No, if there was any kind of karmic justice, the slaver deserved worse than he had been dealt. But to slip the restraints of reason like that had shaken Ferret a great deal. Control of his mind was paramount; elsewise, there was the chance that he might slip into a state of fanaticism. Just like—

Just like his father.

Before he did that, he would rather be dead.

"Thinking about the slaver?"

Ferret continued to look at the holoprojic screens.

A Confed cutter hung against the blackness, waiting to strike should the unthinkable happen and somebody who wasn't supposed to leave or arrive tried to do so. The cutter seemed to flash by as the *Don't Look* flicked past.

"Yes. I was thinking about the slaver."

"I've never seen you like that," Stoll said. "Not in ten years."

Ferret turned his chair slightly, to look at the fat man. "I've never told you about where I came from. What I was before we met."

Stoll laughed softly. "I remember our first meeting. I had to laugh. You, a skinny kid, trying to steal my flitter. I thought surely you were brain-damaged."

Ferret smiled at the memory. "Yeah. I was pretty cocky by then. I'd been in the lanes for five years, and surviving pretty well. I thought the galaxy was my oyster."

"You were lucky."

Ferret nodded. "Very. I could have died a hundred ways. There must be—" He stopped.

"—gods that watch out for fools," Stoll finished. "But you don't like to talk about gods."

"We've never discussed religion," Ferret said. His voice was stiff.

"That's the point, lad. We've been running together for ten years, and we never have talked about such things. Even a fairly stupid fat man such as myself notices such omissions."

Ferret sighed. "I tried to put all that behind me. Where I came from, what I was raised. I try not to think about it."

"Haven't been too successful at it, have you?"

Ferret glanced back at the screens. No help there. Everything was fine on automatic. "Sometimes," he said finally. "But the slaver and his whip brought back an old memory."

Stoll didn't speak. He was very good that way, never pressing. He'd never asked once, not in ten years, about Ferret's past. Ferret had been Stoll's apprentice at first, then his partner, and each of them had kept their own secrets without any prying from the other. They were friends, but not snoopy ones.

Ferret let the silence stretch. He took a deep breath. "I was raised on Cibule," he said. "Son of a dirt-poor farm couple steeped in the God of the Holy Script. It wasn't a pleasant childhood." He glanced over at Stoll, who looked attentive, but not to the point of pulling more than Ferret was willing to give.

Fifteen years, Ferret thought. I guess it can't hurt me anymore. Not with this man who has saved my ass more than once.

"I took it for as long as I could," he said. "Then one day, I decided to leave. . . ."

FOUR

THE MOST VALUABLE things he owned were his boots, and those he wore; otherwise, Mwili took nothing but the money he'd saved and the small backpack that contained his lunch and the coil. Once he got the flitter running, he'd borrow it to get to Toilet Town. The supplies would keep in their hiding place; his father could find them easily enough, and he could tow the flitter behind the tractor when he finally got around to locating it. It would make work for him, but Mwili did not worry too much about that. His father seemed to think that work and God were the only two things in the universe, anyway.

The sun warmed the land some, though it was still cold. He had his gloves today, that helped, and he wore the better of his two gi jackets. His mother had packed him a lunch and water bottle, and he would worry about more food when next he was hungry.

As he walked the lonely road, Mwili felt a mixture of emotions. A small, nagging fear rode him, as if he halfway expected God to hurl some kind of fiery lance at him for daring to go against the Holy Rules. Honor and Obey Thy Father topped the list. There were civil penalties to go with the holier ones. Runaways were dealt harsh justice if caught, and on Cibule, they almost always were caught. That was why he had to get offworld.

On the other hand, there was an elation bubbling from him

21

that the fear could not dampen altogether. He had made a choice. Rather than just plodding through his miserable existence, he had taken a step. It might cost him more grief than anything he'd ever done, but he was willing to risk it. There was a time to stand and wait, and a time to move, and he could no longer bear inaction.

As he walked, the dust powdering up behind him in small cloudy showers, he spun fantasies about what might happen to him. He could stow away on a freighter, get to one of the densely populated planets, and find some kind of work. He was strong, not too stupid, and fairly good with mechanical things. He might get a job in a flitter repair shop. Maybe even become a mechanic and buy his own shop someday. Be a man of substance, find a woman, have a real family, with kids he didn't beat. Not play out his days a dirt raker on God's Rectum.

At that thought, Mwili glanced skyward, again almost expecting a heavenly blast. When Kimo Mchanga had first called Cibule God's Rectum, Mwili had smothered a laugh. None of the other boys listening to Kimo's bragging about how he was going to school offworld had dared to laugh either.

God must be otherwise occupied, for there was no rumble of lordly anger nor blazing line of high-energy flame arcing down to consume him for daring to think such blasphemy.

He began to feel better. If God had meant to stop him, surely he would have cut him down when first the thought had come to him? God, according to his father, seldom allowed a man too much rope, even if he intended to hang himself with it.

Mwili was not sure about God, in a lot of ways.

Halfway to the flitter, Mwili took a break. He sat on a patch of skillweed a few meters from the road, and broke out his lunch. His mother had packed vegetable soup in a self-heater, brown bread, and soycheese, as well as the chilled flask of deepwell water. The food tasted particularly good, and he ate it slowly, savoring the blend of flavors. The skillweed crackled as he shifted his position. Not much of a seat, but it kept the ground chill from his backside.

He thought about his mother as he ate. She would miss him, he felt. His going would leave only the two of them. There had been an older sister, Jana, but Mwili had never known her. She had died at fifteen, before he was born. Something always brought a great sadness to his mother's eyes when she spoke of his sister. There was a hint of some kind of disgrace attached to Jana, but he had never found out what. Once more, he wondered why his mother stayed. It must be out of a sense of duty, he thought. There was no way anybody could love his father. No way.

He finished the meal, repacked the water flask, and started his walking again. He had enough to worry about without calling up memories.

He made better time today than the day before. He reached the flitter in just over three and a half hours. It sat where he had left it, no sign that anybody else had passed by since the breakdown. Just to be sure, he checked the hidden supplies. They also were undisturbed.

For a moment, he was tempted to take some of them. The replacement circuit boards for the watering computer were fairly expensive—he could get maybe a hundred stads for them if he sold them. And there was food, too.

No. He wanted to leave clean. Whatever else his father might do, he wouldn't be able to have him hauled back for stealing. Even Baba could not begrudge him his clothes, and if he took nothing else, he was only a runaway, not a thief. He only planned to borrow the flitter for a little while.

He put the rewound coil into place. The harmonics had to be retuned, and that took nearly an hour. When he was done, he locked the tools back into the chest and fired up the flitter. It ran. No better than before, but it would do to get him to Toilet Town. After that, well, it was his father's problem.

He climbed into the flitter, engaged the lift, and left Three Rocks behind, choking in the ubiquitous dust.

Choo Mji was fairly quiet when Mwili arrived in the late afternoon. He cruised past the spaceport, noting that there were six or eight freighters and the regular passenger liner to Kalk berthed. Good.

He parked the flitter near the police station, and tried to look casual as he strolled away from the small craft. When Baba reported it, it would be easy enough to find. Despite his pose, he walked faster than normal, certain that if anybody looked closely at him, they would see his guilt. Fear rode high in him, making him sweat nervously. If they caught him now, it wouldn't be too bad—he was just sightseeing, stealing a few hours from work. Later, it wouldn't be so easy to wiggle out of, did they snag him.

While it seemed warmer, the sky had grown overcast. It smelled to Mwili like snow coming. He hadn't checked the weathercast, but they were due for a good storm. He walked toward the port ticket office, unsure of exactly what he was going to do.

The first thing he needed was to find out what ships were leaving soon. It didn't much matter where they were going, just so they left before Baba started missing him. He figured he had until dark, at least. Add another hour to that for his father to take the tractor and get to where the flitter was supposed to be, then an hour from there to town. Probably Baba would nose around on his own, looking for him and the flitter, so add another hour or even two before he got angry enough to ask the cools for help. That would put it at about 2100.

Inside the port, Mwili passed the Confed Travel Officer's cube. The Confed didn't think enough of Cibule to have more than a token contingent of administrators onworld, plus a few quads of soldiers. Everybody got a chance to be a trooper, but they took their orders ultimately from civilians, the toplevel aristocracy that considered everybody beneath them less than dog dung. The Travel Officer was a rich man, his wealth mostly accumulated bribes from people who wanted offworld and who couldn't wait six months or more for official permission. He could have pretty much anything he wanted, the TO could, and the rumor was that if you were an attractive woman and didn't have the money to bribe him, something could be worked out.

At the schedule window, Mwili punched his request into the computer. The holoproj lit up with the departures from the port. He smiled. The passenger ship *Drake* left at 1850; there were three freighters scheduled to depart today, too. The first, the *Achilles*, would take off in an hour or so; the others both left after 2100: the *Ragnar* at 2250, the *Willamette* at 2400.

Mwili stepped away from the window, considering his options. According to the computer, the *Achilles* was bound for Krishna, in the Tau System, with a stop at Kalk. He didn't know much about Krishna, except it was a moon orbiting the gas giant planet of Shiva.

The *Drake* also went to Kalk, so he could connect with another ship there from either the *Achilles* or the *Drake*.

The other ships had to be kept in reserve for emergencies only, since it was likely that Baba and the police would be looking for him by then. They might think to check the ships, and he would be caught.

So, which was it to be?

Mwili walked to the chain-link fence surrounding the port, to look at the ships. The passenger ship was a C-class star leaper, would hold two hundred people and their baggage, as well as cargo. Plenty of room to hide there.

The *Achilles*, on the other hand, was a run-down-looking bricklike cargo hauler, and probably had the hold full of *wembe* or potato liquor, Cibule's two main exports. No telling what cargo the ship had dropped off. It was smaller than the passenger ship, probably harder to find a place to hide in, and it was also leaving in about an hour.

The *Drake*, he decided. By the time Baba started searching in earnest, Mwili would be on his way to Kalk. He could hang out there for as long as he needed; Kalk was a lot more settled than Cibule, even if it wasn't all that much larger. The industry on Kalk was mostly underground mining of heavy metals, but there were some fairly large cities. Easy enough for one off-worlder to blend into the background, Mwili figured. So, the *Drake* it was.

Getting on board would be the trick. He had been thinking about it in a theoretical way for six months. Several times, while in town on an errand for his father, he had come to watch the cargo being onloaded. There was a special section for animals, just aft and below the passenger compartment. Caged livestock was conveyored in through a hatch to a robot stacker that worked inside. The livestock cartons came in three sizes, small, medium and large, corresponding roughly to cat, large dog and cattle-sized beasts. Mwili doubted that the stacker robot checked the animals inside closely, if at all. So, all he had to do was find a dog or nguruwe cage large enough and use that. There were several already stacked for loading that might do. He could put the animal into a carton with another one, or maybe tie it somewhere out of sight, and take over the empty carton for himself.

It might be tricky, but he was sure he could pull it off. Getting over the fence would be easy enough. There was a spot behind the repair hangar where nobody would see him scale the wire, and once inside, he'd move fast and carefully. He was sure he could do it.

But not yet. There might be a human worker checking the animals. They did that sometimes, an hour or so before loading. After that, he'd be safe enough.

So. He had a few hours to kill before he made his move.

Mwili turned away from the fence. He didn't want anybody to notice him, maybe remember his face when his father came looking. He was hungry, and there were food vending machines lining the back wall of the freight terminal entrance across the street, under the overhang. He'd spend a couple of his standards to buy some supplies. The jump to Kalk took about thirty hours, being all inner system time on pusher rockets. Eat something now, he thought, and save some for later.

He stowed the rest of the food in his pack, after downing a bulb of fruit juice and a fried soy cutlet. He was waiting for traffic before crossing the street, heading back toward the fence, when he glanced toward the crossroad by the flitter charge station—

And saw his father, driving the ancient tractor, towing the flitter!

Fear froze Mwili. He couldn't move. He couldn't breathe. He couldn't *think*—

Fortunately, Mafuta Kalamu was looking the other way, distracted by the yelling of a hovertrucker behind him, angry at the tractor's slow speed.

Mwili managed to stumble backward until his shoulders were against the rough stucco wall between two of the vending machines. His father! How could it be? Mwili hadn't been gone five hours yet—his father wouldn't have stopped work so soon! He *couldn't* be here!

The tractor went past, some loose attachment clattering on the systone road underneath the old machine. The trucker behind continued yelling, but Mafuta Kalamu pointedly did not look back. Neither did he look to the sides, and so passed his son unknowingly.

Inside Mwili's brain, the voice of catastrophe babbled, a

high, keening whine: *There he is, there he is! You're dead, you're dead—!*

"No!" Mwili yelled. The sound of his own voice startled him into motion. Both his father and the hovertrucker were past, and a short line of flitters and delivery vans followed, blocked by the slow lead vehicle.

As soon as there was a break in the traffic, Mwili darted across the road, toward the port's fence.

He knows! came the voice inside his mind. *He knows you've run away, he's coming to catch you!*

"He can't know!" Mwili said aloud, answering his internal voice.

God must have told him. Baba is tight with God, and you know it's true that God watches you, every day, every second, and he's put your father onto you—

Mwili shook his head as he reached the fence. No, it couldn't be. He wouldn't believe it.

But—how else, Mwili? You know he's come for you. You saw his face. He is angry. Angry at you, boy. The strap will do a mighty dance tonight, Mwili. You'll be so sore you won't be able to bend over for a month! The strap. The strap. The strap . . .

The boy ran, until he reached the spot behind the hangar where he was invisible from both the road and interior of the port. The links of the fence sagged here, from the boots of others who had noticed the protected spot to climb. The fence was bent at the top, four meters up, the supporting bar bowed into a gentle curve.

He started the ascent. As the rough links bit into his fingers, he wondered: what was he going to do now? The passenger ship didn't leave for more than two hours. By then, Baba would have searched the town well enough to know that Mwili must either be gone or still looking for a ride. He would have the police check all transports, local or extee! The cools would only be too happy to help find a runaway for such a fine, upstanding man as Mafuta Kalamu. They'd drag Mwili out of the dog's cage and turn him over to his grim-faced father. And his father would use the strap right then and there, bringing smiles from the cools. Spare the strap, spoil the boy, they all knew it was gospel, the Lord God's Own Truth. And once he got him home, Baba would use the strap again, until his arm was too tired to flail away anymore. And Mwili's life would be hell from now on. His father would never let him forget it. Never.

He cleared the top of the fence, swinging both legs over. He was in such a panic, he almost lost his grip, but managed to hold on until his right boot snagged a bent link. That wouldn't help, to fall and maybe break an arm or leg, and have to lie there waiting for the cools to catch him.

Halfway down the fence, he pushed away and dropped the last meter and a half, landing hard on the packed earth. He stayed in a crouch for a few seconds, looking for some signs of discovery. He saw nobody. He stood.

Why are you running, Mwili? There's no place to go. They'll find you long before the ship leaves. . . .

Wait, wait—wait! The freighter, the *Achilles*!

Mwili shoved the sleeve of his gi back and looked at the cheap black plastic chronograph his mother had given him for his last birthday. What time was it—?

It was 1520. He had eight minutes before the freighter was scheduled to leave. Maybe he could still make it. Maybe it was running late, they did that sometimes, ran late. Where was it parked? To the west of the *Drake*, he remembered. If he could get onboard the freighter, he'd be gone before the cools came looking for him. Yes. The freighter!

Mwili ran, sprinting for all he was worth, not caring who might see him. He passed dins loading freight onto transport trains; ran past two men on a break smoking flicksticks who only smiled at him; ran even faster for all the fear of what awaited him were he caught by his father.

He slid to a stop near the freighter.

His breath came in short gasps as Mwili stared at the ship. The scorch marks of a thousand atmospheric entries lay darkly over the microscratched bow of the old hull. Dull rainbows gleamed from spots where the metal had been partially annealed and retempered by the heat of gaseous friction on God knew how many worlds. The ship was long past its prime, and Mwili had time to wonder why the Confed allowed such a hulk to continue to work between local planets, much less Bender into interstellar warp space. He had time to wonder about that—as he noticed that the ship was buttoned up, except for the crew portal.

Doomed. He was doomed, because there was no way he could sneak into the freighter. It was his only chance, and now it was no chance at all. Hell awaited him at home.

"Hello, sweet boy," came a soft voice from behind Mwili. Mwili spun, feeling tighter than a violin string.

A short, bald, fat man of maybe fifty T.S. stood there, smiling. The smile faded to concern. "Hey, easy, there. I'm everybody's friend."

The farm boy felt himself relax a little.

"That's better, sweet boy. So, what say, you have a problem?" What could he say? Mwili could only nod.

The fat man looked from side to side, as if searching for somebody chasing Mwili. "Got into trouble, hey? Somebody after you?"

Mwili nodded again. He found his voice. To his disgust, it cracked when he spoke. "Y-yessir."

The fat man's smile reappeared. "I see you are interested in my ship. Well, it's not my ship exactly, but I am First Officer, so I have some clout on the *Achilles*."

Mwili felt his hope soar.

"You look like a sweet boy who could use a lift off of this dusty hole, that right?"

"Yessir," Mwili said.

The fat man moved closer, so that he was only a few centimeters away from Mwili. The boy felt a strong urge to turn and run, but he held his ground. After a beat, the man reached up and stroked the side of Mwili's face with one smooth hand. Mwili felt his stomach churn. The man was *kjere!* One of God's worst sins, to be *kjere*, right up there with Murder and Blasphemy. He had heard that such men existed in plenty on other worlds, that it was not considered a sin or even particularly immoral, but he had never seen one, much less met one. Mwili had yet to know his first woman, and here was a man touching his face like a wife. He felt his stomach roil, acid bubbling up into his throat. He swallowed the hot taste.

The fat man's grin spread wider, as he let his hand slide down to cup first Mwili's tight shoulder, then the hard muscle of his chest. "Oh, my," the man said, his face going slack, his eyes widening. "You're a strong one, aren't you?"

Mwili held his voice. He started to shake nervously.

"Come on," the fat man said. "Come with me to the ship. We're going to be great friends, you and I. All the way to Krishna. Two glorious months, with a week on Kalk, too. I can get you past the Confed owls, leave it to me."

For a moment, Mwili almost jerked his arm away from the sweaty grip of the fat man and ran, disgusted with what he knew would happen if he went with him. But only for a moment. He thought of his father, then, and the strap and the long years that lay ahead if he stayed on Cibule.

"What's your name?" the fat man asked.

Mwili glanced back at the fence, fearing he'd see his father standing there, gripping the mesh, calling God's curses down upon his son's evil head. There was no one there, though.

"Your name?"

Mwili turned back to look at the fat man. "Ferret," he said. "Call me Ferret."

He followed the fat man toward the ship, and escape. In this case, he would rather chance the devil he didn't know than the one he did.

FIVE

FERRET COULDN'T REMEMBER clearing the boxcar lanes. He'd told Stoll the story, about his father, about running away, and suddenly it seemed they were in Deep, coming up on a point far enough away to shift into Bender drive. Three more days, and they'd be back in the Tau System, back on Shiva's third moon, Vishnu. Back with Shar Li Vu Ndamase, the most beautiful woman on the moon, if not in the system, and leading star of the erotic dance circuit.

"You never went back?" Stoll said, interrupting his thoughts of Shar.

Ferret brought his mind back to the ship. "Went back? No. Why? My parents had their farm, they didn't really need me."

"Time changes things. You aren't a sixteen-year-old boy anymore."

"No," Ferret said, chuckling, "now I'm a thief and smuggler. I'm sure my parents would be proud. My father would probably either sic the Confed cools on me or turn purple and drop dead of a stroke." He found a small grin. "Now there's a pleasant thought."

"You aren't curious?"

Ferret stared at the viewscreen. Curious? Yes. He wondered at times. About his mother, mostly, but also about his father. The old man would be pushing seventy-five. Had he changed any? Not likely, but it was possible. How were he and God getting along these days? How had Baba ever figured out that I was running that last night on Cibule?

"Not enough to go back," Ferret said.

"Suit yourself."

After that, Stoll said no more about it. That was fine with Ferret.

Vishnu was not an export world; it produced nothing of intrinsic value that could be shipped elsewhere. Vishnuvian industry was sufficient to supply power and essential water and sewer services, but almost all of the food had to be imported. There were several small seas, but fishing had never been that big. And yet, if you were lucky enough to be born there, you had a job waiting when you were old enough. The moon had rigid population controls, and it had become, over the last hundred or so years, *the* place to go.

For what Vishnu sold was pleasure, in myriad forms. The climate over all of the settled areas was warm enough to dispense with clothing, should you so desire, but not so hot as to be uncomfortable. You could gamble in one of thousand casinos, enjoy safe, disease-free sex in five times that many carefully regulated sporting houses, and, if you had sufficient standards, have your every whim satisfied by a legion of servants. The arts were big: song, dance, painting, sculpture, literature, you name it, somebody did it better on Vishnu than anywhere else. You could buy it, sometimes; sometimes, you had to be satisfied just looking or touching. Even the servants were paid salaries beyond what an average Confederation citizen made, by a factor of about five. After ten years of work on Vishnu, a man or woman could retire and live comfortably on almost any other planet in the galaxy for the rest of their lives, although few did. And only natives were allowed to work on Vishnu; offworlders came to play, and they paid handsomely for it. Retired locals got cut rates, of course.

Naturally, the Confed had its fingers into Vishnu, but with the amounts of money that flowed into the planet, the officials in charge of Vishnu were willing to go along with a lot. Posting to Vishnu was considered the juiciest plum a Confederation officer of any rank could be given. Nobody wanted to upset the golden goose, much less kill it.

Ferret smiled at his own thoughts as the *Don't Look Back*

swung into landing orbit around the moon. He had first managed a visit to the pleasure world a little over ten years past. He'd been running the ship lanes as a small-time thief and had managed to save enough money for a three-day stay. When it was done, he didn't want to leave. That was how he had met Stoll.

"Hail the ship *Don't Look Back*," came the voice over the com. "This is Vishnu Orbital Control. That you, Stoll? And Ferret?"

"Copy, Control," Ferret said, his grin widening. "Who else?"

"Hell, you never can tell, Ferret. You might have sold that junk heap for scrap and some poor fool thought he'd try to sneak in here before it fell apart."

"Salt and eat that, Vishnu. This junk heap will still fly circles around that relic of yours."

The voice on the com laughed. It was Stoll's cousin, Renaldo. Like Stoll, he was a native. Not Confed. "Any time you want to bet money on a run to Brahma and around, Ferret, I'll give you thirty seconds and two-to-one."

"If only I could, Renaldo. Your cousin won't let me take advantage of you that way."

"Tell him I'll split it with him."

Ferret glanced at Stoll, who was smiling at the conversation. The fat thief was glad to be home, no matter that he couldn't stay for more than a month without getting itchy. And hungry for food unavailable on the planet.

"Well, I could chat all day," Ferret said, "but I would like to land my battered old crate before it falls apart. You want to see if you can figure out a landing glide, Control?"

"Ah, copy that, *Don't Look*. Gimme your navigation comp. You, ah, still have a computer, don't you? Or are you spacing that can by line-of-sight?"

"What a shame," Ferret said. "Professional actors all over are out of work, and there you sit making bad jokes. I think I'll call the Comedians Guild and report you."

Ferret opened his com channel into the ship's computer, and Vishnu Control took over the flying of the ship. They'd be down in another hour or so.

The pub was called The Naked Singularity, and it was patterned after a terran men's club in old India, from the time of the British Raj. The palm trees were real, cloned and grown from imported stock; the ceiling fans twirled slowly, pushing at the fragrant blue-gray clouds of flickstick, pipe and cigar smoke; the bar itself was of local wood, worked and stained to approximate mahogany. There were reproductions of ancient flat pictures hung on the bamboo and wooden walls—hunters standing over the carcasses of tigers, or riding the backs of elephants.

At the end of the large room was a stage. This was not included in the original model for the pub, but no one seemed to mind. The stage and the performers who appeared on it were what brought the customers in, for the most part.

Ferret walked into the room, wearing the period costume issued to him at the door. The suit was white, neo-silk or some such, with stiff collars and lapels, buttons, and a striped neck-wrap called a tie. The other male patrons wore similar outfits, and women were draped in flowing dresses. It was part of the show, and required for attendance.

The place was packed, but Majilio, the tender, always kept a couple of stools reserved for last-minute special customers. The little man, was, of course, a local, but somewhere along the line, one of his ancestors had come from a world with a lot more sun; his skin was nearly as dark as the ersatz-mahogany bar. For some reason Ferret did not understand, Majilio had the paying customers call him "Wog."

Majilio saw Ferret enter, and smiled at him, revealing white teeth with platinum inlays in a *kipepeo* pattern. He nodded toward the special customer stools. Ferret walked to the nearest vacant stool, aware that some of the customers were watching him, and wondering who he was that he could get such preferential treatment. The waiting list to get into the Singularity usually ran over a week, if you were lucky. He sat, and before he was fully in place, Majilio was there, pushing a glass stein of dark beer across the bar to him.

"Evening, Majilio." He sipped at the beer.

"Evening, Sahib Ferret."

"How's everything?"

Majilio flashed his platinum butterfly tooth overlays. "Shar Li Vu Ndamase is more lovely than ever." He glanced at the stage. "She knows you have returned?"

"I thought I would surprise her."

"You are a brave man Sahib."

Ferret laughed. "Not me. You know what she does when she knows I am here."

"Most men would kill to enjoy that pleasure, Sahib."

"It makes me nervous. And she knows that. That's why she does it."

The little man shook his head. "Ah, I think not. This is her gift to you. She carries much love for you."

Before Ferret could reply, the computer-generated band struck up a fanfare. He turned on the stool to look at the stage. Everyone else in the place had fastened their gazes likewise.

She came out slowly, walking with the beat of the music. She wore a period costume as well, supposedly what the women of Earth wore in England around the end of the Nineteenth Century: the puffy white dress covered her from the throat to the ankles, with long sleeves to the wrists. Only her hands and face were visible, the latter shaded under a wide-brimmed hat. She was looking down, so that her features were in hard shadows from the stage lights.

Ferret swallowed dryly, despite the beer. On his homeworld, women dressed similarly, in that they were mostly covered. Hardly so elegant. During his first stirrings of sexual interest, there had been a young woman caught in a sudden wind. Her skirt had lifted, and he had seen her legs, above the knees. He'd almost tripped over his sudden erection. Clothing had always been more provocative than nudity. Imagination counted for a great deal.

The computer hit a musical sting, and Shar snapped her head up to look at the audience.

Surely, Ferret thought, surely no woman of Earth ever looked so lovely. Her skin was tawny, a shade not quite yellow or brown, but somewhere in between; her eyes were electric blue, an impossible shade, but her own and not due to lenses. When she smiled, it was as if the sun had come up. Ferret heard somebody near him sigh. Every time he saw her, it was like being hit in the solar plexus by a fist.

The music began a driving beat, heavy with percussion.

The woman onstage reached up with her right hand and slowly pulled the hat from her head, revealing jet hair knotted up in a bun. She sailed the hat toward the corner of the stage, and turned slowly, until her back was to the audience. She reached up with both hands this time, and did something to the knot of hair. It showered down over her shoulders like black ink, reaching to the middle of her back. She shook her head slightly, and a ripple ran through the jet. The effect was hard to describe to someone who had not seen it. It was a sexual gesture, potent in a way that was hard to believe—a woman shaking her head to free her hair, and it was as if she had freed the lust of everyone in the room.

Somebody near Ferret said, quietly, "Mother*fucker*."

She turned toward the audience, and looked down at the row of pearl buttons on the front of the dress. Now, it was as if she had forgotten the audience was there. She seemed much too proper in her demeanor to consider exposing herself to the eyes of anyone. Alone in her room, perhaps, about to undress for sleep or a bath. Ferret felt like a spy, peeping at something he had no right to be seeing. Exactly as she intended he and everyone else in the room should feel.

Slowly—it seemed to take hours—she unbuttoned the garment's fastenings. Slowly—it seemed to take years—she shrugged her way out of the dress, allowing it to fall to the floor around her feet.

Underneath the dress, she wore some kind of lacy sheath, like a body suit, that exposed her shoulders and arms, but covered her torso and legs to the ankles. It also had a row of buttons, and she started working on them, turning slowly as she did, so that her back was once again to the audience by the time she finished. Another small series of delicate shrugs, and she stepped out of the body suit. As the garment slid down her bare skin, the audience gasped collectively at the beauty of her nude form. She was a lioness, muscles rippling lightly under the tanned skin. Her arms, back, buttocks and legs were clean and perfect, absolutely perfect.

She turned—it seemed to take centuries—head down and eyes lowered, and faced the audience once more. Another gasp. How could a naked woman, on a world where nudity was commonplace, be so impressive?

The computer hit another musical sting, a sharp sound, and she snapped her face up as she had done earlier. She smiled slowly—it seemed to take eons—and acknowledged the audience. She raised her arms slowly, then suddenly dropped to her knees, legs spreading at the same instant. Kneeling on the stage, she leaned back until her hair formed a black pool on the floor. It was an invitation.

The music changed, going into a harder, faster beat, and she was up, leaping high into the air, landing lightly, breasts bobbing. She spun, fanning her hair outward in a cloud, teeth flashing whitely against that tawny, tawny skin. She danced then, oh, how she danced! It was part ballet, part gymnastics, part something that seemed familiar but looked like nothing anyone could name. She used the entire stage, diving, rolling, leaping, stretching.

Ferret had seen the dance fifty times, and it was never the same twice. She moved in ways he had never seen her move before, close, but not the same. If there were a goddess of Sex, then this was her Dance. This was sensual, erotic, lust-inspiring. This made you want to leap upon the stage and join in, ending in a coupling with this magnificent creature who must be more than human. This was what passion was all about—

Until she stopped.

The music faded, lowering to a gentle melody. The woman onstage came to a complete halt, crouched low, head down. When she lifted her head, she was someone else. Gone was the passion and desire. Now, there was only innocence. She straightened slowly, coming fully upright, and she now looked like a child. Everyone with even a hint of a conscience wanted to protect her, to put an arm around those bare shoulders and keep the bad things of the galaxy from approaching this lovely child.

She danced again, but the moves were peaceful. Full of love, but lacking desire, save to be the dance itself.

Ferret held a sigh back, one that would have been all too close to a sob. If magic could be known, then this woman knew it.

And, as he felt his heart breaking for her loveliness, the woman-child on the stage looked across that crowded pub and saw him.

It seemed impossible, but the joy on her face increased. The smile grew larger, and she seemed to emanate a love that encompassed everybody—but focused on a particular man. Him.

Many of the people in the audience turned, to see the object of this wondrous woman's attention. They couldn't see what it might be—there at the bar sat an ordinary-looking young man

of no great stature, wearing the same type of costume they all
wore. They looked back at the nude woman. They must be
mistaken about her attention.

But no. She moved, walking with languid grace to the edge of
the stage, a yukkuri stroll down the steps and across the floor,
past the crowded tables. Earlier, many men and as many women
would have reached out in lust to touch that perfect body; now,
however, none dared impede her progress.

One did not trifle with a goddess, intent on some Olympian
task.

Ferret sighed, and could not help but return her smile as she
approached him. Naked, she stood for a heartbeat in front of
him. She did not speak, but leaned forward slightly and kissed
him, gently, as a child kisses, save for a small flick of her
tongue between his lips. Then she leaned back, turned, and
returned to the stage. The music followed her moves now,
rather than she the sound.

On the stage, she did a final twirl and spiraled gently down,
to lie on her side. She closed her eyes, and the lights in the
pub went to black. Seconds later, when the lights returned, she
was gone.

There was stunned silence. The audience had come expecting to see a strip, and they certainly had, but none of them had
ever experienced a dancer of such talent. It had to be seen to
be believed, and even then, there was no explanation for it.
Some kind of hypnosis. An optical illusion, maybe. A magic
spell.

Ferret felt the gazes of nearly everyone in the pub weighing
upon him. He met none of the looks, but turned back to the
pubtender. The little brown man flashed his augmented grin,
and Ferret shook his head. "I wish she wouldn't do that," he
said.

"Count your blessings, Sahib. Count your blessings."

He had to smile at that. Oh, yes. Shar was something to be
thankful for, no doubt about it.

Ferret slid from the stool, leaving a ten-stad coin on the bar
as he moved. "See you later," he said.

"Much later, I would wager," the little man said. Platinum
butterflies shined from his mouth as he laughed softly.

SIX _____

FERRET LAY ON his back in Shar's bed, head propped on a thick pillow. He looked down the length of his naked body, but his view was impeded at his lean waist. Shar's unbound hair pooled over his loins, waving gently as she moved her hot mouth on him, one of her tawny arms over his belly, the other under his right thigh.

He groaned with pleasure. She moved faster, using her hands now, too. He felt the pressure build, build . . . crest . . . and hold.

He sighed, and reached down to stroke her head. "Hey," he said, "why don't you come up here?"

She raised her head, releasing him from the warmth of her mouth, and smiled at him. "Aw, you don't like it?"

"Up, woman. You. Up here." He pointed at her face, then at his own.

She laughed at him, and did an exaggerated climb up his form, as if she were scaling a tree. When she reached his face, she kissed him, and sprawled on top of him limply. She faked a sob and then said in a whine, "I work *so* hard, and you don't like it. What's wrong with me? I should have stayed in the hinterlands!"

"It's not you," he said, his voice serious.

She dropped the whine. "I know. It's okay, love. Really. Here, let's try this." She reached down and touched him with her hand, guiding him to her. He found the portal, thrust slightly, and became joined to her, a timeless journey that took only a second. Oh, yes!

She began to rock, crooning deep in her throat, and the pressure in his groin grew, until he thought he would explode. He waited for her, listening to the wordless tune grow more frantic, hearing her breathing turn ragged, feeling her tension increase. When she started to chant, ''oh, oh, oh, oh—'' he relaxed his control.

She began to shudder, her tight and silken muscles clamping and releasing rhythmically, stroking him in waves, calling to his very being.

He sought her depths, yearning to touch the core of her. His groan was contrapuntal to her chant, until she smothered his lips under hers, thrusting her tongue deeply into his mouth, a small balance for his body within hers. They drove into each other, seeking oneness. Then, for the briefest of moments, they found it.

One.

They continued to throb together for another four heartbeats, and then she went limp again, laying her cheek against his lips. He cupped her buttocks, holding her against him, reluctant to allow any space in their connection. The scent of their musk covered them, as did the sweat of their exertions, and both mingled with her perfume, something based on spice, sharp and sweet. The combination smelled to Ferret of more than sex; it was the pungent fragrance of love.

Later, she rolled over and pulled the silk sheet up to cover them. She nestled under his arm, kissing him on the nipple. ''Why didn't you tell me you were coming to the Singularity?''

''I wasn't sure I was going until the last minute.''

''Sheeit,'' she said. She leaned over quickly and jerked one of his chest hairs out with her teeth.

''Hey, ow!''

''You deserve it for lying to me.''

''Well, okay. I wanted to see you dance, but I didn't want you to see me. You always do the same thing when you see me. It—it—''

''—embarrasses you,'' she finished.

''No—'' he began. She leaned over and grabbed a mouthful of his chest hair in her teeth.

"All right, yes, it embarrasses me!"

She let go of his hair and snuggled closer to him. "I love it! Ferret the smuggler, the diamond-hard thief, shy about being kissed in public! You blush every time, it's so cute! You're blushing right now! It makes you appealing, you know."

He growled at her, a mock carnivore rumble, and she squealed and hid her face in his armpit. After a moment, she pulled back and propped herself up on one elbow to look at him. She traced the line of his nose, then his lips with one finger. "Most of the men I have been with would make love to me on the court of a crowded poisonball stadium, and in view of the entire Confed broadcast net without a second thought. They want me that bad. You want me too, but you are so reserved, so proper. Even when we're alone. I find it absolutely charming."

He managed a chuckle. "All my women say that."

She sat up, crosslegged, and glared at him. "What women? You'd better not have any other women!"

"Hey, this is supposed to be an open relationship. You have other men when I'm gone, don't you?"

"Sometimes. But that doesn't count! I don't love them!"

"So, who says I love my other women?"

"I'm going to hit you, Mwili Ferret Rat Turd!" She snatched up the pillow and raised it threateningly over her head.

He laughed. "All right, all right! There aren't any other women!"

"You promise?" She lowered the pillow slightly.

"I promise."

"Any men?"

He shook his head, suddenly serious. "Not for a long time. I have a . . . bad association with that."

She dropped the pillow, immediately contrite, and practically leaped on him, hugging him tightly. "I know. I'm sorry, I shouldn't have said it."

It was Ferret's turn to prop himself away from her. "How do you know? I've never said anything about male lovers I might have had."

"That's how I know."

He shook his head. "Ah, Jesu, you and Stoll, you must get together and compare tapes. He knows things I don't say, too." He paused for a second, remembering.

"Well. There have been a few. Not pleasant memories, most of them."

She reached out to lay one hand on his tight shoulder. She stroked the muscle softly. "You don't have to talk about it," she said.

He opened his eyes and looked at her. She was talented, beautiful, and she loved him. As he did her. Counting Stoll, she made two, the only two real friends he'd ever had. No, that wasn't quite true. There had once been another, met during the years of lane running, but that was down the exhaust a long time ago. If he couldn't trust Shar by now, he never would. They had been lovers for years. He still did not understand what she saw in him.

"It's not that pretty a story," he said. "But I'll tell you, if you want."

"More than anything," she said.

He looked at her perfect face, and he believed her.

"It began when I left Cibule," he said. "On a freighter bound for Krishna . . ."

SEVEN

SEX HAD BEEN a major shock to Mwili.

Sex was not something spoken of on the farm. He had viewed the instruction tapes for his schooling, of course, though they had been rather limited. There had been an illicit info ball passed around among some of the boys his age, and it had described, but not shown, certain practices common between men and women, men and men, and even two women. But seeing a slack-faced man lecture via holoproj was a light-year from the actual experience. The fat First Officer, Benjo, had been as gentle as he could, but it had not been pleasant for Mwili. More than the pain was the shame. He was tainted forever; *kjere*, and damned by God. Much, if not all, of the crew was also damned. Aside from normal male and female relations, men paired with men, women with women, there were *groups*! and casual fornication was the rule rather than the exception. It seemed that nearly everyone on the ship was either *doing* it, bragging about just having done it, or talking about preparing to do it.

Mwili did not doubt that his father would have nodded grimly and knowingly, had he been aware of his son's companions. And, in truth, the boy began to wonder if perhaps his father wasn't right.

It was all so disgusting.

He was ashamed and disgusted, and his first thought was to

jump ship at Kalk. To be away from the perversions he had to endure. But he didn't. He stayed on the ship until it reached Krishna. He did not know why, then.

In her bed, Shar laid a gentle hand on Ferret's shoulder. He looked at her, and his smile was less than happy, but more than bitter.

"You understand why I didn't leave?"

Softly, she said, "I think so."

He nodded. "It took me years to learn why. I couldn't begin to see it at the time, and I didn't want to admit it to myself later when it finally became clear."

She said it for him. "You were excited by it."

He nodded again. "Oh, yes. Backplanet boy that I was, knowing I was going to burn for eternity because of it, even so, yes, I was caught up in it. It was heady. And Benjo was the first person, save for my mother, who had ever demonstrated any real affection for me. Even a perverse love was better than no love at all. He wasn't an evil man, he was even tender with me, in his own way."

"I understand. Go on."

He took a deep breath, remembering the far away time and place. "I grew up fast. There was no choice."

There was an underground of sorts in the space lanes, a network of people and mues who traveled constantly the galactic wastes back and forth between the few habitable planets, moons and wheelworlds. People who fell into the Confed's cracks, faceless, worldless, people who lived on the fringe. The lanes were harsh places, danger could come from the Confed or other laners, because the law did not have a place for such folk. If the cools caught you, it was locktime; if you were hit and hurt by another laner, there was no one to take the complaint—you watched your own ass, first and last, because nobody else would.

It took Ferret awhile to plug into it, to find his way into a lifestyle that was less than luxurious, but more than survival. There were some who did it legally, rich people who were gypsies, never staying in one place for more than a few days, those with enough stads to bribe their way. But mostly, the laners existed by working illegal trades. Many were whores;

some were smugglers; there were scam artists, ticket forgers, stowaways and rebels against the Confed.

And, of course, there were thieves.

One of the first things Ferret learned was the need for proper identification. Benjo had a forged ID cube he gave the boy, one that would allow him basic Confederation passage onto and off of Krishna. But each world was different, aside from the hard and ubiquitous Confederation rules. There were a lot of things he needed to know, things he would have to pay to learn.

Reluctantly, for the First Officer had come to enjoy his company, Benjo put Ferret in touch with a laner he knew on Krishna. The man took his payment from the boy in the same manner as the fat First Officer had done.

Within a month, Ferret was much wiser in the ways of the galaxy than any boy his age on Cibule. Much wiser.

The laner called himself Wall Eye, for a weak muscle that allowed his right eye to drift somewhat when he was tired. He was maybe forty T.S. years old, thin and sharp-featured, with gray hair worn plastered flat to his head in a style popular on Baszel a decade past. His clothes were cheap, but clean, synlin coveralls and fast-track athletic shoes. He always smelled of roses, and Ferret never knew why. He taught Ferret things.

"Y'see that machine, boy?"

Ferret nodded. They were in the main spaceport in the city of Rama, the largest city on Krishna. The machine was a robotic ticket dispenser. A customer inserted his stad cube, punched up his destination, and the proper amount was deducted from his bank balance, while the "ticket" was credited to his cube. Every spaceport had dozens of such devices.

"Watch as Old Hairy takes it for a ride."

Old Hairy was a laner Ferret had met briefly. He was as bald as an egg on top, though he was supposed to be layered with a thick mat of furlike hair everywhere his clothes covered. Ferret didn't know, and didn't want to find out.

The man approached the machine and inserted a cube. Then, before the machine could do more than acknowledge the insertion, Old Hairy punched the retrieve key, removed the cube, and quickly inserted another cube. The small holoproj screen started to clear.

"Lookit his hand."

Ferret looked. "I don't see—"

Old Hairy removed the second cube just as quickly, then
shoved a third cube into the machine. As he did so, Ferret
caught sight of at least two or three more cubes clutched and
mostly hidden in his left hand. The machine's screen flowed
with numbers, but it was not getting to finish a transaction
before Old Hairy started working it again. He moved precisely,
no wasted movements, and Ferret was reminded of a magician
he had seen once on Cibule.

Within a minute, the laner had inserted and removed at least
five cubes into and from the machine. The screen pulsed once,
flashing an amber light.

"Here he goes," Wall Eye said.

Old Hairy began tapping at the keyboard, his fingers flashing
like a champion word processor. The ticket machine emitted a
sharp *bleat*! but the man kept typing. After a moment, he
stopped, sighed deeply, and smiled at the machine. Without
being obvious, Old Hairy looked around. He spotted Wall Eye
and Ferret, and nodded once, acknowledging them. Wall
Eye smiled and nodded back.

The ticket machine clicked, and after a second, Old Hairy
touched the retrieve control and removed a cube. He turned
and walked away, fast, but not excessively so, as might a man
intent on catching a shuttle for which he was running late.

"C'mon," Wall Eye said. "Best we footprint."

"Why?"

"We don't want to be here when the cools come looking for
Old Hairy, that's why."

As they walked, Wall Eye explained.

"Old Hairy's a ticket mechanic, y'see? Them machines got
a programming flaw. Y'know what to do, you can confuse 'em
and get a free ticket."

"Really?"

"Well, you couldn't, but a good mechanic can. All the ticket
machines in a given port are run by a mainframe, so y'got to
know the system and the codes to get past the safeties. Takes
skill and practice, and y'got to keep up with the changes the
Confed and private companies keep making. Old Hairy used
to work for 'em, so he's got an edge."

"Seems like a lot of work for a free ticket."

Wall Eye glanced at Ferret. "Ha! You really are a backrocket
baby, ain'tcha? Like as not, Old Hairy just got an open-ended

ticket for a blank ID. Y'know what a ticket like that is worth, to the right people? Old Hairy can get maybe five, six thousand standards for that cube from an honest man who just wants to travel. A man on the run for killing a cool or blowing away a Confed trooper would give everything he had to be holding a ticket to anywhere."

"It seems too easy."

"Got a lot of 'seems' in you, don'tcha? Yeah, well, there's disadvantages. He has to get rid of the cube pretty fast. They're getting a lot faster at filtering stolen tickets. They'll put a cruncher on it, straining out every ticket sold, and eventually, they'll run it down. It'll take maybe three days 'fore they put a stop on it. Whoever gets the ticket had better use it by then."

They were maybe fifty meters away from the ticket machine Old Hairy had just rascaled. Wall Eye stopped. The long and wide main corridor was thick with passengers, and there was nothing to make him and Ferret stand out. The man with the slicked-down hair twitched his head and pointed back at the machine with his nose. "Take a look," he said.

Ferret did. Two men, dressed in the can't-miss-it flaming orange orthoskin Confed uniform jumpsuits that instantly identified them as spaceport security, had just arrived at the ticket machine. They scanned the nearby passengers.

"Even Old Hairy hasn't figured out a way to bypass the security system. The machine screams when it gets taken. A good mechanic is not only sharp, he's gotta be fast."

Ferret watched the cools for a moment.

A smallish man close to the machine glanced over at the two Confed agents. A mistake.

Before he could move, the small man was grabbed and slammed into the nearest wall, face first. Ferret saw blood spray from the man's smashed nose. One of the Confed men swung his elbow into the man's back, over the right kidney. Ferret could hear the strike, and the man's yell of pain.

"Jesu! What are they doing that for? He didn't do anything!"

"Them's Confed, boy. It don't matter if that cit did anything or not. He's in the wrong place at the wrong time."

The small man took another shot, this time from a knee. He began to slide down the wall, his hands dragging the smooth surface. Blood from his smashed face left a red smear on the plastic.

"That's not right!" Ferret said.

Wall Eye laughed. "Where you from, boy? A cave? Right? Shit, whatever the Confed *does* is right. That cit knows he'll get worse, he complains."

One of the security men kicked the fallen man a final time, then looked to see if anybody nearby was watching. Nobody was. People hurried past, looking away from the brutality.

"They couldn't catch Old Hairy, so they took it out on the first guy they could catch. The lesson's there, boy."

Ferret shook his head, stunned by the violence. Even Baba had to have a reason to strap him. "What lesson?"

"Don't fuck with the Confed, boy. Real simple."

The two security men walked away, moving as if they owned the port, swaggering as if they were gods and the people around them were no more than cattle. Ferret could hear one of them laugh, loud enough to carry even this far. Jesu, damn! How could they get away with it?

Ferret sighed. He had a lot to learn, all right.

"C'mon," Wall Eye said. "Old Hairy'll need a broker, and I just happen to know a man what's looking for a fast exit to points spinward."

Wall Eye turned away from the cools and walked away. That was how he made it in the world of laners. He was a middle man, buying and selling goods and information. He knew most of the scams and most of the scammers, and putting one in touch with another was worth money at times. Ferret followed him, but he kept looking back at the injured man lying sprawled on the cold floor. Nobody stopped to help him. They must be afraid somebody might be watching.

After a month, Ferret knew his path was not going to be either a scam artist or a sexual companion to one. He listened and he learned, and after a month, he made his decision. All right, it was going to be a hard life. Fine. He would be as hard as he needed to be.

It was on Koji, the Holy World, in the Heiwa System, at the spaceport in Rakkaus—called the City of Love, by people who had never been there. He was still traveling with Wall Eye, who liked him well enough, and he wanted to be sure he had the nerve to pull it off before he broke away from the man and moved out on his own.

In the end, it was simple enough to do. Getting up the balls for it was another matter. As when he had left his father's flitter near the police station back on Cibule, Ferret felt as if everyone in the port were watching him. He felt cold sweat beading on his body, and runnels of it flowing down the crease over his spine. His heart thumped so loudly he was sure people could hear it; he had to remember to breathe, and his skin itched and tingled. He stopped at a water fountain, to try and wash the dryness from his mouth.

He went into the public fresher across from the first-class sleeping rooms. The port was a full-service operation: there were shops that sold everything from clothes and food to luggage and livestock; within the main terminal were also restaurants, gymnasiums, theaters and even a casino.

The first-class sleeping rooms on this corridor were plush, if small, units. At fifty stads the quarter-day, only people with means used them for naps. It followed that at least some of the people using the fresher across from the rooms were well-padded.

The fresher was unisex, catering to men and women, and it had privacy stalls, entered by paying a small fee to the fresher's computer. The row of a dozen stalls, each containing a bidet toilet and sink, was set against a long wall, just past the public communal sink and open squat toilets. Each stall was enclosed and had a lockable door, but there was a short gap at the bottom, for cleaning the tile floor; additionally, the top was open, and the walls were only two meters or so high.

Ferret swallowed dryly, and moved to wash his hands at the communal sink. Two men and a woman were also cleaning their hands. After a moment, they left.

Ferret didn't bother to use the air dryers, but instead jammed one hand into his tunic pocket and removed a string gun. It was a simple device. It fired a four-meter-long string; one end remained attached at the barrel, the other end carried a small wad of reusable quikstik. The quikstik was activated by the compressed gas that fired it from the slippery lofric barrel of the gun. Whatever the wad of plastic touched after that became attached to it with an almost unbreakable adhesion, until a let-go solvent was applied.

The boy dropped into a low crouch, almost a crawl, and scuttled past the row of enclosed stalls. He spared a glance

over his shoulder at the fresher's entrance, but concentrated on
looking under the bottom edges of the cubicles. He mostly saw
empty stalls, or the feet of people perched on toilets, coveralls
or kilts pooled around their ankles. Nine was empty, ten was
empty, eleven—ah!

At the second stall from the end of the row, he saw his target.
A blue-anodized aluminum travel case stood next to the man
who sat upon the hard plastic bidet. The case looked expensive, buffed to a dull blue gloss, hardly scratched at all. This
was it.

From his pants pocket, Ferret pulled a popper. He triggered
it, and rolled it under the gap below the tenth stall. It was a
small device, the popper, and the charge was hardly bigger
than a cheap firecracker; however, in the enclosed and hard
floored and walled fresher, the noise it made when it exploded
was more than enough. It would get everybody in the fresher's
attention. The man in number eleven wouldn't be looking down
at his case.

When the popper went off, Ferret extended the string gun
and fired it. The case was less than two meters away, but even
so, he almost missed it, his hand was shaking so bad. But the
clump of quikstik hit the upper edge of the aluminum case.
Ferret looped the remaining string over his hand and jerked,
hard. With the sound of the popper still ringing in his ears, the
case fell flat and slid out from the stall, bumping into Ferret's
boot.

The boy didn't hesitate. He grabbed the case and ran for the
fresher's door. By the time he reached the exit, people inside
the stalls were starting to react.

"—the fuck is going on—?"

"—hey, hey—!"

And finally, the voice of his victim: "My case!"

Ferret rounded the exit and into the hall. He forced himself
to walk. The man in the fresher wasn't likely to chase him with
his pants around his ankles, he might even pause to run the
bidet and wipe, and the service corridor for which Ferret had
bought an entry code loomed just ahead and to his right.

Ferret reached the entrance, and hurriedly punched in the
four-digit entry code.

Behind him, his victim's voice grew louder.

"Help! Police!"

Ferret shoved at the door. It wouldn't budge.

Jesu! Was the code wrong? If so, he was caught! He'd seen what the Confed did to an innocent man—what would they do to him, guilty as sin?

"Help! Stop! Thief!" The man was still inside the fresher, but almost to the exit now—

Ferret tapped the keys again, forcing himself to move more slowly and carefully. Oh, shit, shit, shit! Six. Come on! Nine. Three. Hurry, hurry—! One—

The lock snicked, and the door gave under the pressure of his hand. Ferret's breath was almost a sob as he jammed into the narrow corridor and shoved the door shut behind him. He could hardly breathe, his gut was twisted into a knot, his bowels felt watery.

Had the man seen him? Ferret leaned against the locked door, waiting for a pounding upon it that would announce his pursuer. Oh, God, please—!

Five seconds passed, seeming more like five years. Time for all the police on the planet to converge upon him, guns leveled, ready to burn him into dead cinders. To smash him against a wall and kick him to a pulp.

"Thief!" a voice screamed. But it was dopplering past the service corridor.

He hadn't been seen!

Ferret sighed again and shook his head. The adrenaline pumped through him, and he felt tight, alive, and scared. It was a wild and mixed feeling, fear and the realization that he had pulled it off. A few seconds ago, he would have promised anything to never have to go through this again. Now, now he could see that it wasn't all bad. In fact, he felt like he had when he'd first run away from home. Triumphant. In control. Yeah. It was all right.

Hefting his prize, he started off down the corridor.

Technically, it was not his first theft. He had stolen the string gun and popper from a cubicle on the wheelworld of Volny, where he and Wall Eye had spent a few days, a week past. But the case was his first public venture, and the only one with real risk. The gun and popper belonged to an old junk woman Wall Eye knew, and she probably wouldn't miss them for some time, if ever.

Ferret had a hammer and chisel, but the case wasn't even locked. Hiding in a fresher stall across the port from the score, he opened his treasure chest.

There were some flimsy plastic sheets with numbers and figures inked on them; an expensive reader, inside a genuine leather holder, with several stainless steel info balls nestled in soft rubber sockets; a hand-held flatscreen computer and recorder unit; and several writing instruments—a light pen, paint pencil, and electric coder. There was also a credit cube, shiny translucent plastic, with a gold bar stamped across the corner. Ah. The gold bar meant the owner had plenty. A regulation man, a citizen. The cit would have the cube and case replaced before the local sun went down, and no shit, but this was something for Ferret.

Ferret grinned, and leaned back on the bidet. He didn't know the cube's code, so he couldn't use it without security-locking it into any payment computer. But there were people who specialized in figuring out the codes for stolen cubes, and using them before a stop-pay alert was issued. The cube was worth stads to a codebreaker, although he didn't know how much. Cit money was tricky. He'd seen Wall Eye bargain with other laners over the odd item, and he knew that he'd better be prepared or risk being cheated. He shoved the reader, flatscreen and cube into his tunic pockets. The case he wiped clean with tissue, then dropped into the waste disposal on the way out of the fresher. The case was too large to reach the grinders, and eventually it would block enough trash so that the container overflowed. By then, Ferret figured he would be light-years away.

He spent a pleasant few minutes in an electronics kiosk, pricing readers and flatscreens. The ones he had stolen were expensive enough, retailing at over a hundred standards each. If he was lucky, he could get a quarter of that from a fencer. The cube was something else. He didn't have any idea how much it was worth. Maybe fifty or a hundred standards, no way to tell what the market was like.

He went to make his deals.

Ferret didn't know why, but the woman called herself Warbler. He had met her on Krishna, and seen her in the lanes a couple of times since. She was a hard-faced woman of about twenty-two or -three T.S. years, and, the word was, under the death penalty on Thompson's Gazelle for killing a husband or wife, whichever. He met her in a sleep room she had booked, and they both had to sit on the cot; there was barely enough height to stand erect, but insufficient floor space, in any event.

"So, Ferret. What have you got?"

Ferret produced the reader and flatscreen.

Warbler took the flatscreen first, examined it carefully, clicking it on and running a test pattern to check the graphics. After a minute, she dropped it onto the bed between them. He handed her the reader, and she clicked one of the info balls into it and performed a similar test, to assure that the unit was in good shape.

"Twenty stads for both of them," she said.

"I priced them," he said. "Thirty-five."

She smiled, a brief and amused grimace. "This ain't exactly the Tokyo Electronics Emporium, kid. Twenty-two."

"Thirty."

"Come on. You're fresh, but even you know the lanes better than that. Twenty-four, and that's the top out."

He nodded. "Okay."

"You want a credit or hard curry?"

"Hard. I wasn't planning to open an account here."

She favored him with another smile. "You're a funny kid, you know?" She counted out four five-stad coins and four ones. He took the coins and jingled them before he put them into his pocket.

"Thanks," he said.

"Always open for biz," she said. She started to slide off the bed.

"One more thing," he said. "You seen Bill the Breaker around?"

Warbler stopped her movement. "You got a hot cube?"

He shrugged. "I just need to talk to him."

"You're out of luck, then. Last I saw him was on Farbis. I heard he was heading out toward Rim."

Ferret shrugged again, pretending disinterest. "No big deal."

"I can put you in touch with Raven," she said. "I hear she's around."

"Yeah?"

"For ten percent."

"Shit. I might go two."

"Eight."

"Four percent. You wouldn't want to take advantage of a kid, now would you?"

"Five. If you've got a hot cube, you have to move it today, otherwise it ain't worth the plastic it's made of. I can get you to Raven in an hour."

Ferret thought about it. "All right. Five percent."

She smiled a third time. "I think you're gonna do all right in the lanes, kid."

Raven wore her jet hair cropped short, and there was a jagged scar across her cheek that pulled her mouth up in a perpetual half smile. She must have been beautiful before the scar, Ferret thought, wondering also why she didn't check into a plastic clinic and have the thing fixed. She made pretty good money, he heard. But then, maybe she had her reasons for wanting to look like she did. That was her business, and if he'd learned nothing else in the lanes, he'd learned to avoid asking questions that were too personal. Some didn't mind; others didn't like it, to the point of quick and deadly violence, and cry to the cools if you don't like, kid.

They met in a restaurant on the west side of the main terminal building, a midrange cafeteria with live servers on the line. The place was fairly crowded, but they bought only drinks, then found an empty booth and sat.

Raven said, "Warbler says you have something I might want."

Wordlessly, Ferret produced the cube and handed it to her. She glanced at it, rubbed her thumb over the gold stripe, and nodded. "How long have you had it?"

"About four hours."

She took a sip of her beer and set the plastic can down on the table. "Two thousand," she said.

Ferret blinked. Two thousand *standards*? Jesu! He barely managed to keep from blurting that out loud. He never expected that much, not in a million years! He was all set to leap on the offer with both dotic boots, but instead, he leaned back and sipped at his own drink. It was splash, a mildly alcoholic beverage that had a slightly sour tang. He didn't know as much as he wished he knew about such things, and he automatically doubled the number.

"Four," he said.

"Let's not play," Raven said. "I'm tired, it's been a long day, and I'd just as soon catch a shuttle off this rock. So I'll give you my number and we are at the bottom line. Thirty-seven fifty. Out of which you owe Warbler how much?"

"Five percent."

"Fine. So she gets a hundred and thirty-eight stads from that, unless you want to argue over small change?"

"No. That sounds fair."

"Good." Raven pulled a purse from her belt, a flat rectangle of green plastic, and opened it. She counted out thirty-six hundred standards, in hundred-stad platinum coins, then two fives and two ones.

Ferret hastily stuffed the coins into his pockets.

Raven stuck the cube into her purse and resettled the container onto her belt. She finished her beer, then started to stand. "If you're in a port and need to do biz with me, pull out a call for Fem Black on the com. I'll find you."

"Aren't you going to check the cube and see if it's legit?"

"No need. If it isn't, you're dead next time I see you."

Ferret felt a rush of fear ice his belly. "Uh, look," Ferret began, "we've done the deal and all. Can I ask you something?"

"I suppose."

"How much can you make off that cube?"

"If I start now, maybe six or eight thousand stads. A little in curry, some luxury items I can move, like that."

"Is it risky?"

She laughed. "You looking to get into the biz, kid?"

"Maybe. It doesn't hurt to know things."

"Risky enough. I've been lucky. Two out of three hot cubers do locktime. They get careless."

"Thanks for the information."

"No charge, kid." She started to walk away. "You still with Wall Eye?"

Ferret was very much aware of the weight of the three thousand stads in his pocket. "Not anymore," he said.

Not anymore.

EIGHT

"I CAN UNDERSTAND why you might not like sex with men,"
Shar said.

Ferret shook his head. "It wasn't so much the acts as the
reasons for them. I was bought, I didn't have a choice. It was
my only coin. Later, I met a boy my age, and we got along
okay. For a time. We were together, but out of choice. Nobody
was selling anything, nobody had to, that was the difference.
But that came to a bad end, too. Not because of the sex, but
for . . . other reasons."

"Another story?"

Ferret took a deep breath and let it out. "Might as well,
since I'm baring my soul."

But the com chimed at that moment, interrupting the intended revelation.

Shar said, "Yes?"

From the com came the voice of Stoll, somewhat tinny for
the small speaker that reproduced it. "If you two are done with
your sweaty athletic endeavors, Ferret and I have work to do."

"Work?" Ferret said. "I just got here!"

"Sorry, m'boy, but biz waits for nobody. We're talking six
months."

Ferret sat up and stared at the com. It was preset to a nopix
transmission, but he wished he could see Stoll's face, to know
if he was serious. Six months meant just that: his half of the

profits on the venture, whatever it was, would buy him six months on Vishnu. At an average cost of nineteen thousand standards a month to stay on the pleasure world, six months was nothing to hiss at. That meant the total score for the caper had to run close to half a million, taking out Stoll's cut, the finder's fee, and assorted bribes and expenses. Not a small bit of biz.

"You wouldn't be trying to damp my drive, now would you Shanti?"

"If only I could," Stoll said. "But in this case, no, the biz is legit. *If* we can manage to stir ourselves from Shar's passionate embrace and move our ass to get to it."

Shar laughed. "Is that 'we' a hint of latent desire, Shanti? Would you like to join us next time?"

"Alas, dear one, you tempt me. But no. My own passions lie in another plane, as you well know."

Ferret chuckled. Indeed. Food was Stoll's mistress. He had a particular bent: while he was as plebeian as the next man in his drinking habits, he never ate the same item prepared the same way twice. Every meal the fat man consumed was different, a new experience each time. Which accounted for his bulk. If he liked something, he ate much of it at a sitting, knowing he would never have it again. Ferret had once seen him consume two kilos of *kipande cha nyama*, meat from dwarf cattle found only on Bibi Arusi's Green Moon. These were exceedingly rare animals, raised by hand, and fed nothing but highest quality honeyed grain and vintage smoked eel wine. The cost of that single meal had been worth two weeks' stay on Vishnu, ten thousand standards, counting the bribe for illegal importation. Stoll lived to eat, and he allowed no other desires to interfere.

"I bet I could make you skip a meal," Shar said.

"Have you nothing better to do than bedevil an old man, child? What a horrible thought!"

Ferret and Shar smiled at each other. Ferret continued to look at her as he said, "I am on my way, Lord Glutton. I'll see you in fifteen minutes."

Shar frowned at him and shook her head.

"I meant thirty minutes," Ferret amended hastily.

She smiled at him, and it was a thing of joy.

"Or maybe forty-five minutes," Ferret said.

From the com, Stoll said, "Ah, you young people. No sense of tomorrow." Ferret could almost see him shaking his head in mock dismay. But five seconds later, Stoll had left his mind completely.

As Ferret took the pedway to Stoll's cube, he felt almost unbearably happy. Stoll and Shar were his friends, the kind who would come at his call to help him bury a body, no questions asked. And Shar loved him in a way he had never expected to be loved, something that amazed him still at least once daily. Sure, she was beautiful, but anybody with enough money could buy surgical beauty; it was what shined from within that counted. Were she to turn haggish-looking tomorrow, it wouldn't matter. Shar lived behind the face, and while it was the face and body that had first called to him, it was the woman beneath who kept him in thrall. He sometimes felt that if Shar were given a featureless body, a lump of protoplasm, it would naturally grow beautiful to match her inner self. He could not begin to understand why she favored him as she did. He was but a thief, not all that clever or rich. She had tried to tell him that she felt an essential connection, but he didn't understand what she meant. Something to do with his soul and hers, she said, and he didn't question it too closely for fear of spoiling it.

A group of chattering tourists zipped by on the opposite walkway, pointing and snapping holograms with their cameras. Probably they had saved for years to enjoy a few days on Vishnu, while he lived here almost permanently. That was something to be thankful for, too. To be with the galaxy's most perfect woman, on the galaxy's most perfect world, was something most men could only dream of. And here he was, a self-educated farm boy from nowhere, who had the dream as reality. True, he was a thief and smuggler, a dangerous occupation, but he did not harm anybody by being such. He stole from those who could afford it, or insurance companies who covered them; he smuggled items forbidden by arcane and foolish laws, never dealing in addictive drugs, weapons, or slavery. One might even say he performed an essential service—keeping cools and Confed patrols in business, and supplying illegal—but not particularly immoral—items to fulfill people's desires. It was a rationalization with which he could live.

The exit to Stoll's cube loomed, and Ferret crosstracked to the slower outer belt of the pedway. The morning sun shined warmly, and he took a deep breath of the city's clean air as he regained the dead sidewalk bordering the pedway. If God existed, Ferret figured He had decided to allow this particular sinner some measure of joy. Ferret figured he was way ahead, even after the hard years on Cibule. Only a few men found Paradise while still alive.

"So," Ferret said, "what is this enriching biz you have for us?"

Stoll was eating a midmorning snack, some kind of candied fruit, looked like. Any curiosity Ferret had about what the meal might be, he kept to himself. Stoll would wax on about his food for hours, telling Ferret everything he wanted to know about it, and a lot more he could care less about. Stoll knew his meals like a good mother knew her children.

The fat man held up one hand, a signal for his partner to wait a moment. Ferret smiled. He knew better than to interrupt Stoll while eating, but he did it anyway, to mildly annoy him. It was part of the long-running game they played, and both of them enjoyed it.

There was a story about Stoll, something that had happened before he and Ferret had met. Supposedly, a restaurant in which Stoll was eating had caught fire, but the man had refused to leave until he'd finished his meal. With the place burning down all around him, and frantic firefighters spraying disox foam hither and yon, Stoll had calmly finished his dinner. Singed, but satisfied, Stoll had approached the payment computer to settle his tab, but the computer had been melted into slag by the fire, along with most of the restaurant. It was probably apocryphal, but it was a good story, and Ferret wouldn't put it past his partner.

The younger man looked around the inside of Stoll's cube while the other finished his snack. The cube was spare, almost stark in its lack of decoration. A table, four chairs, and a couch occupied the circular central room. There were three spokes, short hallways, leading from the center wheel to a bedroom, fresher, and, of course, a kitchen. Stoll was not above preparing his own meals, and was an excellent cook, especially considering he never made the same dish twice. Not a particularly good way to get culinary practice. The other rooms were no better appointed than the center room; Stoll spent his money on one thing, and had for most of his life.

"Wonderful stuff," Stoll said.

Ferret glanced at him. "Don't tell me. I don't want to know."

A shadow of annoyance crossed Stoll's face, and Ferret could not stop the smile. Stoll caught him in it.

"You're joking. How can you joke about such things?"

"I am sorry," Ferret said, his voice grave. "I don't know what came over me. Tell me about the snack." This too was part of the game. A partner should enjoy his partner's passions, even if he ragged him about them.

Stoll lit up, a fat and happy human lamp. "Blue Chungwa, from Earth, actually. It's a citrus fruit, crossbred up from kumquats and lime, originally. This particular batch came from clone stock grown on Flamind—that's one of the Hothouse Islands on Aqua, in the Sto System. Amazing places, the Islands. There are almost nine hundred of them, the largest only a kilometer or so across, dotted across the Inghetata Sea, in the Gheata Latitudes. They're the only place on the entire planet warm enough to grow semitropical vegetation. Most of Aqua's crops are waterculture, you know."

"I seem to recall," Ferret said dryly, pretending to be bored.

"Yes, well, the dish is prepared with walnut butter and fireweed thimblebee honey, with a dash of sour cream and three drops of wormwood brandy."

"Fascinating," Ferret said, deadpan.

"I give it an eighty-three," Stoll said.

Ferret raised an eyebrow. A very good score. He had eaten with Stoll at places where the food only rated fifty, and it had been some of the best Ferret had ever tasted. The scale ran from one to a hundred, with most of Stoll's meals falling around the midrange. Stoll had yet to taste anything he would rate over ninety-one. His criteria were passing strange: A meal scoring a hundred would cause the eater to pass out from pure bliss— comparable to a few dozen orgasms, one after another, Stoll had told him. A meal that caused nausea and projectile vomiting usually rated around ten. Anything below that was usually too vile to look at or smell to consider eating; a food rated at one would be something one could not remain in the same room with for more than a few seconds, without fainting from revulsion. But there were a lot of people on a lot of worlds, and all manner of diets, so Stoll had a lot better than such fare from which to choose.

"This is wonderful and all, Shanti, but I left Shar's bed to come here, and I hope it is for a better reason that a lecture on candied fruits you have recently consumed."

"Your taste is all in your dick, boy."

"I'll tell Shar Li you said that."

"Considering that she finds you attractive, her tastes could use improvement, too."

"Shanti . . ."

"All right. Have you heard of the Immelhoffs?"

"The emerald mining family on Lee, in the Delta System?"

"The same. Well, as it happens, one of the daughters is about to be wed. She is a rather artless girl of tender years, pushing sixty T.S. Her father has finally found her a match that won't compromise the family integrity. He had to go offworld to do it; she's marrying a boy of fifty-one, from the planet next door, Rift. He's the scion of a rich waste disposal dynasty; the family's money comes mainly from the development of a rather complex protozoa of the suctoria class, whose chief function is the ingestion and conversion of common sewage on the less well-developed planets."

Ferret shook his head. "I suppose it would kill you to get to the point."

"Out of deference to the high society types in the Delta System, the wedding is to be held on the more civilized world of Thompson's Gazelle." Stoll continued his monologue as though Ferret had not spoken. "The bride, groom and assorted family and friends are spacing there for the ceremony and attendant celebration, courtesy of the doting fathers. It is to be a week-long bash, at the system-famous luxury casino and hotel, the Woodwind, in the capital city of Kazehi, on the subcontinent."

Ferret stood. "I'm going back to Shar's. Call me when you get to the end of your long, slow, epic broadcast."

"Sit down," Stoll said, shaking his head.

Ferret sat. "Jesu, Shanti, you're an old man! You don't have that much time left, you could be eating something instead of boring me.'' But he smiled, giving the lie to his words.

''I'll dance at your funeral, brat! Now shut up and listen!''

''Yes, master. To hear is to obey.'' Ferret grinned widely. He loved this fat thief, had thought of him as an older brother, maybe even the father he wished he'd had.

''As I was saying, the guests will be staying at the Woodwind. They will all want to dress up to the place's elegant reputation, not to mention trying to impress both the dirt diggers and the sewage magnates. The baubles will come out.''

''Ah,'' Ferret said, ''at last we get to it.''

''There is a particular jewel which will likely make its appearance attendant to the festivities. It will be on one of the guests, a sheep rancher from Lee by the name of Petur Tagir. The item is a bracelet of bottle labradorite, carved into the shape of a supine woman.''

Ferret was puzzled. ''Labradorite? That's only a semiprecious stone, isn't it? What is it worth?''

''Intrinsically, not all that much. It's an antique, and the workmanship is fairly good, but the bracelet would probably only bring something around forty or fifty thousand stads on the open market.''

''Then how are we supposed to get a quarter of a million out of it? Not counting expenses?''

''If you'll quit interrupting, I'll tell you.''

Ferret stared at the ceiling and gave a mock sigh. ''Go on.''

''Thank you. It seems that Herr Tagir's father acquired the bracelet from a competitor as part of a transaction that was somewhat less than scrupulous. The competitor then fell upon hard times, and it was a number of years before he could regain his financial footing. At this point, he offered to buy the bracelet back from the senior Tagir. Despite what was a generous offer, Tagir refused to sell.

''This bracelet became a point of conflict for the competitor and Tagir. Both men continued to grow quite wealthy, and eventually, both men passed on. The bracelet was left to the younger Tagir, who fancied it as much as his father. But the son of the competitor had been charged by his father to retrieve the family heirloom, or suffer eternal shame. Which is where we come in.''

"We are working for the son of the competitor?" Ferret said.

"Just so. The sentimental value of this trinket is worth over half a million stads to our client."

"Tagir will know who took it."

"Knowledge is not proof. And certain clues will be provided to the local cools that will point a suspicious finger elsewhere." Stoll grinned widely. "Our contract with our client is to return the bracelet. I'm afraid I might have underestimated somewhat when I told you the value of this caper."

"Huh?"

"Well, there will be other baubles there, now won't there? In order to throw the cools off the scent, we'll *have* to take some of them, don't you agree?"

Ferret laughed. "Of course."

Stoll's face grew serious. "We've got some protection on this one, Willy. Our client has covered some holes for us. These people like precious rocks, and they like to show them off. Emeralds, rubies, diamonds, pulsestones. If we walk carefully, this could be the caper that lets us retire. We might pull five million out of it."

Ferret's mouth seemed dry, of a moment. He had trouble swallowing the lump in his throat. Five million! He could stick his half in a bank and live on Vishnu almost permanently, on the interest alone! Never have to leave the world except for an immigration day every few months, if he didn't want to, never have to leave Shar Li. He could be a rich man, respectable, living high and comfortable. That would be quite a rise, to millionaire from a dirt farm runaway and thief. The excitement flowed through him in epinephrinic waves, filling him with a desire to run and shout and dance.

But he thought he sounded quite calm when he spoke. Quite calm. "I see. So—when do we go?"

NINE _____

SHAR'S BODYSUIT WAS soaked with sweat, as was her hair, despite its being tied up on top of her head with a scarf. A cloth band around her forehead kept the perspiration from her eyes, but it, too, was heavy with moisture. As Ferret watched her, he marveled at how much work went into making something look effortless.

She finished the sequence of steps, shook her head in dissatisfaction, and walked to the edge of the stage where Ferret sat, his back to the wall and his arms wrapped around his knees. She grabbed a towel lying on the floor next to him and used it to wipe her face.

"It looks great," he said.

"It stinks," she said. "My timing is off, my balance is for shit, and I feel as stiff as a day-old road-killed slatcrawler."

"Colorful metaphor."

"It's all your fault."

He raised an eyebrow. "My fault?"

"I wish you wouldn't go on this caper. I'm worried."

"Hey, come on, you know what my job is."

"This is out of your league."

"Thanks a whole lot. I should stick to fifth and demistad petty theft, huh?"

"I didn't mean that." She dropped into a squat next to him, then sat back and extended her legs to the sides in a stretch.

Easily, she rocked forward into a full side split, her crotch touching the stage floor. She leaned farther forward, stretching her lower back muscles.

"What exactly *did* you mean?" He heard the anger in his own voice, and felt fully justified at it.

She continued to work at her muscles. "This is for big stads and there's a lot of risk in it."

"Not all that much if Shanti is right. We've got inside help on a lot of it."

"*If* Shanti is right. You don't dance in and lift five million in jewels and dance away, just like that."

"All of a sudden you're an expert on my business?"

She stopped her stretching and sat up. She reached out and took his hands in hers. "No, you know that's not true. I realize that you're good at what you do, but something rings wrong about this one. A feeling."

He couldn't argue with that. More than once, he'd had bad feelings about a situation. Sometimes he was wrong, but sometimes, he was right. He'd learned to start trusting his gut-level reactions when they came up. Maybe it helped keep him out of trouble, maybe not, it was hard to tell. Once, he backed away from a simple job, made some excuse, and the thing had gone sour. Confed troopers had shown up, and two of the people on the caper had been fried, the others caught and sent to the Cage on Kontrau'lega. Sometimes called Omega—the end of the line—the place was hellish and desolate, and the Cage was the worst spot on the prison planet. Nobody ever came back and nobody had ever escaped from the Omega Cage. Maybe if he'd gone, the job would have run the way it should have, and things would have been different. There was no way to tell.

He didn't get any glimmerings of a problem with this one. Maybe that was because the shine of precious stones was too loud and bright. Whatever. There was excitement, yes, but no rumblings of disaster. He could trust his feelings, but—should he trust hers?

"Listen," he said, "it'll be all right."

She pulled her hands away from his, and cradled his face. "I love you," she said softly. "You're the best thing that's ever come along in my life. It doesn't make sense, I know, but we're connected, here." She touched his chest over his heart, then pressed her hand to her own breast. "I have had better lovers—"

"Oh, thank you so much—"

"Hush and listen to me. It isn't your looks or your cocky attitude or anything physical, no matter what you think. From the first minute Shanti brought you by, I knew you were for me and I for you. Maybe it's just chemical, but I don't think so. For me, it is spiritual. Yes, I know that makes you uncomfortable, talking about spirit, but it's true. You threw that part of yourself away when you left your home, but I have enough for both of us. I don't know what I would do if I lost you."

He caught her hand and pulled it to his chest. "I'll be back in a few weeks, and it will be for good, this time. I won't have to go offplanet to make enough to stay here ever again."

"You don't have to do it," she said. "I would go to another world with you. I can dance anywhere there's enough gravity and a place to stand. Anywhere."

He shook his head. "No, love. This is your world, and I am about to make it mine. It'll be all right. Really."

They sat there for a moment, not speaking. Then, she stood, and tossed the towel at him. "You have a mind like a stone," she said. "Is there anything I can do to talk you out of it?"

He smiled at her, but did not speak. There was one thing. She held a hammer that would shatter his resolve like a thrown rock would break fine thincris dinnerware. She had only to say she would not be waiting when he got back, and he would call it off. But, maybe she didn't know how much he needed and wanted her. Maybe she didn't know he would do anything to keep her. Anything. She had the hammer, but—she didn't know to use it.

He wasn't going to tell her, either.

She went back to her dance, and he watched her, in awe of her talent, knowing he would soon have her and her world forever. That was worth a little risk. That was worth almost any risk.

During the Bender trip to Thompson's Gazelle, Ferret and Stoll went over the portions of the plan they had developed thus far. Naturally, the final pieces of the picture had to wait until the surveillance and investigation of the hotel itself: where the guests would be, the security and so forth, but there were some basic lines to be developed in advance.

The ship was one of the newer luxury A-class intersystem starliners, the *Muto Kato*, built and registered out of the planet of the same name. The layout was much like an ocean-style luxury vessel, with multiple decks, shops, and the amenities of a small town. The people on board were mostly very important souls, else they would not be able to afford the trip or be allowed to make it. And, since most of them were cits, Ferret knew that they would assume he and Shanti must be important, too. Traveling first class tended to allay suspicion, simply because it was so hard to do without a lot of money or a lot of influence, or both. Naturally, one had to keep a watchful eye out for suspicious Confed agents, who could be anywhere, but the risks were small when one had a six-deep fabricated background, bought from and built by computer experts.

The two men sat amidst the tiny bit of greenery the starliner called a park, little more than three small trees and some shrubbery, surrounding a bench perched on the lip of a bathtub-sized pond containing five or six lethargic goldfish. On the off chance that somebody might have decided to record the conversations at the bench, they both wore scramble transceivers, earplug and throat patches, and sub-vocalized their conversation. A passerby would have heard nothing, but to Stoll and Ferret, it was as if they were talking aloud.

"Have you arranged for passage for us offworld and extrasystem?" Stoll asked.

"Yes. I got Holley and his legit hauler. He's kept the ship clean, and he's arranged for some innocuous cargo as a cover. We're listed as exit crew."

"Good. I have plugged into the Wandering Leos on Rift and Thompson's Gazelle, and we'll have all the local small backup we'll need."

Ferret nodded. The way offworld was the most important, win or lose the caper. With the Wandering Leos as ground clutter, the local cools would have their hands full straining the dross. And Confed controllers had been greased for insurance, even though Holley's hauler was ostensibly legal. "What about the hotel plans?"

"It's in my personal comp," Stoll said. "We'll expand it up

tonight and start the drill. The place is big, but laid out with a thought for lost guests, so we won't have any trouble learning the codes and hallways."

"That's a relief. I'm remembering that convention center in Fee'n Exe. I didn't think we'd ever get clear of the place."

Stoll laughed, and the amplified sound of it deafened Ferret.

"Hey, let's keep the decibel level down, fatso!"

"Sorry. I keep seeing you running up and down the halls like a beheaded fowl, yelling, 'Which way? Which way?' "

"You didn't think it was so funny when that private guard nearly shot your ass off."

"That was different."

"Yeah. It always is when it's you and not me."

"So bitter for such tender years. Tsk, tsk. Shall we get back to the matter at hand?"

Ferret grinned. "Yeah, might as well. Beats you talking about whatever gut rot you had for breakfast this morning."

"You wound me," Stoll said, sounding altogether unwounded. "Now, some of the guests will keep their stuff in the hotel vault, that's out. But some of them will trust their own security. . . ."

Ferret listened, absorbing the information Stoll fed him. A lot of things were covered, but there would still be more than a little risk. But nothing worth having was ever easy, he had learned.

Ferret looked up and saw a Confed factor and three attendants walk past, a lord of all he surveyed. Ferret glanced away quickly, to avoid giving any appearance of offense. Cats might look at kings, but anyone lower than those fortunates who wore the Confed mantle had best be very careful about how or when they watched. Like ancient samurai, the elite of the Confed could slay with a wave of a hand, and be inconvenienced little by such actions. Ferret was not political, but one did not need to be a weatherman to know which way the wind blew. Once he was rich, he could buy respect; until then, he'd seen too many people get squashed by being insolent—or stupid. Best to take care; even a fringe dweller could be caught short.

The city of Kazehi had a sharp-edged newness to it found on a lot of the later-settled planets. Time and the elements had yet to smooth the burrs from the pre-fab plastic and local stone and wood. Like a fresh chapel painting in a candlelit church, the colors were still bright and unsmoked. Thompson's Gazelle had been settled all of fifty years before Rift and Lee, the only other two inhabited worlds in the system, and the footprints of man and mue had yet to settle too deeply into the fertile soil.

Here stood rows of giant warehouses, squat blocks of stressed plastic, full of grain and other foodstuffs, baking in the tropical sunshine. There, apartment cubes littered the hillsides like children's blocks dropped in a hurry.

The streets ran thick with electric carts and flitters, windows open to the humid heat, drivers cursing each other for various infractions. The crisp aromatic stink of partially utilized fossil fuels lay over the city like a miasma, rich in hydrocarbons and unnoticed by the inhabitants. Confed troopers walked in pairs, Parker .177s slung over their shoulders, artificially alert, but hardly worried. There was little danger of rebellion here. Life was too easy. There were fortunes to be pulled out of the ground and seas here—war was for the hungry. Confed oppression was everywhere, but conscription and regulation and the killing taxes were bearable on such a world. As it had always done, money talked, and what it said was, "Leave me alone and I'll pay you well."

Ferret grinned at the sights, sounds and smells. There was a bristling aliveness about frontier worlds, a taking-care-of-business attitude that permeated the air and made such places more exciting than the worn worlds of Earth or Titan or Alpha Point, places he had visited in his lane days. What the new planets lacked in culture, they made up for in brashness, and he felt much more at home in this city than he could ever feel in Earth's New York.

"There's Volny," Stoll said, interrupting Ferret's philosophical ruminations.

Volny was a short and slender man of indeterminate age; he could have been forty or seventy, his face seamless and bland. He made his living as a fixer, somebody who could put together intricate puzzles of the right people with the right caper at the right time, and he had a good record. With Volny working the background, you didn't have to worry about trying to find your haul-ass ship when you got to the port. It would be there.

Volny spotted the two thieves and nodded to them. They

would speak to him later, in the opaqued privacy of their hotel room, the anti-bugging also courtesy of Volny. For now, it was enough to know he knew they had arrived.

The Woodwind was the best the planet had to offer, and like the city, was brash and colorful. The architect had tried to make the buildings look organic, as if they had somehow grown up from the land, but the hotel looked more like rocks in a garden than plants. No matter. The Woodwind boasted all the conveniences stads could buy, and its very complexity was the only thing that made the caper possible. No matter what anybody said, Stoll was convinced that an alert guard with a gun was a lot harder to fool than a computer chock full of security programs. He was telling Ferret this for perhaps the hundredth time since they had met, but he was preaching to the converted. No laner worth his body metals felt any different.

"We have two-level police insurance," Stoll said.

Ferret nodded. That meant not only the first cools to get the call, but their immediate supervisors were being paid to respond somewhat slower than normal. A good cool was hard to buy outright, but who could point a finger at a man whose flitter took a couple of tries to start because of a wobbly converter? Or one with a bad transceiver that garbled a call? Thirty seconds, a minute, success was often measured in far less time, and a few thousand stads for a few seconds was a good investment. Nobody was asking for an honest police officer to do anything other than his job, save that he stop to buckle his belt correctly on the way. It was a powerful rationalization, and Ferret and Stoll had used it more than once. No guarantee, but an edge, and edges were what allowed a fringer to survive and prosper.

Ferret had made some calls on his own. He said, "Winkler is in to rascal the room comps."

From the plush leather chair in the room's corner, Stoll smiled. "She's good. They might as well leave the stuff sitting in the halls and save us the trouble of opening the doors."

"Don't be too sure. Billy Boy says about half of the check-ins so far have been hauling personal squeals and screamers. And not a few lock boxes."

Stoll waved one plump hand in dismissal. "Don't bother me with trifles. We have Reason's best can opener and suppressor.

Sixty-three thousand standards each. Money back if they don't
work to level seven complexity.''

"I'll be sure to tell the judge that. And the jailer."

"You worry too much, m'boy."

"And you don't worry enough, fat man."

The noon sun beat down upon the city, and suddenly, it was
time. Too soon for Ferret, in that he was always sure something
major had been forgotten. But as Stoll pointed out, they were
as ready as they were ever going to be, and after the wedding,
all those jewels and precious trinkets were going back to their
respective worlds. The happy couple would be united on the
morrow, the evening remaining between would be filled with
parties, dinners and other social gatherings, with the valuables
hanging from wrists, necks, ears, noses, breasts, and assorted
clothing. The job would have to be done during the day, when
people were out and jewels were not.

As the two men started to leave their room, Stoll said, "You
forgot something."

I knew it, Ferret thought, I knew it. "What?"

"Here." Stoll held out a small, multiple-charge hand wand.

Ferret stared at the weapon. It looked innocuous enough.
The wand was a thin cylinder, eighteen centimeters long and
maybe twelve or thirteen in diameter. About the size and shape
of a good erection—there were offbeat weapon makers who
sometimes designed wands to look precisely like that particular
organ, surely bespeaking psychological volumes about the man
or woman who would buy such a design. The one Stoll held
out was merely a cast aircraft-aluminum tube, featureless save
for the operating stud. Point the thing, press the button, and
any complex animal within range was knocked unconscious by
the combination of ultrasonics and neomagnetic resonance. The
parasympathetic nervous system did not understand the particular energies of the wand, and shut down a whole shitload of
functions to protect itself. It was a humane weapon, in that it
did not ordinarily kill its victims. Fifteen minutes of uncon-
sciousness and a splitting headache for several hours thereafter
was the usual result of being flashed by a hand wand. As such
things went, being alive to gripe about it was infinitely better
than your friends gathering for your funeral.

Ferret glanced at Stoll's face, which was uncharacteristically hard. "Take it," Stoll said.

Ferret nodded, and took the weapon. He felt the smooth metal, warmed by the touch of Stoll's hand, and he stared at it for a second before he thrust it into his jacket pocket. It would stay there until the job was over. He had never used a wand or any other hand weapon since he and Stoll had started their partnership. He only carried them because Stoll insisted. It had been the only major point of contention between them over the years.

Stoll refused to work with anybody who went unarmed on a caper. Even after ten years, Ferret had not been able to convince the fat man that he was no good with weapons, and would just as soon not have one. Stoll never seemed to believe him, and Ferret knew deep down that Stoll was not convinced because he could hear the truth buried under the protestations. Even though he had not fired a tight beam hand wand in more than a dozen years, he knew he could outshoot Stoll, who practiced regularly. Like as not, he could outshoot any but the most expert, for when it came to small arms, Ferret was a natural; he was a master. No matter that he tried to deny it, it would not stay down, and Stoll somehow knew his protests were lies.

The wand tugged old memories from Ferret's past into the fore, memories he would just as soon not have come up now. But once started, that particular flood would not be dammed. Could not be, not by Ferret.

It was the year before he had met Stoll.

The year he had run with Bennet Gworn.

TEN

THE SPACEPORT ON Gebay was the worst Ferret had seen in over three years of running the lanes. Some said Spandle was worse, and some said the wheelworld of Golda, circling Rim in the Beta System, was the bottom, but they were wrong. Ferret had seen Spandle and Golda, and neither came close to Gebay, for sheer boring. To be posted to Gebay by the Confed was considered just short of being jailed—and the word was, prison anywhere except the Omega Cage was better.

Ferret sat in the VIP lounge, courtesy of a hotwired upgrade on his ticket. This was supposedly the best the port could offer, a bare room, sporting a dozen hard-backed plastic chairs and an empty table. Word was, the Gebayans didn't think much of travelers, those so idle they had no work to keep them home. There was no provision for food or diversion in the VIP area. Chairs, so you could sit; a table, so you could put your work on it, that was it. At least there weren't a dozen armed guards staring over your shoulder, eager to protect the industrious citizens from the influence of slothful offworlders. According to what he'd heard, the standard greeting on Gebay was, "Why aren't you working?" It didn't matter if you *were* working when you heard it—if you have enough time to listen, you were probably a slacker. Nice attitude, these folk. Next to them, Confed cools were soft rods.

The main entrance to the lounge slid open, and Bennet Gworn walked inside, looking as arrogant as always.

Ferret had brushed by Gworn a few times in the last couple of years. Lane runners were a fairly loose group, but there weren't that many of them. They shuffled from world to world, yanked as they were caught doing one form of rascal biz or the other, or sometimes just getting tired and dropping out, finding a spot to stay. Some tried local crime and some even gave it a try as cits. Ferret couldn't see that, himself. The Confed sat on honest citizens, made life hard for them, while fringers had almost total freedom. At a price, of course. Hardcore runners numbered maybe a thousand, and Ferret had met more than half of them at one port or another. Gworn had been around at some of the hot spots that inevitably brought clusters of laners. Sometimes it was the rumor of easy money; sometimes the word was that the local cools had gone slack. Different reasons.

They were the only two passengers in the lounge. After looking around, Gworn ambled over toward Ferret. He was taller than Ferret by six centimeters, probably that many kilos heavier, and had chocolate skin and kinky black hair. He wore a civilian copy of jumpship trooper leathers, tight but flexible, and orthodotic molded slippers with nail-grip soles. Fast on his feet, Gworn was. A thief, like Ferret, specializing in break in and barrel ass.

"Nice place you got here," Gworn said, gesturing at the inside of the lounge.

"Glad you like it," Ferret said, his tone matching Gworn's sarcasm. This was standard laner-speak, all surface tension and no depth. "I had it upgraded when I heard you were coming. You shoulda seen it before."

Gworn dropped onto a chair nearby. He slouched, resting on his backbone well above his buttocks, legs extended straight and locked. "Yeah, well, you shouldn't have. It's all too flash, you know what I'm saying?"

"Anything for a laner."

"So, how'd you get stuck on this dirtball? Bad connect?"

Ferret shrugged. "I snatched a half-system ticket with a penalty for re-route. I was heading toward Three-One-Three-Cee but it was here or come up with stads for a change. I'm glued here for two days."

"You going to Ohshit? How come?"

Ferret shrugged again. The Nu System had one world, a heavy gee planet that exported mostly heavy metals. Officially, it was called #313-C, a number its discoverer had hung on it and then never gotten to change before he died in a windstorm. The popular name came from what the majority of new visitors said when first they felt the gee-and-a-half and saw the surface of the world, which seemed at first glance all bare rock and stubby plant life. Then on second glance, it *really* looked bad.

"I hear there's a change in the local Confed government. The new people are looking for tourists, so there are ticket points and freestarch at every spaceport. Supposed to be seven ports."

"Eight," Gworn said. "I touched down there last year. They built a new one."

"Whatever. I thought I'd take it easy and spend a month or two there."

Gworn bent his legs and sat up straighter. He looked tired all of a sudden.

"You ever think about quittin'?" he asked.

The question surprised Ferret. It sounded sincere, and sincere was something you usually didn't hear from other laners. Everybody had a blade to sharpen, and if you didn't watch close, you'd get it in the back. But Gworn's question didn't sound like a knife being honed. For a moment, he almost dropped his guard. Not quite.

"Sometimes. But what would I do? I don't have anything anybody wants to buy, leastways nothing I want to sell."

Gworn leaned back and sighed. "Yeah. I hear you."

Ferret felt uncomfortable. This was not a conversation he'd had before, and not one that led to pleasant thoughts. The road ahead loomed long and tricky, and while it was the only thing he knew how to do, he was pretty sure it eventually would take him nowhere. Free, all right, but at a price, always. There was the danger, sure, but more than that, there was worse, the being alone. Trusting anybody else usually got you hurt. It was one against the universe and fuck you pal if you get in my way.

But something about Gworn touched him, made him feel, if only for a moment, somehow safer. As though Gworn had *risked* something by talking to him.

"Uh, look," Gworn said. "I got a place. Not much, but it'll sleep two. If you're interested. No wires on the offer."

Ferret looked at Gworn. Jesu, he was no more than a boy underneath all that leather and dazzle. And what Gworn was feeling had to be the same thing he was feeling: lonely. It was a big galaxy, and the lanes weren't places to be vulnerable. They'd eat you alive out there, and smile around your splintered bones. So you toughened or you didn't make it. Ferret was tough, and he knew Gworn had to be tough, too, and yet what he felt at this moment was what he saw from Gworn. He was tired and he was lonely. Maybe, just maybe, they could trust each other. Eventually. It was risk, more than theft, but what the fuck—*every*thing was a risk. Gworn just happened to come along at the right place and the right time. Maybe it was more than coincidence. Maybe it was like fate or something.

"Sure," Ferret said, his voice clear of sarcasm. "Why the hell not?"

So it began. At first, it was warm bodies together, hands and mouths and nerve endings, touching, but with eyes open, giving, but holding back, taking, but with caution.

After a time, it seemed more comfortable, two against the road, and so keeping the dark at bay was only half as hard.

A few months later, they loosened up, and began to see that they could trust each other. And why not? They had nobody else, and everybody needed somebody.

So they slept together, though it was no big deal; ran together; stole together. They laughed while running from vigilantes on Hadiya; got stoned stupid and nearly drowned while on Maro; scored high on a theft of suckee powder on Kaplan, then lost the money gambling. They were young and invincible, nothing could stop them, now that they were together. They were Ferret and Gworn: touch one and the other would be on your back. It built up into something, something more than they'd had before. It was scary at times, exposing yourself, but Ferret learned to enjoy it. A friend was something he had never had, and he was sure he would have cut off his arm for Gworn.

Nearly a year after they met, Gworn disappeared for a few days on the frontier world of Greaves. At first, Ferret didn't worry; they didn't dog each other's shadow, and there were spaces in their togetherness. But after nearly a week, he began to get really nervous. They were due to meet on the spinward outbound ship, and it was leaving in two hours. Where was he? Had something happened to him?

Finally, Gworn showed up, grinning like a wirehead and looking five kilos lighter.

"Where the fuck have you been?" Ferret managed, his voice quivering from the relief of tension. A minute earlier, he had been scared; now, he was angry.

"Hey, flo'man, I spent some time in the woods. I hit a mark with some pull, and he had sniffers all over the place looking for me."

"Yeah, well, you could have let me know you were doing something stretchy, you know? I would have helped." His anger warred with his relief, and the relief won. Gworn was all right. An asslick nodick, but that was fine, as long as he was okay.

Gworn grinned, white teeth against chocolate skin. "Nope. This was my caper, Willie. Had to be. It's your birthday today, check?"

Ferret stared at him. "How'd you know that? I never said."

"I might have accidentally viewed your old ID or something. You know, while you were asleep."

"You turd." It was said without heat, and as much a part of their normal conversation as insulting each other's penis size and sexual abilities.

"Hey, don't spaz up, pal. I . . . got something for you."

Ferret was curious. "Yeah?"

"Yeah. A present."

They sat in the small cube they'd rented at the port. It was bigger than a sleep stall, but not much. Both of them sat on the bed, and Gworn tendered a heavy cloth bag. "Here."

Ferret took the bag, then glanced at Gworn's face. The white teeth shone against the dark skin, the smile full of anticipation. "We got to get to the liner," Ferret said.

"We'll make it. Look at what I got you."

Ferret opened the bag. Inside was a small plastic box, heavy, and it rattled when he shook it. Next to it was what looked like a natural fabric skinshirt, soaked with some kind of aromatic lube oil. Whatever was inside the oily cloth was real heavy. He unwrapped it.

The room's light gleamed from a polished metal surface. Ferret felt his breath catch.

"It's a gun," Gworn said.

Ferret looked up from the handgun at his friend. "I know that. Think I'm stupid?"

"Yeah, I truly do. They could write tapes about it, Ferret. Volumes and volumes—How Stupid Ferret Is, In Fifty-one Languages. It'd be like a never-ending story, they could keep adding to it for years."

"Where'd you get this?"

"Where you think I been all week? There's a collector in the Outbrush, he's got a whole room full of these. Not like this, but different kinds. Going back seven or eight hundred years, some of them."

Ferret lifted the weapon. It was bigger than the cheap hand wands he'd carried and never even fired in practice. The handle was of some close-grained dark wood, and the weapon was plated in some shiny metal, nickel or stainfree, he figured. There was a trigger, surrounded by a small loop of metal, a fluted cylinder set in a frame, and an external cocking mechanism. The barrel was about twelve or thirteen centimeters long, with a rounded delta-shaped ridge on the top end. As he moved the weapon around, to look at the other side, Ferret felt a sense of power and of rightness about its being in his hand. It was as if it belonged there, somehow. He had never felt such a sensation of fitness about any object before. How odd.

There was writing engraved along the length of the barrel: on the top, it said: COLT'S PT. F.A. MFG. CO. HARTFORD CT. U.S.A. Along the side, in smaller characters, it said: COLT SINGLE ACTION FRONTIER SCOUT .22 CAL. This last, .22, was repeated on the cylinder, next to the symbols L.R.; underneath the loop surrounding the trigger were some numbers; there was a tiny picture of some four-footed animal standing on its hind legs, holding something in its teeth, on the left side of the frame.

Ferret was flushed with excitement when he turned to grin at Gworn. It had to be worth a fortune. "What do the words mean? I recognize some of the symbols, but I don't know the language."

"Old style Terran," Gworn said. "I couldn't find the instruction manual for this model, but I did find a data ball on how to fire one similar."

Ferret waved the gun around, getting used to the feel of it. "Is it charged?" He pointed the gun at the wall.

"No. You have to use these." Gworn opened the box and removed some tiny cylinders. They were shiny metal or hard plastic, flat on one end and cone-shaped on the other.

Ferret glanced at the small bits of metal. Almost unconsciously, he thumbed back the protruding mechanism on the rear of the gun. It clicked several times before it caught and locked into place. He pointed the gun at the end of the bed and squeezed the trigger. The vaguely hammer-shaped cocking lever snapped down with a sharp *click*! and a fine spray of lube showered from the impact point.

Ferret looked back at Gworn, and grinned widely. He reached out to hug the other young man. "Jesu, Benny, it's— it's, I, Jesu—!"

"Hey, don't get maud on me, shitbrain." But he didn't move away from Ferret's embrace. He put his hand on Ferret's shoulder and rubbed gently at the muscle.

"Nobody ever gave me anything this valuable before."

"It's okay, pal. Really."

"Where's that data ball? I want to see how to operate it."

"We'll miss the outbound. Can't do that, can we?"

"Fuck the outbound!"

"Right! The lanes are always open."

Ferret looked at his friend, his face serious. This was important, the effort that went into it. Nobody had ever cared enough to do something like this before, not even his mother. When he spoke, his voice trembled, almost as if he might cry. Not that he would cry, of course, it just sounded like that. "Thanks, Benny. Thanks a lot."

Gworn looked uncomfortable, as if embarrassed by Ferret's gratitude, and for a moment, Ferret was pretty sure he saw Benny's eyes begin to tear, before the dark youth blinked and turned to glance at the door, like maybe he heard somebody there. "Yeah, well, I wanted you to have something special, you know? Something from me."

Gworn turned back toward Ferret and they both smiled at each other. Ferret said softly, "Yeah, just wait until your birthday, asslick."

"You don't even know when that is, micro-cock."

"Hell I don't. You sleep too, pal."

Both of them laughed, and life felt really good to Ferret. As good as it had ever gotten.

The data ball was of some help. The loading of the chambers was somewhat different, being from the right side of the weapon, called a "revolver," instead of the left, as in the demo. The small cartridges consisted of a metal shell, filled with explosive, and a lead pellet or "bullet," also rigged to explode when it connected with its target. The revolver held six of these cartridges when fully charged, although the data ball warned that leaving an empty chamber under the hammer was a wise precaution, in case the weapon was jolted or even dropped, to prevent accidental discharge.

Ferret couldn't wait to try it. He and Gworn stole a flitter and took a ride into the forest that came nearly to the edge of the port. Greaves was a frontier planet, and wood was thick all over the place. The two drove thirty or forty klicks away from the port town into a desolate area, and hid the flitter out of sight from the road. From the data ball, it was apparent that the revolver would make some noise when discharged, and they didn't want to be noticed.

They set up a dozen plastic food containers taken from a restaurant, ranging in size from a drink can to ten liters. Ferret loaded five of the cartridges into the revolver, being careful to omit the one under the hammer. As the weapon was cocked, the cylinder revolved, placing a loaded chamber under the firing pin.

"Well, go ahead," Gworn said.

"No. You go first."

"Hey, it's your gun. I gave it to you."

"You nearly got nailed taking it. You should do it first."

Gworn nodded. "Okay."

He took the weapon.

"You're supposed to line up the front ramp with the notch in the rear," Ferret said. "And align that on the target."

"Hey, I saw the fucking data ball, jerk-oh. I know what to do."

He extended the weapon to arm's length and pointed it

vaguely in the direction of the lined-up containers, which were about six or seven meters away.

"Okay, here goes—"

A bomb went off.

Ferret dropped into a crouch, looking for the trouble, as the gun fell from Gworn's surprised fingers and thumped onto the thick humus.

Ferret straightened as he realized the source of the explosion. The gun.

Gworn stared at the fallen weapon. "Did it explode?"

Ferret lifted the gun and dusted the bits of moss and leaf from it. There was no sign of damage. "I think that's the sound it always makes."

"You're damping my drive! Hell, you set that thing off in civilization and every cool for five klicks would come running."

"Right about that. What were you firing at?"

"The biggest juice can."

Ferret walked to the row of containers. "No marks on it. I guess you missed."

"Anybody would. All that noise. And it jumped in my hand, too."

"Want to try it again?"

Gworn took a breath and let it out. "Sure."

He managed to shoot four more of the live rounds, flinching against the sound and recoil. None of the containers, however, had been in any danger. They were unmarked. There was a crater on the ground about five meters behind the targets, though, where one of the explosive slugs had impacted.

"It isn't very accurate," Gworn said. "I can do a lot better with a hand wand or a spring gun. And without all that ear-fucking racket."

His own ears ringing, Ferret said, "Let me try it." He removed the empty shells from the revolver, using a spring-loaded rod built in for that purpose, then recharged the weapon. He faced the row of targets, the gun held loosely, barrel pointing at the ground next to his leg. Then in a motion that seemed as natural as breathing, he whipped the gun up and started firing it—

Once, when he was about twelve, his mother had taken him to a prayer meeting in Toilet Town. His father disapproved of the traveling Reverend who took his tent from village to village, and his mother had done it without telling her husband. The sermon had been somewhat more lively than at the local church, but seemed to deviate little from standard doctrine. But afterward, there were the five collection baskets, and the Man Who Threw Money.

Out and out entertaining was not allowed in church, even one that was no more than a synlin tent, but the Reverend had included some things intended to pull in the crowd. Mwili didn't remember the Reverend's name, nor that of the Man Who Threw Money, but he always remembered that part of the service.

Five people with collection baskets stood in a row near the front of the tent, while the Reverend exhorted the congregation to dig deep and help keep the Lord's Work going. Mwili sometimes wondered what the Lord did with all that money—wasn't God supposed to be able to make anything? Why didn't he just mint his own stads?

In the back of the tent, a good twenty meters from the basket holders, a man stood up. He was ordinary looking, dressed in slightly better than average fashion, but he hardly had the look of a rich man. He yelled, "I got twenty-five standards for the Lord, Reverend!" He held up five five-stad coins. They glittered in the hard glare of the tent's lighting rig.

That brought a gasp from the crowd. Twenty-five stads was nothing to spit at. That was a lot of money to be throwing around. As they were about to find out.

"I'll send a basket, brother!" the Reverend said.

"No need, Reverend! The Lord can collect his own money! He knows what's His!" And with that, the man started flinging the coins. He sailed them backhand, like Mwili had once seen a friend sail playing cards. Twenty meters if it was a centimeter, and the baskets no bigger than a loaf of bread each. Five throws, so fast Mwili couldn't follow all the coins, and five coins each plunked into a different basket, as if they'd been pulled there by invisible strings.

Oh, man!

Now, Mwili, like a lot of children his age, was a fair rock thrower. There wasn't a lot to do and there were a lot of rocks on Cibule. At twenty meters, he might hit a target the size of those baskets one out of five. Two, were he particularly lucky.

But five for five? And backhand? No way! It was more than just impressive. At that moment, Mwili was certain there must be a God and that He had his gaze fastened to this particular congregation. How else could those coins hit those baskets unless God Himself called them in? Nobody was that good, not without some kind of magical aid.

The effect on the gathering started the baskets moving and money flowing. Mwili was sure that for as long as he lived, he would remember the Man Who Threw Money as his first experience that miracles were possible. Years later, when he was older, he realized that it was more skill than magic, that the man was demonstrating a trick at which he was adept, probably through much practice, or at the very least, through some fluke of natural talent.

It had been more than seven years, and he hadn't thought about it in a long time, but he thought about it now. For as Ferret fired the antique sidearm, the Colt .22 Frontier Scout Revolver, it was as if he were watching and not doing it.

Five times he fired, as fast as he could cock and squeeze, the gun held low, just past his hip. He did not aim, as the data ball instructed. He just watched the targets and shot, pointing as a man would point a finger.

Five times he fired, and five containers exploded into plastic sleet, showering the woods with shards and the remains of juice or food. Two of the containers were the larger ones, but three of them were the smallest. And with that sense of knowledge that sometimes came to him like it was inborn, Ferret knew he could have hit five targets half the size of the smallest drink can; more, he could have done it all day long without missing. No doubt in his mind.

With the sound of the reports echoing in his ears, Ferret realized he was standing totally relaxed, the gun once again pointing to the ground by his right leg.

Like the Man Who Threw Money, Ferret had found his trick.

Gworn moved closer to Ferret, staring at his friend. "Mother Hairy Asshole, Ferret! How did you do that?"

Ferret shook his head. "I don't know. It's like it was no big deal."

"Yeah, well, don't let me make you mad, you got that thing around."

Ferret looked at the gun. It felt as natural as his fingers. It felt so right.

"You want to try it again, Benny?"

"No way, flo'man. It's yours. It likes you."

Ferret raised the gun and looked at it. "Yeah. I guess it does." He grinned, remembering the Man Who Threw Money. Well, well. Maybe God had come up with *two* miracles. Not bad for less than twenty years.

ELEVEN

"WHAT'S THE MATTER, Ferret? Am I boring you to sleep?"

Ferret blinked at Stoll. "What? Oh, sorry. I was just remembering something. Real old input."

"How nice for you. Do you suppose we might land your memory ship and put its wings on *this* caper and get it into the air?"

"Sure. I'm ready."

"I'm *so* glad. Let's try and stay awake, shall we?"

For the first three rooms, it moved as slick as a lubed finger across polished denscris. Winkler's rascalling of the room's security comps was perfect; the admit override code opened the hotel locks without a hitch; the can opener and suppressor built and supplied by Jersey Reason, the best machineman in the biz, popped the personal locks and squashed the electronic squeals and screamers as easy as thumbing a control. So far, they had collected about a kilo and a half of jewelry, not to mention maybe a hundred thousand stads in loose hard curry. They did like feelie money on these frontier worlds.

There were three rooms left, the target bracelet being in the fourth and next one, and then they were rich and gone. This would be the last caper, and it was going down like fine wine.

At the door to the target room, Ferret got a cold rush.

It was as hard a chill as if someone had opened a door to a

freezer next to him. He stopped. The hall was empty, there was no alarm from the watchers keeping tabs on security, and absolutely no reason to worry. But the hairs on his neck were stirring and Ferret felt his belly clutch as it did in free fall. *Wrongness.*

"What?" Stoll said. He was already extending a hand to punch in the override code.

"Something's wrong."

"What?"

"I don't know. Bad vibes."

Stoll nodded. "Okay. We go in high and low, you take the right, I'll take the left."

"Shanti, we've got maybe a million each, why don't we just—"

"This is the target, Ferret. This is why we're here."

Ferret knew. On one level, the money was the thing; on another level, the contract was more important. Even if they never ran another caper, there was their reputation. They had to deliver, if at all possible.

"Okay. I'm high and right."

Stoll pulled his hand wand. Reluctantly, Ferret withdrew his own weapon from his pocket and gently touched the firing stud. It wasn't a killing weapon, he told himself. The chill grew harder; his skin felt itchy and crawly.

Stoll tapped the first key on the override code. "On three." He started punching the numbers in. "One. Two—" He hit the last number and the door clicked and slid open. "Three—!"

Ferret jumped into the room in a high stance and spun slightly to cover the right side of the suite. Stoll was a heartbeat behind him, crouched low, his arm extended, wand moving back and forth in a short arc, covering the left.

Nobody home.

The door slid shut behind them. Stoll raised slightly from his low stance, and nodded toward the bedroom.

The two men did a fast search. The closets were empty, the fresher vacant, nobody hiding under the form chairs or beds. They were alone.

Stoll put his hand wand away. "False signal," he said.

Ferret sighed, pocketing his own weapon. "Looks like." But the feeling persisted. There was some kind of atavistic rumble going on he couldn't placate with reason. Look, no one is here, he told himself. See? We checked everywhere. Nothing to worry about.

The beast in him continued to growl. *Run*, it said. *Danger is here. Death. Run.*

They found the small lock box and powered it open. Inside was a cache of rings, pins and bracelets, including the one they'd been sent to steal. It had an interesting look to it, and Ferret impulsively slipped it over his wrist and under his jacket sleeve.

"Four down, three to go," Stoll said, grinning.

"Look, Shanti, let's barrel."

"That feeling still there?"

"Yeah."

Stoll looked around, then nodded. "I hear you. I'm getting something like that, too. We've got enough. No point in being greedy. We're covered with four rooms. Come on."

Stoll touched his throat mike. "We still clean?"

"Like a surgery," Ferret heard the voice of the watcher say over his earpiece. Halfway home.

Stoll reached the door first, and the door slid wide. Ferret was behind him. It saved his life.

The hall turned into noise and fire. Ferret heard the sounds of carbines blasting on full auto, felt the impact of the explosive slugs as they rocked Stoll back into him. The stench of propellant reached him, along with shouts.

Shanti fell to the floor.

Moving almost instinctively, Ferret jerked the hand wand out of his pocket and thumbed the firing stud down and pointed it. The weapon thrummed in his hand as he waved it back and forth, tapping the control. The attackers in the hall were preternaturally clear and sharp, he could see their faces in minute detail, as if he had studied them for hours. There were too many of them, they were getting in each other's way, and they couldn't shoot straight enough.

The wand fired six charges before it ran dry, and four men and two women went down, as though his hand had a target computer of its own directing the weapon. There were five or six more of them still up and shooting as Ferret spun and slapped the door controls. Something spanged off the door frame, sparking and ringing, and Ferret felt a spray of hot particles sleet against one arm.

The door slid shut with painful slowness. When it clicked into lock mode, Ferret snap-kicked the mechanism, destroying it.

Stoll!

Ferret dropped the weapon and fell to his knees. The front of Stoll's tunic was ruptured with fist-sized holes rapidly filling with blood. He lay on his back, his eyes shut. He opened his eyes and blinked once at Ferret.

"Shit—!" Stoll said. And died. There could be no doubt.

Ferret stared at his friend, his brain burning and screaming in panic. Outside, men yelled, and the door began to shudder under the impact of explosive fire. The door wouldn't hold for more than a few seconds.

Ferret stood. Shanti was dead, he couldn't help him now. He ran toward the room's outside balcony, picking up a form chair as he moved. Without pausing, he slung the chair at the thincris door. The clear crystal shattered outward; the chair tumbled, then caught on the metal rail bordering the small balcony; and Ferret was right behind it.

The room was on the fourth floor, too far to jump to the ground, but the room just under it also sported a railed balcony, as did all the rooms above ground level on this wing. A good thief always thought about ways to run, should biz go sour, and this caper was shattered.

As the room door behind him began to splinter, Ferret leaped over the metal rail and hung by his hands. He swung himself back and forth like a pendulum, then let go his hold. His feet were two meters over the next balcony, and he landed hard, falling to one shoulder. He didn't hesitate, but repeated his movements from the third to the second-floor balcony, nearly landing on a woman sunning herself. He twisted to avoid her, and hit his side on the rail, scraping a long patch of skin loose. He thought he heard a rib crack, and he could feel the blood start to seep into his clothes.

The woman screamed, but he ignored her, bounded over the railing and to the manicured lawn below. He landed hard, tumbled forward in a shoulder roll and came up scrambling.

Behind him, he heard the men who had killed Shanti yelling as they reached the balcony. He sprinted for a row of bushes,

broke his stride to make a harder target, and felt the wind of
bullets passing him as he reached the cover. Despite his fear,
and in amazement, he had time to notice the overpowering
bananalike scent of the flowering shrubbery as he crashed
through it. He moved, he felt, as if in slow motion, a bug
trapped in hardening amber. It was all a dream, choreographed
by some mad dancer, held together with bloody glue and icy
fear—it couldn't be real.

"Hold your fire!" somebody yelled from four flights up.
"There are civilians down there!"

And, as Ferret cut to his right, running crouched and burning adrenaline, bowels clenched against the expected hammer
of an explosive round, he heard another voice yell something
at him. Or, rather, to him:

"I'll find you, Ferret! You're dead!"

The recognition of the voice made him stumble. He nearly
fell, but managed to recover. In another few seconds, he was
out of line-of-sight of the burgled room. He was safe, for the
moment, and there were lines of retreat laid. Ahead, on the
road passing the hotel, he saw a traffic jam. At least the Wandering Leos hadn't been altogether compromised. His chances
were good that all of the escape conduits weren't burned. It
was possible he could still get away. That should have made
him feel better, safer, but it didn't. Not with that voice still
echoing in his mind. *I'll find you, Ferret! You're dead!*

It was impossible, of course. There was no way. No way,
but he didn't doubt it for a second. Retribution had found him,
half a galaxy away and more than a decade later, and the fear
he felt had nothing to do with being captured or even killed
for this particular caper. It was his past that had caught up with
Ferret, and a debt now called due for a crime much worse,
committed in a moment of fear so long ago. On some deep
level, he had always feared it would happen. And now, it finally had.

Bennet Gworn had come for him, at last.

He lay numb on the bunk in the escape ship, staring at the
spring frame of the bed above his. They were in Bender space
now, and Thompson's Gazelle was light-years behind. He was
safe from immediate pursuit, but Ferret knew he couldn't outrun the fear.

Volny had thoughtfully provided a military diagnoster for the ship, and the broken rib had been orthobonded, the torn skin repaired. There was a dull ache in his side, but he didn't want painkillers to fuzz his thoughts. He wished none of it had happened, but there was no avoiding thinking of it. Shanti was dead, the caper was flayed, and Gworn would be coming for him. Somehow, he had found him, and Ferret didn't think that his old friend had stumbled on him accidentally. It had taken time and money to subvert the hall watchers and to set up the assassination. He must have known about the biz long in advance, and if he did, then that meant he probably knew where Ferret had been before.

And, maybe he knew about Shar.

That was the thought twisting his gut the most. Shanti was dead, and he deserved grief and maybe some kind of revenge. But Shar, Shar was alive and unsuspecting, and if Gworn knew about her . . .

Ferret had to get back to Vishnu. He would have made a straight run, but the ship had other business that could not be changed, and he didn't need the Confed on top of Gworn. So he lay on the bunk, riding the edge of panic, more afraid for Shar than for himself.

God, he thought, if you are out there somewhere and bothering to take an interest in any of this, hear me now. I haven't paid you much mind, and maybe I deserve some heat for that, but if you will keep an eye on Shar, keep her safe, I will give you any price you want. Just this once, I'm asking for something. I'll never ask again. Please.

God chose not to reply in any way Ferret could understand, and the inner pain he felt continued unabated.

Gworn. After all these years. Come to exact payment.

I've already paid, Bennet. A thousand nights I dreamed of it, a thousand times I wished I could go back and change it. It was a mistake, but I can't undo it, Gworn. I can't. I would give almost anything if I could. But not Shar.

God, don't let him get there before I do. Please.

TWELVE _____

CARRYING A STOLEN and valuable antique gun from planet to planet was an interesting proposition. On a couple of the desolate frontier worlds, Ferret could have walked the streets with it openly and nobody would have cared, because everybody was armed. If all the dirtbreakers and timberjacks killed each other off, well, to hell with them, as far as the Confed was concerned. They had plenty more where they came from—not all conscriptees had to be soldiers.

On a couple of worlds, many people would hardly have recognized what the revolver *was*, unless they were history buffs. But on most planets, while they might not know precisely what model Ferret's gun was, they knew enough to discern its function in a hurry. Where the Confed gave a damn, going armed-unlicensed was worth a few years locktime, and maybe a brain scramble, just for the hell of it. Local regs could be added to that, for good measure.

After Gworn gave it to him, Ferret had found some old flat-style vids and watched them, stories of the frontier days on Earth. The men wore funny costumes and virtually all of them had carried weapons very similar to his revolver. They spent a lot of time shooting each other, too, but those were vids, and fiction.

Ferret hadn't been a laner for almost five years without learning a few tricks. There were smugglers who would take any-

91

thing anywhere, for the right price. Sometimes they owed him favors, sometimes he paid them to move his six-gun, as the vidmen called it. Once, he dressed as a junker, and had the disassembled handgun all over his costume: the frame and barrel formed a belt buckle; the cylinder was part of a bracelet; and he wore a necklace of a hundred bullets, each gas-plated in silver, so they looked fake. He had long since learned how to take the gun apart for cleaning. And every chance he got, on any planet with an Outbrush, he practiced with the weapon. Refill cartridges were relatively easy to come by. Apparently there were quite a number of antique weapons around chambered for that particular charge.

He wasn't as good as the best of the gunslingers in the old vids, but he could toss a plastic drink can into the air and hit it consistently. He learned to protect his ears with plugs, and he carried the assembled revolver with him on all the break-and-barrel capers he and Gworn did from then on. Not that he would ever really shoot anybody, but it gave him a sense of confidence.

On Mwanamamke, in the Bibi Arusi System, Gworn had bought a set-up caper, a sure thing. The pair arrived and took a room at a local inn.

It was spring in this hemisphere, and the town was called Dhoruba. It was a spread-out place, the buildings mostly single or double level, the kind of city frontier worlds with lots of space could afford, sprawling outward instead of upward.

The deal had been with Milk Face, an albino Exotic from Rim, fifth planet in the Beta System. Rim was also called the Darkworld, for the mostly prevailing night that was due to a combination of an unusual axial tilt and the single continental land mass where most people lived. Ordinarily, Albino Exotics were beautiful, and they exuded sexual allure that was almost irresistible to an ordinary human or mue. Milk Face, however, was ugly, deliberately made so by surgery, and he took special drugs to damp his pheromonic output. Nobody felt any particular pull to Milk Face. He made his living selling set-ups, background information on potential capers. He had a good reputation, Milk Face did, and he wasn't cheap. Then again, if you were willing to take the risks involved, you could still clear a nice profit after he was paid, and he only took a quarter down and the balance after the job was done.

Gworn explained the caper: "The guy's a coin collector. He's got a shitload of gold, silver, iridium, platinum, you name it, some of the stuff more than five hundred years old. We could clip a couple of kilos, easy, and Mickey Metal will turn it into ingot for ten percent. We could clear eight or ten thousand stads, we're lucky, untraceable."

Ferret nodded. "What's the beegee?"

"Guy runs a Stacey-Hillerman house alarm, with the coin room hardwired into the system. Microwave-connect to a private guard service, armed response in one minute, plus or minus fifteen seconds."

"Can we get in and out that fast?"

Gworn grinned. "Don't have to. Milk Face has the interrupt test code. We can pulse a false signal and clear the system for five minutes of testing. In five minutes, we can be halfway to the fucking Green Moon."

"What's the floor plan?"

Gworn produced a cheap reader and thumbed it into life. A small holoproj lit the air over the reader. The two young men leaned back on the bed as Gworn dialed the image up larger.

"All right, there's the main entry, over there, the secondary. Down this hall and to the left, there's the coin room. The guy lives alone, no watch animals. Here's his sleeping quarters. . . ."

Ferret watched and listened, taking it all in. It seemed a simple enough caper. They'd stall the alarm system, pop a door or window, and hit the coin room, shattering the thincris cases and scooping up the most valuable coins. In and out in three minutes, longest. By the time the guards responded to the continued "test" of the alarm system, they'd be nearly back to the port. When things finally got sorted out, the mark figured out what was missing and the local cools got called in, Mickey would have the furnace fired up and the coins would likely be molten and bubbling, stopping any possible identification. Mickey was a pro, he had the formulae for half a dozen standard compositions of official Confed free trade nonferrous metals, and counterfeit molds for each one. In a few hours, there'd be a stack of gleaming hundred-gram rectangles clinking together in Gworn and Ferret's pockets. They'd pay Mickey, deposit the balance of the caper fee into Milk Face's account, and be on a first-class ticket to points elsewhere. A good night's work, and maybe a week's holiday in some pleasure kiosk. Biz, O biz, we love it!

Ferret grinned. He could hardly remember the fear he'd often felt before he met Gworn. This was the way to live, fast, exciting, dangerous. He and Gworn were charmed, it would go on forever. They couldn't lose, he was certain of it. They had something. Maybe not as potent as God had been back on Cibule, but something.

"There it is," Gworn said.

They sat inside the stolen ground car, looking at the house. Ferret drove past slowly. Both the interior and exterior of the house was dark, except for the glow of street lights. As they cruised by in the quiet electric car, Gworn leaned out through his open window and aimed a surgetube slingshot at the pole light closest to the mark's house. Ferret heard the *thwack*! of the elastic tubes as they hit the metal frame of the slingshot.

"Fuck!" Gworn said, as the lead ball he fired missed the light. He quickly reloaded the slingshot. "Slow down, fireball."

Ferret grinned tightly, feeling that crawly skin sensation he got on every caper. He was sharp, he felt light and itchy, he was pumping dangerblood.

Ferret slowed the car to a crawl.

Gworn fired another lead ball. There came a tinkle of glass and the light crackled and died, fading to a dull orange before winking out.

There was a house four down from the mark's, a place owned by a man who traveled a lot. He would be away tonight, according to Milk Face's information. They could park the car in front of that house. Not coincidentally, the model they had stolen matched that belonging to the traveling man. If anybody happened to notice the vehicle, they'd think it belonged there. Not that anybody was likely to notice: this was a quiet residential area, and it was nearly oh-two-double-oh in the morning. Decent folk were asleep, and shift-changers would have already come and gone. Still, Milk Face was nothing if not complete. DFY planning he called it: Don't Fuck Yourself. There were plenty of people out there who'd do it for you.

Ferret parked the car. His mouth was dry, but he smiled at Gworn. "You ready?"

Gworn nervously returned the smile. "Yeah."

"Let's dance, buddy."

They leaned toward each other and hugged. Ferret felt the wirelike tenseness in Gworn's back and shoulders under his hands, then they were out of the car and casually strolling along the street. This was the most dangerous time. Both wore dark coveralls and sprinting boots; Ferret felt comforted by the weight of the revolver in his pocket.

Insects flitted around the exterior lights of the house next to the mark's, casting giant but faint shadows on the lawn. The dark was thicker due to the broken light, and Ferret felt safer when they were standing in the bushes next to the house. They had decided to spring the window in the hallway that ran between the kitchen and the utility room. A flowering fruit tree mostly hid the window from the street, and with the light out, it was unlikely anybody would see them. Everything smelled plant-green to Ferret.

"Start the timer," Gworn said.

Ferret lifted his left arm and touched the timer button on his chronograph. The seconds started to flash off.

From his pocket, Gworn pulled the small transmitter that would send the test signal to the guard service. He took a deep breath. "Here goes." He pushed the control stud; it clicked, loud in the quiet night.

Ferret counted aloud, his voice soft. "—seven, eight, nine and ten. Go!"

They ran to the window. It was just as Milk Face had said—wired, but with a single snap latch. Gworn jammed the shim under the plastic sealant on the separating ledges and triggered the vibrator. The snap latch jiggled in a half circle and opened, as easily as if someone had done it from inside. Ferret and Gworn grinned at each other.

Down the hall they went. Instrument lights from the kitchen machinery and utility room cast enough of a glow to show them the way. They moved quickly, careful of their steps, the soft cushions of their boot soles making almost no sound on the tile floor.

The door to the coin room was closed and locked, and a blinking red diode showed that the alarm was armed. Gworn produced a short pry bar and levered it into the jamb next to the bolt. The mark put his faith in the alarm and not the lock, which was more for show than effect. The bolt popped free of its track with a *grinch* and the door swung outward on plastic hinges.

Ferret pulled a battery-powered light and dialed the beam to flood. They were in.

Behind thin sheets of clear crystal, precious metal disks gleamed in the light. Gworn lifted the pry bar, to smash the closest case, but Ferret caught his arm. "Wait," he whispered. "Look." He lifted the edge of the thincris, and it opened. There were no locks on the covers.

Gworn laughed softly. "Nice of him to make it so easy!"

They started taking the coins, dropping the plastic-wrapped circles of bright metal into their pockets. "Stay away from the aluminum and copper," Gworn said. "Gold and platinum are the best."

"Hey, eat shit, Bennet. You think I'm stupid?"

"I truly do. They could write tapes on how stupid you are, Ferret—"

"Who's there?" a deep voice said.

The lights went on.

Ferret spun, aware of Gworn diving for cover behind a display case as he turned. A big man stood there, naked, but holding a spring pistol in one hand and some kind of electronic control device in the other. Ferret had time to notice that the man was well built, save for too much belly, covered with a layer of curly, black body hair, and just as startled to see them as they were to see him.

Gworn's movement drew the man's attention. He tracked left with the spring pistol, yelled, "Hold still!" and fired the weapon. The *twang* of the weapon seemed loud in the room. The dart hit one of the display cases; thincris shattered, chips flew. Ferret felt as if he were mired in thick gel, moving in a nightmare, so slowly that he might die of old age before he finished his action.

Later, he would have all the time there was to remember his moves; later, he would think endlessly about what he did; now, however, his mind went blank, and his instinct to live surged forth and took control.

He jerked the revolver from his pocket and cocked it, then

thrust it toward the man and fired. It was a single, smooth move, as if he had practiced it a thousand times.

The explosion filled the room, lapping against the walls and bouncing back against Ferret's ears, making them ring.

The bullet hit the man just over the bridge of his nose, snapping his head back, knocking him backward. The naked man collapsed onto the floor. The sound of his fall was loud in the silence after the shots.

Ferret lowered the gun and stared at the man. He blinked, and for a moment, couldn't track. What—? Where was he—?

Gworn ran to the down man and kicked the spring pistol away, then kneeled. After a few seconds, he stood again.

"Oh, shit, Willie, he's dead. You killed the fucker."

Ferret shook his head. Killed him? No, that wasn't possible. He didn't kill people. He walked over to where the man lay and looked down. The front of the man's head was a dark red and grayish-pink edged hole, big enough to stick your hand into. Ferret felt his stomach churn.

In all his years, on the farm and in the lanes, Ferret had never seen a dead man this close. Sure, he'd been on Pentr'ado when a boxcar crashed and spewed thirty people all over the landscape, but he'd been a half-klick away from that. They had just been distant lumps on the landscape, not like this. And *he* hadn't killed them—

"Come on, come on, we got to get the fuck out of here!" Gworn grabbed Ferret's arm and tugged him away from the dead man. Ferret pulled his arm free, stuck the revolver into his pocket, and bent to see what the man had held in his other hand. He lifted the small rectangular box and stared at it.

"Fuck, that's a screamer!" Gworn yelled. "He's called the cools! Come *on*, man! We have to barrel *now*!"

They ran for the door, it was faster than the window, and inside ten seconds were sprinting toward the stolen electric car. Another ten seconds, and they would be there and gone—

Too long. The first flitter fanned around the corner, blue lights blinking, but no sound from the hooter.

Ferret had come back from his initial shock. He pivoted to his left and sprinted for the gap between the nearest houses. "This way, Benny!" he yelled.

A second police flitter thrummed into view behind the running pair, lights dancing over the houses. An amplified voice

boomed out into the darkness: "POLICE! STOP WHERE
YOU ARE!"

Like fuck I will. Ferret darted past between the houses,
jumped a child's unicycle lying on the ground, and cut to the
right behind the corner of the carport. He heard Gworn's heavy
breathing right behind him. There was a wooden fence just
ahead. It was a good two meters tall, but if they could get over
it, they had a chance.

Ferret reached the fence, caught the top and hurled himself
upward. He swung himself over it, dropped, and hit a hard
surface. He rolled and came up, just as Gworn flew over the
top, barely touching the wood. Ferret was already sprinting
away when he heard and felt Gworn hit, hard.

"Ow, oh, shit, my leg!"

Ferret skidded to a stop. He heard the cools hollering on the
other side of the fence. He looked at Gworn, who was sprawled
on the plastcrete next to the fence. "Come on, Benny—!"

"I can't! My leg, I think it's broke! I can't get up! You gotta
help me, Willie!"

Ferret stood frozen. His heart thumped wildly, and his breath
came hard and fast. Of course. He had to help Gworn. No
question.

"Over that fence," one of the cools yelled. Beams of hand-
held lights waved and stabbed the air not three meters away.
Only the wooden fence stood between Ferret and Gworn and
the oncoming cools.

"Willie!"

Ferret started to move toward Gworn. He took three quick
steps, got within a meter and was bending to pull his friend up
when the first cool clambered up the fence and threw one leg
over. He crested the top and saw the two young men. "There
they are!" He cleared his other hand, showing a military-class
stun beamer. He pointed the weapon at Ferret. The hole in the
end looked big enough to swallow him. Ferret's breath caught
in his throat. He was going to die!

Ferret pulled the revolver from his pocket and fired at the
cool. He didn't know if he hit him or not, but the man fell
backward, screaming. By then, the light beams showed at least
four or five more cools were at the fence. One of them tossed
a sleepgas grenade over the top. The throw was too hard; the
grenade trailed an arc of thin smoke and bounced on the plast-

crete, rolling to a stop ten meters past Ferret. It oozed narco-genic smoke.

It was a timeless moment and it was all too intense. It seemed to last his whole lifetime. Ferret felt sick, as if he might vomit. He had killed a man, maybe two men, and half the cools on the planet were on the other side of that fence. In another few seconds, they would surround him, and he would be caught. A primal fear gripped him, fear of dying, fear of spending his life in a cage, fear of having his mind deleted by drugs and reconditioning. How could this be happening? It wasn't real, it couldn't be real.

Even so, he was not going to leave Benny. He stretched out his free hand. "Come on, Benny! Give me your hand—!"

One of the cools threw something over the top of the fence, something that dangled over the edge and swung back and forth against the wood, scraping it lightly. Ferret never knew what it was, not for sure, not as many times as he would replay that scene, but what it looked like in that hot microsecond of his life was . . . a strap.

Just like the one his father used to beat him with.

The strap.

The already overwhelming fear only took an instant to es-calate into full, mindless, mewling panic. Nothing rational could stand before that feeling, it was the final touch of frost, the deadly chill, reaching for Ferret with icy talons, coated with all the guilt he had ever felt.

Time to meet God, Ferret. Come with me—!

"No!" The sound was raw, from his bowels, and when it left him, so did his reason. Human no longer, he was an animal with only one thing left to him, only one thing:

Ferret turned and ran. He ran until he couldn't see for the red haze pounding in his eyes; he ran until his legs turned to jelly; he ran until he couldn't breathe, then he stopped and was sick. He puked until he felt as if he would turn inside out. His pants were wet, he didn't remember doing that, and he had no idea of where he was or how he had gotten there.

He must have been five kilometers away when he finally dropped, exhausted, but he could still hear Gworn's cries echo-ing in his mind. "Willie! Willie, don't leave me! Willie—!"

Ferret had saved his life and freedom, but in that moment

of cowardice, in that panicked flight, he had lost something: his image of himself as a live-forever hero.

He left Bennet Gworn, his only friend, to a vengeful justice. He would never get over that. Not in a billion years.

He had deserted his only friend to save himself, and what it had cost was more than he could stand.

THIRTEEN

AFTER WHAT SEEMED a billion years, the ship put down on Vishnu, and Ferret hurried away from it. With the jewels he had collected during the theft on Thompson's Gazelle, he was likely a millionaire, even after paying everybody's share. He still wore the bracelet they had been sent to steal; he would have to return it to the rightful owner later.

Ferret had sent messages to Shar; she would be hiding, if she believed the frantic tone of his pleading to do so. They had time-shares in a kiosk owned by Stoll's nephew; it was in the gentle hills that passed for mountains, a hundred klicks from the city. It was unlikely that Gworn would know of the place, and Shar would be safe there.

Meanwhile, he had to decide what he was going to do about Gworn.

He hailed a public flitter, and climbed in. The driver was a programmed din. He told it to take him to his cube. The flitter pulled smoothly away from the private section of the space-port.

His first thought was that he could try to buy Gworn off. It was appealing, but it didn't scan. If Gworn could put together the kind of trap that had killed Shanti, he didn't need money. Mercenary troopers didn't come cheap, and the buy-off for local cools and hotel staff would have also been expensive.

However he had gotten them, Gworn had more than a few stads.

How had he escaped from prison or brainwipe? How long had Gworn been looking for him? How had he *found* him?

Too many questions, no answers.

Maybe he could sit down and explain to Gworn about how he had panicked, and try to show his own remorse. Gworn had a valid grievance, but he had killed Ferret's partner, maybe he could let it go at that.

Right. Ferret had heard his ex-friend screaming at him as he ran from the hotel. Just as he had heard him screaming that night when Ferret had run and left him to be captured.

Gworn didn't want justice, he wanted vengeance.

Ferret had suffered over this for more than ten years, and now it had cost Shanti his life. Gworn might have good reason to be bitter, but it shouldn't extend to anybody else. It was between the two of them, only Gworn wanted more.

He could, Ferret supposed, hire guards. With the money he now had, he could get top, skilled people.

No. Guards weren't the answer. If Gworn had money, and it was obvious he did, then he could bribe somebody someday. What might feel like an impervious shield could have a fatal crack hidden in it, and Ferret did not trust his and Shar's life to some stranger. His recent experience was a testimony to that. Shanti was dead, and the people they had trusted had betrayed them.

Abruptly, Ferret leaned forward and spoke to the din.

"Reprogram destination. To the Intergalos Bank, Main Branch."

The din acknowledged the order, and Ferret leaned back against the seat cushion. His gut was still clenched with the fear that had stabbed him on Thompson's Gazelle. He was afraid, but he was not going to roll onto his back and die. He had regrets, but he wasn't willing to pay with his life for a mistake born of panic. Or pay with anybody else's.

At the bank, Ferret removed his lock box from the vault and went to one of the small enclosed privacy rooms with it. The box had been unopened for a decade, ever since he had first come to Vishnu.

As the footsteps of the bank officer retreated, he unlocked

the lid of the box, to reveal the contents: the handgun Gworn had given him, and a single carton of ammunition, both sealed in blocks of stripgel.

Ferret stared at the weapon with mixed emotions. He had also had mixed emotions when he'd put it here, years past. He hated the thing for what he had caused it to do. The gun was a killing machine, and he was forever a homicidist because of it. He would have destroyed it, but he had not been able to bring himself to it. It was too valuable, he had told himself then. It was his only link with Gworn, and it was a concrete reminder of what he could never forget. Good reasons to keep it.

But more than this, the revolver held a fascination for him. Despite what it represented, he *liked* the thing, he enjoyed the touch and heft of it, the way it felt in his hand, the actual firing of it. Though he had not held it since first he'd put it here, he remembered it as if it had been but a few moments.

Until the recently botched caper, he hadn't fired any weapon since the night he'd run from Gworn. He had carried one only at Stoll's insistence. He was a thief, a smuggler, and he had fought more than a few men with his hands, but he did not want to kill another human or mue again. Somehow, along the way, he had acquired a reverence for life, even before the killing. It made no sense, given his background, but it was there. Some holdover from the Holy Rules, maybe; some pounded-in reverence he hadn't noticed sticking at the time. Whatever. More than once, a weapon would have saved him personal grief. Six years back, his left knee had been lasered during a hovertruck theft, and if he had shot the guard first, he could have saved himself weeks of pain and effort after the new joint had been built. Another time, Little Gib had been caught by the cools on a counterfeit wine caper, and he'd be free if Ferret had thought to bring even a hand wand.

Maybe it was because he didn't trust himself. Maybe it was because he connected Gworn's capture with killing, and couldn't reconcile the two. Maybe it didn't matter, because here he was, staring down at the goddamned gun again. And, despite his resolve about using a weapon, feeling a thrill of anticipation. Damn. It was the wrong thing to be feeling, he should be sickened at the sight of the fucking thing. But he wasn't.

Damn.

He stripped the preservative away and checked the action. The ammunition would normally go bad after so long, but it had been sealed against moisture and temperature change, and was supposed to retain its potency.

He loaded the weapon, five rounds, and slipped it into his belt, under his jacket. He put the remainder of the ammunition into his pocket. He found that when he stood, he was shaking. He might try to get Gworn to listen to reason. But, if the man would not, he would be able to protect himself.

And he would protect Shar Li.

The kiosk lay at the end of a winding road through a forest thick with evergreens. Tall trees reached for the sun, armored bark stalks sheathed in dark greenery, rising from a blanket of dried needles that carpeted the earth beneath them. Ferret drove a rented flitter along the narrow road, watching the rear screens for any sign of pursuit. He had learned about running over the years, and there was no indication of a tail.

There were other recreational kiosks in the area, but none close to the one he sought. He arrived, shut the flitter down, and hurried to the small wooden building. He had sent a message that he would be arriving, and he expected to find Shar waiting for him.

She was gone. She had left a note:

"Willie—the day is too perfect to waste. I've gone for a hike, and I should be back by evening. Love, Shar."

Ferret walked out into the sunshine. It *was* a beautiful day. A few fleecy clouds marred the otherwise clear blue sky; Krishna and Brahma hung in space, pearly blue-green globes, while Shiva was below the horizon and not visible; everything in delicate gravitational balance. Birds and insects peeped and buzzed in the greenery, and the scene held no sense of danger. Maybe he could even relax and enjoy it until Shar returned from her hike.

He found a chair leaning against the kiosk and sat in it, under the shade of the rustic wooden building's overhang. It was warm, with a gentle breeze blowing the woody smells about him. But the gun weighed heavy under his belt, and the knot inside him would not relax under the gentle ministrations of the forest's quiet beauty. He slipped off the jacket and carefully laid it next to the chair where he could reach it easily. He wished that Shar would hurry her return.

Despite himself, Ferret dozed. He awoke to find that the day had wound down into the beginnings of dusk. A thunderstorm built in the distance, the clouds mushrooming up and flattening at the top, going from white to gray to almost purple at the bottom. There was a smell of impending rain in the air.

Where was Shar?

He stood, and worked the kinked muscles of his back and legs loose. There was a cut-off point at which he would begin to worry, but her note had said "evening," and that covered a wide stretch. It could mean by dark, it could mean midnight. Shar had little concept of time; she was almost always late for any meeting.

He found a package of cutlets in the freezer and a loaf of bread. He popped the thick slice of soypro into the microwave oven. When it was done, he made a sandwich and ate it slowly, washing it down with sips of splash from a can he found in the cooler. His stomach felt jittery, and the food was nourishing, but tasteless.

He heard a rattle at the back door, and he went to check it, gun in hand. Some small catlike creature with dark-striped fur stood there on its hind legs, begging for food. He smiled at it, and tossed it the last of his sandwich. The thing caught the quarter-slice of bread and soypro, and darted out into the darkness. Apparently the local animals were used to man's encroachment on their territory. Can't beat 'em, make 'em feed you. There were probably worse philosophies.

Ferret powered up the unit's holoproj and tuned it to an entertainment broadcast. The story, as nearly as he was able to tell, involved a rich athlete and his sexual conquests. He watched it with half his attention.

By nineteen hundred, despite his resolve, he began to worry. The storm was apparently moving this way; the wind had picked up, and the nearby trees swayed and rustled under the gusts. He shut off the holoproj and stared through one of the windows into the windy night.

Shar arrived just before the storm broke over the kiosk. The wind was so loud by then, he didn't hear her open the door.

He was startled by the sight of her, and he had the gun halfway up before he managed to smile and put it away.

Her smile matched his, but only for a moment.

"All right," she said, suddenly serious. "What is going on, Willie?" She pointed at the gun. "What are you doing with that?"

"Come sit down, love. I've got a story to tell you."

He hugged her first, then began to unwind the whole thing, starting when he'd first met Gworn and working through to that bungled theft on Mwanamamke, ending with the death of Stoll on Thompson's Gazelle.

She had known about Stoll—he'd included that in his first message, to assure that she'd hide like he asked. Even so, her tears flowed when he talked about it. He found himself starting to cry, too. The grief that had been blocked by the fear broke through, and the two of them clutched each other like children.

The rain began a wavelike pounding on the roof of the kiosk; lightning flashes sparked in the night, and close thunder rumbled, vibrating the air with its deep voice.

The external storm continued, while the one inside the two of them abated somewhat. Shar sat nestled next to Ferret, with his arm draped over her shoulders.

"So, what now?"

He shook his head. "I came to make sure you were all right. I'll have to find Gworn, before he finds me. I want the advantages to be on my side, this time."

"And what will you do when you find him?"

"Whatever it takes to end this."

"It doesn't sound like he'll listen to reason," she said.

"No. Probably not."

"And you want me to stay here until it's settled." It was not a question.

"Yes."

"It might take months."

"No. Gworn was never particularly patient. Besides, I'll find him."

"How do you know where to look? It's a big moon, and a bigger galaxy."

"I know where to look."

"Where—?" she began. Lightning flared and thunder ripped the rainy night, the light and sound almost together.

"Close," he said. "Are there arrestors on this place?"

"Yes." A beat. "I knew you shouldn't have gone on that caper."

"If it hadn't happened there, it would have happened somewhere else," he said. What he didn't say was that if it had happened somewhere else, Shanti Stoll might still be alive, and he might be dead in his place. He didn't need to say that.

The storm started to move off, taking the high energy of its electrical fury, but leaving the comforting sounds of the rain pattering on the roof. "Let's go to bed," Ferret said. "I need to feel you next to me."

She turned her head slightly and kissed his arm. "Yes."

There was less passion in their connection than there was clinging and stroking. Feeling her aliveness, the taut muscles and smooth skin, that was what he wanted more than sex. Eventually, the two of them reached a peak, after a long, slow rocking he wished would never end. More than anything, he wanted to keep her here, making love and being together. If he'd thought he could run and hide, he would have already been gone, hand in hand with Shar. But she would have to dance, somewhere, in front of some audience, and word would travel. If Gworn had found him once, he might find him again. That was no way to live, looking over your shoulder for the rest of your life. No, he would have to find his old friend and somehow settle what lay between them.

Somehow.

FOURTEEN _____

THE MORNING SHOWED few traces of the night's rain; the sun
bathed the kiosk in gentle light, and the air was only a little
muggy. Ferret and Shar ate breakfast outside.

"So you'll be going soon?" she said.

He swallowed a mouthful of poached egg. "Yes. I'll call
you, to keep you up to date."

"Got time for a walk before you go? There's a lake a couple
of klicks from here. It's lovely in the morning."

"Sure." He didn't want to leave. Not ever.

They finished eating, and stood. She smiled at him and said,
"Let me wash my face and—oh!" He heard a sound like a taut
string being plucked.

Her smile fell, replaced by puzzlement.

"Shar?"

Her features went slack. "Oh. Willie, I—it's so cold. . . ."

She started to collapse. He grabbed her, but she was slack,
almost boneless, and it was like trying to hold a sack of sand.
He slowed her fall, and his hand scraped something sharp on
her back. Quickly, he turned her, to see a spring dart sticking
up from just under her left shoulder blade. The metal dart was
fletched with a spiral of plastic, bright with a black stripe, stark
against the white of her shirt. Red with a black stripe: poison.

"Shar!"

By the time he jerked the dart free and tossed it away, she was already going gray.

She said, "Willie . . . I—I—love . . . you . . ."

"Shar, it'll be all right. I'll get a medic!"

He picked her up and started for the house.

He could hear somebody moving through the bushes behind him, but he didn't pause. He ran into the house, put her down, and started punching the phone.

It took a second for it to register that the unit was without power.

The flitter! He would get her to a hospital!

But when he looked at her, lying on the floor next to the phone, he knew it was too late. Frantically, he searched for a pulse. Nothing. He started CPR, breathing for her, pumping her heart with his hands on her chest.

Time passed. He could not say how long. He stopped finally, when he was exhausted. It was obvious he was wasting his time. She was gone.

Shar Li Vu Ndamase would dance no more in this life.

Shock hit him, as if he had been slammed with a giant boot. He sat next to Shar, his mind stalled, body limp. She couldn't be dead. Couldn't be. He stared at her. What had happened?

As through a dark haze, he remembered pulling the spring dart from her back. And, all of a piece, knew what had been done, and who was responsible.

Gworn. Gworn had killed her.

He was up, and the gun was in his hand, killing magic. He hit the door with one shoulder, breaking it from its hinges, and tumbled to the damp ground. He rolled up, screaming.

"Gworn! Where are you, Gworn!"

He ran into the brush, heedless of the branches that scratched him. "Goddamn you, Gworn!"

Ten minutes of searching the brush gave him nothing. Gworn was gone.

But he knew where.

He put Shar's body into the bed they had shared the night before, covered it, and left a note next to her. It said, "The man who did this is Bennet Gworn. I have gone to find him." Then, using the name he hadn't called himself in fifteen years, he signed it, "Mwili Kalamu."

The bracelet he had slipped onto his wrist on another world—another lifetime—gleamed in the room's light. He pulled the carved semiprecious stone from his arm and slid it over Shar's cold hand. *Take my last gift, my little dancer. I will miss you more than I can say.*

He went to the flitter. He found the tracker, stuck to the underside of the frame. Gworn hadn't had to follow him; he only had to follow the signal. He had led the man here himself. Stupid. Even though it was a rental, he should have checked. Ferret gave the kiosk one last look, then left. He knew exactly where he was going. Gworn would be at the spaceport. Waiting for him.

Well. The time for talk was past. He would find Gworn, and he would kill him. No questions, no hesitation. Bennet Gworn, whatever his grievance, was a dead man.

They were both dead men now, each in their own way.

He had been in the main port two dozen times, as a laner and since. Jumping on- and offplanet, picking up friends of Shar's, seeing people off, the place was familiar. Gworn couldn't know it as well.

He spotted laners, all new faces, but with the same look they all had. They saw him, and knew that he knew them for what they were. He stopped a kid of maybe nineteen. "Do you know Gworn?"

"Piss off, Rickie," the kid said, sneering.

Ferret grabbed the kid by the wrist, and dug a knuckle into a pressure point on the back of his hand. It was painful. From three meters away, he looked as if he were shaking the boy's hand in greeting.

"Ow, shit, cut it, cut it!"

Ferret eased up. "I don't have time to play games with you, laner. If you know Gworn, spill it!"

"I don't know him! Straight shit, Rickie, I swear!"

"He's death, kid. If I find out you lied to me, you're final chill with him, you copy that?"

"Yeah, yeah, I hear you!"

Ferret dropped the boy's hand and turned away. He stalked off, and did not look back. The boy would be afraid. Laners were always afraid, but Ferret had added more to it. He didn't care, it didn't matter. Nothing mattered.

Where would Gworn be? Think. It's been more than ten years, but you knew him once. You know how he thought then. He might have changed, but you ran together. Come on, Ferret, use your brain!

He considered the layout of the port. The main terminal was multileveled, a major level, with three terraces above and two below. And the basement, where the air exchangers and power transmission bars were—

The basement.

It was that quick, and that certain. That's where Gworn was. He wants to kill me, and he'll want privacy for it. He'll know I'm coming.

Ferret found an access door, and waited until somebody came out through it. Before the door could close, he had it. The man who had just exited said, "Hey, you can't do that!"

"Yes, I can. You don't want to get involved in this, citizen."

The man must have seen something in his face. He backed away warily. "Yeah. Right, I-I can see that."

Ferret started into the access tunnel, the door closing softly behind him. Maybe the man would call security, maybe not. It didn't matter. Nothing mattered. He was going to find Gworn. Find him and kill him.

The basement walls were thick, to keep the droning of the machineries from reaching the passengers four floors above, but this close the sound was a constant thrum.

He passed several dins, tending circuitry and mechanical devices, but they took no notice of him. Apparently the place was run by robots. Good.

He wound his way down a narrow corridor, between stacks of thick pipes. Some of them were covered with a thin layer of frost; others were warm to the touch. The air stank of lube, and a musty odor, something like mushrooms.

There were a lot of corridors, and few rooms walled off in the basement, but it was a big place. It might take days to search it properly. Fuck it.

"Gworn! I'm here!"

The yell was lost in the throb of machines.

"Gworn! Where the fuck are you, you bastard!?"

Only the whirring of metal blades, the hum of greased bearings, the whine of power, answered him. At first.

Then: "I'm sorry about the girl," came the yell. "I wanted

you to suffer. I went to see her dance, once. Too bad it had to be her.''

The voice seemed to come from his left. Ferret took the revolver from his pocket and circled that way.

''You left me there, Ferret! Left me to the cools! I spent six years in a cage!''

The voice was definitely just ahead. Ferret thumbed the hammer back on the gun. He moved faster.

''You were my friend, Ferret! I loved you!''

Gworn had moved by the time Ferret reached the place where he thought the voice was coming from. To the right, now. Yeah, I loved you, Benny. But that was then.

''So you have to pay,'' Gworn yelled. ''First your partner, then your woman. Are you suffering, Ferret? I want you to suffer, like I did!''

Gworn was moving as he talked, away and to the right again. Ferret circled to cut him off. He nearly ran into a shielded fan belt. Better watch where he was going, or the basement would get him instead of Gworn.

''I had six years to think about it, Ferret. You ran off and left me, and I learned to hate you above everything in the universe. I'm going to kill you a little at a time! I'll make it last, Ferret. I'm better than you, now. I've practiced with this spring gun for four years, almost every day! Your antique doesn't scare me! You still have it, don't you?''

Ferret almost answered him, but caught himself. I won't talk to you, Gworn. You killed Shanti and you killed Shar, and I'm going to kill you. My face will be the last thing you ever see.

''Ferret? Are you there? Or did you run away again? You're a *coward*, Ferret! But it doesn't matter if you run, because I will find you! I'm your shadow forever!''

He was closer, Ferret knew. Just ahead was a row of holding tanks, shunting some kind of liquid back and forth, gurgling and vibrating. The tanks were tall enough to conceal a man.

''Ferret! Goddammit, where the fuck *are* you?''

Ferret rounded the end of the row of tanks. There Gworn was, back to him. Ferret lowered the revolver, so that the barrel pointed straight down. ''Right here, Gworn,'' he said, his voice quiet against the background drone.

The black man spun, dropping into a shooting crouch, shoving the spring gun out in front of himself. He was screaming something wordless, something primal and full of rage.

Ferret's gun hand came up, as if it had a life of its own. He never took his gaze from Gworn's snarling face. Even the shot sounded quiet against the overlay of machine noise. Gworn's spring gun *twanged*, but the dart went high; Gworn was already falling from the impact of the bullet. He fell, and dropped the spring gun. It clattered and slid three meters away. He clutched at his chest with both hands.

Ferret moved in, and stood over the prostrate man, staring down at him. Gworn was bleeding from around the edges of his hands, the fluid oozing bright red.

"It . . . wasn't—wasn't supposed to be like this."

"No," Ferret said.

Gworn blinked, and tears streamed from the corners of his eyes back and into his ears. "I hate you. I—I used to—to . . . love you, Ferret. I truly did."

"Yeah."

"I'm dying."

"Yeah."

"Well, fuck you, Ferret! You—you hear?" He coughed, and his leaking blood increased its flow.

Ferret looked at the bleeding man, then at the gun in his hand. Another killing. Everybody was dead or dying. He felt hollow, as if all his insides had been scooped out, leaving nothing but a thin shell, with no emotions, nothing but dull grayness, not even pain.

"Fuck you! Fuck you! Fuck—" Gworn stopped abruptly, as if the words had been measured and then cut with a razor-edged sword. His eyes rolled back and he let the last breath he would ever take escape in a bubbly moan.

Dead, Ferret knew. Now they are all gone. The only three friends I ever had. And it's my fault. I betrayed one and that cost me the other two. Now there is nothing. I'm nobody, I have nobody. They are all dead. I should be dead, too.

He raised the gun and stuck the end of the barrel under his chin. Just pull the trigger, Ferret. Make it six people you have killed. The mark, the cop, Shanti, Shar, Gworn and yourself. Go ahead, it'll be easy. A gentle squeeze, that's all it will take. It'll blast your damned head right off . . .

He stood there for five minutes, though it seemed like only

an instant. Then he lowered the gun. He couldn't do it. Gworn was right. He was a coward. He didn't have the guts to do it. He didn't deserve to live, but he was afraid to die. He was running again, just like he had done before.

Like he had always done. Only this time, he couldn't outrun his pursuer. It wasn't his father and it wasn't Gworn, it was himself. He would never be fast enough to escape that follower, the shade of his own soul. No matter where he ran, no matter how far, it would be right next to him, whispering into his ear day or night, whenever he paused to listen: *Right here, coward. I will always be right here.*

Forever and ever and ever. . . .

He looked at the gun again, and realized what a fatal attraction it had held for him. As if it were possessed of some magical lure, a Siren of polished steel and wood, calling to the killer in his soul. But no more. He tossed the weapon at Gworn's body. It hit the dead man on the leg, bounced onto the floor and slid ten centimeters.

Gworn had given it to him, let Gworn have it back.

Part of Ferret turned and walked away.

Part of him would stay there in the basement.

Forever.

FIFTEEN _____

So FERRET WAS rich, but almost everybody who had ever meant anything to him was dead. All the money in the galaxy couldn't buy them back for even a minute.

There was nothing for him on Vishnu, and at least one corpse the cools would attribute to him. The gun next to Gworn was covered with his chemical and finger prints; he'd made no effort to wipe them away. He might make a case for self-defense, maybe even beat the illegal weapon charge, using some of his money-as-power, but it wasn't worth the effort. Nothing was worth the effort. Everything was down the tubes. He couldn't stand being on Vishnu for another day, another hour. He had to get away.

He left his own ship and caught the first commercial liner leaving. He bought an open ticket, paid for it, and boarded. He didn't care where he was bound. It wasn't until they were half a dozen light-years away that he even bothered to ask what the next port of call was. Kalk, the steward had told him. In the Svare System.

Ferret sat in his tiny cabin, staring at the walls. The cosmic finger had jammed itself up his ass again. His home world, the giant moon Cibule, orbited Kalk. Actually, they might be said to orbit each other, given the size and gravity ratio, no matter that they were called moons, but that didn't matter.

It had been over fifteen years since he'd been on Cibule, and since it didn't matter where he was going, he figured he might as well be there as anywhere. Over the years, he had wondered about his parents. Well. Now was the time to find out what had happened to them. The finger was urging him that way, and he had no better plans. He had no plans at all.

It was the only thought that even briefly stirred him from his depression, and then only with a dull curiosity. That was a measure of how he felt: the only destination he could think of now was a dirt-farm he had hated.

He stayed in his cabin, he stared at the wall, he ate if he remembered it. The blanket of grief that covered him was of thick lead, and it was an effort to do anything. He sat bowed under the weight of it, and thought about Stoll and Shar and Gworn. He had fucked it up and they were all dead. It was all his fault and there was no way to repair it, no way to make it right.

Nothing would ever be right again.

Part Two

The Siblings of the Shroud

Recognition of one's ignorance is the first step toward enlightenment.

—JINSOKU

SIXTEEN _____

THE EVERWEAR PLASTIC of the house belied its name—it looked worn; the green color of it had faded with the years and sunlight, and pieces of the topcoat had flaked away from the thicker base, giving the place a mottled appearance.

The house itself looked much smaller than Ferret remembered. There was a flitter parked under the open-walled shed and a tractor outside, next to it. The vehicles were not the same ones he had left, but by no twist of the imagination could they be called new. The flower and vegetable garden his mother had always kept so well tended was a stretch of dead and dried stalks, overcome by weeds. The *wembe* patch closest to the house was in similar condition, the gray-green of the spiked foliage dead or dying, with many of the tubers pulled up and left to rot.

Jesu, it looked terrible. What had happened?

Ferret parked the flitter he had bought and climbed out. The stink was the same, though somehow less intense.

He didn't bother to touch the announcer button. The door was unlocked, and he opened it and walked into the house in which he had been born.

Inside looked worse than outside. Cobwebs laden with dust fuzzed the corners; more dust lay on every exposed surface like fine powder; trash was strewn over the floor—empty food cartons, paper, drink containers. He couldn't believe his mother would allow it to deteriorate so, were she still capable of taking care of it.

He wandered through the house and his memories of it, failing to reconcile the two. This wreck had no place in his scenario—he had never lived *here*.

His father was in the kitchen, sitting at the table, a cup of tea in his hands. He sat so still that at first Ferret thought he might be asleep. After a moment, however, the man looked up.

He had weathered much like the house, Ferret saw. He was only in his seventies, still middle-aged, but he looked closer to a hundred. His hair, what there was of it, had gone white; his skin had been baked by the sun into a mass of wrinkled leather, spotted with darker pigment that made him look paint-spattered. The sclera of his eyes were dirty yellow, and shot through with spidery vessels. Like the house, he had also shrunk with the years. Ferret felt a sense of amazement: How could he have ever feared this pitiful man?

Though his body had suffered, Mafuta Kalamu's mind had not fled into senility. Ferret saw his father recognize him.

"So. You've come back." The old man's voice was flat, almost a monotone.

"Yes." He looked around. The kitchen was in no better shape than the rest of the house. "Where is mother?"

"Dead."

Ferret nodded. He had suspected. He was surprised at the feeling that suddenly touched him. He hadn't seen her in more than fifteen years, and had thought about her only a few times, but he found that knowing she was dead brought up feelings of unfinished business. There were things he should have said, questions he should have asked. As God had once ridden his shoulder, now it seemed Death had replaced Him. In an odd way, he took some comfort that his father was still alive.

Ferret said, "How long?"

"A year and a month. She caught a fever. It was a short illness. The medic says she should have lived."

There were a thousand things Ferret could say, a thousand more questions he could ask. He settled on the one that had dogged him the most over the years:

"On the day that I left, how did you know?"

The old man looked away from his son and stared at the cup of cold tea. "She told me. She knew."

"Why?"

His father sat there unspeaking for what seemed a long time before he answered. "To punish me, of course. She didn't think I would go after you. I did, you know."

"I know. I saw you."

"She hated me. Because of Jana."

For a moment, Ferret couldn't place the name. Then he remembered. "My sister?"

"She killed herself," the old man said.

Ferret blinked, surprised. His mother had always told him that Jana had died from pneumonia. "Why?"

His father twirled the teacup slowly in his hands. "She was going to run away. There was a boy."

"That's not worth suicide," Ferret said.

"I found out. She kept a diary. I had the boy arrested for having sex with her—she wrote of it, she boasted of it! It was a sin."

There was something there, in his father's voice, something he was not saying. Ferret had become a better judge of such things than he had been as a boy. "What else?" His voice sounded harsh in the small kitchen.

The old man seemed lost in his thoughts. He spoke as if seeing through time, as if from a great distance. "She had no right to leave me. No right."

Ferret felt the hair stir on his neck. The meaning of the statement gave him a chill. "No right to leave *you*?"

His father looked up at Ferret. His face had aged even more in just a few moments. Tears gathered in his eyes. "She and I . . . we had, we were . . ." He trailed off.

There was no need to finish. Ferret knew.

"You molested my sister. Your own daughter."

"No. She loved me. She *did* love me."

"You hypocritical bastard! You were so goddamned holy and pure, strapping me if I breathed wrong, and you did *that*?"

"After she died, your mother was going to leave. But she didn't. She stayed. To torment me."

"How could she have allowed you to ever touch her again?"

The old man stared at his tea. "She did not."

"Then how . . . ?" Ferret stopped. The enormity of it struck

him like a physical blow. The room sharpened around him, as
if he had taken a potent psychedelic. The universe was filled
with razors, whirling, whirling, slicing and nicking him in a
wind of steel, catching his attention, making him *aware*. He
could see with absolute clarity.

His voice, when he found it again, was much more steady
than he felt. "Who is my father?"

"I don't know. She never said. That was part of her punish-
ment. It could be any man I met. Do you know how that made
me feel? That any stranger who laughed could be laughing
at me?"

Ferret turned away, suddenly unable to bear the sight of the
man he had always thought of as his father.

Behind him, the voice continued: "I repented. I tried to
wash my soul clean with prayer and humility. But I couldn't
forget. Every time I looked at you, I was reminded."

Ferret felt the emotion well in him. He had thought his feelings crushed by the deaths of Stoll and Shar. He had thought
that nothing could touch him. Now his mother was gone, and
he had lost—for whatever it was worth—his father, too. Could
there be a God? If so, he must surely have angered Him, to be
cursed so. What had he done to deserve this?

"Even after you left, she stayed. I had destroyed both of her
children, you see, and she made sure I knew it. We did not
speak of it, but her every gesture, her every breath conveyed
it to me. It was my cross."

Ferret turned back to face the old man. "You built it yourself."

The old man nodded slowly. "Of course. We all build our
own crosses." He looked up into Ferret's steady gaze. "Didn't
you know that?"

He left the flitter he had bought at the spaceport, left it parked
with the ignition card sticking from the slot. Somebody would
take it, but it wouldn't be stealing, as far as Ferret was concerned. He had no need for the vehicle; he would never set
foot on this world again.

On the ship—where was it going? It didn't matter—he used
the room dispense to dial up various liquors. He drank without
tasting the stuff, drank until he was fogged with alcohol,
wrapped in a warm haze that shut out everything but the need

o maintain it. Sometime later, he began ordering other drugs:
powders, poppers, even one of the high-intensity radiants. It
didn't matter. His credit was thick, and the machine dutifully
supplied whatever he ordered. He didn't need food, he didn't
need contact with anybody, he didn't need anything.

In communion with the dispense, Ferret lost himself, while
the light-years of distance sped past. Entombed inside a high-
tech miracle of a vessel he sped, faster than light, traversing
the near vacuum of it all—but it was never fast enough. He
could not get away, save for the drugs.

Chem was slower, but it helped. He lost them, left Mwili
behind, forgot for yawning spans of time who Ferret was as he
swirled into chemical byways, spiraling away from his conscious mind into fantasy. The dispense was his only friend and
he worshipped at its altar, praying for the machine's promise
of oblivion.

Occasionally, he had a moment of lucidity, why or how he
could not say, and he would wonder what he was going to do
when the ship reached its final destination. Then, some chem
would kick in, and he would smile. It didn't matter. There
were other ships, other destinations. He could keep moving as
long as his money lasted, and that would last long enough.
Long enough for what? To forget?

To forget what?

Time passed. Exactly how much, Ferret did not know, but
it felt like months, maybe even years. In a fresher somewhere,
he washed his face; when he raised up to look into the mirror,
he saw a stranger. The man looking back at him was gaunt, his
clothes hanging loosely on him; this man had sharp features,
the flesh honed away, leaving little more than skin over bone.
The eyes were bloodshot and bleary, the mouth a thin-lipped
line. His hair was straggly and dirty, and the beard-suppressant
was beginning to wear off, allowing a few days' growth of
whiskers to pattern his face. The man's hands shook as though
he had palsy.

A rare moment of clarity settled upon him. Where was he?

He wandered from the fresher out into a pub. The room was
long and narrow, focused around a polished wooden bar backed
by racks of liquor and chem, reflected in a floor-to-ceiling
mirror behind the gleaming bar. A smallish man tended the

patrons there, and maybe two dozen additional customers sat at tables nearby, drinking, eating, talking—doing the things ordinary people did. A neon sign against the mirror had been shaped into the words: Electric Eel, obviously the name of the place.

Why was he sober? He must have mixed his chem or drinks wrong. Sometimes that happened. One chem would balance another, like an acid with a base, and the net result was that neither accomplished anything. Well. He could remedy that fast enough. Although it might be mildly amusing to find out just where he was.

Ferret moved to the bar, and perched upon an empty stool. Before the tender spotted him, he turned to the man seated next to him. "Pardon, flo'man, but I've become a little disoriented. Could you tell me where I am?"

The man was big and dark-haired, wearing a freight handler's coverall. He grinned, showing stainless steel teeth. "The Electric Eel, pard. Smoketown."

"Thank you. Ah—what planet?"

The big man laughed, stainless steel flashing. "You are far orbit, pard. Thompson's Gazelle. You need the system, too?"

"Thanks, no. Let me buy you something."

Well. That was some twist of cosmic comedy. Back on Thompson's Gazelle. He felt no particular worry. Benny was dead, and his hired mercs would be long gone. Nobody would be looking for him under any name but the fake one he had used to pull the caper. However long ago it had been. He thought about asking the freight handler what the date was, but decided against it. The man might decide he was loopy enough to take outside to shake loose his credit cube. He had lost a few that way, and then had to stay sober long enough to get them replaced. A bad scene.

"Tender, get my friend here whatever he's consuming."

The pubtender moved toward them. Ferret turned back to acknowledge the freight handler's smile when he caught a movement peripherally. He reacted without thinking, thrusting his left hand up, fingers stiffened and extended, his thumb curled tightly against the palm under the base of his forefinger.

The block was sloppy, slow, and weak, but it stopped the open-handed slap the pubtender had thrown. The man pulled his hand back.

"Well," he said, "at least you aren't so far gone you can't remember any of your training."

Ferret stared at the little man behind the bar, the freight handler forgotten. Recognition came, breaking through the months of alcoholic and rec chem overlay, and from under the weight of years since last he'd seen him.

Elvin Dindabe. His Gura for nearly a year in the art of *Sengat*, the fasthand sting of power fighting from the Indonesian colony on Titan. Startled as he was, Ferret managed a grin of joy at seeing his old teacher.

For a time, Dindabe had walked the Musashi Flex, a loose association of professional combat artists. The Flex moved from world to world, the fights were sometimes to the death, all in the name of some kind of modern *bushido*. A Flex player might run into another in some pub or alley somewhere and if there was a chance of an even fight, there would be one. Sometimes they were unarmed, sometimes weapons figured into it. The winner was the last player standing. Or breathing. Male, female, human, mues, there were all kinds of players, and it was not a pastime for the cowardly.

The fighters reported the matches, honor was a big part in it, and somebody somewhere kept score. For a time, Dindabe Gura had been among the top five players on the circuit, and as such, had been one of the deadliest men in the Confed. Most worlds had little tolerance for the game, and it was illegal as well as dangerous.

Dindabe had retired, spent a year on Vishnu where he had been born, enjoying monies he had won as a player. He'd taught classes to help keep his hand in. His rates were high, but he was the best available, and Ferret had felt the need to sharpen his own close combat skills. The techniques he had learned had saved his skin more than once, especially given his reluctance to use deadlier weapons.

"What has happened to you?" Dindabe said.

"It's a long story, Gura."

Dindabe waved one hand. A tall and thick woman appeared and walked toward him. "Watch the bar," he said. "I have something to do."

Ferret raised an eyebrow. "You the manager?"

"I own the place. And five others. Come with me."

Ferret would have preferred not to, but there was no arguing with Dindabe Gura. Nobody ever argued with him.

Dindabe circled around the bar, and Ferret followed him. The small man did not look back, nor was there need to do so. Ferret followed, afraid for what was to come.

As well he should be: in *Sengat*, if a student failed at something, his teacher might feel responsible, depending on how much time and energy he had put into the student. Dindabe had worked with Ferret for a year. Ferret wondered how that stacked up in the code of the art.

SEVENTEEN

THERE WAS NO point in even trying to block, this time. The smaller man's hand lanced in and cracked against Ferret's face, hard enough to sting, but not to injure. It was to get his attention. Ferret knew this, and he accepted the impact and subsequent heat without rancor. If Dindabe had wanted to hurt him, he would already be in pain.

"I spent a year training you," the smaller man said. "Best you have a good excuse for your present state."

Ferret remembered a student who had studied with him on Vishnu, a woman who was better than he, but prone to two-day chem voyages. Dindabe had disapproved. He had too few years left to waste his teaching on anybody who didn't appreciate it, the Gura had said. After one binge, the woman had returned to class and had five of her ribs broken while sparring with Dindabe. He had danced to one side and flat-slapped her, a strike that looked like nothing. Now, he'd said, *now* you have a reason to take chem.

Recalling that incident did not make Ferret's unease slacken. He took a deep breath, and began the story.

The months of chemical abuse sloughed away as he spoke, and the wound was as fresh as it had been. Even as he spoke, Ferret knew his actions had been a waste of time. He had not faced his grief, but had only covered it. It lay buried under a thin layer of false forgetfulness, waiting for its chance. He cried as he spoke, not so much from self-pity, but from a sense of loss that time had not been allowed to dull. Finally, now, he grieved.

When he finished, he heard Dindabe sigh.

"I remember the dancer. She could have been a master as a fighter, had she chosen that road. And the fat thief had skill his bulk could not hide. But you went the wrong way, Ferret. The arts could have focused you, you could have burned the sorrow away in a righteous fire; instead, you took the easy way."

"I know, Gura. I was weak."

Dindabe nodded. "A mistake need not follow you forever. How long since you worked out?"

"I don't know. A few days before the caper."

"Too long. Have you training clothes?"

"No."

"My sekolah is not far. All that you need is there. You are *kaki*, starting tomorrow. Six hundred. Tonight, you sleep here."

Ferret felt his mouth go dry, and he nodded dumbly. There was no point in arguing. Dindabe would always be in training, and it seemed he had a school—sekolah—here. The literal translation of *kaki* was "foot," but what it meant in *Sengat*-style fighting was low student. Not a pleasant place to be, since such a position involved not only intense training every day, it also meant doing whatever chores the Gura chose to assign. Cleaning the sekolah's mats and mirrors, caring for the weapons, scrubbing the sidewalks, did the Gura desire that. It was a hard place to be, and the last time he'd been there, he'd been younger and in better shape. With the months of dissipation and chem, Ferret was in poor condition for even the lightest of exercises; no one had ever accused Dindabe of pampering his students.

Ferret was afraid. At the same time, he felt a lifting of the burden he had been trying to pretend he could not feel. When Dindabe Gura was through with him, he would either be in top condition physically or dead; either way, it felt good in a way he had never hoped to feel again. A man can only stay down so long before he rises or loses everything that he is. At the very least, the choice was about to be made.

Ferret wondered which it would be.

• • •

One of the students—there were only three others—was a smuggler named Lyle Gatridge. He was a muscular man a few years younger than Ferret, and called "Red," for the usual reason. He moved well, and he had a fondness for the back-of-the-hand dart gun called spetsdöd. A Flex player had to know weapons since some used them, and the spetsdöd required a lot more skill than a hand wand or shot pistol. The little flechettes the thing fired could be loaded with half a dozen chems, ranging from simple to stun statics to killing poisons. It was rumored that the military had even developed a load that would cause more or less total voluntary muscular contractures for several months.

As *kaki*, Ferret was not allowed to touch weapons, save to clean them, which was just as well. Even if he had the inclination, he was too tired to indulge it. Most of what Ferret did produced sweat and exhaustion.

He was free-sparring with Red, and being kicked around the mat for his efforts. Dindabe did not believe in body armor or protective cups, and a missed block could cost bruises, broken bones or teeth. It was amazing how fast the basic self-defense moves came back to Ferret.

Red danced in and threw a smooth series of kicks and punches, snapping his feet and hands out sharply.

Ferret's blocks were less skilled than they once had been, but effective despite that. He backed away, making no attempt to counterpunch, happy to keep from being beaten senseless.

The two men circled slowly, just out of each other's range. Red said, "You shouldn't be *kaki*, you're better than that."

"I used to be," Ferret said. His breath came hard. He'd been training for six weeks, and it was only in the last few days that Dindabe had allowed him to spar with the other students. "Besides, it doesn't matter how good you are when you start with the Gura. He puts you where he wants to."

Red slid in and threw a crossover sidekick. It was a powerful strike, but what it held in force, it lost in speed. Ferret was able to jerk himself to one side, firing off a backfist. Red danced away from the counterpunch.

"You should have followed up," Red said.

"So should you."

Ferret circled to his left.

Red bore in, lancing at him with a snap kick, a spinning back kick, a hammerfist and a flat punch. Ferret managed to backpedal away from the two kicks, then block the hammerfist. The flat punch got through, however, nailing him just below his solar plexus. He was knocked almost breathless, but he spun away and slashed with a stiffened right hand. The chop bounced from Red's muscular lat, doing little damage, but hitting hard enough to elicit a grunt of pain.

Facing Red two meters away, Ferret couldn't breathe. He tried to take small sips of air through his lips, striving to appear uninjured. Never let them see you are hurt, Dindabe had taught him. You may be on death's doorstep, but pretend you are invincible and impervious to pain. If you take the best shot an opponent can throw at you and are able to laugh, it will unnerve him greatly.

Ferret didn't have enough air to manage a laugh, but he did force a tight smile. What wind he had recovered, he spent in speaking: "Good shot."

From behind Ferret, Dindabe's voice came. "Enough," he said.

Ferret and Red essayed military bows, choppy nods, and relaxed from their fighting stance. They turned and bowed to the Gura, who nodded in return then went back to showing a block to the school's other student, a big yellow-skinned woman named Zholti.

Quietly, Red said, "You wearing body armor under your shirt? That hit should have grounded you."

Ferret dredged up another smile, as much for being able to breathe again as anything. "Maybe you ought to work the punching *ita* a little more, Red. I hardly felt that little shove you gave me."

Red nodded, and went to do just that. Ferret began to practice one of the complicated fighting dances called *kata*, or *tari*, watching himself move in the plastic mirror. He was nowhere near his old form, but he was in better shape than he had been in for a long time. That was something, at least.

But as he danced with imaginary opponents striking at him, Ferret felt a sense of defeat in his moves. He was sober, but that didn't bring Shar or Shanti back. There was an emptiness where they had been, and he did not see that anything would ever fill that space.

• • •

After almost three local months, Dindabe put him to work
in the pub, tending the bar. Ferret was allowed to mix drinks,
if not to consume them, and he spent at least one shift a day
serving patrons in the Electric Eel. It wasn't that he needed
the money, certainly. It was more that Gura thought idleness
high on the list of things to be avoided; since becoming sober,
Ferret could handle his training at the school capably, if not
easily; more, the Gura had taken in another student, and she
was given the position of foot.

He was working the bar on a rainy Threeday evening when
his life took another abrupt turning.

Ferret sloshed thirty cc's of rum into a mixing glass, added
equal amounts each of vodka and bourbon, a squirt of havman-
jani fireoil and sparkling wine as a mixer. The drink was called
a Kohler Killer, and two of them would put most men into a
drunken stupor. The man who ordered this one was a local,
and he could put down three of them and still walk a straight
line. Amazing the tolerance one could attain for chem.

Most of the people who came to the Eel were locals, and
the place had a reputation for being reasonably priced and
peaceful. There was no bouncer, per se, but Dindabe usually
had one of his students working when he wasn't there himself.
The locals knew who Dindabe was, knew too that he preferred
peace in his pub, and was willing to do whatever it took to
keep it that way. Locals didn't fight or even raise their voices
too loudly in the Eel when Dindabe was around. On that particular evening, however, a starliner in need of major repair
hung overhead in high orbit. The liner's ship-to-ground lighter
had landed and discharged a fair-sized load of passengers while
the necessary modifications were being effected on the vessel.
A dozen or so passengers had somehow found their way to the
Electric Eel, and now sat at the tables and bar. The smell of
flickstick smoke drifted over the bar to Ferret, the pleasant
aroma of burned cashews made into purple plumes by the
smokers of the mild hallucinogen.

There was trouble in the pub's atmosphere, Ferret could feel
it upon his skin like damp tropical air, but he was too busy
mixing drinks and chem to worry much about it. Besides, the
Gura was there, chatting with the regular customers, and Ferret

had no doubts about Dindabe being able to handle any problems that might arise.

There came a lull when everybody was happy with his or her current beverage or smoke or powder, and Ferret had a moment to rest. He took the time to pinpoint the disturbance that had been bothering him.

At a table close to the door, four men sat drinking Sting from small porcelain cups. The drink was native to Simba(.)Numa in the CinqueKirli System, and was a hard-edged concoction that tended to make the drinker nasty when too much was imbibed. The four were on their second cup, and Ferret had no intention of selling them a third. They were spacers, ship's crew, and he figured them for shore leave from the starliner. Two of them were average-sized, the other two larger, and all four of them had the muscular look of men who worked with heavy machinery. They wore blue sweats and workboots, and talked quietly among themselves, giving no overt signs of trouble.

Three meters away from the four, a single figure sat at a table meant for six. Though the place was crowded, no one made any move to share the table. This character was part of the problem, Ferret felt, the focus of the four shippers' attention. And an interesting figure it was, too.

The person at the table alone was smallish, and draped in folds of some silky, dark gray cloth from head to feet. The robe left bare only the hands and a swathe over the eyes; the former were thin and well-formed, but showed no rings or jewelry. It was impossible to tell if the person under that covering was male or female, human or mue. Occasionally, he or she would raise a cup of splash and, using a straw pushed under a fold of cloth, would sip at the liquid.

"Something?" Dindabe said, suddenly standing right next to him.

Ferret managed to keep from starting. The Gura had a way of sneaking up on him without being seen or heard. "Maybe."

"The four by the door," Dindabe said.

Ferret nodded. Naturally Dindabe would have seen the potential problem. Ferret felt a sudden need to show his teacher that he had not lost all of his former abilities. "They're watching that one," he said, nodding slightly and pointing with his nose. "There, all wrapped in the dark blanket."

"A Sibling of the Shroud," Dindabe said. "A priestess."

A woman, then. That Dindabe could tell did not surprise Ferret. But he now felt itchy. His scalp tightened. Action threatened. "Do you want me to ask them to leave?"

"No."

Even as his teacher spoke, one of the four men stood, the largest of the group. He sauntered toward the robed figure Dindabe had named priestess. The other three men also left their chairs, and drifted away from the table in different directions. They were surrounding the woman, trying not to be obvious, but failing. Half the pub's patrons were aware of the action now. The *wa* inside the Eel had been disturbed.

"Gura—" Ferret began.

"Watch. Watch and learn."

The largest of the four men stood looming over the seated woman. From behind the bar, Ferret couldn't make out the words, but the man's tone was angry and challenging. The woman looked up, inscrutable under her robed cover.

Around the pair, the other shippers converged, moving closer, shifting into fighting stances.

Ferret risked a glance at Dindabe. What was he doing? The priestess would be catfood before he or Ferret could get there, if they didn't move now—

"Watch them, not me," Dindabe ordered. He smiled, as if enjoying a private joke.

Ferret returned his gaze to the shrouded woman just as the shipper reached down with one big hand to grab the costume. Here it was—!

Later, when he had time to reconstruct it, Ferret's amazement was even more profound; but even in the moment, there was no lack of awe.

The small woman danced. For an instant, it seemed as if Shar had been reborn, so smooth and light were the robed woman's moves. She spun up from her chair as if she were lighter than air, spun away from the big shipper, who suddenly seemed to think it necessary to dive facedown upon the table, breaking the thing under the weight of his jump.

The others moved in, lancing at the woman with kicks and punches, cursing as they attacked. These men were fighters, more than ordinarily adept, and they flowed smoothly in their strike patterns. Ferret recognized skill, likely born of theoretical training tested in dozens of practical pub brawls, as the three moved in for the kill.

They might as well have been standing still, asleep on their feet. The woman danced around them like a butterfly around rooted flowers. She twirled, twisted, leaped, and each time she passed one of the attackers, that man seemed suddenly intent on learning to fly. But they were not birds, these shippers, and they flew like boulders in heavy gravity, smashing into walls and onto the floor.

Ten seconds after it began, the fight was ended. The four attackers lay sprawled like damp paper dolls, and the priestess stood quietly in the center of the pub, her arms by her sides, the pale brown of her eyes calm and impassive from within the gray shroud she wore. An apt name, shroud, Ferret felt. He had never seen anything so impressive. Even the coin thrower of his youth paled beside this fighter.

He tried to think of something clever to say. "Not what you'd call a passive order, are they?"

Next to him, Dindabe's smile still shined. "One of the four players who could beat me at my prime was an arrogant bastard named Zoner," he said. "The rest of us hated him, but we respected his skills. Siblings don't walk the Flex, but those of us who did heard rumors of their art. It is called sumito, and they have developed a complex and intricate system, as you have just seen. Zoner was hot to try one of the martial priests. Against the rules, he challenged one of them. That isn't done with civilians, you know, it's bad form to even defend seriously against one, much less *attack* a nonplayer. But Zoner loaded himself up with weapons and to Perdition with the rules."

Dindabe continued to look at the woman, who returned to her seat and lifted her drink to sip at it.

"Zoner bought himself a quick loss unarmed, like you just saw. So he pulled a poisoned dart. The shrouder took him out without working up a sweat. Zoner could beat me nine of ten, and a nonplayer handled him like a mother does a small child. It was the most amazing thing I had ever seen. Zoner never had a real chance."

"Dead?"

Dindabe nodded. "Stabbed himself with his own dart trying to kill the priest. Karma."

Ferret thought about that for a moment.

Dindabe said, "Come on. There's trash to be thrown out. And you should meet the priestess."

"Me? Why?"

"A feeling."

After helping Gura move the unconscious men outside, where a medical van shortly arrived and loaded them, Ferret and the Gura went back into the pub. Ferret followed his teacher to where the robed figure sat.

"I am Elvin Dindabe, I own this place, Sister. I am sorry you were bothered here."

Though he could not see it behind the face wrap, Ferret was sure the woman smiled. When she spoke, her voice was deep, but definitely feminine. "Had you prevented it here, I would have had to deal with it later."

Ferret got the sudden impression he was only catching part of the conversation. It was almost as if they were speaking a foreign language; or, rather, some higher form of speech with nuances he could not quite catch. He thought he heard Dindabe apologizing for not preventing the fight, though the Gura didn't say exactly that; he also thought he heard the woman acknowledge that Dindabe could have short-circuited the attack, but chose not to do so, and was forgiven for it. How very odd—

"This is Ferret. My student."

Ferret snapped himself from his inattention. The woman regarded him for several seconds, her brown eyes unblinking, before she inclined her head in the slightest of nods.

"Ah," she finally said. "And now mine, I see."

Huh?

Dindabe smiled. "You honor me, Sister."

"Not at all. It is you who honor me." She and Dindabe gave each other slow nods, bows, and the woman looked back at Ferret. "In the order, I am called Moon," she said. "Welcome to the Siblings of the Shroud."

Ferret stared at her, uncomprehending. What was she talking about?

What in all the Seven Levels of Hell was going on here?

EIGHTEEN _____

DINDABE AND FERRET left the pub and went to the school, leaving Moon sipping at her drink. He might be a lot of things, Ferret thought, but a candidate for any kind of priesthood was not among them. At the school, he said so. But even as he did, he heard a defensiveness in his voice. It was almost a whine.

The two of them stood on the rubbery mats, the mirrors casting their reflections back at them. The background smell of old sweat draped the walls, a testimony to the neuromuscular skills practiced within the school.

"You don't understand," Dindabe said. "The Siblings are very selective. They don't take just anyone." He stared off at the wall for a second. "I would have given anything to learn their art after I first saw it, anything. They wouldn't accept my application."

"I'm sorry, Gura, but—"

"But *what*? Who are you? You're a man who wears the name of an animal as a disguise. A thief, a drifter, a man who has money but nothing else! What *good* are you? What purpose do you serve?"

Beneath the anger, Ferret felt Dindabe's pain, and it resonated with his own like the strings of some hurtful musical instrument. Dindabe had examined his own life, that was obvious, and he now played part of his wonderment song aloud, revealing his personal fears: Who am I? Why am I here?

That chord touched Ferret to his depths. Those were the questions he had not dared ask, after the deaths of the only people who had ever meant anything to him. They had been his prostheses, his crutches against having to find out about himself. When they were gone, he had nothing to hide behind.

Who was he?

Why was he here?

Dindabe wasn't finished yet. "No, I don't think you're priest material either. I can't see what she sees in you. But it's your choice, Ferret. You don't have to go with her. You don't have to do anything. You can go back to being the way you were. You can drink or chem yourself into a warm stupor and let your life ebb back into what it was before: nothing. It's up to you. No man can make a choice like this for another, you have to decide. Do you want to risk becoming something more than a ferret? Or would you rather stay what you are, a pretense of a man?"

"Shut up!"

Ferret was stunned, both by Dindabe's longest-ever speech to him, and by his own outburst. His anger overwhelmed him, and his fear of Dindabe as a deadly foe fled before the rage. Yelling at the Gura was tantamount to suicide.

"Ah," Dindabe said, his voice softer, "I am sorry. Maybe I don't have the right to say these things to you."

Ferret shook his head. It was as if a door had been opened within his mind, showing passage to another land, a place so different from where he had lived before that it was more alien than any real planet in the galaxy. He could see into the new land, it was frightening, more terrifying than anything he had ever experienced, and it would never go away. Closing the door might hide the view, but it would not stop the memory. Therein lay a new way, and the risk to him was great. It would take more from him than anything he had to back away—or to go forward.

"You're right," Ferret said. "Truth cuts deep and it hurts, but you're right. I've fucked my life up pretty good, Gura." That, at least, was no revelation.

Dindabe put a calloused hand on Ferret's shoulder and shook him gently. "It's not too late, son. You have a chance to fix it. Not everybody gets that."

Ferret stared through his teacher, a far look that focused on infinity. Of a moment, he remembered what it had been like when first he had been taught of God. Of how good it had felt to think somebody wiser, more powerful and lovingly benevolent was in charge, watching out for him. And he recalled how he had felt when he rejected that concept. Something had been lacking since, though he had never consciously acknowledged it to himself. He missed God. He did not miss the piety of his father, neither the trappings of organized religion—those were the reasons he had first thrown God away—but he missed the warmth of something greater than himself. Maybe this was what had been lacking. Maybe he could find it again. Maybe this priesthood had some answers.

Maybe.

A day later, Ferret sat in Moon's private cabin onboard the starliner bound for Earth, watching the woman. He had determined from her voice and movements that she was young, his age or maybe a little one way or the other. He had not seen her face.

"Do you wear that shroud always?"

"Not always. We are allowed to remove them in private, for bathing or certain kinds of work, or in the presence of . . . loved ones."

"What is the point in wearing them?"

"Anonymity, for one. We take new names on entering the order, and we present a uniform appearance to outsiders. Our founder, Diamond, thought it appropriate to show our worth by our actions, and not our appearances."

"How interesting."

She laughed, a throaty and happy sound. "Oh, there are pragmatic reasons, as well. From time to time, the Siblings engage in actions that are somewhat . . . irregular. One might even say illegal. Wearing face cover and having generic names makes it somewhat difficult for certain oppressive authorities to know whom to detain."

"Somehow, I'm not getting a picture of typical holy men and women here. A highly effective combat form, skulking around in disguises, using phony names—it sounds a little odd. Surprising the Confed allows it to exist."

"What do you know about the Confederation government?"

"Not much," he admitted. "I've never been very political."

"You have much to learn, Ferret. Much to learn."

"All right. Indulge my curiosity. What was the fight in the Eel all about?"

"One of the crew members of this ship wanted to see what was under my robes. He chose to make his desire known in an out of the way part of the vessel where he found me alone. He was insistent. I discouraged him."

Ferret smiled. He could imagine. "And his friends thought to get even."

"Apparently so."

"Dindabe thinks highly of your fighting system. After seeing it, I understand why."

"It is a small part of our order, but necessary—we could accomplish little did we have to spend all of our time hiding from aggressors."

Ferret nodded. Her speech had a formal tang to it, it seemed very proper and aloof, and yet, beneath her words, he felt a current mixed of both humor and warmth. Here was a woman who was competent and dangerous, and, somehow, amused over something. That was an intriguing combination, not one he had ever run across in quite this way. While he was more curious about her, he also wondered about the system that produced such a woman.

Whatever else these Siblings might be, he doubted they would be dull.

The Confed's interstellar travel net was flung wide; sometimes, the net gaped. Bender ships had been assigned routes that, to the casual observer, often made no sense. Generally, travel between major systems was relatively short and direct, as might be expected. But sometimes, due to unexplained machinations generated by those who controlled such things, a trip that should be a single long jump became a series of shorter hops. For instance, a reasonable man would likely assume that a liner running from the Delta System (wherein Thompson's Gazelle spun around its primary star) would go straight to the Solar System, and Earth. The space in light-years was, as such things went, relatively short, and the Deltanian worlds exported a number of goods to the vicinity of Sol. But, no. Instead, a person traveling from Thompson's Gazelle to Earth via commercial starship would first bend space to the Haradali System, change ships at Wu or Tatsu, then be routed to either Dirisha or Mti, in the Ndama System and *then* Earth; or, worse, one could waste twice the time while parked in various orbits of the four-world Bruna System as passengers were ferried up. A direct jump that would take four or five days thus became a leisurely and roundabout slow-ship tour that took instead anywhere from two to three weeks.

Not, Ferret thought, as he sparred with the mirror in the ship's gym, that he was in any great hurry. The more he thought about it, and the more he heard about it, it seemed that this group was some kind of radical organization. He had always been apolitical, at least to the point of worrying little about local governments or Confederation intents, save where they intersected with his business. Somebody was always going to be in charge, and who they were and what they did had never bothered him greatly. Yeah, the Confed was nasty, but he had always played outside of its bounds. Dancing on the fringe, it was called. They would squash him if they caught him, but that was the game, not being caught. Who gave a crap what the Confed did to citizens? A man with a name like Ferret was never going to be upstanding; let the cits worry about politics.

He shifted backward, watching his mirror-brother watch him. He blew out stale air, set himself, and made another run toward his image. Punch, punch, slide, step, kick, kick, and drop, ridge hand to the groin, there—!

Whatever laws the Confed spawned, Ferret intended to obey only the ones he chose. Yes, civilians were always bitching about repressive this and unjust that, but he had largely turned an uncaring ear to such noises. Cits were bound by things that laners and thieves shrugged off like a *kookileigh* shrugged off snow. There were, in Ferret's experience, two kinds of law: one law ruled the poor, an altogether different one more gently guided the rich. Enough money kept nearly everybody at bay. A sufficient bribe could almost always calm the most agitated official, and if it did not, that money could buy you a fast ship to points elsewhere. It was a big galaxy.

His mirror doppelganger looked knowingly at him. True enough, brother. Fuck politics, you got crime.

Ferret raised from his crouch, having just defeated another

invisible enemy, and shuffled back a few meters. He set himself for another attack series.

Radical groups, however, tended to get themselves shut down. It was one thing to harbor opinions, another thing to stand up and speak them aloud. The Confed was not particularly tolerant when it came to dissent. So, if the shrouders were fire-breathing anarchists, they must be careful about where they blew their smoke, elsewise, they would be history. Moon had not exactly advocated any kind of military overthrow, though she had hinted that the order played fast and rather loose now and again. Not too bright, that, Ferret thought. For all she knew, he could be a Confed agent, looking to infiltrate the Siblings.

Jump, punch, chop, chop, spin, heel kick, hook kick and poke to the eyes—!

Ferret relaxed, shook tightness from his shoulders, and took a deep breath, letting it out with almost a sigh. Everything the woman said made him more curious. There was, it seemed, a whole galaxy full of things he had never even wondered about before, things he had not thought worth considering. He had died when Shar and then Gworn had died, and it was surprising to find out that he still cared about anything else.

The man in the mirror stared. What have we gotten ourselves into? Ferret wondered.

He watched Moon again, and shook his head. They were in the gym, and the dance seemed always the same; still, he could not follow it for more than a dozen steps before he lost the thread of it and became entranced with the beauty and complexity of the twirling, leaping figure. Some of the *kata* he had learned during his fight training had been intricate—in one set, he fought nine imaginary opponents at once—but those maneuvers seemed dull and slow compared to hers. Moon's steps were not merely light and quick and in perfect balance; they seemed to flow liquidly without pause. Her arms and hands fluttered and flitted in concert with her legs and feet, but the circles and waves thus described seemed not so much for balance as a kind of naturalistic art. Shar would have loved this priestess. They would have understood each other.

As Moon spun into another repetition of her wondrous flight, Ferret's unease gathered itself into a hard knot in his belly.

They were nearing the Solar System, and Earth. Soon, they would be approaching the home of the order to which Moon belonged. Ferret was, he realized, afraid; of what, he could not say. Moon had given him some bare facts: the form which she so beautifully practiced was called the Ninety-seven Steps, supposedly encompassing all of the most efficient fighting movements of which a human was capable. The commune to which they traveled was in Earth's Southern Hemisphere—an island in the Bismarck Sea, three hundred kilometers north and east of Wewak, New Guinea, a larger island itself north of the Australian continent. The names meant nothing to him, but with a thief's memory for detail, Ferret had filed them away. Manus was a tropical land, living in an eternal summer, too hot during the days, and slightly less hot during the nights. The place boasted dank swamps, steep hills, fast-running muddy streams, large amounts of rain, and thick forests, all buzzing with pestiferous insects and assorted small vermin. Only the coastal regions were habitable by other than a crazed recluse.

Why, Ferret had asked, had the Siblings established themselves on such a hellhole?

Moon had smiled. He could not see her face, but there was a wrinkling and slight movement of the shroud covering her features that he was certain indicated a smile. For just that reason, she had said. Nobody else wanted it. The towns that had been there before lay largely abandoned; the property owners had been more than willing to sell to some insane collection of priests and priestesses willing to lay out a lot of stads for such real estate. The grateful populace took their money and moved quickly, before the mad priests could change their minds and renege. They fled to more hospitable climates, shaking their heads over the brain-damaged ones who actually *wanted* to live there!

The Siblings wanted privacy, Ferret said, understanding.

Just so. The order pays its taxes promptly and is largely left alone. To be official, the Confed sends a rep twice a year. The rep does a cursory inspection, gets stoned on local hemp, and takes a bribe to report what he would report anyway: the thick shrouds have made them all crazy with the heat—they're harmless.

A mistake, I take it?

Again, the hidden smile. But no answer, other than that.

The knot in his belly grew larger and more icy.

Whatever was going on here was much more than some splinter religious group in the middle of nowhere. He felt it in his gut, coiling around like some kind of slithery reptile. Whatever it was, he was going to find out pretty soon.

NINETEEN _____

THE QUESTION "WHY was he here?" took on a more specific
meaning as Ferret and Moon left the air-conditioned coolness
of the local port. The station was automated; he and Moon
were the only people in it. When they exited, he didn't see any
other pedestrians there, either. And no city, to speak of. There
were some weathered orange prefab buildings, storage sheds,
they looked like, that clashed with the surrounding riot of
greenery. A couple of other structures: a pub, what seemed to
be a market. The air was heavy with heat and dampness, laced
with tropical and alien smells. Ferret had been to Earth while
running the lanes, but in another hemisphere and a different
season. Within seconds, his light tunic and pants were wet with
sweat, despite the polypropyl fabric guaranteed to wick away
perspiration. Gods, Moon must be roasting under that wrap
she wore!

"Transportation?" he asked.

"No. We walk. It's only a few kilometers. Somebody will
bring our baggage later."

Overhead, a few klicks away, an afternoon thunderhead was
nearly finished building, dark purple-gray clouds at the bottom, with the cottony-white top high enough to be shredded
by substratospheric winds. He had been in the tropics of several worlds, and he didn't much care for them. This place
seemed worse than most.

Ferret found himself enveloped in a sudden fog. It bit him. Damn, where had all these insects come from? He slapped at the bugs, his efforts doing little except to swirl them about him in buzzing clouds. They didn't seem to be bothering the priestess, even if they could have gotten at her through all that cloth.

"Here," Moon said.

She held out a dark blue hand-sized plastic rectangle.

"A repel-field generator," she said. "The low setting will keep the insects away. The high setting will stop most precipitation."

Ferret took the device, slid the control tab up to the low power setting, and was gratified to see his surrounding bug-smoke dissipate. He slipped the generator onto his belt. It made no sound or vibration he could feel.

"So, the order doesn't believe in wasting its money on such frills as ground cars or flitters, eh?"

Moon continued her long strides without looking at him. "That little device I just gave you cost eight thousand stads," she said. "About the same as a two-passenger flitter runs in a major metropolitan area. Here, with shipping, the flitter would cost half again as much. This island is only a little over thirty by ninety klicks, around sixteen hundred and forty square kilometers altogether. Most of it is inaccessible by ground car or flitter."

She was interrupted by a strobe of lightning and a tearing boom of thunder fast following. Almost immediately, it began to rain. The drops were fat, spattering the plastcrete and nearby bushes with a sound like pebbles falling. Within seconds, a driving tropical wind sent rain sweeping over Ferret and Moon in slanting angular waves.

Ferret fumbled with the control tab on his belt generator, and the waterfall deluging him turned into a fine mist, powdery light, hardly enough to dampen him more than he already was.

Moon leaned close to him, and their fields intersected. He felt his hair stir slightly. Some kind of reaction to the two fields clashing, he figured. A few drops of rain slanted through, confirming his guess. Moon said, "It rains like this almost every afternoon. Between the rain and the insects, which would you rather have—the generator or a ground car you can't drive anywhere?"

"I take your point."

She retreated a pace, and his hair fell back into place. The fine mist continued, no more stray drops hitting him. They walked along the road, skirting puddles. The noise of the rain made casual conversation difficult, so they hiked without speaking. At least it was cooler, Ferret thought.

The few kilometers turned out to be about six. The storm had swept away by the time they reached the gate to the complex, the wind gone and thunder diminished to distant grumbles. Vapor rose under the sun's renewed touch, and already Ferret could feel the heat returning despite the five centimeters of rain.

He had seen a map in the travel station, another item to be committed to memory, and he mentally reviewed it, trying to determine their position. The island's profile was roughly fish-shaped, tapering from the "head" on the east to a sort of squashed, flukelike tail on the west. The fish would have a hook-shaped "nose," if fish had such, an upturned crescent-shaped horn that was actually another small island. This horn was separated from the main body by a strait that seemed narrow enough to span with a thrown rock, judging by the map. At the tail end, tiny islands dribbled away into the sea, looking like small bits of excreta from the larger fish. The travel station was somewhere in the vicinity of the fish's eye, and they walked northeast away from it, as nearly as he could tell—he recalled that Earth's sun set in the west. From the top of a rise a klick back, he had seen the sea, maybe another six or eight kilometers ahead.

Around the compound, a fence stretched in both directions, a metal chain interlink hung with signs warning of high voltage and danger in several languages. Trees and foliage had been cleared from the mesh for five meters on either side. Nobody was going to shinny up a tree and clear the fence, from inside or out. The gate itself was thickly barred and the frame heavy plastcrete; a guard kiosk stood to the left of the entrance, manned by the first person Ferret had seen since arriving. The guard wore a shroud identical to Moon's, but controlled no weapons Ferret could see. Why didn't the Confed notice this place? Some stads must have changed hands somewhere, and not just a few.

Ferret eyed the fence, his thief's instincts curious. "How do you keep it lit during all the rain? Any problem with shorts?"

"No. The carrier is broadcast and triggered by heavy weight—small animals can climb it, but a man will set it off. The charge is a high volt, low amp, come-see-me."

Ferret kept his face impassive as he nodded. Talking very sophisticated gear, a come-see-me zapper. The fence was dead, except for wherever somebody tried to scale it. That particular spot would light up, and while it probably wasn't set to kill, a climber would be lucky to be knocked off and able to consider his mistake in trying it. Otherwise, he'd hang there, clamped to the wire by his own electrically clenched muscles, until somebody came to get him down. Behold my sticky web, stupid bug. . . .

"Hello, Clip," Moon said, interrupting Ferret's professional thought train.

"Moon. Welcome home," the guard said.

"Good to be back. This is the new palliate."

Ferret looked at the man. He must be a permanent guard, he figured. Otherwise, how could she have known who he was?

"Von will be glad to see you," the man called Clip said.

"And I him."

Ferret caught a new undertone in her voice, a happy note he hadn't noticed before. Did Moon and this Von have something going?

Abruptly, he found that thought disquieting. He did not want Moon to be attached.

Oh? And why is that, Ferret old pal? Don't tell me you've got hormones for this tent-covered priestess? Jesu, she could look like a tree stump under that rig!

Ferret suppressed a grin at his inner voice's carping.

Clip touched a control and the gate slid open. Moon walked into the compound, Ferret following.

"What's a palliate?"

"A new student," she said. "Someone who is uncloaked, and starting with the First Layer."

"First Layer?"

"Part of the Undershroud. You have to earn each layer of clothing. There are two divisions, Under and Over, and each has Three Layers. First, Second and Third Under; First, Second and Third Over."

Oh, sister, he thought. Mumbo-jumbo.

She seemed to hear his thought. "Think of it as a kind of pin or belt in a martial art."

Hmm. Put that way, it didn't sound so bad. Actually, it kind of made sense. You'd know who knew what just by looking. All right, he could live with that.

They moved from the gate along a walk that seemed to be made of marble, toward a small building straight ahead. The door slid open, and Moon entered, Ferret right behind her.

He followed her down a narrow hallway to a larger room that stood empty, save for a holoproj inset into the wall. After a beat, another Sibling entered, enwrapped as Moon and Clip were. The figure moved to Moon, said something Ferret did not catch, then stood waiting as Moon turned to Ferret.

"You have to surrender your weapons," she said.

"Weapons? I don't have any weapons."

"You have a plastic HO scan-transparent buckle blade and a stun-grade slap cap ring," she said.

"Huh?" Ferret was at a loss for a moment. Jesu, he had forgotten all about the ring and belt knife. He had been carrying them for years, had never used either one, and tended to dismiss them, as neither were killing devices. How did she know?

"Our detector is efficient," she said, again as if in answer to his unspoken question.

Maybe they were telepaths? "Right about that. Sorry, I forgot all about them."

He tendered the ring and unsnapped the blade from his belt buckle, handing it to her, too. She in turn passed the weapons to the silent figure standing behind her.

They walked from the antechamber down a short stretch of the marble path to a second, larger building, a T-shaped structure of stone, with a lot of windows.

"This is Admin," Moon said. "Von is waiting for us here. He is the Elder Brother of our order."

The Admin building's air was conditioned, and Ferret enjoyed the cooler and drier air as Moon led him along a hallway lined with a dozen doors, most of them open. He could see people inside the rooms—offices, actually—and while some of them were dressed like Moon, others wore fewer garments. All the costumes had a similar look—the wearers' faces and heads were covered, as were their torsos—but those of lower rank had thin, silky masks that stopped at the neck, and some had bare arms or legs, their clothing being little more than dark bodysuits and slippers.

So far, the layout seemed both modern and well constructed. There were computer and holoproj consoles, high-tech climate exchanger strips and liberal use of decorative wood and stone, often polished and carefully worked into intricate patterns. Whoever had designed the place hadn't stinted on material or workmanship, and Ferret had lived well enough to know an expensive structure when he saw one. This was not a poor order.

They passed the entrance to a library, shelves stacked with tapes, disks, recording spheres and actual books. Ferret was even more impressed. Hard copy books were usually rare and valuable, and for them to be kept in that space-consuming fashion must mean they were special indeed.

Another turning brought them to an office that seemed no different than any of the others at first glance. A second look revealed some finer touches, however. The wood of the walls inside this room was thick and full of buried knots, darker concentric patterns against the dark wood itself. The wood had been overlaid with something that gave it a dull gleam, more like satin than glass. Several paintings hung on the polished walls, one a magnificent woman, nude, caught in a pose that indicated both triumph and supplication, almost as if she had somehow found and now stood before God, having overcome great obstacles to do so. The painting so caught his attention that he hardly noticed the robed figure standing to one side.

"Ah. Moon."

Ferret tore his attention away from the painting. The man's voice was vibrant, deep, alive with power. This was the Elder Brother? It must be a title, for surely this was no old man. That bothered him a little.

"Hello, Von." Again, there was that sound in Moon's voice, a current that Ferret could not quite recognize. Affection, to be sure. Maybe respect? Love, perhaps?

"Whom have you brought to us?"

"He calls himself Ferret," she said, as if he were not there and listening. "One of Dindabe's students. Fallen on hard times."

Von shifted his attention from the priestess to Ferret. Ferret felt the man's gaze almost as if it were a touch. "Dindabe. He is well, I trust?"

Ferret said, "Yes. You know him?"

Ferret was sure that Von smiled under his covering. "We met some years ago. He would have joined us, but his intent was altogether too martial, I'm afraid."

Ferret stared at the man. His fear surged. "I don't know what my own intent is," he said. "I'm not sure I belong here."

"Moon seems to think you do," Von said. "And Moon is seldom wrong about these things."

Ferret turned to look at Moon. He tried for sarcasm. "Oh, really?"

"In truth," Von said, ignoring Ferret's attempt at irony. "Well. What shall we call him? Moon?"

"I thought 'Pen' might fit him." Her voice was quieter than usual, softer.

"Ah. You aim high."

"He has the potential."

"Hold on, what are we talking about here?"

"You think so?" Von continued, ignoring Ferret's question. The priest sounded surprised, and at the same time, most interested.

"Yes. I think so."

"Good. Pen it shall be."

"Excuse me," Ferret said, "but would somebody explain?"

Moon said, "When you join the Siblings of the Shroud, you leave your old identity behind. You take on a name that has meaning in the order. No one else can use the name as long as you are a member. We have not had a Brother Pen for some time."

Ferret felt a curious lightness. He tested the word in his mind. Pen. Pen. It was as if he could shed his past with his name. He had done it before, as a boy of sixteen, when he left Mwili and became Ferret. There was something appealing about it, being able to start anew. In the church, there had been a parallel, being born again. He was too old and too cynical to be reborn, but he could start fresh here with this siblinghood, with a new name and a clean screen. Before he spoke, he was aware that he had made his decision, had actually made it when Dindabe had first suggested it to him.

Pen. It was just a word. A simple sound.
He looked at Von.
"Welcome to the Siblings of the Shroud, Pen."
Pen.
And Ferret no longer.

TWENTY

THE FIRST SURPRISE came when Pen stripped away his old clothes and dressed in the skimpy tunic, briefs, pullover mask and boots they gave him. The cloth was like air. He could hardly even feel it on his skin.

"It's called *kawa*," Moon said, when he emerged from the dressing room. "An offshoot of orthoskin. It's one-way osmotic, but waterproof the other way; one-quarter as heavy as purest spider silk, twice as strong. *Kawa* has a rip-stop weave that will turn all but the sharpest knife; it sheds dirt, and it can be layered in such a way as to dissipate or hold virtually all your body heat—keeps you cool in summer, warm in winter. A shroud of *kawa* worn daily will last ten years with minimal care, more with special cleaning and draping. It feels almost alive, doesn't it?"

Pen rubbed the smoothness of the cloth over his chest, fascinated by the feel of it. "I've never even heard of it. Where do you buy it?"

"We don't. It was created by a team of our biotechs more than twenty years ago."

"You could make a fortune marketing it."

"No doubt. But *kawa* is used exclusively for the shrouds."

Pen continued stroking the silky material.

"What you are wearing is the First Layer. For Second Layer, you add a short-sleeved shirt and shorts; Third Layer is a long-

sleeved shirt and pants. After that, you start the Outer Layers.
But that's not something you need concern yourself with for a
time. It takes awhile to reach that level.''

"How long?"

She smiled—he was sure of it—and said, ''Depends on you.
The average is three years. Some take longer, some less. Attitude and work blend together. We work on the mi-
cro/macrocosmic principle, the 'As above, so below' dictum.
Theoretically, you could master all we teach in a few months.''

"But practically?" he said.

"Practically, the average is three years."

"How long did it take you to get fully dressed?"

"Two years to the First Outer Layer, two more years to Full
Shroud.''

Four years. A long time, he thought. But only two years for
her to do what averaged three. Interesting. Then again, what
was she, exactly? And what would he be at the end, assuming
he stuck around? He realized he didn't know anything about
this order, save they could kick heads with unequaled efficiency
when they so desired.

Well. He was about to find out, wasn't he?

The compound that comprised the quarters of the Siblings
of the Shroud was extensive. Moon took him on a tour of the
grounds. Within the confines of the high electric fence lay
something just under seventy hectares. There were woods,
meadows, carefully tended gardens; an auditorium and gymnasium combined was the largest building, more or less centered in the compound. From the gym, which included a full
medical facility, one could take marble walkways to the other
buildings. Northward lay the barracks, two buildings, one for
students, the other for instructors. Private rooms.

"We have forty students at various levels," Moon said.

"How many instructors?"

"Forty. Each palliate starts with a personal teacher. You will
learn from others, of course, but you are paired with a primary
Brother or Sister at the beginning, and you stay with them until
you are done with your training.''

"And you are my teacher?"

"I am."

That pleased him as much as anything had for months. He

felt honored that Moon, obviously a woman of skill and talent, had chosen him to be her student. "Why" was a good question, but he was afraid to ask. And he wondered why he was afraid.

To the east of the gym was the power station. It broadcast energy for the complex, as well as for certain exterior operations run by the order. Nearby were the stores and mech shop buildings.

South of the central gym lay the swimming pool, a large rectangular in-ground unit, complete with diving boards and platforms. East of the pool were the dining hall and Admin; north of them, the biotech labs, central courtyard and gardens, and a bit farther, the meditation dome. There were three gates in the fence, always guarded. Pen and Moon had entered by the main gate, set in the southwest corner of the fence; other, smaller entrances stood at the northeast and southeast corners.

Quite the small town, Pen noted. Self-contained, laid out efficiently, and very private.

As they walked along, Pen noticed recurring patterns of footsteps, painted or stained on the marble outwalks or floors of buildings. In the gym, there were no less than a dozen such patterns laid side by side on the rockfoam flooring. He counted the steps, and was not surprised to find that each pattern held the same number: ninety-seven.

He saw people walking or trying to walk the forms. Some seemed to move flawlessly, as he had seen Moon move; others could only manage a portion of the dance before losing their balance, stumbling or falling, then returning to the start to begin again.

Moon led him to his room. His bags were there ahead of him.

"I'll give you a few minutes to shower and settle in," she said. "Then we'll begin."

After she left, Pen looked around. It was a smallish room, but not too small. Aside from the bed, there was a closet and built-in set of drawers; a chair was parked next to a table with a comp terminal and holoproj screen on it. A lamp stood over the table, another next to the bed. There was a fair-sized window with an exchange strip under it. He dialed the opaque thincris to clarity, and found he was looking north, through a stand of thinly spaced trees at the fence, maybe fifty meters away. He darkened the window, and moved to a heavy plastic door on the wall at right angles to the window. He slid it aside and discovered a fresher with a mirror, sink, bidet and shower stall. A small window of frosted glass opened out to the same view as the main window.

Well. He had lived in a lot worse places. The room wouldn't win any awards for opulence but it was clean and comfortable.

Pen removed the mask. Odd how quickly he had gotten adjusted to it. The eye slit was generous, extended to the ears, and did not block central or peripheral vision in any way. He skinned the bodysuit off, noting that it felt clean and dry, and went to shower.

By the time Moon returned, he had redressed, still feeling almost naked under the whisper-thin cloth. The sensation caused him some discomfort. And arousal. He had been with more than a few people sexually, mostly women, and nudity did not particularly bother him. Then again, he had no idea what Moon even looked like under her shroud, and any stirring of sexual interest on his part would be only too obvious. He did not want to be at that disadvantage.

Naturally, the more he determined to avoid it, the faster his penis swelled and hardened. Great, just fucking great. Why did this happen? Moon was as visually stimulating as a pile of blankets! Down, boy!

If Moon noticed, she did not speak of it, and when she was looking away, he shifted his cursed erection within the bodysuit as best he could. It did not peek one-eyed down his leg from the tight crotch of the sensual material as it had threatened, but it did make an unsightly lump running up toward his navel. Dammit.

His hormones faded soon, though. Beneath the shade of a thick-boled tree between the barracks and meditation dome was a sheet of outdoor rockfoam. Upon the springy material were sets of footprints, with maybe a dozen students trying to walk them. Ferret—no, Pen—was about to get his first experience as a student of sumito.

"Walk the pattern," Moon said.

He felt a sudden surge of panic. "Just like that? No instruction?" He looked around, but none of the other teachers or students seemed to be paying any attention to him and Moon.

" 'The pattern is the teacher,' " she said, and her voice had the sound of ritual in it. "The pattern is fixed, but you are not. How can I tell you how to move? I am not you."

Pen looked at the line of footsteps on the rockfoam surface. "Yeah. Right." Well, the first four or five moves didn't look too hard. After that, the angles got tricky. He tried to picture in his mind how to go at it, and realized he couldn't. Until you got there, you wouldn't know what your balance would be, which muscles would be taking the load. The last few weeks with Dindabe had given him some of his old strength and centering back, but he was nowhere near top shape. Then again, he had seen Moon dance this dance, as well as a few others since he'd arrived. The trick was to keep moving—some of the steps had to be done with the help of fast inertia, because a slow move wouldn't allow enough stretch.

Pen took a deep breath, and put his feet on the first two steps. He bent his knees slightly, shifted his weight, and moved. Third step, okay, twist a little, pivot on the back foot, fourth step, lean right and shift, fifth step. Six and seven took a kind of hop, and then he was moving fast enough to hit eight, off a half centimeter, but not bad, it felt good, he had the flow of it, now—nine, ten, use your arms and hands for balance! crouch and bounce, eleven, twelve is short, got to slow down and pull up, but thirteen, watch it, watch it! oh, Jesu, no way—!

He tangled his right instep behind his left ankle and his dance became a fall. He managed to twist and get one arm out, and finished the tumble in a half-assed roll. He hit hard on his right shoulder. The rockfoam was forgiving, however. He came up, and shook his head.

Moon stood impassively, her arms crossed, none of her visible except the swath of her eyes. What did she think? Was she disappointed in him? He wanted to impress her, wanted her to think well of him, and he had fallen an eighth of the way through. Pretty bad.

"I'm sorry," he said. "I'll try it again."

"No. That's enough for today."

He tried to think of some excuse. "I'm a little off, from—from the trip and all. I'm sure I can do better, Moon." It sounded lame, it sounded whiney, and he regretted saying it as it left his mouth. *That's the way to impress her, fool! Fuck up and then make excuses!*

"Tomorrow. It's almost time for supper. You don't want to be late."

"*I* don't want to be late? Don't you eat?"

"I am dining more privately tonight."

Instant suspicion flared in him. Privately. With Von, he didn't doubt. There *was* something going on there.

"I'll see you in the morning," she said. "Get some rest after supper. Tomorrow will be a long day."

There were about sixty-five people in the dining hall when Pen arrived. About half of them were in full shroud, the others in various degrees of dress. A couple wore the same kind of outfit he wore. Robot dins stood behind a line of dispense trays. The smells of the cooked food wafted to Pen, and he found he was very hungry.

He moved down the line, taking portions from the dins. Vegetables, soypro cutlets, fruits, cheese, iced tea. They set a nice table here.

There were a number of vacant spots at the tables. Pen chose one next to a muscular man dressed in mask and short shirt and pants—Second Layer, he recalled—with darkly tanned bare arms and legs, indicating that the man had been here long enough to get some sun.

As he sat, the other man spoke. "Ah, you'd be the new palliate. I'm Spiral. Welcome to the order."

"They call me Pen."

"Good name. You must be something special."

"Not so's you could tell," Pen said. "Why do you say that?"

"You'll get it in history. They don't give out Pens easy. Last one wound up running a planet somewhere. Big achievers, the Pens. The original was there with Diamond when the order was established. Diamond gets the official credit for a whole shitload of things, but the story is that Pen was the one who actually came up with the Ninety-seven Steps."

Pen took a bite of the orange vegetable. Delicious. "Yeah, well, I didn't inherit his talent. I fell all over myself trying to walk the pattern today."

Spiral laughed around a mouthful of cutlet. "Hey, *everybody* falls, brother. Right up to Full Shrouds, they fall. That's one of the Final Layer tests, to walk the pattern consistently without falling. How far'd you get?"

''Not very. Twelve steps.''

Spiral choked on something. He coughed, spat a lump of soypro out, and coughed some more.

''You okay?''

Spiral caught his breath and nodded. He sipped at his tea, then looked at Pen. ''Twelve steps, you said?''

''Yeah, I feel kind of stupid. I'm glad Moon didn't laugh at me.''

''Moon? You got *Moon* as a Sister?''

''Yeah, so?''

''Holy fuck! Twelve steps and Moon. You ought not to be sitting next to *me*, brother. *You* are somebody!''

''What in the hell are you talking about?''

''Well, first, Moon is gearing up to be Elder Sister, when Von leaves. She's the best there is. The Elder doesn't have to teach, he or she doesn't want to, and for somebody about to take over to pick up a new student is a big deal. You *got* something, pal.''

''Right, I'm an ex-thief and drunk, I got null.''

''Listen, my first day here I made six steps on the pattern before I fell. I got black pins in two arts, I can do a full split without a warm-up, and my resting pulse is forty-two. That's not brag, it's just so you know. I'm in shape, I trained hard before I ever got to this world. Six steps is pretty damn good; three or four is average. Nobody since I've been here has done more than seven on the first day. Moon is the best there is, they say she did nine on her initial try. And *you* did twelve, without a warm-up. Almost all the way to Twisted Star. Shitso, pal, there are people who've been here six months before they made twelve!''

Pen stared at his plate. He felt a cold chill touch his neck under the pullover mask. Something was frightening about hearing this from Spiral. He wasn't anything special. He was a thief, a man who had drifted through his life so far doing nothing, wasting his allotted time, destroying those close to him. Something was wrong about this. He didn't feel special.

He didn't *want* to feel special!

And Moon, Moon had never indicated a thing. If what Spiral said was true—and he would check it out before he believed it—then why hadn't Moon reacted? It was as if she expected him to do better than he had, and he had disappointed her.

What was going on here? What did it all mean?

He was afraid to find out. And yet, he wanted to find out more than anything.

TWENTY-ONE _____

HE COULD NOT sleep. The impact of it all finally hit him like a falling tower of rigidcast blocks, knocking away any chance at rest and filling him with dread.

What was he doing here?

Since he had fired the explosive bullet that killed Gworn, he had been floating in a kind of nonthinking sea of limbo, allowing himself to be swept along with whatever current chose to take him. Not only had he not fought against it, he had tried to numb himself and sink into oblivion. As with most of his life, he had failed. He had obeyed Dindabe mindlessly, and now he was light-years away on the motherworld, as docile as a trained pet, following directions again. Why? To what end?

He shifted from the bed and walked to the window. He dialed the thincris to clear and stared out at the night.

A tropical moon hung somewhere out of sight, but its thin light lay over the compound palely; there, thirty meters away, an outdoor lamp projecting a yellow-orange glow drew a shifting cloud of insects, a shade of light he suspected was not supposed to attract such creatures. Only they didn't know that. As he watched the flitting bugs, he was reminded of an old entcom joke he had seen a long time ago: Two pioneers are perched atop a rocky hill jutting up from some alien landscape. The base of the rock is surrounded by large fang-bearing creatures that look very hungry. "Don't worry," one of the settlers is saying, "the Confed exploration report says they don't have claws and can't climb." Meanwhile, behind the settlers, unseen by them, a dozen of the hungry beasts are scaling the sheer wall, using everything from old-style pitons and ropes to motorized line crawlers and boosting jets. Dinner is about to be served.

He turned away from the window, not bothering to opaque it again. Why had he thought of that? Was it because he felt trapped? Or maybe because he somehow felt that things were not what they seemed? He wondered how many times men had died with the words, "They're not supposed to be able to do that!" on their lips.

Who was not supposed to be able to do *what*?

First he had been Mwili. Then Ferret. Now, he was Pen. Why? To what end? What was he supposed to be doing? What the hell did any of it *mean*?

He returned to the bed, his despair covering him like the shrouds that hid the brothers and sisters of the order in which he now found himself. Was life simply inertia? Move until you couldn't move anymore?

He leaned back against the wall, his legs outstretched on the bed, and stared at the distant light, aswarm in creatures drawn to it for reasons they could not possibly understand. He envied those people who had faith. It was so much easier than thinking. Let God handle the big questions. Trust something higher, watch where you step, mind your manners, and it will all be for some glorious end. Someday, all your questions will be answered, as you sit at the throneside of the Omnipotent, basking in His supernal light, secure eternally in bliss. Someday, you will have the big payoff. How much easier it would be to have that prosthesis as a prop, supporting you where your own shaky legs could not. Even the harshest religion could be adhered to, given that you believed in the payoff. What were a few years of denial compared to eternal happiness?

Pen sighed, and all his life was in the breath as it came and went. Why was he on this island, this planet, in this galaxy?

Well, come to it, he supposed it didn't matter. Everybody had to be someplace, and in the end, one place was as good as another. Might as well ride the currents a little longer.

After all, it was not as if he had somewhere else to go.

• • •

Moon mysterious, the woman who by virtue of her hidden
features could be anything and perhaps all things, met him for
breakfast. She began to answer his questions before he could
ask them, but like an oracle, her words were wrapped in layers
as opaque as her robes.

"There was an actor," she began, as he sipped at a tumbler
full of cold and acidic fruit juice, "who lived several hundred
years ago. Very famous in his time. Once, he was talking to a
younger actor about criticism they had received on a performance. The younger actor was disturbed over the comments,
and smiling ruefully said, 'Well, I guess you just have to ignore
the bad reviews, eh?' The older actor returned the smile, and
shook his head. 'Dear boy,' he said, 'you must also ignore the
good ones.' "

Pen stared at her from behind his training shroud, certain
she could see through it to recognize both the ignorance and
stupidity on his face. More than anything else in his recent
life, he felt a desire to please this deep-voiced woman. He
wanted to be able to nod sagely, instantly understanding the
meaning of her parable, to be able to say, "I see," and dazzle
her with his brilliance as he explained the deeper meaning of
it. Instead, all he could manage was, "Ah," because he had
absolutely no idea what she was talking about.

And she knew, of course. With that eye-crinkle he had
quickly learned meant she was smiling, she said, "There are
some introductory lectures we have recorded for new students.
I'll take you to the hall so you can run them. It's basic stuff,
but we need to make certain you have it. Our courses are relatively informal, as such things go, but everybody starts new
here. There are requirements, naturally, but you progress at
your own speed. What takes some students a week will take
others a month; our curricula are tailored to fit individual
needs."

Pen nodded. *Why did you choose me, Moon?* he wanted to
ask. But he could not.

"Eventually, you will learn for the right reasons; to begin
with, it is only necessary that you learn at all."

Another of her ambiguous and mud-clear comments. Pen
could see that impressing Moon was going to be a difficult job,
especially given the fact that he felt like an idiot.

The holoproj took the form of a sibling, fully enshrouded, standing on an otherwise empty stage in a small classroom. Pen was alone, watching the projection, unsure as to the figure's sex even after it began to speak. The voice was midrange and neuter, and he figured they did that on purpose.

It said:

"The Siblings of the Shroud came into being in the year 2275, founded by Diamond. He did so to promote what is a complex and diverse philosophy. To the outside world, the Siblings have been thought of and called many things: existential humanist/pacifists; elitist intellectual pantheists/positivists; meddling sons-of-bezelworts. There is some truth in all of these, but no simple statement can encompass the entire range of the Siblings. Essentially a humanist order, the Shroud's beliefs and actions are eclectic and far-ranging. Siblinghood asks much, but demands little.

"There may or may not be a God or gods; the Siblings do not concern themselves with proving or disproving such a thing. By definition, gods are more powerful than men, and thus quite able to fend for themselves without help. Worship may fulfill a human need, but it is not a primary function of the Shroud to speak to this need. Other religions may do so as they see it.

"We believe that all life is sacred, but that some lives are more sacred than others. A conscious and reasoning human mind is, until shown to be otherwise, the peak of galactic evolution as we now know it. There have been alien intelligences before us and may be more after, but neither are they our concern—humankind, in all its altered forms, is. Nurturing of the human mind and spirit lies at the core of the Shroud. Natural evolution has brought people to the point of being able to effect their own evolution through intent. As a sibling, this is a primary drive: if one can help, one must. To do less is to beggar one's humanity. We believe in faith, but it is for each person to find that faith in him or herself, and extrapolate it into faith in humankind."

Pen shifted in the plastic chair. It was not uncomfortable, but he was. All this talk about helping humanity caused it. The thief's rule was to look out for yourself, first, last and ever. That didn't fit in too well with this altruistic stuff.

As if the holoproj could hear his thoughts, it spoke to them, startling him.

"More important, however, than helping others is helping one's self. A medic with a fatal disease is apt to be a poor one; without a sound mind in a sound body, urging someone else to that state is difficult at best. Self-knowledge and self-development are therefore the first goals of a sibling. 'When you know who you are, you know what to do.' This is wisdom old when Diamond came to understand it. A person drowning can save no one else."

Pen nodded. That was reasonable. So the Shroud wasn't altogether some head-in-the-vacuum organization.

" 'As above, so below,' " the anonymous sibling said. "The microcosm is the macrocosm, the disk spins from the center outward, the wheel turns eternally. These are truths, but each is only a part of the larger whole. In your training, you will learn to take the longer view, you will be taught to understand as much as possible, to reach for the overview. Small things often represent larger things, and the totality teaches more than the singularity. Ideas are linked, and even the smallest particle has a place in the cosmic schematic. Learning that place is paramount."

Whoops, it's starting to slide off into mumbo-jumbo, Pen thought. He wondered how much longer the introductory lesson was going to take.

"Welcome, then, to the Siblings of the Shroud. Your journey will be personal and at times intense. Remember through it that there is a reason for everything. Your purpose as a sibling is to learn what you can, and to pass it along. Good luck be with you."

The projection faded slowly, the figure misting into ghostly gray before it vanished completely.

That's it? The Siblings were some kind of cosmic do-gooders? Some purpose.

Well, said his inner cynic, *at least they have a purpose. That puts them several hundred parsecs ahead of you, doesn't it?*

Pen sighed. He couldn't argue with that.

The next recording was an introduction to Confederation politics, and a short history thereof. He found it very interesting, since he had never paid particular attention to the Confed's machinations before. There was more iron in the Confed's grip than he had thought, if this lecture had it right. As a thief, he had always carried his paranoia of authority with him, it was as natural as his clothing. They *were* after him, in truth, and circumventing laws was how he survived and prospered. According to this, many honest and standup citizens felt the same way. The Confed was repressive to ordinary folk in ways more heavy-handed than it was to outlaws. Odd. He had always accepted living with the small dread that there might come a knock at the door to any room in which he was staying; he had assumed that civilians had no such worries. If anything, it was worse for them. They could not simply catch a boxcar to a starliner and fade, as he often had. They had responsibilities, families, homes, and such things made them prisoners in a way he had never been. There was something basically wrong with that. The rules by which he had played the game gave the authorities the right to staple him, could they catch him; he understood and accepted that. But it hardly seemed fair that the Confed could, if it so desired, come down on anybody. Civilians, the honest standups, deserved to be let alone. They should have some kind of recourse. According to this lecture, the Confed was like a gigantic dinosaur, crushing anyone foolish enough to wander into its path, unseeing and uncaring about those beneath its massive feet. Great to be a citizen.

Pen grinned at the sexless lecturer. We're talking sedition here, pal. Conspiracy. If the Confed knew about this, it would squash the Siblings like a troublesome beetle. And me along with it.

That brought up an interesting question: Why didn't the Confed know? Something that big had to have blind spots, of course, but couldn't some disgruntled brother or sister have gone carrying tales? Surely there must be dropouts. Spies, even. How did the order get around that?

As the lecture ended, he resolved to ask Moon about that at an appropriate moment.

More time had passed than he had realized. As Pen left the classroom, which was in the second level of the auditorium, he saw that the afternoon's heat had been tempered with a shower. The building bordered on the central courtyard and gardens, and the tropical flowers were in brilliant bloom. Reds, yellows, blues, a riot of colors festooned the greenery. He thought about going to get something to eat, but found he wasn't particularly hungry. Moon had not specified when she would meet him again, so he wandered into the gardens, strolling along the pathways, enjoying the smell of the plants and rain-swept air. He stopped to observe a particularly electric flower, a blend of red and violet and orange. The bell-like blossom was upturned toward the sun, and a long and flat fuzzy stalk emerged from the flower like a tongue.

"Beautiful, isn't it?" came Moon's voice from behind him. "It comes from Dirisha, in the Ndama System. It's called *kinywa-ororo*—the 'soft mouth flower.' "

"I've never been a particular fan of such things, but it is beautiful."

"It's a carnivore."

He glanced at Moon, unsure he had heard her correctly. An insect buzzed past him. "Excuse me?"

"Watch."

He turned, in time to see the insect, a fly-sized and shimmery green creature, alight upon the fuzzy tongue extending from the flower. Almost immediately, the fly began to buzz again, beating its wings as it attempted to take off. It could not, however. Something in the fuzz of the extrusion held it fast. As Pen watched, the tongue began to move. Slowly, to be sure, but within seconds, the trapped fly was reeled into the flower. The blossom began to fold inward, the "lips" of it meeting, until it formed a closed cup. The flower shook, as the vibrating fly tried to escape. Abruptly, the flower expanded, almost as if someone had pumped air up the stem, as a child might blow up a balloon. After a beat, the flower deflated. The lips began to open, slowly.

"The flower produces a caustic gas," Moon said. "A strong base. The interior is, naturally, impervious. But the fly is now a partially digested mass embedded upon a series of thornlike projections near the base of its tongue. In a few hours, it will be no more than protein soup, feeding the flower. The gas, incidentally, can cause severe burns to an unprotected finger or hand. You don't want to pick these blossoms."

Involuntarily, Pen found himself taking a step back away from the flower. "Nice," he said. "Real nice."

Under her shroud, Moon shrugged. "Everything alive wants

to survive. The *kinywa-ororo* uses its beauty to catch prey. Things are not always what they seem.''

He regarded her. ''Ah,'' he said with mock gravity, ''a lesson!''

She laughed, and he felt joy for having amused her. ''A small one.''

''What now, teacher?''

''With your mind bedazzled, perhaps we should work on your body.''

Don't I wish! ''My body?''

''The Ninety-seven Steps.''

''Ah.'' Well, it was too much to hope for that she would rip off her robes and attack him sexually. Not that he would fight too hard. At the same time, he was still surprised that he felt such desires. In the months since Shar, he had been with people that way, but he remembered little about those encounters. Certainly they had brought him no joy. Right now, he would give everything he owned just to see Moon's undraped face, smiling at him, either in anticipation or satisfaction.

''Of course. I'll try to do better today.'' Knowing what he had learned from Spiral gave him a confidence and certain amount of pride. A dozen steps was something, after all.

''I hope so,'' Moon said. Her tone of voice carried no admiration, and his confidence and pride melted, a shard of ice left in the hot sun. Then his resolution firmed: whatever it took, he was going to impress this woman.

Whatever it took.

TWENTY-TWO _____

TODAY WAS SWAMP Day.

As the light of morning broke into the still-warm night, Pen, along with another nine students still ranked in Undershroud, found himself circumfused in the fetid miasma of the mangrove swamp that lay to the west of the Siblings' compound.

Cold and thin-barked trees rose from the muck, and the air was alive with the hum and buzz of insects and the calls of various avian species. Altogether as unpleasant a place as Pen had ever been.

Pen slogged through a stretch of soupy ground, his mud-boots whining as the hydraulics fought to keep him from sinking into the ooze. The boots were built somewhat like an outrigger canoe, with flaps that jutted from the soles at right angles, giving a wider surface area. Fortunately, the students had been allowed to keep their repellors, elsewise Pen was certain his bare arms and legs would be covered with insect bites. As it was, his skin had been scratched in a dozen places by assorted brambles. He would have given a lot for a snag-proof skinsuit.

Swamp Day supposedly came but once a year, and this was Pen's first experience of it. He had been at the compound for nearly six months when the test of HSP—Higher Sensory Perception—began, and he could not say that he was enjoying the procedure.

Moon had explained it easily enough. "One of the instructors will hide somewhere in the large expanse of the mangrove swamp; the object is for the students to find the brother or sister."

"Is that all?" he'd asked. "How does that test HSP?"

"The swamp is five kilometers by seven. The instructor will be hiding in such a way that you aren't apt to blunder into him or her."

Wonderful, he had thought. Slogging around in a swamp, looking for somebody who wanted to be found, but was hiding carefully enough to avoid it. Great.

Moon continued. "It isn't a perfect test, but the swamp is isolated enough so that only the students and instructor will be there. The instructor's *ki* will be easier to sense without the interference of too many others."

Pen altered his heavy-footed steps to avoid a stretch of open water. The boots weren't that good.

Despite his willingness to believe almost anything Moon said, he'd been more than a little skeptical when she'd started talking about *ki* and auras and telepathy. It had been a little easier to think of it in more scientific terms. Electrochemical brainwave activity, magnetoencephaloemissions, truthscan electropophy—those were things one could see demonstrated with sensory gear, charts, graphs, holoprojic reads. Tuning into another person at a distance by some kind of radiopathic reception was more difficult to grasp, despite his own experiences with sixth-sense feelings as a thief.

"Call it what you will," Moon had said. "The fact is that it exists. *Ki*, auras, whatever. That a human brain can do what a relatively simple machine can shouldn't be so hard to believe."

Maybe not. But he had trouble buying it. The exercises Moon had taught him for HSP were weird. She would have him sit and defocus his eyes while staring at her, trying to "see without seeing" her aura. Or he would stand in a darkened and soundproofed room, "listening without listening" for Moon's movements. There were half a dozen such tricks he practiced, and sometimes they worked, sometimes they didn't. When they *did* do what they were supposed to do, he couldn't understand why.

A lot of his questions about the Siblings had been answered

in the last few months, though. They were not a celibate order, for instance. Many of the students paired or tripled. Before Von left, he and Moon had spent a lot of time together. Pen had been glad to see the Elder Brother leave. Although Moon had less personal time for Pen, now that she was Elder Sister, he felt a sense of relief at Von's departure. How could a mere student compete with a Full Brother?

Not, he thought, as he watched a snake slither across a muddy patch of ground, that Moon had ever indicated the slightest interest in him as a sexual partner. Or anything other than a student.

Behind him, Pen heard a splashing. One of the other students, he figured, likely feeling as foolish as he did.

Some of the teachings made sense. The Ninety-seven Steps, for instance. He could fumble the pattern fairly well by now. Twice, he had made it through to the end without even a small bobble, a cause of justifiable pride. There were some who had been here for years who were still unable to reach the end in any fashion, much less smoothly. In fact, according to Pen's research on the house computer, no one had *ever* progressed as rapidly as he had. The sumito sparring sessions had seemed almost natural to him, as if he had found some hidden talent he'd never imagined before. The art was unlike the fighting system he'd learned from Dindabe. Pen looked forward to each workout, eager to learn more. It was nice to be the best at something, especially something everybody here wanted to be good at.

He put his right foot down at a bad angle, and the whining boot shoved him crooked, nearly toppling him into the mud. Careful, O master of balance!

He grinned, amused at himself. What was it Moon had said? Pride goes before a fall? Something like that.

This little trip into the swamp was something else, though. He had his doubts.

Ahead lay a thickly wooded stand of trees and suckery underbrush, angling down a steep hillside. Someone had come this way before, because there was a faint trace of a path leading around the coppice. A wise move, Pen figured, since working one's way through that steep underbrush was surely an invitation to disaster. One was apt to slip and fall on such a slope, and the only advantage to the thick growth was that it would probably stop a nasty tumble down the hillside. Small consolation.

But as he started along the path, Pen stopped and stood still. What was that? Some faint sound came, something he could not pin down. Another student? Not likely, coming from that section of woods. No marks of passage marred that dense living wall. He strained to hear the sound again. Nothing. He wasn't even sure he had heard anything. It might have been his imagination. He started to turn away.

Wait. There it was again. As if someone were calling him. . . . Then, he was certain he heard a faint voice—"Pen!"

The sun had risen high enough to send stray, slanting beams down through the dense canopy of trees, heating the swamp around Pen. In the distance, thunder grumbled as the sun assembled its first electrical storm of the day. The stink of decaying plants was all around Pen, a rich, rotten stench. But he forgot his eyes and ears and nose as the truth of the call touched him: he had not heard the sound.

He had felt the call in his mind.

A chill danced over him, frosting his arms and legs and neck with prickles, stirring his hairs in some atavistic danger signal. He shivered as he stared at the wall of wood before him. Not just a call, but one from Moon. He was as sure of that as he'd ever been of anything. She hadn't told him she would be the instructor hiding in the swamp, but he knew it was her. Knew it in a way he could not begin to explain. There was no denying it, it was a simple fact, as real as the sunlight and swampstink. More real.

The fabric of his undershroud withstood the passage into the copse better than his own skin did. Within moments, he was abraded and scratched in a half-dozen new spots. If this section of wood continued this thick for much longer, he would be raw everywhere his flesh was exposed.

After a hundred meters, the woods thinned. The downslope was not so steep, and after another hundred meters, pretty much leveled out. Here, the ground was drier, and there was a path of sorts, winding around a muddy stream and another small hill.

When he circled the hill, he saw something that made him stop and stare in amazement.

It was difficult to comprehend, at first. The ground was less thickly wooded, a clearing that had gone back to nature. Here were set two squarish structures, built of wood and plastic; there, a large, concentric circle of ground had been cleared and remained mostly so, with only thin patches of brush marring it. Amazing enough, here in the middle of a swamp, but the main attraction sat upon the cleared circle: a full-sized model of an old-style atmosphere ship.

The ship and buildings had suffered under the weather. Holes gaped in the structures, revealing the bracing inside; moss grew thickly in spots; rot had made large inroads. Whoever had built these things had done so long past. But—for what purpose had this imitation of a landing field been constructed? Pen had no doubt that's what this was—a crude mock-up of a rocket port. Pre-Bender, maybe, certainly long before boxcars were common.

"Cargo cult," came Moon's voice from behind him.

He turned, not surprised.

Moon stood watching him, enigmatic as always in her shroud.

"It's a religious belief," she said. "Originally, it had to do with primitives and their observations of more advanced cultures. Civilization came to the remote islands, usually during wars. The natives watched the outsiders build runways or rocket pads, and then miraculously, aircraft would appear from the skies, bearing valuable cargo. So the natives built their own such places, hoping to lure the gods into bringing them a share of the wealth. Much like a hunter uses a decoy to trick prey."

"They must have been real primitive."

"Actually, the cult ran in cycles. It took on more mystical significance, had undertones unrelated to the original purposes. This particular construction was built less than a hundred years ago, by locals who were probably living in prefab houses with holoproj and full powercasts."

Pen shook his head. "Why build it in the middle of a swamp? I wouldn't think that would be particularly attractive to a god."

"This area wasn't a swamp when they built it. This is probably fourth or fifth forest cycle. The weather is a potent force here, as you may have noticed."

"I've been meaning to ask you about that. Why isn't there weather control on this planet?"

"Two reasons: the technology has to be imported and the

local government doesn't want to spend the money, or admit they have to buy it offworld. The Confed allows them a certain leeway, a sop to homeworld politics.''

Pen stared at the fake rocket. He was aware that this entire conversation was unreal. What they should have been talking about was how he had known Moon was here; how he had burrowed his way through that wall of vegetation and come straight to her. How impossible it was.

Then again, maybe not. Moon believed in HSP; this demonstration had convinced Pen, too. One did not have to know the physics of a repulsion engine in order to ride on a flitter. There was something here, all right.

"Come," she said. "Let's get back to the compound. There's an easier path, this way."

"What about the other students?"

"They've already been called back. They were never meant to find this place. The test was for you. The others were only window shading."

Pen digested that morsel as he followed Moon along the path away from the remains of the ersatz rocket port. They were a devious group, the Siblings. He wondered what other circuitous teachings they had simmering.

In the "winter," the heat abated somewhat, but not all that much. Pen had advanced, so that his undershroud was more complete, but he still had a way to travel before he was entirely covered. Even with the chemical sunscreen he wore, he had developed a deep tan on his exposed flesh, presenting what he considered a comical sight in the mirror as he undressed for bed. Light here, dark there. Not that anyone had seen him bare, save at the pool, and even there, the hood and briefs were always worn; since his arrival at the order, he had yet to enjoy sexual congress with a sister or brother student—or a teacher. Solitary masturbation relieved the physical pressure, but that wasn't particularly joyful. And he hadn't been without a bedmate for such a long period since he'd left home as a teenager. Odd.

It was amazing how much he could tell about Moon's moods, considering he had primarily her voice and eyes to work with. There were days when she was tired, days when she was angry, days when she seemed filled with inner light and peace. He was sensitive to her in a way that seemed telepathic. More HSP, he figured.

On this particular day, however, he had no warning of the trauma she was about to inflict. It came as they walked past the power plant.

From under her robes, Moon produced a gun.

Pen stared at it as if she held a live serpent. She could not see his face, but his body betrayed him.

"What's the matter? It's only an airgun. It shoots low-velocity steel pellets."

"What are you doing with it?"

"You need to learn how to shoot—"

"No." His voice had a whiplike crack to it, surprising him with its intensity.

"What?"

"I don't use guns."

"It is part of your training. All the siblings must have a basic knowledge of hand weapons."

"I know about hand weapons. I know what they can do."

"It is required."

He stared at the air pistol. It was an innocuous weapon, probably capable of stinging, but unless its projectile hit an eye, not dangerous to a human. Even so, he felt a chill dance over him as he considered the gun.

Pen drew in a deep breath. "I'm sorry. I don't handle guns. A wand, a slap cap, those are okay. Not guns."

"Why?"

Ah, there was the question, the one neither Dindabe nor anyone at the order had ever asked. "It's . . . personal."

After what seemed a long time, Moon said, "I have a lot of flexibility in my teaching, but there is an overall curriculum. You must demonstrate a basic proficiency with this"—she waved the gun gently—"to gain rank. If you cannot progress in rank . . ."

The rest need not be said. Failure at any rank for more than three tests meant expulsion from the order. It almost never happened, but it had. And, it seemed, would happen at least once more.

Pen sighed. "Then I guess I'll have to leave."

"What?" Her surprise seemed potent, he wished he could see her face. More than anything, he wished at this moment to be able to see Moon's features. "You would leave over something like this? You were a thief, Pen. Surely you did worse things than fire a gun."

Her surprise and disturbance bothered him almost as much as the sight of the gun. Almost. He did not want to upset his teacher. He would do anything for her. Almost anything.

"No. I never did anything worse than firing a gun."

"Then you are familiar with them?"

"Yes." All too familiar.

A long time elapsed. Half an eon, at least.

"All right," she said. "I will take your word for it. You need not show me. I'll pass you on this test."

The rest of the eon ran past. Pen blinked, understanding what it was that Moon was doing. True, she was the Elder Sister and her word carried much weight; still, he understood that she was risking herself by her words and actions. If she lied for him, was willing to trust him on this, she would be putting herself into jeopardy. It might be small, no one might ever know, but the thought of it further filled him with dread. Why would she do this? Take his statement at face value? He was not someone to trust.

Emotions warred within him. Memory and loathing fought against respect and devotion. The old fortress stood firm against the new attack. The last time he had carried a gun, it had cost him everyone he had ever loved. It had destroyed the life he had built. Intellectually, he understood it was the hand that fired the weapon, the mind that moved the hand, those things were responsible. But his gut clenched at the sight of the gun, because that was the external object upon which he could hang the blame. He knew this with his brain, but his belly would not accept it. It might never accept it.

As time ran down, entropy and energy exchanging their souls, Pen/Ferret/Mwili took a deep breath, knowing what he had to do, what he *must* do, were he to survive as anything other than a shell of his old self.

He could not allow Moon to cover for him.

"Give me the pistol," he said.

"You don't have to—"

"Please."

Moon tendered the weapon.

The plastic handle was warm from her hand. He hefted the

gun, felt the balance and point of it, and checked the mechanism. The safety, there by his thumb, the trigger, the power pack charge reading. In an instant, he knew the weapon, instinctively felt the heart of it. It was his talent, one he despised, but also one he could not deny.

To his left, ten meters away, was a small citrus tree, a *yemlat*. The fruit was a yellow-green obloid, similar in size and shape to a lemon, but thinner skinned and juicier. Pen snapped the pistol up into firing position, thumbed the safety off, and started shooting, as fast as he could pull the trigger. The first two pellets clipped one of the *yemlats* from its branch; as the fruit fell, the next half dozen rounds smacked into the fruit, spraying pinkish juice in all directions. The ruined *yemlat* hit the ground, and Pen continued firing, moving his wrist slightly, sending a stream of pellets into the squishy mass. He fired until the pistol ran empty, clicking several times. He raised the weapon, twirled it in his hand, and extended it butt-first to Moon.

The *yemlat* was little more than a pulpy spot on the ground, pounded flat, as if smashed by a hammer.

Silently, Moon took the weapon.

Pen felt the adrenaline surge ebb, and he felt himself shaking slightly. What he had feared had happened: the lure of the gun was as strong as ever. It was almost mystical in its power, calling hypnotically to him: *This is what you were destined to do, man. Your fate is with the gun. Admit it. Enjoy it. Glory in it!*

No!

But it wouldn't go away, the feeling. And the fear had an insistent voice, telling him what he wished he could not hear. *Did you do it for Moon? Or did you do it because you lusted after it? We know the truth you and I. You can't fool us . . . .*

"I'll see you later," Moon said quietly. And she left him there, staring at the fruit he had slaughtered.

It was just as well. He had a lot to think about.

TWENTY-THREE _____

THE REST OF the afternoon passed without Pen's seeing Moon again. He trudged away from the pulped fruit he'd slaughtered with the air pistol, and attended a live-teach lecture on Confederation history. The information rolled over him in the instructor's monotonic drone: A sixty-year stretch starting in the year 2195 was known as the Expansion. It was a period of intense colonization and galactic exploration. Such things continued after the Expansion, of course, but much abated. The next historical block, lasting from 2295 to 2375, was generally known as The Consolidation.

Pen sighed as the teacher paused for breath. What would Moon think of his display? She had been subdued when they'd parted, he could see that—

The lecture began again:

During the Consolidation, the Confed settled into control, forming a galactic association whose membership was mandatory. Power was centered on Earth, and those in power gave up none of it willingly. A large space-going Navy was built, and a larger Army conscripted to fill the troop carriers and ships-of-the-line. To draw the Confed's ire was to find oneself in very deep excreta, indeed. Those in control had no qualms about using military force to quell even the slightest deviation from official policy. The planets and wheelworlds either toed the line or had their feet cut from under them, as simple as that. After a time, a kind of status quo evolved; don't rock the boat and draw attention and you can do what you want—within limits. Make too much noise, however, and you get squashed. Squeaky wheels got replaced and not lubricated.

And, the instructor continued, while no official publication listed it as such, the recent turn of the Twenty-fourth Century marked what the Siblings considered the beginning of a time to be known unofficially as the Declination. No one could say for certain, but according to integratic predictions, this phase of galactic history would mark the fall of the Confed, and either chaos or some interim form of voluntary planetary association would exist until a new system came to power. History, the teacher said, is as cyclic as a sine wave. What rises eventually falls.

Pen listened with half his attention. Before coming here, he had never paid much mind to politics, and while he had been becoming more and more interested, the incident with the gun loomed over him with the intensity of one of the afternoon tropical storms. The intricate dealings of power theory paled against the hard plastics and spun fibers of a gun in one's hand. Besides, the practice of integratics was restricted to those in Full Shroud, a state which had, before today, lain years ahead of him. After today . . . ?

Eventually, the class ended. Pen hoped it was recorded somewhere so he could restudy it later, for he retained only a small part of the teaching. Assuming, of course, that he would be around to study anything after today.

Outside, the last rays of sunshine were fading into a fast-arriving tropical night. He didn't feel much like eating, so he went back to his room. He carried a sense of foreboding with him, as tangible as the mask he wore.

The door was open, as he'd left it, but as he approached, he felt the presence of someone inside.

It was Moon.

She stood at the window, back to him, but he knew it was her. Despite the shroud, he could have picked her out of a dozen other siblings in full array, simply by the way she held herself while standing still.

Moon turned, sensing or hearing him arrive.

He was surprised to see her. She had never come to his room before.

"Your door was open," she said.

He nodded. "I leave it that way most of the time. An old habit."

"Would you close it, please?"

Uh-oh. She wanted this private, and that made his scrotum shrink and ridge, going cold. The gun. It had to do with the gun. Was she going to throw him out of the order for his reluctance to use it? Or, worse—for his ability to use it so fucking well?

When he had closed the door and turned back to face her, Moon said, "We know all about your past, Pen."

With that, she reached first to her side, then her neck, and unfastened the closure strips that kept her *manto*, the outer cloak, in place. She unwrapped the sheetlike garment and allowed it to drop onto the floor.

Pen could not have been more stunned if she had sprouted wings and flown around the room. She stood there in jacket and pants, with the pouched utility belt, the *yuyo obi*, wrapped around her waist. After three heartbeats, she untabbed the belt and lowered it to the floor next to the cloak.

"We know about the killings. Your lover, your partner, your ex-friend."

With that, she untabbed the *gi* jacket and shrugged it off.

"We know all about your days as a thief, and your travels as a laner. We also know how hard you tried to help Bennet Gworn after he was captured."

She pulled the scoop-necked long-sleeved shirt over her head and tossed it aside, then bent slightly and removed her long pants. Now, she was dressed identically to Pen, in First and Second Layer Undershroud: a short-sleeved shirt and short pants, boots, an undertunic, briefs, and *zukin*, the thin and silky hood. As he watched, she continued to remove these articles of unique, almost alive fabric. It was as erotic as anything Shar had ever done in her strip dances, and his erection throbbed against his belly, feeling like a block of wood. What the hell was going on here? His excitement was tempered with dry-mouthed fear. What was she *doing*?

"We have all the psyche reports on you since you arrived, plus the deepsleep and narcoscan tests. We suspected how you would react to a handgun. We were prepared for you to refuse to use it."

She was down to tunic, briefs and hood, now, the boots just having joined the pile of clothes on the floor next to her. Her legs were shapely, and he could see the muscles slide and dance under the skin when she shifted her weight. Her skin itself was so pale veins made blue lines under it. Most of her body hair had been depilated, and she looked as smooth as a newborn baby.

Dry? Pen's mouth was sand and ashes and the dust of centuries when he tried to speak. "Th-the gun. It was a test? The order was checking to see if I could overcome my revulsion for it?"

She pulled the tunic off over her head. Her stomach was flat and hard-ridged, her arms well defined, her breasts small and underlaid with thick pectoral muscle. She hooked her thumbs into the briefs and slid them down, stepping out of them and letting them lie in a black pool at her feet. Her undepilated pubic hair was jet, tight curls that made a stark contrast to her white skin, a dark and willowy nest.

Save for the hood, she now stood naked before him.

He wanted her more than he had ever wanted anybody, anywhere, any time.

She reached up and caught the fastenings on the left side of the hood. "The test was personal," she said. "It was to see if you would be able to overcome your distaste of the weapon to avoid compromising *me*. And you did."

Moon unfastened the closures on the hood and unwrapped it from around her face. Her hair was cut short, but it was as dark as her pubis, black and curly. She smiled. His eye for detail catalogued her features and they were less than perfect: her nose was thin and slightly askew, as though it had once been broken and not repaired. Her teeth were straight and white, but her mouth was a trifle wide. She had high cheekbones, almost an Oriental cast, and laugh lines crinkled deeply the corners of her eyes. Nothing about her was classically beautiful; taken together, however, the overall effect of her facial features was striking. Whatever objectivity he might have had fled when first she had removed her cloak. Staring stupidly at the nude woman now in front of him, Pen could not recall ever seeing anyone more lovely, not even Shar. Beauty came in different forms, and Moon's was unique.

She dropped the *zukin*, took a deep breath, let it out, and smiled. "You have the potential to be the most extraordinary sibling in a long time, Pen. And I know you want me." She turned and walked to his bed, sat on it, then lay down.

Later, when he thought about it, Pen thought he must have surely set some kind of record for getting undressed. It seemed that one second, he was standing there feeling a mixture of awe, lust, stupidity and absolute surprise, and a second later, he was lying naked next to Moon, grinning like a wirehead on full pulse current. He thought about that later—when his mind returned.

Moon lay next to him, propped on one elbow. She idly stroked his shoulder. Pen responded by leaning over to kiss her, feeling her mouth flower beneath his again.

After a time, he leaned back and smiled at her.

"So, I take it you enjoyed yourself?" she said.

"Any more fun than that would have killed me," Pen said, grinning. He chuckled. "Of course, I've been practicing mentally for months."

"I know. I felt the wind from your panting on my back often."

"It showed, huh?"

"Some."

She lay back, keeping one hand on his arm, and stared at the ceiling. Pen could not have said how much time had passed, but it was full dark outside, and it felt late. As if he cared about anything outside this room.

"Why do you leave your door open?" she asked.

He rolled slightly to one side and nuzzled her armpit. The dark hair there was silkier than that between her legs.

"That tickles!"

He pulled back slightly, then slid one hand down the length of her body, then back up to touch her face. He felt like a man who had been awarded his heart's desire, and for no reason he could readily understand. That she would be here, relaxed under his touch, actually enjoying it. It amazed him. "It's funny," he began, "you'd think a thief would lock up everything. Not me. I grew up in a house where doors were never shut inside. My father used to say nothing could be hidden from God, so there was no point. I didn't know at the time that my mother had refused to sleep with him for years, so he had nothing to hide, either from God or me. I rejected God, along with a lot of what my father tried to beat into me, but I never dropped that one habit. Odd, isn't it?''

She dragged her fingertips down, over his chest and then his lower belly. It gave him a chill.

''I have a question for you,'' he said.

''Sure.''

''Why did you do this? Make love to me?''

''Because I wanted to. Because there is something about you that attracted me from the first time I saw you.''

''Yeah? So, why'd you wait so long?'' The question was not serious, but she gave him a serious answer.

''I had to be sure. I've felt attracted to a lot of people, but it takes too much energy to pursue that very far. For me, sex has to be part of something else.''

''Such as?''

''Such as love.''

That one rocked him. Love? He didn't know what that was. He felt desire for Moon, even now, when the flesh was certainly too weak to do more than smile and remember. He felt good to be around her. He respected her abilities, as a fighter and teacher. And now, as a lover. It had been intense. But love?

''I don't think I'm worthy of that,'' he said. It made him sad to say this, because he was afraid it would destroy this precious moment in his life; sad, because he wanted very much to please this woman, as long as she would have him. Sad, because he thought it was true. He was unworthy.

''I know you don't think so,'' she said. ''But you are, nonetheless. You haven't learned how to love yourself yet. You don't know who you are.'' She sat up and swung her legs around tailor-fashion, to face him. ''Have you ever heard of Emery, the Earth philosopher? Twentieth or Twenty-first Century. 'When you know who you are, you know what to do. You know when and where to do it, and with whom.' ''

''Never heard of him. Interesting philosophy. Did this guy tell you how to get to know who you are?''

''In a way. That's part of what we're trying to do with the Siblings. First, we try to teach each other; then, we try it on the rest of the galaxy.''

''Doesn't sound easy.''

"No," she said, bending down. She did something with her hands, a soft and fluttery motion.

"I think you're wasting your time there—" he began. After a few seconds, he grinned down at her uplifted face. "Jesu, it's a miracle! You've brought it back from the dead!"

"Dead? Ah, Pen, it was only a little tired. I'll see if I can't kill it this time. . . ."

She laughed then, and he joined her. To hell with philosophy. Some things had to be experienced directly, and words only got in the way.

"Oh, yes!"

If there was a Heaven, surely he had achieved it.

But even through his pleasure, he heard that tiny voice in his mind—the voice that belonged to the part of him that watched all that he did, and would never be still.

You have thought that before, Mwili. Or Ferret. Or Pen, whatever you choose to call yourself. And it has never lasted, has it? And it never will, either. Face it.

No, he told it mentally. Go away. Leave me alone!

Perhaps the voice stilled. Perhaps not. Either way, he lost the sound of it in the surging wave that crested and carried him to new places with this new woman. For a few moments, at least, the sound went away, along with the darkness, the worry, the memories. He and Moon danced the oldest man and woman dance, yin and yang, and all else was less than a shadow.

For a few moments.

TWENTY-FOUR _____

PEN AND SPIRAL were on their way into "town." A shipment of electronic parts had arrived at the port, and as the two were on maintenance detail this week, it fell to them to fetch the supplies. Spiral drove the four-wheeled ground vehicle, a lumbering relic that jolted the two men at every bump or hole on the ill-kept surface of the road.

"What are you grinning at?" Spiral asked.

The top of the GV was down and the breeze from their motion was soggy, but welcome. Pen now wore all eight items of Undershroud, the long-sleeved shirt and long pants of the Third Layer covering the First and Second, and despite the breathability of the fabric, was warm in the direct sunlight of the morning. "Grinning? Was I grinning?"

Spiral laughed. "Like a cheetah with a fresh kill. You could be wearing three hoods and it would show. You've been doing that a lot the last few months. Staring off into space and looking like you've discovered the punchline to some grand cosmic joke."

Pen chuckled. "Not me."

Spiral hit a particularly deep rut, and the GV jolted its two passengers. If not for the restraining safety belt, Pen would have been bounced clear of the seat.

"You hit that same hole every time—does it have some special significance for you?"

"Reminds me of a girl I used to know," Spiral said. He accelerated the GV on one of the few straight stretches of road between the order and their destination. "I don't suppose that Moon would have anything to do with your attitude lately?"

"Moon?"

"Come, come, Pen old boy, you don't really think the rest of us are all blind, do you? You've been discrete, but—really! I suspect if we could harness the sexual energy you two have been spending, we could shut down the power station."

"Spoken like a true Second Layer retard," Pen said. Unlike Pen, Spiral still wore the short shirt and pants of Second Layer.

"Ooh, nasty! Well, my lord lofty and mighty Third Layer Pen, you won't see these arms and legs except in the swimming pool, come next week."

Pen glanced at Spiral, interested. "Really?"

"I test in three days. Want to get in on the score pool? Take a hundred percent and you'll clean up."

"I'll clean up the kitchens for a week with that kind of brainlock. A hundred? Hah! Who do you think you are—Von?"

"Well. Ninety-five, maybe."

"Yeah, sure. Eighty, maybe."

"You cut me deeply, Pen."

"I was there when you asked Jade the difference between a Confederation factor and a senator, Spiral."

"It was a joke."

"I'm sure the class thought so. We had to sit and listen to Jade drone on for another forty minutes."

"You have no sense of humor."

"I think I'll take seventy-five for your score."

"Your dick should rot off."

Pen smiled. He liked Spiral. Hell, he liked everybody these days. The man was right—Moon was the difference. Not just the sex, though that was fine, but the whole process of being with someone, sharing parts of the day, talking about things that meant nothing to anyone else. And she was teaching him things. He wanted to please her, so he studied with renewed intensity, worked to learn all the things she thought he should know. It was a strange mix of teacher-lover-friend, his relationship with Moon. He had never known anything like it.

The GV rounded the last turn before the prefab orange storage sheds appeared. As civilization went, the enclave of the

Siblings was head and shoulders above the port and its sur-
roundings. A few of the natives had stayed on the island, and
they seemed to gravitate to the port. There was a small store,
a bar, and little else, outside the port, save for the storage
sheds, and those usually empty. The Siblings did export small
amounts of food—copra and wine, mostly—more for appearances than for need. The order had a way of finding money.
Although no one had ever asked him to do it, Pen had eventually deposited most of the stads he had stolen into the order's
account. This was his home now, these were his people, and
what was theirs was his. It only seemed fair that it work the
other way. The biotech lab had an expensive cell injection gun
now, due to his contribution. And the newest students carried
bug and rain repellors courtesy of a jewel theft on a planet
light- and real-time years away. It made Pen feel good to do
that.

"Uh-oh."

Pen pulled himself from his mental wanderings to see what
had disturbed Spiral. The cause would have been impossible
to miss.

Just ahead were four Confederation Jumptroopers, wearing
tropical whites, and carrying short, brutal-looking carbines.
As Pen watched, two of the troopers, a man and a woman,
detached themselves from the other two and walked toward the
local bar. Spiral drove the GV past the remaining two troopers,
who watched it pass. Next to the main building of the port,
Spiral pulled the GV to a halt, stopping the electric motor. The
cooling metal ticked as the two siblings looked back at the
troopers.

"The Confed rep must be here," Spiral said. "He comes
out a couple of times a year."

"I've never seen him," Pen said.

"Usually Von—Moon, now—sends somebody to take care
of him. He gets a 'gift,' drinks or tokes until he's moronic,
then leaves. Looks like he brings an escort squad to fly him
home. I've never seen troops here before, either. He's probably
in the pub."

"Moon didn't mention that he'd be here," Pen said.

"Think because you two share a pillow she tells you everything?" It was another of Spiral's jokes, but Pen felt somehow

as if he'd been slighted. Why hadn't Moon told him, since she knew he was going to the port?

"Come on. Let's get the supplies and get back."

Pen glanced away from the troopers at Spiral. "You sound nervous."

"Nah, not me. I just don't much like being around soldiers." He was silent for a moment, then, "I used to be one."

"Yeah?"

"Yeah. Impress, standard tour. I was young and stupid, and even so, I found the Confed military mind to be something less than flexible. If something moves, they tend to shoot it and then examine the remains for answers."

"Nice thought pattern."

"And you being a Three Layer man and all, you didn't know that."

"In my former line of work, *every*body was likely to trigger a few blasts in my direction if I stood still too long. Confed, local cools, property owners, it didn't matter. Who looks at the face behind a weapon pointed at them?"

The two alighted and moved toward the cargo area. Spiral said, "You ever miss it? Life in the speed channel?"

"Not for a San Yubi second."

That's what he said, but he felt that old familiar crawl of epinephrine along his nerve endings as he had passed the soldiers, hormonal urges to duck and cover. It had been a big part of him once, those stretched and tight-skinned rushes. He glanced at the troopers, measuring them, very much aware of them, watching him and Spiral. No, he told himself. I don't miss it. Not really.

They had the GV loaded with the supplies when the Confederation Representative emerged from the town's pub, escorted by two of his four troopers. The rep, resplendent in patterned-silk kilts and tunic, walked with the care of a man on a tight-rope. He wasn't weaving or stumbling, but to anyone who'd spent more than a few hours in a pub, his physiological state was only too apparent. The grin he wore could consume a carload of excreta.

The pair of troopers had obviously had this duty before. They boxed the rep, side and side, and moved at his pace. To call it slow would have been kind. A slug would have had little difficulty moving from the procession's path.

Pen and Spiral were about to enter their car and depart when the rep spied them. The group of three Confeders was about ten meters away.

"Ah, it's more of the blanket-covered brothers. Or is it sisters?" He laughed, a braying haw-haw-haw, and nearly stumbled as he stopped his already slow motion. "You boys—or is it girls?—really know how to show a man a good time. Except for one thing. C'mere!" The man waved, an exaggerated motion that nearly unbalanced him. One of the troopers leaned in a little and, with one hand, braced the rep.

Pen and Spiral glanced at each other.

"Great," Spiral said. "We get to play with the drunk."

"Just stay calm," Pen said. "You can humor him for a couple of minutes." The two siblings walked toward the others.

"You males or females under those shrouds? I mean, just left whatshisname, the old man with the tea-colored skin and black eyes, Cube, is it? And he's male, right enough. How about you?"

The soldiers were grinning.

"We're male, Honored Representative," Pen said.

The man haw-hawed again. "Really? Sure, your voice sounds deep, but you could be a woman anyway. Who could tell? I used to know a whore in Sidney could sing bass. How can I be sure?"

"You have our solemn word," Spiral said.

The rep shook his head. "Nope, nope, nope, won't do. The only way to be sure is to see for myself. Myself. Tell you what, shuck off those covers and let's take a quick peek, hey?"

Pen smiled nervously under his hood. He turned slightly to favor one of the soldiers with his attention, even though he spoke to the rep. "Sorry, Honored Representative, but we are not allowed to remove our shrouds in public."

"Hey, hey, no problem. There's nobody around but us. And if anybody wanders by, I can have my troops clear 'em out and it'll be as private as a security-sealed vault."

Pen felt sweat running down his back under the dark clothing. This didn't sound good, not in the least.

"I am sorry, sir, but we cannot—"

"Listen, holy-roly, you can do exactly as I tell you!" He turned slightly, to face the soldier on his left. "Lars!"

The trooper, a tall blond man of twenty-five or so, stepped toward Pen, stopping two meters away. "You heard the rep," he said. "Strip. Now, you pross?"

Pen and Spiral glanced at each other. Things had gone sour awfully fast. What the hell were they supposed to do here? How much trouble was this guy? Should they comply, and avoid the hassle? That would be the easy thing.

Pen thought about what Moon would do. She wouldn't back down from this toad and his warts. She'd tell him to stuff it. Then again, he was not Moon.

"Pen?" Spiral's voice was low, almost a whisper.

Pen looked at his friend and fellow sibling. He shook his head slightly. "I think maybe it's time we left," he said, keeping his voice low.

The rep heard this, and his grin increased. "You weren't thinking of going yet, were you? Take a look at your cart."

Pen tried to keep the rep and his two troopers in his peripheral vision as he glanced back over one shoulder at their GV. His stomach fluttered suddenly as he saw the other two troopers standing by the vehicle, weapons held loosely but pointed more or less in Spiral and Pen's direction.

The rep said. "Lars, why don't you and the troops show these clowns how the Confederation's finest takes care of recalcitrants?"

Lars smiled at this. He unslung his Parker carbine and for a brief moment, Pen thought the man was going to shoot them. But no, he lowered the weapon carefully to the road, and indicated for his fellow trooper to do the same.

Lars said, "The rumor is you dark sheets learn how to fight as part of your training. Suppose we see how that stacks up against Confed hand-to-hand?"

As he spoke, Lars edged to Pen's left, and the other soldiers moved to the right. Pen was aware of the other two troopers, a man and a woman, moving in to encircle them.

Quietly, almost under his breath, Spiral said, "Oh, man."

Pen said, "Honored Representative, we don't want any trouble—"

"Well, you *got* it, boy. You think a few drinks and some smoke buys me? You priests are getting too big for your covers, you don't move when I say move! Do it, Lars. Hurt them. And then strip 'em naked.''

He seemed a lot more sober than he'd been. They had been set up, Pen realized. Given an option, he would have run, but those two by the GV had been sent there to prevent it. And it took a really fast man to outstep a bullet. Something was going on here, Pen wasn't sure just what, but he and Spiral had been trapped, and altogether too neatly for it to be a drunken lark.

Pen only had a second to worry about this when Lars lunged, a quick shuffle step in, followed by a powerful straight punch at Pen's face.

Almost absently, Pen twirled to his left, around the incoming punch. Lars, expecting the resistance of Pen's nose against his knuckles, overbalanced and stumbled past.

"Fuck!" the quad leader said as he recovered his attack stance. He spun a quarter turn to face Pen again.

Pen tried a final time. "Listen, we don't have to fight—"

One of the other troopers screamed in fear. Pen shifted his gaze a hair. The trooper seemed to be trying to learn in a fraction of a second what it had taken birds millions of years of evolution to accomplish. The man's flight began well enough, but judging from his glide path it was certainly going to end badly. He flew past the startled rep, aided by Spiral's execution of the middle steps of The Flower Unfolding, the second dance of the Ninety-seven Steps.

The startled soldier slammed into the ground, hard.

Pen had time to notice that while the throw was effective, Spiral's form was off, and his left foot was a good five degrees aslant to where it was supposed to be. He would have to rag Spiral about that—

Lars, bellowing, charged again. This time, he fired two punches, left and right, followed by an elbow strike and a knee at Pen's groin. This was probably his best shot, and no doubt had worked well for him in bars around the galaxy. Not this time, though. Pen shifted, danced, twisted, and launched a spinning hammerfist. The tightened edge of his hand smashed into the base of Lars' skull, straightening the man into a racing dive. Lars hit the street outstretched, skidded on the hard surface, and abraded his nose and chin to the bone. He was going to have one hell of a road tattoo, Pen thought. When he woke up.

The woman trooper darted in at him. Pen shifted and caught her outstretched leg at the ankle as she kicked at his crotch, continuing the move upward, so she sprawled flat on her back. Her head bounced from the road's surface as she hit, and she went boneless, out cold.

As Pen turned to see what Spiral was doing, the last trooper stumbled into a fall that ended when he smacked into the Confed rep's horrified grasp, knocking them both flat.

The rep managed to untangle himself from the soldier, only to begin vomiting.

"I think maybe we'd better leave," Pen said to Spiral.

"I copy that, brother. We sure stepped in it this time. What are we gonna tell Moon?"

Pen shook his head. Hell if he knew. Maybe these guys would just forget about it and go home. Sure. Well, at least they didn't see our faces.

The Confed rep and his troops were less than ten minutes behind Pen and Spiral, but that was enough time to prepare Moon. She hadn't asked a lot of questions, but had listened to Pen's report, nodding occasionally.

"It seems too pat," Pen said. "Like they had planned it all along. Maybe all that cover the Siblings are supposed to have bought is wearing thin. I got the feeling they wanted to do more than just pound on us a little for kicks. I think maybe they might have wanted to ask us some questions after we had been tenderized a little."

"All right," she said, when he finished. "I'll handle it."

He would have questioned her further, but she turned and swept away in a swirl of her cloak. For a moment, Pen felt a deep sense of dread, watching her. He shrugged the feeling off. He was just coming down from the fight, he figured.

Pen watched, along with the other assembled siblings, as Moon told the man she could not identify the two assailants.

"You and this whole pack of dustcovers will be fucking sorry!" the rep yelled. "I am going to have this place razed and planted in sugar cane! I'll have all of you jailed!"

Moon was unmoved.

The man foamed and raged some more, but in the end, left.

Later, when he and Moon were alone, in bed, Pen asked her about it.

"It was an unfortunate event," she said. "You couldn't have known it would happen. We'd just as soon the Confed didn't know how well sumito works—we try to avoid using it under official surveillance."

"Nobody told me."

"That usually gets covered later. I guess we'll have to start teaching it sooner."

"Can he do that?" Pen asked. "Can he wreck the order here?"

"Possibly. But he won't."

"Can we blackmail him? About the bribes?"

"No. That's a standard method of operation for backrocket reps. Everybody does it, and at worst, he'd get a few months' suspension."

"Then how do you know he won't give us a hard time?"

"He won't. Take my word for it."

Pen had been content to do just that, snuggling up against her and putting the incident from his mind as he thought about more pleasant things.

A few days later, Pen was crossing the compound when he saw Spiral approaching, wearing the new garments that showed he'd passed his next level test.

"How you do in the score pool?" Spiral asked.

"Not too bad. Got beat by Shell. She guessed eighty-four on the nose."

"Yeah, what'd you pick?"

"Eighty-seven."

"No shit? Hey, thanks for the confidence."

"After you heaved that trooper into the Confed rep, how could I do less? Even though your foot *was* off on the first throw."

"So *you* say. Um. Got to run, I don't want to be late for history." He started off, then paused. "Too bad about what happened to the rep and his troops."

Pen shook his head. "What happened to them? Something nasty, I hope?"

"You didn't hear? Their ship crashed into the Pacific on the way back to Port Moresby."

Pen stared at Spiral. "What?"

"Blew a repellor or something. Hit the water just under cruising speed, splashed the ship over a two-klick area. Everybody died."

Spiral started off, and Pen stared at his retreating back, stunned. He remembered lying in bed with Moon, his naked body pressed against hers. The rep wouldn't cause them any trouble, she'd said. How did she know that?

Take my word for it, she'd said.

No, he thought, it was an accident.

Fortunate timing, wasn't it?

Pen shook his head. It had to be an accident.

But—what if it wasn't? What if Moon—?

Don't even think it, he told himself. But the thought would not go away. He recalled the feeling of dread he'd felt before the rep and his quad had arrived. At the time, he'd paid it little mind, but now, it felt as if maybe his HSP had kicked in somehow, as if maybe he'd somehow sensed their doom. Impossible, of course, even HSP couldn't foretell the future. He couldn't have picked that up, unless . . . unless maybe he was somehow reading something from Moon. Moon, who was the focus for his odd insights more often than not. When it worked, it usually worked around her. Could he maybe have been picking up her thoughts or feelings? He had thought that kind of thing had happened a time or two before.

No. Because that would mean that Moon . . . he turned away from that thought, feeling a hollow sensation, and the flutter of something trying to escape from deep inside his belly.

What had Moon done?

TWENTY-FIVE

FUGUE.

In the order, as in other parts of the galaxy, the word had taken on a different meaning from the musical term from which it had come. An adept in conversational fugue was an expert in, literally, double-talk. When a fugue master spoke, it would mean something else entirely. Like a game of *Go*, fugue could be as complex as the speaker's ability allowed. The simplest of phrases could carry worlds of meaning, and a fugue player used not only words, but inflection, tone, body language and gestures to enhance his play. Two experts ostensibly talking about the weather could well be carrying on a conversation about particle physics—not that anybody of lesser ability in the art could understand them.

Fugue had arisen partially in response to the technological advances in lie-detection gear. When multi-channel stress analyzers and electrophy equipment were brought to bear, it was nearly impossible to prevaricate and not be detected. Since such machineries could be utilized without the subject's knowledge in many cases, those in the public eye had learned to speak a thousand shadings of the truth. Even a simple yes-or-no question might be fielded as one wished by a skillful rendering of strict truth. "Do you know where this wanted criminal is?" could be answered negatively by using precise thought patterns: "No," and the unspoken tag line, "I don't know where he is *at this moment*." Such questions required more precision on the part of the questioner: "Did you know where he was at seven hundred hours local time this morning?" to be countered by, "No." *Not exactly. I knew about where, but you didn't ask that.* . . .

This kind of exacting dance became more and more difficult. Like trying to pin a blob of mercury to a table with a knife point, the ascertaining of truth turned into a slippery devil indeed when questioning a fugue master.

Such uses of fugue were limited, of course. And it quickly became more a diplomatic tool than a resource for criminals. Proper fugue wasn't easy to learn, after all, and a better player could almost always best a lesser one. Most of the real experts eventually wound up in Confederation service, and that tended to stop the use of fugue by most in trying to fool the Confed.

Eventually, the complicated double-speak became a toy of the upper classes, much as certain uncommon languages had been for years; still, even the most esoteric of recorded languages could be translated by a properly programmed viral matrix computer. No one had yet devised an artificial brain that could play fugue with the best. Some were trying.

Pen listened to this lecture, as he had countless others, but with more interest than usual. Fugue was part of the Siblings' training, and there were things he wanted to learn to say without doing so directly.

In the six months since the Confederation rep's ship had gone down, killing him and his quad of soldiers, Pen had yet to find the courage to speak to Moon about it. He was afraid—not of her reaction—but of what he would learn.

Had she coldly had them killed? Five people, just like that? Moon, his oh-so-gentle lover?

Pen's reaction was, he knew, absurd. If she didn't say it aloud then it wasn't real? Foolish. Certainly Moon was capable of it. He had seen her cripple the spacers back in Dindabe's pub. How long ago was that? Three years? Gods, how the time had flown.

He loved her. No doubt of that. That she might have killed to protect herself or the Siblings shouldn't change his feelings. But he was afraid it would, somehow, especially if he confronted her with it. He both wanted to know for sure, and he did not want to know. It could have been an accident. A coincidence that she had said what she said. The galaxy was full of things more coincidental than that, they happened every day, didn't they? Certainly.

So . . . fugue. Perhaps if he learned it well enough, he could ask without asking, and she might answer without answering. A poor solution, perhaps, but it was better than none.

And maybe better than the bare truth.

"So, Pen, how are you feeling?" That was the teacher's statement. Cube was one of the older siblings at the order, and the highest of them in fugue ability. Watching the man's hands, listening to the tone of his voice and his inflection of the words, Pen made the fugue-analog out to be: *Something is bothering you, is it not?* Easy enough.

Pen thought about his reply, composed the layers of speech and action, and smiled under his shroud. He said, "I feel quite well, Brother Cube." His fugue-intent was: *No, nothing bothers me, honored teacher.*

"Good to hear. I had thought you looked a bit tense." *Really? I still don't think so. But I defer—for now.*

"Well, I am testing for my next layer in a month, perhaps I am a bit nervous about that." *Nope, I'm not nervous about anything.* A lie, and blatant, because he could see the old man smile under his hood, not buying it for a minute. Cube didn't even need to speak. *That wasn't very subtle, Pen. Surely you can do better?*

Pen felt very much out of his depth. It was worse than learning a new language, because it was so encompassing. He could see how easy it was to get lost, and this was the simplest of conversations. Maybe his idea of trying to find out things from Moon by this method was not all that clever. She was not as good as Cube, but she was far advanced in this game over Pen. He remembered the conversation she had had with Dindabe, what seemed like half his lifetime past. They had been dancing fugue, and he had missed it, save for the faintest of suspicions that something was going on. How had Dindabe known fugue? It didn't matter. He had known, somehow, and that was how he had passed the then-Ferret off to Moon, Pen was now certain of it. It had seemed magic at the time.

"You seem pensive," Cube said. *Have I lost your attention, Pen?*

Pen was at a loss. Fugue required at least as much concentration as the Ninety-seven Steps, and by wandering off mentally, he had lost the thread.

"Uh," he began, "uh . . ."

Cube laughed. That needed no fugue to translate.

Damn.

Integratics.

Here was another subject, one even more slippery than fugue. The butterfly-and-tornado aspect of it seemed unlikely to Pen, when first he began to study it. That events so small *here* could eventually connect and cause things so much larger *there* seemed altogether unrealistic. If ever a god wished to construct a complicated dance, surely this theory was it. Electronic tarot cards or a fiberoptic gel crystal ball seemed to make as much sense.

According to the theory, everything affected everything else, and if one looked long and hard enough, one would eventually see the connection.

In Pen's mind, stars might burn down and die while he looked for some of the connections.

The teachers were fond of using colorful metaphors in describing the science, if science it was. They talked of spinning disks, of expanding balloons, and of fossil footprints in rock. It did not take Pen long to realize that even a basic understanding (not to even speak of mastery) of integratics would require as much as or more time than fugue. Statistical analyses had to be coupled with sociobiological projections; politics with troop movements; the latest galactic music trends with the literature of a hundred years past. And all of these had to connect to each other. The resulting picture, if indeed there was one, was so large as to be outside Pen's scope of vision. He could see pieces now and then, and a major example used by his teachers was, he had to admit, quite astonishing:

On Maro, a low-level watchman fell asleep while monitoring a safety computer for a crystal mine. During his slumber, a gas leak occurred, pressure built up, and there was an explosion that killed six men and destroyed sixty-nine mining dins.

This mining disaster on Maro caused an immediate shortage of compounds used in making densecris on the sister world of Nazo, the result of which was a drop in stock values of a major manufacturing concern. Said concern scurried to raise the stock price by engaging in quasi-legal and illegal transactions, got caught at it, and thus wound up causing a shipload of Confed auditors to bend to Maro from Earth.

This ship's engines malfunctioned upon leaving subspace, and the ship exploded, killing all onboard.

One of the auditors on the destroyed ship was the lover of the holoproj star, Kerri Cherry, who, in a fit of depression, jumped off a building in Tokyo.

Unfortunately, Cherry's leap ended on the roof of a chauffeured aircar carrying the Supreme Commander of Confederation Ground Forces, Carstair Immeler. The armored car crashed, the S.C.'s restraint system failed, and he was splattered all over the inside of his vehicle, quite dead.

Immeler's death caused a scurry of political and military activity as the potential successors fought to be chosen, resulting in the assassinations of two Over-Befalhavares by poison, and a mysterious disappearance of a Systems Marshal.

In the end, the new S.C. picked was Pram Abel Reilly, a Confed hard-liner, known as the Hammer. One of the Hammer's first actions was to reinterpret the Confed Standing Orders about rebellion and treason. During a peaceful anti-Confed demonstration at Macumba University on Mason, a handful of students carried placards in front of the campus security building. Reilly ordered his local commanders to stop them. As these things sometimes do, it got out of hand. Violence escalated. Rocks and bottles were thrown, shots fired.

Most of the student body, irate over the deaths of their fellows, stormed over the campus and occupied several major buildings.

Troops moved in with riot gas.

Somebody stole a shipment of military weaponry, carbines, and the students started shooting back.

It was time for some serious negotiation, but the Hammer decided to bring things to a quick end—by using tactical nukes. For all practical purposes, the university was destroyed in the ensuing explosions, along with more than twelve thousand students, two hundred professors, five hundred support staff, and more than a thousand local residents. Not counting Confed troops, whose casualties were kept secret.

An object lesson, Reilly said, it will make the dissenters sit up and take notice, by God.

It had certainly done that. If the Confed had seemed asleep, the action against the students had shown that awakened, the wrath of the beast could be mighty. Blind, maybe, but nonetheless effective for that.

So, a man falling asleep on one world might be said to be responsible for the deaths of thousands on another world, not to mention a new policy of Confederation repression throughout the entire civilized galaxy.

Butterfly and tornado, indeed. Hindsight showed it, but how in any kind of rational galaxy could anybody *begin* to predict something like that in advance? It sounded to Pen like mysticism, pure and simple. He could see the linkage only when shown from the now, and moving backward.

And had they spotted that one in advance? Not precisely, but they had managed to get glimmerings of something like it.

At that, his teacher had wandered off into charts and numbers again, and while fine in theory, it sounded like so much mumbo-jumbo to Pen in actual practice. According to their projections, which admittedly were still sketchy, something of major galactic importance loomed out there somewhere. And somewhen. So far, the best computer-augmented crunchings had narrowed it—whatever *it* was—to one of four stellar systems. As for time, well, they had that down to a mere hundred years—plus or minus fifty or sixty.

Precision was not their forte at this stage of the game, Pen thought. But he did not say that aloud.

Throughout the complex studies, Pen was still, by and large, a happy man. He had progressed to the Overshroud, and now wore the First Layer, the gi. He had only to gain the utility belt, the *yuyo obi*, and the *manto*, the cloak, to be a full-fledged Sibling.

And there was Moon.

As he got better at fugue, there were times when Pen considered asking about the destruction of the Confed rep's ship. But, as time passed, the event grew dimmer. His link with Moon strengthened, and he could usually tell where she was in the compound simply by intuition, the same sense that had led him to her in the swamp that first time. His exercises in

HSP began to work more often than not, although mostly when it was Moon with whom he practiced. Not magic, but still something he had trouble understanding.

Together in bed, Pen and his teacher were a tangle of passionate limbs, tingly and warm, and hearts pounding. There was, he figured, too much joy there to risk by overturning old rocks. Rationalization, sure, but why the hell not? His life had been full of dark places—was it so much to ask that he allow himself to stay in the light as long as he could? Wouldn't any reasonable man do the same?

So the time went, Pen learning, loving, and content for the second time in his life. Not every man got another chance. He was willing to stay here studying for the rest of his life. It was simple, but he was learning that the good things were. He didn't need a pleasure condo on Vishnu to be happy.

He had everything he needed right here.

TWENTY-SIX _____

PEN LAY IN Moon's bed next to her, sated and comfortable. A night bird chittered outside in the warm darkness. The only light came from the power control panel on Moon's desktop computer console, green and red diodes that gave the room a dim, ghostly glow. The scent of musk lay heavy in the air.

"You're happy, aren't you?" she said.

He grinned at her, barely able to make out her face under the panel's sensor lamps. He could see faint reflections mirrored in her eyes. He started to say something flip, but at the last moment, realized it was a serious question. "Yes," he said. "I'm happy."

"Why?"

He wasn't ready for that one. Now he did try a joke. "Why? Have you so little self-confidence? No mirrors around?"

Moon did not speak to that. The silence stretched uncomfortably, and Pen felt as if he had somehow disappointed her. He tried to make amends. "Look at all that I have. You are a very special woman, Moon. And all this"—he gestured with one hand, taking in the compound and the totality of the Siblings—"it's everything a man could wish for."

"So, as long as you have me and the order, you're happy." It was not really a question.

He imagined sharpness in her tone, felt her displeasure. What was wrong? Was she trying some kind of fugue on him? His belly clutched at itself in cold fear. "Have I done something wrong, Moon?"

Another long silence fell upon them, as tangible as a blanket. Then, "No, not you. *I* have done something wrong." She rolled up onto one elbow and faced him. He copied her motion. She said, "Before and after you practice sumito, do you do your meditations?"

"Certainly."

"What do you feel when you meditate?"

He was at a loss. What was she after? "Uh, well, I feel a sense of calmness, of—of—relaxation—"

"Really?"

He paused. She wasn't going to be put off by anything other than truth. "Sometimes. Sometimes, I don't feel anything. I wonder what we're going to have for lunch, I think about you, I worry about a cramp in my foot. All of us have distractions, you taught me that."

"But when the meditation is going well, when you get lost in it, what then, Pen? What do you feel then?"

He was confused, afraid, and he didn't know what she wanted him to say. "I don't understand."

She leaned back, and sat up, looking down at him. "What is the most important thing in your life?"

He took a deep breath. That one he could answer, no question about it. "You are," he said.

Moon reached out and put her hands on the sides of his face. Her touch was gentle, loving, and somehow, sad. She said, "Forgive me for that, Pen. We all have our flaws, and mine has been a blind spot where you are."

"Moon, I don't understand. Why wouldn't that make you happy? To know you are the most important thing in my life? I love you!" He sat up, shaking the gel pad of their bed, and reached for her. She came into his arms, unresisting, and hugged him tightly. It was all right, whatever it was, they could work it out—

"I love you, too," she said. "But not nearly as well as I should have. Not nearly enough."

She would say no more. They made love again, and her passion seemed undiminished, but there was a core of sadness within her he could not touch. What was wrong? What had he done? In that few minutes, he had gone from being almost unbearably happy to feeling an almost absolute dread. Somehow, he had fucked up, and he had the conviction that it was going to cost him Moon. He hadn't known what love was before, and now he did. Or thought he did. Given what others said about it, and what he had read, what he felt for her had to be love. But that was threatened, all in an instant. How could that be? What had he done wrong?

She put him to work in the wine cellar under the Stores building. There, Pen learned the ancient art of riddling, the manual turning of wine bottles.

His teacher was Bolt, a solid priest of maybe sixty, gone gray by the look of the hair on the backs of his hands, and as efficient at small movements as any man Pen had ever seen. One had to be, he learned, to be a riddler.

The cellar was dimly lit, the overhead lamps giving out no more than a soft glow that barely allowed one to move safely among the rows of aging wine bottles.

"We make only about a hundred and fifty cases of sparkling wine a year," Bolt said, as he led Pen down a dusty corridor. "Eighteen hundred bottles. Use three different kinds of grapes for the press. Can't call it champagne, that's only allowed in one of the old Euro districts, but it's the same method. Yeast eats the sugar right in the bottle, makes alcohol, and dies. That's where we come in. The dead yeasts and sediment have to be removed."

The two of them reached a turning in the corridor. Rounding it, Pen saw a different row of racks. These were angled so the bottles pointed down at about forty-five degrees, bottoms up.

"Here's how it works," Bolt said. "Each bottle has to be turned, every hour. See the pulse-paint on the outer bottles?"

Pen nodded. The top row of a dozen bottles had small specks of glowing orange on the outer rims of the two outermost bottles. The paint was at six o'clock, throbbing softly to its timed bacterial pulse.

Bolt said, "They have to be turned, like this."

The priest reached up and grabbed two of the bottles and twisted them slightly. Then he moved his hands and turned two more. Pen watched, amazed, as the man rapidly gave each bottle in the rack a similar turn, working in pairs. It only took a moment to move all the bottles. There were about a hundred or so of them in the rack.

"An hour from now, we move them again, this way." He demonstrated. "There is a sequence we use, it's similar in all champagne wineries, though not exactly the same. Here, here, here, then this way, like this, like so."

"What's the purpose?" Pen asked.

"To settle the dead yeast into the neck, next to the cap. In a month, all of the sediment will be there. We quick-freeze the end of the neck, allow the pressure to extrude the plug, add some sugar, and cork the bottle."

Pen nodded.

"Be very careful," Bolt said. "The pressure of the carbon dioxide inside the bottles is between six and eight atmospheres. Jostling a bottle or dropping it might result in an explosion. Such a glass bomb can be very dangerous."

"Why not do this with machinery, then? Surely there are such devices?"

"Yes. But hardly cost effective for such a small operation. Besides, hand riddling is better, no matter what anyone tells you. Machines have no souls."

So Pen learned the sequence for riddling, moving down the row of eighteen racks, twisting bottles. It was not the most intellectually stimulating job, and the near-darkness of the cool cellar was both quiet and, at times, spooky.

The actual turning took less and less time, as he learned the sequence, and Bolt left him alone to his task. It did not take long for Pen to spend only a few minutes to finish the entire chore; this left large blocks of empty time, waiting for the next turn. He was encouraged to practice meditation during these spaces, and he tried. In the cool dark, he kept expecting to see the shade of some long-dead priest stalking the corridors. No such spectre intruded on his boredom, however. Pity.

When he wasn't turning the maturing bottles of sparkling wine, Pen had another job: working with the bonsai garden just west of the gymnasium. He would emerge from the cellar blinking against the tropical sunshine and walk to the miniature forest, feeling like a giant as he moved among the twisted and tiny trees.

Pruning and shaping bonsai were more exacting than turning wine bottles, but slower still. His teacher here was called Agate, and she was, surprisingly, younger than Pen, a woman with a soft voice and a lilting laugh. She had been born here, she said. He supposed that explained her youth. It brought up all kinds of questions, but he refrained from asking. It might be some kind of test. Virtually everything might be a test these days, and he did not want to make any mistakes. He had already done something to make Moon unhappy with him, though he had yet to figure out what it had been.

Agate taught him the subtle method of using heavy wire to wrap and bend the tiny trees, and how to cut the smallest foliage away without damaging the plants. She showed him how to balance the shapes, to mimic the effect of wind or sun, and she drew diagrams of the garden overall, so that he could see the totality of it, as opposed to mere individual trees. There was, Pen saw, a kind of beauty to working in such a small arena. But very slow sculpture, indeed.

"It can take fifty or a hundred years to bring a bonsai to its essence," she said. "One may not live to see the final product."

"That's discouraging," Pen said. He kept his voice light, a half-joke.

Her answer was a poem—he found out later that she was the most accomplished poet among the siblings—and he puzzled over its meaning for a long time.

> Anticipation—
> It's a ticklish thing really,
> quivering, exciting, waiting,
> until it dies—
>   killed by its own self
> Lost through virtue of being there.

He wondered, but he did not ask, thinking it might be another test. Instead, he bent wire and urged the limbs of the bonsai into new ways under the young woman's direction.

So went his days for the next month, turning bottles and working with bonsai, both endeavors designed, so he often thought, for a man with less than full mental batteries. Neither sediment settling nor photosynthetic adaptation produced much in the way of visible results, and a man who would do such

things full time would have to have the patience of a small
stream wearing down a mountain of granite. Still, he did the
chores without complaining. At night, he still had Moon, and
that made up for whatever mindless drudgery the days might
hold. Besides, there was some kind of purpose in the work,
some reason Moon had put him to it. Maybe he would figure
it out someday.

Almost another year passed.

Pen lay on his bed, alone, staring at the featureless ceiling.
Something was missing.

The test had gone well. Pen had known most of the answers
to the oral questions put to him by the panel of instructors. His
dance of the pattern had been flawless, if he did say so himself.
The written exam had been difficult, but no more so than expected, and overall, his score was nearly ninety percent. Not
as high as Von's, nor in the same league with some of the early
brothers and sisters, but as high as anybody else had scored in
the last fifteen years—and that included Moon. Certainly it was
something to be proud of. The ceremony for full enshroudment
would be held in the morning. He would be surrounded by his
friends and teachers, the *manto* would be draped over his
shoulders by the Elder Sister—his lover Moon—and he would
be a Full Brother, with all the rights and privileges attached
thereto. He had been at the compound for nearly four years.
During that time, he had seldom left the grounds, and he had
never left the small island of Manus itself, save for short boat
trips around the perimeter. He had no desire to ever leave, for
this was his home in a way no other place had ever been.
Everything should be perfect, and yet—

Something was missing.

There was a lack, some feeling or energy or something he
could not pin down. Like a mosquito buzzing just outside his
reach, it drew his attention, but when he turned to look directly
at it, this *thing*, whatever it was, was no longer there.

What was it? He had Moon, he had status, he had a sense
of accomplishment unlike anything he had ever done. His
knowledge had increased tremendously, his physical powers
were at their peak, he had learned to calm his mind and spirit
through quiet meditations. Or so he had thought.

He should be at peace, and yet, he was not. Some unrest bubbled in the caldron of his soul, and he could not see or touch or hear what it was. He only knew that it was there.

He would have asked Moon, but she had withdrawn from him. Not physically, and she was as responsive as ever to his questions, but there was a wall there that had not existed before. He was afraid to thicken the barrier by admitting to a flaw, by being less than perfect. If she knew, it might make things worse, and yet, there was no one else he could talk to about it:

Tomorrow should be the greatest day of his life. Full Shroud, entry into the siblinghood, and the respect and admiration of all who aspired to that same state. But that invisible mosquito buzzed and would not be still, and the faint hum of its wings threatened to become the roar of a giant waterfall in his mind, engulfing and drowning him.

There was something he was missing. He was incomplete, somehow, a piece of truth about him lay hidden. It was within him, he felt, beneath the murk of who he thought he was, and he had to find it or he would never be whole. The thought of it frightened him as much as anything ever had. What if, as he suspected, he figured out how to get to the center of who he was, and—his core was rotten? How would he live with that?

And what would Moon do if she knew?

TWENTY-SEVEN

HE STOOD ON the raised platform in front of the other students and instructors as Moon draped the *manto* over his shoulders.

"Not an end, but a beginning," Moon said. It was the ritual statement that always accompanied the cloak. Now Pen understood at least a part of its implication. He, for one, did not have all of the answers.

The students cheered as Pen wrapped the cloak around himself and fastened the closures. For the first time, he stood completely dressed in the costume of his order, Full Shroud at last. There was a power in it, despite his newly discovered worry about his spiritual lack. It was what he had worked for all this time. He had come much further than ever he had expected. From a farm boy to thief, to vagrant to priest. How odd life was.

Yes, came his nagging inner voice, *and now what?*

"So, now what?" Spiral asked. "Off to save the galaxy?"

Pen sat across the cafeteria table from his friend, who was maybe six or eight months away from earning his own *manto*. A few other students and faculty sat at nearby tables or moved out after finishing their lunches. The smell of roast duck, a special meal prepared in honor of Pen's promotion, wafted through the room.

"I expect I'll stay and teach slow learners such as yourself how to walk the pattern without falling," Pen said.

"Hey, you haven't seen *me* fall in two months, pal."

"Probably only because I haven't been watching you."

"Funny." Spiral paused to chew thoughtfully at a mouthful of duck in cherry sauce. Despite his joking, Spiral seemed to have an inner peace that radiated outward from him. Pen hadn't noticed it before.

"You seem rather calm these days," Pen said.

Spiral swallowed his food and nodded. "Mmm. I've been having some real clear meditation. Sort of dancing on the edge of a real powerful feeling. Like I'm about to cross over into the promised land. But you know all about that."

Pen nodded mechanically. No. He didn't know. His own meditation had never produced those blissful states some of the siblings achieved. You could see them, glowing like spiritual lamps plugged into the cosmic generator. It was called many things: *Relampago*, the lightning; Zen-mind; siddhi-spirit; samadhi; the Buddha-Christ-Baba soul; cosmic consciousness. They were, according to the teachings, all the same. His physiology teacher had been more pragmatic, talking about hyperoxygenated brains and self-hypnosis, but no one who was around a man or woman burning with the cosmic fire could deny their power: they had been touched by the Finger of God.

A delusion, perhaps, but none the less potent for that. And Spiral assumed that because Pen was higher in rank he was also higher in spiritual achievement. It was not so. Part of his problem, Pen knew. He *should* be higher, he felt, but he had somehow failed.

One of the newer students, dressed only in first layer undershroud, approached their table.

"Pen?" the young woman asked tentatively. Pen smiled under his hood—she had not been here long enough to pierce the shrouds and recognize the people under them. He remembered when he had been unable to do so. It seemed like such a long time ago.

"Yes?"

"Moon would see you in her office, at your convenience."

"Thank you."

The girl scurried off. Pen stood. "I'd better go see what the old lady wants."

"Who told you we call her that?"

"Nobody, to my face. But I'm not altogether deaf."

As Pen started away, Spiral said, "She probably wants to take back your cloak, Pen. It was all a joke, letting you have it."

It was supposed to be funny, but Pen did not feel like laughing. He had thought the same thing, and the fear it brought up was altogether too real.

Moon stood by the window of her office, staring out through the thincris at something Pen could not see. She did not turn when he entered.

"You wanted to see me?"

Still facing away from him, she said, "Yes." Then she turned, slowly, and from her body language, he knew whatever it was she wanted was bad.

"You have learned all we can teach you here," she said. Was that a quaver in her voice? No, it couldn't be. Not Moon. "What you need can't be gotten cooped up in our private world. I—I wish that it could."

Pen stood stock still, feeling rooted to the floor. He knew what was coming. His worst fear, that which he dreaded more than failure, more than death itself.

Moon took a deep breath. It was ragged. Almost a sob.

"You have to leave," she said.

Pen's voice, when he spoke, was as calm as deep vacuum. "I see."

Moon shook her head. "No, you don't. That's my fault. I bound you to me, I wanted what you offered, and I allowed myself to lose my own center. I knew better."

"You regret what we have had together?"

"No. Never that. Only my selfishness. I measured what you needed against what I wanted, and I filled my own cup. I warmed myself by your fire."

"So. You made some kind of mistake—not that I understand what the hell it was—and I have to leave because of it?" He felt the anger fill him with heat.

Moon stood silent for a moment, then closed her eyes. "Yes. Now we both pay the price."

"I am being kicked out of my home! What are *you* losing,

Moon?" The rage flowed now, unchecked, a torrent. *"What the fuck are you losing?!"*

Her answer, when it finally came, was soft, a single word: "You."

You. It killed his anger, flash-froze the heat like a bath of liquid air.

You. The power of a single word, backed by truth of Moon's emotion and he could not deny the love he felt from her, could not protest, for all her soul seemed wrapped in that word.

"Oh, God, Moon!"

She came to him and they embraced, both crying, like children confronted with the death of loved parents. Tears and sobs and mindless groping for comfort. Somewhere in it, Pen felt a moment of empathy. He did not understand why she was sending him away, but he understood that she truly loved him. That making him leave was done from that love, and that it was the hardest thing Moon had ever faced.

He did not understand, but because he could feel her pain, he accepted it.

Not that he had any choice.

TWENTY-EIGHT

THERE WASN'T MUCH to do to get ready. There was no deadline, no admonition to be gone before the sun set, but the implication was clear enough: the sooner the better.

What Pen owned could be put into a small bag. A second shroud, that was the extent of his wardrobe. He had long since recycled his "civilian" clothing. He hadn't gathered much in the way of *things*: he had a reader and a dozen or so marble-sized recording spheres he could call his own; a piece of sculpture Moon had given him, a nude female dancer cast in bronze, not much larger than his hand; pocket tools, which he carried in his utility pouch. His old credit cube, much depleted, but with enough stads still banked to live on for a year or two, provided he was frugal. Small odds and ends.

The things he carried would not weigh him down. The memories were what lay heavily upon him. Especially when he began to say his good-byes.

He was dry-eyed and numb through most of it. Smiling under his hood, nodding at his teachers. In the kitchen and wine cellar and storeroom and powerhouse, he smiled and nodded, shook hands, embraced some, slapped others on the back. He exercised the ritual of leaving, performed the dance robotically, and he tried to sit *atman* upon his own shoulder to watch it. Tried, and failed. It was hard.

• • •

Spiral was harder. They danced around it.

"You know, I'm going to miss you, Pen."

"Yeah. Me, too, you."

"Now I know there was a better way, a more peaceful method, but I'll never forget taking out that Confed quad."

"We had some good times, all right."

"You give 'em hell out there, Pen. If anybody can, it's you. I'm sure it's all for the best."

"Sure, Spiral. You take care of yourself."

In the bonsai garden, among the tiny trees he'd never see reach maturity, he found Agate. They walked among the small and ancient plants. Pen felt a catch in his throat as he realized he might never see this garden again.

Next to a small recycled stream, Agate perched upon one of the three rocks—granite, pumice and quartz—and asked if she might recite a poem for him.

"Yes, of course," he said.

"I didn't write this one," she said. "But I offered to say it."

Pen took a deep breath and let it escape. He didn't ask who wrote the poem before he heard it.

Afterward, he didn't need to ask.

> There is no comfort in change
> but also no learning in the
> > steady
> > > drone
> > > > of
> > > > > peace
> There will be no greater sorrow
> than watching you go—
> > except
> for watching you grow old
> > and tired here—
> > > clarity awaits
> > > elsewhere.

It was short, pithy, bittersweet, and he fought to keep the tears from welling as he thanked her. Part of it he understood, part of it still not. But it touched him, nonetheless.

• • •

Surprising how little time it actually took to make the rounds.
A few hours to close out four years. They were both sad and
happy for him, most of them, and he appreciated that, though
none of them understood how he felt. No mixture of emotions
for him, no joy of leaving. He would have done anything to be
able to stay.

Moon was not inside the compound. He didn't need anybody
to tell him that, he felt her distance, just as he knew where to
go to find her.

He left by the Northwest Gate, and walked north toward the
ocean. The sound of the breaking waves droned in the salty,
fishy air as he climbed a small hill that overlooked a steep drop
to the blue-gray water. There he found Moon, staring out to
sea, the wind trying vainly to unravel her wrappings with its
chilly and insistent fingers.

He moved to stand next to her. For a long time, neither
spoke. Only the wind sang, and its voice was no more than a
moan.

After several eons, Moon pointed at the spot on the water a
few hundred meters offshore. "That's a Langmuir slick," she
said. "Do you know about them?"

"No."

"It's a spot where dust and debris, seaweed and such, collect. An odd circulation habit of surface water under a steady
wind. Doesn't seem to matter how hard the wind blows; in
anything short of a hurricane, you get that kind of dead spot."
Her voice was deliberate, as if she were lecturing to a class.

Pen didn't say anything.

"You wouldn't think that such things would exist. There's a
place in one of the Earth's oceans hundreds of kilometers in
area where it does that. Called the Sargasso Sea. Old-time
sailors used to fear being trapped in the seaweed that collected
there."

"Moon—"

Her voice changed. Pain entered it. "That's what this place
has become for you, Pen. A Langmuir slick." She turned to
face him. "If you stayed here, you'd only stagnate, spinning
in the eddy of our order, going nowhere, learning nothing. You
have to go."

"I—"

"No. Don't say anything. I want you to stay. More than almost anything I don't want you to leave. I would have you be here, with me. But if I keep you, you will never be as much as you should be. Some day, you'd blink away the scales and see what I had done to you, and you would hate me for it."

"I'd never hate you," he said.

"You would. And I couldn't bear it. So, what I'm doing isn't particularly noble or altruistic. You're missing a part of yourself, Pen, and I want you whole, more than I want you to stay. They don't teach us about love here. Maybe it can't be taught. I don't know. If I could love you a little less, I could keep you. But I *can't*, Pen. I have enough of my center, and I know the truth of it."

He felt very small in that moment. The universe was too daunting, too hard, too overwhelming to bear. He could hear the love in her voice, and yet, she was sending him away. There was something wrong with him. He had failed her. He had failed himself, and there was nothing he could do to fix it. Never had he felt so helpless, not as a boy under his father's lash, not when Stoll and Shar had died. In the depths of his drunken odyssey, he had not been so alone as he was right now. He was a man who had found Paradise—twice!—and had been thrown out both times. Once in anger and death, and now again, with love. Why? What god had he offended so, to be punished this way?

What was he going to do?

For once, his sarcastic inner voice remained quiet, even that part of him crushed and silenced under this new weight. He had to find the truth, whatever it was that Moon wanted him to find, no matter how much work nor how long it took, but— how was he going to do it?

How?

Part Three
The Ninety-Seventh Step

The truth waits for eyes unclouded by longing.
—ANONYMOUS

TWENTY-NINE _____

MOON HAD ARRANGED for him to receive a new credit cube. It identified him as "Pen," and the number of stads so credited was easily twice that in his old account. The name he'd used for the old cube was an alias and unlikely to be in anybody's look-for comp, but according to the new cube, he was a fully accredited member of the Siblings of the Shroud, with all of the rights and privileges attendant thereto. As far as the Confed was concerned, he was a new man. The brainwave pattern imprinted on the read-only chip imbedded in the cube was almost legitimate, slightly different than that recorded for the twelve-year-old Mwili Kalamu—enough to keep a Confed computer from matching the two on first pass, but close enough so that an encephaloscan would probably be forgiving. Tolerances were pretty slim, but there was a range the machines were programmed to allow.

A new man—but one with the same old dreads.

He busied himself with mundane tasks as long as he could, but eventually it was time. All that he owned was packed in a bag hung over his shoulder. One of the palliates had been detailed to drive him to the port, a boy who seemed still in his teens. He made Pen feel old.

"Thanks just the same," Pen said. "I'll walk. Might as well go out the same way I came in."

The palliate seemed altogether too respectful, as if Pen were some kind of awe-inspiring figure, and that raised a sad smile under the shroud. If only you knew, boy.

Moon was gone. He had not seen her since they had stood together by the cliff, watching the sea. He reached for some feel of her, but wherever she was was beyond his range to sense. Just as well; a tearful parting scene might undo him completely. Better to remember the Moon of before.

So, with the day's first thunderheads building over him, Pen walked away from the place he had called home for the past four years. As time went, four years wasn't all that long, even in a man's life. He was, by biological reckoning, still young. He had skills and knowledge he hadn't had before, and money enough to keep him for a time. And once again, none of it deadened the echoes inside of him, that empty, hollow feeling.

Down the road he walked, wrapped in an emotional flux as tangible as his clothing. He managed only a few hundred meters before he had to stop and look back.

Gathered inside the gate stood maybe fifteen shrouded forms, watching him.

Pen's indrawn breath was nearly a sob. His teachers and friends had turned out to watch him leave. The sense of what he was losing almost had him then, washing over him like a breaker. He managed to turn away without waving, but he felt a sense of bittersweetness as he began walking again, something he hadn't thought of before.

Maybe they were going to miss him a little, too.

He had attended to all the little details, to keep himself occupied, but he had neglected an important one:

Where was he going to go?

True, he didn't have to decide here, since he would only be taking a connecting boxcar to a major port in Australia. Still, sooner or later, he'd need a destination. There was never any question of his staying on Earth. He couldn't be that close and not find excuses to flit back and see Moon and the others. Assuming she would allow it.

He thought briefly of retracing his earlier paths. Going home to Cibule, to see if his father still lived. Maybe going to Vishnu, even Thompson's Gazelle, to look up Dindabe. But—no. Old paths were just that. He knew on some level there was nothing to be gained that way.

So, which way, O wandering priest?

In the back of his mind, he had a glimmering that he'd played with: Koji. The single planet of the Heiwa System was known through the galaxy as the center for religion. Millions of pilgrims found their way to Koji every year, to study, to teach, to seek out answers to questions beyond logic's ability to adequately cover. If a religion was organized above the stone-age level, it probably had a branch on Koji. Buddhists, Jesuits, Tillbedjare, Libhobers, Trimenagists, Mothers, Fathers, Sisters, Brothers—Koji welcomed them all; more, a de facto truce existed with the Confed—somebody was bright enough to realize that movements with billions of followers might be best left alone as much as possible. Maintaining civil order was difficult enough; fighting religious wars did not greatly interest the Confed. Fanatics would stand until the last man—witness the Battle of Mwanamamke in the Bibi Arusi System, led by Thomas Reserve Shamba and his Right-to-Freedom sect in the late 22nd Century. The Confed had won, but the victory had been pyrrhic. It had been expensive, time consuming and bad press, too. No, the Confed treaded lightly on Koji when it walked there at all, and it watched very carefully for bare and holy toes where it stepped.

So—Koji?

Might as well.

The ship bent and warped normal space, courtesy of the Scates-Waller Augmented Reality Analog Instigation Construct, more popularly known as the bender drive. The math and metaphysics of the drive were both highly unlikely and, according to some, downright impossible, but they had given man interstellar space. Some had it that it was mere illusion, but then some had it that all was *maya*, and in the end, arguing philosophy was mostly a waste of time, illusion or no.

Pen sat at a table onboard the starliner, sipping at ginseng tea, watching a couple try to keep a three-year-old girl occupied. It looked to be a full-time job. Pen had wondered about children, whether to take on the responsibility of them, but he had little confidence in his ability to guide a life other than his own. How could he teach when he had yet to discover the purpose of his own existence?

The little girl managed to slip the controls of her parents. She made straight for Pen.

"Why are you all covered up?" she asked. No guile there, just simple curiosity.

How to explain *that* to a small child?

"Because I'm hiding," Pen said.

"Who are you hiding from?"

"Myself." Saying that spooked him. He hadn't realized how much truth was in that simple statement.

The girl shook her head, disturbing her fine, blond hair. "Won't work," she said. "You can't hide from yourself. You're right there with you."

She's got our number, hasn't she? came Pen's inner voice. *You can't run and you can't hide.*

The child's mother arrived and dragged the little girl away, murmuring an apology, while carefully appraising Pen's shrouded figure for possible danger to her offspring. The mother could not realize that the child was more dangerous to Pen than he could ever be to her.

One other memorable event happened on that voyage through bent space. Actually, it took place several weeks earlier on a world twenty light-years away, but the news of it only arrived at Pen's ship when it docked for passengers on the way to Koji. Once in realspace, the liner uploaded newscasts and passengers could replay them when they so desired. Pen had been out of touch for a long time, not caring what happened anywhere except on Manus. He sat at a holoproj table and flicked the unit on, to see what the Confed was allowing its subjects to see these days.

The event had been covered in great detail, for the Confed wanted it shown. There must have been a platoon of camera operators working to capture it all.

On the world of Wu, said the voiceover, in the Haradali System, two local factions fought over control of a prime piece of real estate, property used for growing a particular kind of grape that would only flourish in a narrow latitude. The grapes were used in making Timbalee wines, some of the best wines ever devised, according to experts, no matter what vintage you might choose.

Unfortunately during the legal battle, somebody forgot to

pay the Confed its triple-tithe tax. Somebody got quite heated about it, somebody essentially told the Confed to go away and leave them alone, this was serious business.

So, the Confed decided, somebody needed a lesson, and it was one of which everyone should be aware.

The recorded images were very sharp. Troopers gathered up the arguing factions, maybe five hundred people who were either directly involved or working for those who were. The soldiers were not gentle in their work. Pen watched a close shot of a man's head being smashed by a carbine's butt, thoughtfully done in slow motion so no viewer could miss the effect of heavy plastic on scalp and skull. Blood sprayed, and the camera was close enough so that the red mist fogged the lens. An artful image, they must have thought.

There were other such scenes. Boots driven into stomachs or groins, elbows into noses, weapons used to batter heads. No one was shot—they were saving them for the grand finale, and needed them alive for that.

Cut to a Confederation Dreadnought hung against the starry pinprick of space. The Fourth Fleet's flagship, the voiceover explained, the *Indomitable*. Mounting (classified number) banks of (classified) gigawatt laser weaponry. The camera held the shot long enough to show a ten-passenger lighter arc from under the belly of the mothership, to give it scale.

It was a big ship, all right. Bigger than a couple of the smallest wheelworlds.

The camera pushed in on the ship, and faded through it, back to the five hundred people on Wu. The shot was high, from a flitter or thopter, but a zoom showed a remarkable close up. Those who were still able to run did so. Panic flowed from those people like their screams, the sounds of which were produced with clean fidelity despite the camera's distance.

Pen felt his stomach churn. He knew what was coming, even though the announcer tastefully avoided speaking it aloud.

They cut to the *Indomitable*. The camera held it a beat.

They resumed the crowd, but long. Pen could see they were people. Then, of a moment, they weren't people anymore. The scene was washed out in red, boiling clouds of red, reaching even to the camera so high above.

There was a time-dissolve to a glassy landscape of muddy brown green, glittering under a clear sky and bright sunshine.

Pen recognized it as laserglass, and a big patch of it. The camera pulled back, way back, and added in a scale on the screen to show just how big it was. Two kilometers by almost three. What used to be the center of the wine country in contention. And the tomb for five hundred people.

Pen turned away from the screen. It didn't track for a moment. How could anybody be so—so—*insane*? To kill that many people, to destroy that much valuable property, just to make a point? Insanity was too gentle a term. It was screaming madness, foaming and gibbering. It was hammering a tack with a piledriver. It was—was—fucking *crazy*!

From years past came the memory of Wall Eye, and the day the two of them had watched Confed security smash the face of a man whose only crime had been to be in the wrong place at the wrong time. And what Wall Eye had said to the boy who called himself Ferret: *The lesson's there, boy. Don't fuck with the Confed. . . .*

Pen shook his head. That hadn't changed. Maybe it wouldn't ever change. Something was wrong about that.

On an entire planet whose reputation had come to be intertwined with the supernatural—and one could argue about the natural or magical etiology of various gods until the local sun burned out—the highest concentration of seekers and believers was in Shtotsanto, the Holy City. The place sat inside a ring of mountains, a protected valley accessible primarily by air. For those who didn't mind a two-week hike followed by a climb and descent of a moderately tall mountain, there were foot caravans leaving the port daily. The terrain was mostly high desert along the Shtotsanto Road, the better part of the climb was through year-round snow, and the reward was a greened plateau with mild temperatures and several large freshwater lakes. The town ran to single- or double-story buildings, mostly, and the reason given was that no one wanted to block the sun from his or her neighbor. According to the information Pen had read, the population generally numbered about half a million in the Holy City, but that figure was largely transient.

Many people took the walk, it being considered a good way to calm one's spirit before achieving the Holy City.

Pen took the airbus.

Two weeks of eating dust did not particularly appeal to him, and he doubted that such a hike would do much other than strengthen his legs and give him a few blisters. He was in a hurry. Something was missing in his life—what he wasn't sure of—and he wanted to find it as quickly as possible. He had fair physical control, and a hard-earned humanistic outlook, but he needed more.

It would be his ticket back to Moon, he knew that much.

While he wasn't sure, he felt that what he lacked was the holy fire, the Finger of God, that sense of purpose some of the siblings seemed to have. People in the godlike state always seemed to know precisely what to do, there never seemed to be any doubt for them. And kicking up sand seemed unlikely to be a part of it. Better he should get straight to the city and start studying. Getting to God was a big project.

If a place might be said to feel holy, Shtotsanto did. The local season was either later summer or early fall, and the air was crisp with impending winter and expectation. People smiled at him on the sidewalks, waved and nodded, and seemed to take no notice of his garb. No, that wasn't the problem. The problem was in finding a proper instructor.

The city was an interesting mix of old and new, and laid out, it seemed, for pedestrians. There was no lack of wheeled or air-cushioned vehicle traffic, but a lot more people walked.

It was not as though there was any lack of teachers. Pen found that out when he stopped at a public compucom booth and tapped in a request for information on religious instruction. The holoproj lit and began scrolling names at fastscan speed. He watched for a minute, fascinated, before he stopped the scan and requested a total of the names.

Twelve thousand eight hundred and sixty-nine, the holoproj informed him.

Twelve *thousand*? Damn! How was he going to come up with the right choice out of that number? There were supposed to be many paths up the mountain, but this was absurd. He might spend years moving from teacher to teacher before he found one who had what he wanted.

He was staring stupidly at the pulsing holoproj when a voice behind him said, "Lost, pilgrim?"

Pen turned. The speaker was a tall black-haired man, gone

gray at the temples, who wore crinkly smile lines and a matching grin. He was maybe forty T.S., dressed in loose-weave pale blue orthoskins and dotic boots, and from his carriage, looked to be in good shape.

Pen returned the smile, then realized the other probably could not know he did so under the shroud. "I guess I am," he said. "I'm looking for a teacher and it seems there are more than a few around."

The man laughed. He held his right hand palm forward in greeting. "To be sure," he said. "I've been here awhile. Perhaps I can help. I'm Armahno Vaughn."

Pen regarded the man. There was something familiar about him, but Pen knew he had never seen that face before, he'd remember it. What did he want? Pen felt no fear, not with the Ninety-seven Steps at his call, but this character might be trying to set him up for some kind of con.

After a beat, Pen decided that wasn't likely. His street-senses were rusty, but Vaughn tripped no alarms. No sense of menace or malice came from the man. This was the Holy City, after all, and people here were more apt to be helpful, weren't they?

"I'm looking for God," Pen said.

Vaughn did not laugh at this. He said, "Yes." He paused for a few seconds, then added, "You're one of the Siblings of the Shroud." It wasn't a question.

"I am."

"A priest."

Pen nodded. "A title. Our order concerns itself more with the redemption of man than the seeking of his Creator. Assuming there is such a thing."

"Doubts are good," Vaughn said. "If a belief can't stand questioning, it isn't apt to be much."

"You know something of these matters?"

Vaughn smiled again, and the smile lines showed that it was something he must have done a great deal of over the years. "Something. I am a teacher, of sorts."

"Would I find your name listed here?" Pen waved at the holoproj.

"Near the end. The listings are alphabetical."

Pen looked at the three-dimensional image floating before him. Well. He had come to learn, and here was a teacher. Coincidence, likely, but he had to start somewhere. And a man

who smiled that much either found a lot of humor in life or
was spacing with a damped drive. He didn't seem crazy. What
the hell.

"Will you teach me?" Pen asked.

"Of course."

As easy as that? Well. Maybe not. But it was a place to
begin, wasn't it? It was time something came easy to him, Pen
thought. It seemed like everything he had ever learned had
been with sweat and blood and emotional pain. Maybe he
should search for another teacher, but, to hell with it. He could
always do that if this guy didn't work out. And who knew?
Maybe this character had some answers.

Pen certainly had enough questions.

THIRTY

PEN SAT *seiza*, his eyes closed, meditating.

The word "easy" might as well be stricken from his vocabulary, Pen thought. And that thought was a mistake—he wasn't supposed to *be* thinking, he was supposed to be following his breath in meditation—

Vaughn brought the bamboo cane down to lightly touch Pen's shoulder. Ah, shit. Pen leaned forward in a bow, then resumed *seiza*. It seemed like hours before the strike came. Whack! The sound and force of it jolted Pen. Damn. How does he *know* when I lose my concentration? He never seems to miss it!

Even with his eyes closed, Pen was aware of Vaughn moving away. The man walked like a ghost, and it was not Pen's ears that gave him Vaughn's location, only that slippery sixth sense he'd developed over the years of training on Earth. Were it not for feeling Vaughn's *ki*, Pen would never know where the man was. Higher sensory perception, indeed. It seldom worked as it had when Moon was—no, don't think about that.

Zen meditation, the sitting practice of which was sometimes called *zazen*, was but one more method Vaughn used in his teaching. The system was called Zendu, and it was, as nearly as Pen could tell, a kind of mish-mash of Buddhism and Hinduism, with assorted odds and ends thrown in. Eclectic was the term Vaughn used to describe it, and it was certainly that. Some of it he had heard and dealt with in his training on Earth.

Sure, Pen had studied religions, but that had been academic, had been intellectual. Reading about that goddamned bamboo stick was altogether different than feeling it sting your trapezius when your monkey brain wandered off through the trees, chittering stupidly. It was not the pain, it was the embarrassment of being found wanting.

The stick touched his other shoulder this time. Pen bowed, and the *thwack*! came again. Hell of a time concentrating today.

Maybe it was because there was trouble in paradise.

In the months since he'd been studying with Vaughn, the Holy City and Koji in general had been peaceful. There was a kind of quiet, but intense atmosphere that permeated the air here, an attitude of learning that seeped into everything, filling virtually every act with a kind of optimism and good cheer. It was everywhere—walk into a restaurant, and that man working behind the counter might well hold multiple doctorates in assorted philosophies; the woman sweeping the floor might be wiser than a college full of scholars; the mue repairing the room heater could be a potential saint. People in the Holy City were seldom what they seemed at first glance. But lately, there had been unrest amongst the teachers and learners. Confed spies lurked about, so the rumors went, and while nothing overt seemed to be happening, the stories had it that the Confederation was up to something on Koji. And if the Confed was up to anything, it certainly meant no good would come of it. The status quo that was the Confed had altered somewhat over the years. There were always the small repressions, of course, the swaggering petty officials everywhere one looked. The military boot did not stomp down all that often, but when it did, it came down hard. Pen could not forget the splash of laser-glass on Wu.

Meanwhile, here on Koji, Babaji Ananda, one of the shining lights of the local Zendu contingent, a human spiritual lamp who lit the darkness for more than a few followers, had disappeared. True, Babaji sometimes wandered off if not watched, he was less than adept on the physical plane, what with the Light of Truth shining through him the way it did, but he was not a man who could be misplaced for long. According to those who knew such things, Babaji would be harder to hide than a thunderstorm in the desert. And according to those who claimed the ability to sense psychic power, Babaji was not in the Holy City. Not alive, anyway.

Based on his own mental ability to locate Moon when she

was within his range, Pen believed that others could do the same. It would be foolish to deny something that worked simply because one did not know *how* it worked. One did not need an advanced degree in physics to push a button.

Then again, a holy man was missing—so? It might be unusual, but even here there was some crime. Maybe the man had been waylaid and stretched out by some hardstick thug for his credit cube, or that expensive pulsestone timepiece his followers had given him as a sign of their devotion. Babaji had a drawer full of expensive trinkets, so Pen had heard. People were sometimes robbed of such items—stranger things had happened. But while one part of Pen was willing to accept that, another part of him believed the stories. The Confed had some nefarious plan working on Koji, and woe to those who dared get in the way. Not that anybody could figure out how Babaji Ananda could get in anybody's way. It was said the man could call birds from the trees to perch upon his fingers, so innocent of threat was he.

Thwack!

Come on, Pen, he told himself. Concentrate!

No use. He wasn't going to achieve satori today.

Life was certainly more complex than Pen had once thought. Veils within veils, onionlike layers. Pierce through one layer, and another waited beneath. If one bought into the concept of *Maya*, then all the levels were merely illusory, nothing existed save the God-mind, and the manifestations of matter and energy were so much cosmic smoke, cleverly designed to fool the unwary. Pen knew the theory, and after his months with Vaughn, he was coming to know some of the practices. Meditation, breathing, chanting, lessons. Vaughn was not, thank all the gods, big on koans, but Pen had been given a few to chew on: the stone woman's dance, the sound of the single hand clap, the glass spaceship. The theory he knew—intellectual stall-out, allowing for the intuitive breakthrough—but theory and practice were once again two different things. In his experience, it had always seemed to be so. The theoretical celestial mathematician and the synlube-stained Bender mechanic were opposite poles of the workings of a stellar drive, and who was to say which, if either, was more necessary to the process? Thought and action were equally balanced, according to some. But thought was more than the monkey brain, playing with its logic, smug in its certainty that it knew all there was to know. There were other senses, other ways of "thinking," and those who refused to consider that it might be so merely crippled themselves. The hard-headed rationalists who sneered at the gods cut themselves off from large parts of themselves. So Vaughn said—as did at least twelve thousand others in the Holy City, with variations, Pen was sure. He was willing to be agnostic enough to listen, at least, although a tangible sign on the physical plane wouldn't hurt, either. So far, nothing along that line had happened. Nor had he come up with satisfactory answers to the koans—

Thwack.

Good and evil, here was another concept Vaughn had draped over Pen like a lead quilt. In *Maya*, the concept of good and evil were also illusions. At least in that the inability to see the illusion for what it was was the evil, and good lay simply in getting the point. Now, the yin and yang of the *illusion* was something else. For instance, even though all might be nothing more than a delusion, within the game of the delusion, certain rules applied.

Vaughn told the story of the teacher, his disciple and the elephant:

"The teacher and his student were walking in a rural area of old Earth, during a time when animals were still used as work beasts. Suddenly, an injured elephant burst forth from the nearby wood, trumpeting in anger and rage, and charged for the two men.

" 'Look out!' the teacher yelled, and leaped aside.

"The student on the other hand, smiled at the charging beast and stood his ground. The elephant snatched up the student with his trunk and hurled him aside, doing no small damage in the process.

"After the elephant had stalked off, looking for other targets upon which to vent his rage, the teacher hurried to the student, who was badly shaken and nursing a broken arm.

" 'Why didn't you run?' the teacher asked.

" 'Because the elephant is nothing but an illusion,' the student said. 'I was trying to pierce the veil of *Maya*, as you taught me!'

" 'Did not you hear me yell at you to flee?'

" 'Yes, but—'

" 'My son, the elephant is *Maya*, but so are we. The flesh we wear conforms to the rules of the illusion. Until you learn to manipulate matter through mind, you must recognize this fact: the elephant is not real, but we are also not real, and our unreality is of the same quality as the elephant's on this plane. Even a ghost can be touched by another ghost.' ''

Nothing was simple, Pen thought. All he wanted was to return to Manus Island, to Moon, but to do that, he had to be able to convince her he had become more than he was. He did not think he could fool her, so he actually had to do it. And it seemed more than obvious that one simply did not pick up a comset and give God—or whatever passed for that entity—a direct call. Hi, God. How's it going? Listen, can you alter my consciousness so I'm clear and centered? There's this woman, see, a priestess, one of the Siblings of the Shroud, and she and I, we, that is—

Sure.

Thwack.

Pen opened his eyes to see the impassive face of Vaughn looking at him. "I think I'm wasting our time here today, Vaughn."

"Never that," the other man said. "You may not be able to maintain your concentration properly, but it is no waste of time. You are learning."

What? Pen wondered. But he did not say it aloud. Instead, he glanced at the old-style flat picture Vaughn had mounted on the wall across from the mats. It was an odd thing, the picture. The tones of it were sepia, ranging from a near-white to dark brown, lifeless when compared to the living color of a holoproj or hologram. And yet, despite its flat and monochromatic scheme, the picture was dynamic. The scene was some mountainous region, on Earth, Vaughn had told Pen. A tall spire of rock stood against the sky, with a tablelike boulder balanced upon it like a hand calculator on the tip of a light pen. A wonder that it could do so.

Perhaps five meters away from the edge of the balanced boulder was a sharp precipice, a cliff slightly higher in elevation. The ground under these rocky abutments was not within the frame, but it was at least twenty or thirty meters below, judging from the height of the leaping man.

And here was the crux of the picture. In midair, halfway between the cliff and table rock, flew a man. He wore clothing from a period several hundred years in the past—a wide-brimmed hat, billowy shirt and dark trousers and heavy boots with thick heels. It was apparent from his posture that the man had jumped from the cliff toward the table rock. The camera, while ancient, had been of sufficient quality to stop the man's motion, so that he hung in the sky, slightly blurred, frozen forever in midleap.

The first time Pen had seen the picture, he had stared at it, struck by half a dozen questions: who was the man? Why had he dared the deadly jump? Had he made it? If so, how would he get down? There was no room to build up speed on the rock for a return jump, which was upward, in any event, and he could not do it standing. Through the Ninety-seven Steps, Pen had learned a lot about human motion, and there was no way the man could jump back. Would the rock be unbalanced by the man's landing, toppling from the spire? Who had operated the camera?

That such a simple flatgraph could call up such curiosity was, to Pen, as interesting as the picture itself. Here was a dynamic event, provoking questions about someone who had died before his great-grandfather had been born, performing an act for which Pen could think of no good rationale.

He had asked Vaughn, who had shrugged. He knew none of the answers. The picture had been a gift from someone close; it had been given without a history. Yes, he had wondered about it. No doubt that had been the reason it had been tendered, to provoke such thoughts. But there were no answers to be had. Maybe that was the point. To have questions that could not be answered was a lesson sometimes needed.

Intellectually, Pen could understand the reasoning. Emotionally, it frustrated him. He sometimes felt a kinship to the leaping man. He, too, was in midjump, unsure of his trajectory or landing, knowing he could not turn back. And if he survived the leap, what then? Where would he be? Where would he go from there?

He focused on the picture almost like a mandala, drawn into it. If he knew why that man had taken it upon himself to jump from one rock to another, he was sure he could learn something of great importance. He was sure of it.

Vaughn had moved off, was gone from the room. After a time, Pen arose stiffly from his heel-sitting pose. He needed to move. He would go outside into the crisp fall air and practice sumito. There was a security in the motions of his art, something he could do well. His meditations had always been best when he moved, and he was certain there was some deep lesson to be learned from that, too. But he would think on that another time.

With a final glance at the leaping man, Pen left the zendo.

THIRTY-ONE _____

DURING THE NIGHT, winter layered the city with powdery snow, now swept by chill winds into drifts a meter high in places. Pen looked out at it through the warmth of a heat exchanger window. The white blanket had turned the houses and streets into a pristine wonder, achingly clean and reflective under the now clear and icy blue skies. Although Pen seldom was cold within the folds of his shroud, he was not a winter person. The temperature outside was well below water's freezing point, and it bit the lungs to breathe air that cold. He tended to sleep late when it was like this, burrowing under the covers like some animal intent on hibernating until spring. A holdover from his days on the farm, when morning's first light meant trudging out into the cold fields to work the crops.

"There'll be snow on the ground for a couple of months," came Vaughn's voice from behind him. "Mild, compared to the outlying mountains, but it's all relative."

Pen turned away from the window. Vaughn was dressed in heavy orthoskins; he also held gloves and a multifab thermal hat.

"You going out?"

Vaughn smiled. "And I thought you were a slow student. Yes. Actually, I'll be gone for a few days."

Pen nodded, but did not ask where. His teacher sometimes did that, took off for a couple of days, a week once. He never offered an explanation, and Pen had not asked before. He had his shroud and his past, let Vaughn have his secrets if he so desired.

"Anything in particular you'd like me to work on while you're gone?"

"Yes. Spend some time on the Good and Evil Paradox. There's a moral dilemma there I'd like you to address."

Pen nodded. "All right. Have a good trip."

"Thank you."

Two days after Vaughn left, Pen sat in front of his holoproj, again reading the lesson Vaughn had left in the computer's memory for him. He'd been working steadily on it. The question was, as usual, simply expressed:

"If all is illusion, then what is the point of striving either to do good or evil? Why bother to live at all?"

Simply written, yes, but here was a question better philosophers than he had failed to resolved satisfactorily. There was a zen answer, of course, and it and its many variants had been duly recorded: Why bother to live at all? "Well, why not?" Or, "Because." Or "The Buddha is a toad." That, of course, was the problem with zen. Mountains were mountains, streams were streams, and forests were forests, except when they were not. And then were again. To someone who *knew* zen, on the proper intuitive level, it all made perfect sense. To someone who did not know zen, it made no sense at all.

So, here was Vaughn's question: If evil is an illusion, then why bother to resist it?

Pen knew he could try and fake a zen answer, but he had tried before and failed. "Because the post was tired" sounded properly esoteric to someone uninitiated in the ways of the slippery philosophy; to a Master, it was gibberish, though Pen was damned if he could figure out how anybody could tell.

There were other ways. As Zendu had many branches, so did the mind, and while reasoning logically was not always the proper solution for all questions—when the only tool you have is a hammer, then every problem looks like a nail—there were times when the monkey brain could be made to serve. Maybe this was one of them.

The story of the elephant and the student figured into it. About all being part of the same illusion. Until one could rise above it—as certain masters in a number of religions were reputed to have done by learning control of *Maya*—then one had to deal with the other ghosts as being like one's self. Pen was sure of that point.

Now, given that the stuff of *Maya* was consistent within a plane, as with the elephant and student, then the *illusion* of evil could be dealt with on that basis. Ghosts versus ghosts, as it were. And, since one had to play by the rules of a particular plane, then using smoke to fight smoke was certainly valid as a technique. As to whether one should or not, it all depended upon what one was trying to accomplish.

Working off karma certainly was justification. Trying to serve others as a path would do it. Or just for the pure hell of it. The zen answer was there: Why? Well, why not? Sure, one got to it in a rather circuitous manner, but if the idea was to reach the mountain's top, then a flitter was as good as a pack beast, was it not? He could justify to himself, and that ought to be enough—

A cold wind ruffled Pen's shroud, and the sound of someone entering the next room reached him. Vaughn? Yes, but there was something more than his instructor's *ki*—somebody was with Vaughn. Somebody with power. With a sense he could not precisely define, Pen felt the other person's energy, and it burned brightly, brighter than did Vaughn's. Who—?

Pen stood and walked toward the doorway. Yes, there was another man—

He only had a second to notice the second figure before he saw the blood on Vaughn's clothing. A large spot of it glistened on the man's right side, and Vaughn was hunched that way protectively.

Pen moved fast. He reached his teacher just as Vaughn started to collapse. From his utility belt, Pen pulled his pocket knife. He flicked the short curved blade out and quickly cut away Vaughn's shirt to reveal the wound. He wiped blood away and found the injury—a fingertip-sized hole, clean, angling in about ten centimeters above the hip, and emerging from the man's back a couple of centimeters short of the spine.

Pen was no doctor, but he had been instructed in fairly intensive first aid by the Siblings—not to mention having seen a fair collection of gunshot wounds in his days as a thief. The pellet had missed the spine, and it looked high enough to have missed the kidney. Even so, it needed a competent medic to make certain. He could stop the bleeding, bandage it, and go from there. He stood and went to the fresher, returning in a moment with the aid kit. He pumped lympocytic iodofoam into the wound, slapped stikseals over the holes, and sponged away the rest of the blood.

"Do you want a medic?"

Vaughn shook his head. "No medics. It's not bad, I think it cleared the kidney."

"He will be well," came a soft voice from behind Pen.

Pen turned. "If you're a medic, why weren't you here doing this?"

"I am no medic, my son. But I know."

It took a second for Pen to recognize the man. Babaji Ananda! He must have spoken it aloud, for the man said, "Yes." Then Babaji looked at the injured Vaughn. "You will recover. Even now, you improve." He waved one hand at Vaughn, as if blessing him.

"Thank you, Babaji."

Pen looked at the two men. Something passed between them, he could feel it, but he could not have said what it was. "Somebody want to tell me what's going on?"

"I must go and meditate," Babaji said, smiling. He turned and walked away.

Vaughn managed to prop himself into a sitting position. "I owe you an explanation. But first—did you work on the problem I left you?"

Pen stared at Vaughn as if the man had suddenly grown horns and a tail. "Vaughn—!"

"Indulge me, please."

"Yes, I worked on the problem."

"And your conclusions?"

"Christo, Vaughn—!"

"Pen . . ."

"All right. It is morally justified to oppose evil. Satisfied?"

"Why?"

"Because I *say* so!"

Vaughn smiled. "Most satisfactory. We always knew you had the potential."

We? Since when did Vaughn begin using the royal "we"? "Come on, Vaughn. That's a through-and-through gunshot wound in your side. You want to tell me about it? And how you came by Babaji Ananda, who has wandered into the bedroom and back off into lotus land?"

"One more question. What would you consider the major evil in our galaxy today?"

"I should have let you bleed to death." Pen paused, took a deep breath, and said, "Ignorance. Or the Confed, I suppose. Both together."

"Good."

"Dammit, Vaughn—!"

"The Confed kidnapped Babaji. I went to fetch him. They were not happy with my actions, and sought to stop me. Hence, this." He pointed at the bandage on his side.

Pen knew an incomplete explanation when he heard one. And he wasn't about to let it pass. "Why did you go after Babaji? And how did you know where he was? And how did you manage to get him away from what I suspect were heavily armed guards?"

"Always questions."

"But never enough answers. Come on, Vaughn."

So Vaughn explained. "There is a faction of Confederation Intelligence that would like very much to establish itself on Koji. You may not know that a fair number of criminals find their way here, looking for sanctuary. Since the Confed must be careful nosing around after such people on the Holy World, many of these criminals remain free. Some repent, change their ways, and follow one Way or another. Some merely wait until they think it safe to flee back into the galaxy at large."

"All right, the Confed wants to catch crooks. So?"

"Many of these escapees have committed political crimes. Not moral wrongs, but actions deemed treasonable by the state. Some of these men and women have champions on Koji. That makes it difficult for them to be captured."

"You aren't trying to tell me that sweet-faced saint in the other room harbors political criminals?"

"Babaji? Hardly. He sees good in everyone, regardless, but he doesn't have the guile to hide anything. No, not Babaji, but some of his more militant followers dabble in politics. The Confed thought to slay several birds with a single stone by taking Babaji. A trade, for certain badly wanted fugitives, and a free hand to plant several sub rosa agents within the Zendu community, for the little father's safe return."

"Not the most legal of maneuvers, was it?"

"The Confed seldom worries itself over niceties such as law

when it wants something, Pen. You should have learned that by now.''

''Maybe so. I expect I've learned something else from this conversation, too. I take it that you are one of Babaji's more militant followers?''

Vaughn smiled. ''I confess that I am.''

''Great. I go looking for a holy teacher and wind up with a revolutionary. I don't much like it, Vaughn.''

''You are not required to like it. Merely understand it.''

''Yeah, well, I appreciate your position, but I have better things to do than fight the Confed.''

''I doubt it. I don't think there is anything more important for men of conscience to be doing these days.''

''The morality of opposing evil?''

''Just so.''

''It won't buy me a ticket back to Moon.'' He had told Vaughn all about Moon, of course.

''It might. It might take you to a place where you can find out what you need to know.''

Pen shook his head. ''You don't understand, about Moon, about me and the Siblings. You couldn't.''

Vaughn smiled, and stood.

''You okay? You ought not to be moving around.''

Vaughn's smile faded slightly, then held. ''I am sore, stiff and more than a little tired, but these will all pass. I'm going to my room, to change clothes. When I come back, I think I can convince you I know what I'm talking about.''

''Good luck,'' Pen said, his voice sarcastic.

Vaughn left him alone in the central room, and Pen fought the urge to pace as he waited. Another twist in his convoluted life—Jesu, couldn't things stay simple, just for a little while? For just a little fucking while, couldn't it all slow down? He couldn't think of anything more surprising than to find out his teacher, supposedly a holy man, was some kind of insurgent. Nothing could have rocked him any harder, he thought.

He was wrong. He found that out when he looked and saw Vaughn standing in the doorway. He knew it was Vaughn, from the eyes and hands, all that he could see of his teacher. The reason he couldn't see any more was simple:

Vaughn stood wrapped in the full costume of the Siblings of the Shroud.

THIRTY-TWO

PEN STARED, UNABLE to speak. At first, he thought it might be some kind of joke, but even from here, he could see that the cloth of the shroud was the unique shimmery-gray found only in true *kawa*. The only way to get that material was from the Siblings. It was sent to members of the order on request, but to no one else. Even if a clever thief could steal a shroud, unlikely he would be able to wear it with the sense of rightness that Vaughn had. One had to grow into the costume over time. On the man Pen faced, the drape of the cloak was perfect.

Finally, Pen found his voice. "Vaughn . . . ?"

"Close," the man said.

That was the final clue. The rest of it came to Pen, all in a rush. The use of "we" when talking about his potential. That early sense of having seen or known Vaughn before. And the name—of course—how could he have missed it? Armahno Vaughn. Armahno—hermano—brother.

Brother Vaughn.

No, not quite.

Brother *Von*.

Oh, shit!

"It is you, isn't it? Von?"

"Yes. I hope you will pardon the masquerade. I'll explain as best I can."

240

Pen shook his head. He had the feeling this was going to be one hell of an explanation.

It was.

Von said, "Sometimes the best disguise is no disguise at all. I have been a sibling for nearly twenty years. The shroud is almost like a second skin to me. Siblings do not remove their garb in public, the Confed knows that."

Pen said, "So the best way to hide a sibling is to shed the identifiable clothing."

"Just so. Early on, Diamond's decision to enshroud the order was debated rather hotly. Someone wearing full sibling costume is altogether too obvious, and there are some drawbacks to being so ostentatious. Sometimes, it is easier to hide a thing in plain view. Sometimes the best disguise is an obvious disguise."

"All right. I can see that."

"You have been taught much about the Confed and our general attitude of passive opposition to its policies."

"Yes. I used to wonder about that. What happened to those who washed out—about how they'd be dangerous to the order. A word in the right ear and all."

"But you don't wonder anymore?"

"In the four years I was there, nobody ever washed out."

"That's because we choose our trainees carefully. It has happened, no system is perfect, but when it has, certain memories of their experiences have been . . . deleted."

Pen thought about that. Brain scrambling. That was bad enough, to have some simadam rummaging around in your mind, erasing chunks of it. But he also remembered the Confed rep and his quad, who had smashed into the ocean like a big rock. Moon had caused that—

Moon. God, Von and Moon had been lovers before he had arrived. Even afterward. And here he had been for the last few months filling Von's ears with stories of Moon, how much he loved her, and how he would do anything to get back to her. Jesu damn! How must that have made Von feel? He might still have longings for Moon himself. Knowing Moon, how could he not?

"But we are not passive," Von continued. "When a brother or sister is at a stage where we feel they can know the truth, they are told. We actively oppose the Confed. We know it

cannot endure, and by opposing it, we seek to hasten its down-
fall. Our integratic projections are less than perfect at this point,
but we know it will happen relatively soon. Within the next
fifty to seventy-five years.''

"Pinpoint accuracy isn't one of our strong points, is it?''
Pen said.

Von grinned under the shroud. Easy enough to see.

"We'll get better.''

There was a short pause, and the question welling inside Pen
since he had first seen Vaughn-as-Von finally surfaced.

"My being here is no accident, is it? Not coincidence.''

Von moved to the window, and looked out at the snow.
"Perhaps we should go for a walk,'' he said.

"All right.''

Outside, the cold tried and failed to chill Pen under his
shroud. He and Von walked; their boots made squeaky sounds
on the dry snow, and their breaths fogged the crisp air.

They moved along mostly empty streets, occasionally passed
by a fan car that blew white powder up in frozen clouds.

"Moon loves you, you know,'' Von said.

"How does that make *you* feel?'' Pen asked.

"Privileged. She loves me, too. How can I begrudge her
another, or a dozen others? Love isn't finite, you must understand. You don't run out of it. The more you give, the more
you have.''

"That's very idealistic.''

"And you don't believe it. Well, you'll learn. True, one only
has so much time, and that has to be apportioned, sometimes
a difficult task. But I left and Moon stayed. What could it
matter to me whether she slept with you or alone? It was all
the same to me—I couldn't enjoy her favors.''

"I still have trouble with that, Von.''

Von shrugged.

"And what's Moon loving me got to do with being here with
you?''

"We—she—knew you were coming to Koji.''

"Don't try to tell me integratics gave her that.''

"Not at all. Psychology. You were her student as well as
lover, Pen. She knew. And she knew I was here.''

"And the two of you set me up for all this.''

"In a manner of speaking.''

Another car slowly fanned past. Tiny crystals blew into his eyes. Pen blinked them away. "Why?"

"You needed more training, but not on Earth. Sort of post-graduate work."

"Why the disguise? I can't see any reason at all for that."

They reached a corner, and Von turned to the left. At the end of the narrow street was the Confed garrison. It contained only a token number of troops, but even on Koji the Confed had to be contended with, in essence if not physical presence.

"Because," Von said, "she didn't want your brain scrambled."

"What!?"

"If my teaching as Vaughn didn't take, there would be no problem. I could be a revolutionary and if I failed to sway you, the Siblings lost nothing. As Von, it would be a different story."

"You would have had me mindwiped?"

"Certainly."

Pen walked silently, save for snow squeaks. Then, "How do you know you can trust me? I don't come from the most reliable of stock!" He was angry, at being fooled, at being so blind, for still not understanding.

"I know," Von said. "I can trust you with my life, and the lives of our entire order."

"How? How can you know?"

"Babaji told me."

"Babaji?" Pen stopped. They were only a few hundred meters from the garrison's entrance, staffed by a pair of cold-looking guards in overcoats and hats. "Babaji is a sweet old man, a mystic!"

"That's how he knows. He's connected to the cosmic in a way you and I aren't. I couldn't tell about you, Pen. I had a feeling you were ready, but the lessons were going slowly. You weren't getting what *you* wanted, and that clouded my vision. But not Babaji's. He *knows*."

"Shit."

"You don't believe, that's your problem. You've never believed in anything, not really. Without faith, you can do a lot, but with it, you can do miracles. Babaji can see the soul of a person in a way I can't. He knows what we've always suspected about you, Pen. You have much more to give than you know."

Pen saw the pair of gate guards look at them. How odd we must look, two figures wrapped in grays, arguing in the cold.

"I don't see how being a revolutionary enters into anything."

"The opposition of evil, remember?" Von said. "Spiritually, the Siblings make few claims. Pragmatics is another topic. What do you think all of your training has been for, save to put it to use? We concern ourselves with the evolution of man. Through our work, some of the brothers and sisters achieve a cosmic connection, but that is not our main intent. That kind of thing is up to the individual. Your path up the mountain personally is your problem. As a group, we must think of every human and mue's path. On the most basic of levels, we must first try to give everyone the chance to grow. Under the lash of the Confed, too many people never get that chance."

"And that's our job? Bootstrapping humanity?"

"Just so."

"We're supposed to wipe out the Confed." It was not a question.

"In a manner of speaking, yes. It might be by education and evolution, it might be by revolution. We aren't sure. What we are certain of is when there's a sword hanging low over your head, it is impossible to stand up and look around."

Pen thought about it. Certainly he had learned about the evil that the Confed did, directly and otherwise. No argument that the Confederation as it stood was a bad thing. But it was huge! How did an order the size of the Siblings expect to *do* anything about it? A gnat against a dinosaur?

His anger, meanwhile, was unabated.

"You manipulated me. You, and ¯ . . Moon."

"Indeed. When there is a job to be done, the proper tool must be utilized to do it correctly."

"So that's what I am. A tool."

"There is no need to be bitter, Pen. We are all tools. Each of us has a purpose. You did not know yours. We strived to offer you one."

"So you twisted me, warped me, tricked me!"

"You tricked yourself, Pen. We only gave you the opportunity to learn how to be a part of something larger than yourself.

You have wanted that since you left home. You have said as much."

"To Moon. Not to the Siblings, but to Moon! I loved her. I still love her."

"No. She loves you. That's why she has been helping you. You only *think* you love her."

Pen glared at Von, his anger riding high and hot in him. "What the fuck are you talking about? What do you know about it?!"

Von's answer was soft, almost too low to hear. "You can't love another unless you love yourself. And you can't love yourself until you know who you are. You haven't discovered that yet, Pen. Otherwise, why would you be here, with me? You are still looking for answers."

"Fuck the answers!" His voice must have carried to the sentries, for they both stared at him. With effort, Pen lowered his speaking volume. "How can you know that?"

"Your focus has always been elsewhere. You told Moon she was the most important thing in your life."

"She told *you* that?" Pen's anger was swallowed by a surge of weariness. His and Moon's intimate talk, words given while lying naked together, and Von knew them. He felt betrayed, felt suddenly as gray as his shroud. How could she?

"Before Moon, there was the dancer, and your partner in crime. You were happy when you were with them."

"Yes. I was."

"But Pen—*have you ever been happy when you were alone*?"

Pen stared at a snow drift, piled against a plastcrete wall. Sunlight sparkled from crystals, tiny bits of silver against the white. His anger steamed, but he listened.

"As a boy on Cibule?" Von continued, his voice still very quiet.

Pen's voice matched Von's. "No. Not then."

"As a lane runner?"

"Sometimes, when Gworn and I first got together—" He stopped, realizing what he was saying. With Gworn. Not alone.

"As a thief?"

He fought to remember. With Shar Li, with Shanti . . . Then, "Yes, I can recall a time when I was happy alone."

"Really?"

"I remember a moment on Vishnu, I was on the walkway,

by myself. I had just left Shar Li, I was on my way to see
Stoll.''

''And what were you thinking about?''

''Paradise. I had a friend and a lover and such a beautiful
world as Vishnu. . . .'' He trailed off again, realizing what
Von meant. He had been alone, but his thoughts were of things
outside himself. Jesu be damned.

''And at the island on Earth, I had Moon, the others, the
ritual of work and learning,'' Pen said.

''You begin to understand.''

Yes. He did. Always, his happiness rode on another's shoulders. If Moon was pleased with him, he was happy. When he
did the Ninety-seven Steps, if she said his performance of the
Braided Laser had been correct, or the transition from Neon
Chain into Vacuum Cage had been smooth, he was secure—in
pleasing her. And when he was working, intent on accomplish-
ing a given task, he didn't think about it at all. Even the thrill
and rightness of handling a gun required that external focus.
He felt cold, suddenly, but not from the air around him. It
came from within. So simple. How could he have missed it all
this time?

''What difference would it make, opposing the Confed?'' he
asked. ''I would still be doing someone else's task. Doing what
I had been led to do.''

''No. This time, you have a choice. We sharpened you and
gave you a direction, but the choice must be yours, and it must
be conscious. You can take another path, live any way that you
choose. Your will is your own. While we hope you see the
rightness of it, what we want—both Moon and I want—is for
you to achieve your own goals, no matter what they turn out
to be.''

''Are you telling me Moon wouldn't be disappointed if I
turned away from this?''

''If Moon thought that joining the Confed and *opposing* us
was what you *truly* desired, she would be happy for you. You
see, most of the time, Moon knows who she is. She can love
another *because* she knows. She wants the best for you. Anyone who truly loves another wants the best for his or her be-
loved, even if it excludes the lover in the end.''

''You really believe that?''

Von nodded. ''I *know* that. That's why I could smile at the thought of Moon with another lover. It was making her happy, and that's what I want.''

"No shit?''

Von paused for a moment before answering. "There are times when it's harder to maintain that purity than other times. I'm not a saint, only a man. But I try.''

"It's still hard for me to believe.''

"You might not be able to control what you think or feel,'' Von said, "but you *can* control what you do. I'm not perfect, don't claim to be. When I'm centered, I'm fine. When I'm off, I'm off. That's the way the game is played. I keep trying, though, and that's the important part. Sometimes I win, sometimes I lose. That's the way of it.''

Pen nodded, but did not speak to that. There was a lot here to think about. Things he hadn't ever wondered about before. He had no long-term goals, save to get back to Moon. Listening to Von, he understood that goal to be out of his reach. Moon would not accept him as an extension of herself. Until he learned about his own center, she would not have him. And after he learned . . . ?

In a moment of clarity he knew. Were he centered, he would not *need* Moon. The choice to return would be no less important, but it would not be all-consuming.

What was it Von kept harping about in his teaching? To achieve a want, you had to give it up? Intellectually, he understood that; emotionally and, he guessed, spiritually, it still didn't make sense; still, he had a stronger feel for it in this moment than ever before, that idea of nonattachment. As though the clouds had parted for a moment and allowed a single ray of sunlight into the darkness. He could almost see it. Almost.

But—what was to be done? Should he join with Von in his quiet war against the Confed? Rescuing holy teachers and passing on bits of wisdom to fools such as himself?

No, that wasn't his path. He was a loner, had always been so, despite his attachments to others. Fighting the Confed might be worthwhile, he knew that, but not Von's way. He would have to find out how to do that on his own.

Pen glanced up at the two soldiers, who had turned away from the shrouded priests. No problem there, they must have figured.

Maybe they were wrong, he thought.

Maybe they had turned their backs on the very man who could topple the Confed like a laser cutter slices through the thickest tree. For an ambition, he could do worse. To be the man who brought down a corrupt and repressive governing system. Maybe not the worst rule men had ever lived under, but certainly one that deserved to be changed.

Now there was a goal.

It *felt* right. No matter that Moon and Von had manipulated him into it. Hadn't he been thinking the same thing earlier, about getting to the top of the mountain? Trek or flitter, what did it matter if the end *did* justify the means? It did that sometimes. Not always, perhaps, but in this case, maybe, just maybe, it did.

He looked at the representatives of the Confed, secure in their invulnerability, then back at Von, impassive behind his shroud. He could still search for that sense of inner peace, but he could also do other things along the way. After all, God was patient. God could wait.

Odd how such major changes in a man's life could come about so quickly, based on such flimsy things as feelings.

In the flick of an eye, he made his decision. A new direction, bam, just like that? Yes. Just like that.

Damn.

THIRTY-THREE

So Pen left, perhaps not certain that he finally knew his path, but convinced he at least had a valid reason for moving. The Confed was an evil thing, and illusion or not, according to the rules of the cosmic game, part of *his* reality. Therefore, he was justified in doing something about it. What? Why, he would bring it down, a simple enough goal. Not an easy task, but then few things worth doing were easy. A man's reach should exceed his grasp, after all, and one against billions was certainly a stretch, for any man. Despite that, he felt confident. He would do it. He had learned skills, he could learn others, he could find the way. For the first time in his memory, he had a real goal. That meant something.

What to replace it with? Well, that might be harder, but by the time he got to that point, he was sure he could figure something out.

He got a job tending bar on Hadiya. The Shin System was one of the majors, even if Hadiya was one of the less advanced of the six worlds in it. He built and served drinks in a spaceport pub called the Nocturnal Eye, and he spent his off-time fomenting revolution. His converts were mostly students, the young and idealistic, and they knew him only as Mwili. Once away from the pub, he had a formidable disguise: he wore a throat inducer that changed his voice, and a thin-layered skinmask. More important, he used Von's trick—he left his shroud at home. Anybody who knew anything about the Siblings knew they never went unshrouded in public. Pen still shook his head when he thought about Vaughn/Von. He had never suspected, and he had *known* the man under the layers of near-living *kawa*.

He studied the subject of revolution. He read political texts, ranging from Mao Zedong and Machiavelli on old Earth to Carlos Perito on Alpha Point, to Lord Shamba and his doomed army; he watched holoprojic program balls on revolution, dug from dusty library sockets; he began to learn the mechanics of guerrilla war. It was not so much shooting as ideological conversion. He had to convince people that the Confed was evil, which should be no problem; more, he had to convince them they should *do* something about it, and that might be a bit tougher. He was confident.

The pub he worked in was seldom without a contingent of troopers, either waiting to ship out or in a holding pattern on Hadiya itself. There were others who frequented the Nocturnal Eye, men and women who spent a lot of time looking over their shoulders. To all of them, Pen listened.

"—damn uplevels twat thinks she knows it all," said one soldier over his spiked wine. "Just because she's a fucking *officer*. Well, she wasn't so know-it-all when we were rolling around in bed together."

Pen nodded, pouring the man more wine. "On the house, trooper," he said. "Man like you deserves a free one."

And likely a man like you won't be around much longer, bragging about sleeping with a superior officer. Either she would take care of it or the Confed military would.

"Goddamn straight, pal. Thanks."

The man spilled half of the free drink, sloshing it all over his uniform as he tried to down it. Drunk. But that was okay with Pen. Drunks were a great source of information. The soldiers had a word-of-mouth comline that was faster than White Radio, and all kinds of classified scat got into it. And what drunk trooper couldn't trust a tender who gave him free drinks?

"—yeah, well, the fucking uplevel toad heads is doing it to us again," the soldier continued, "spacing us to squash some kinda student unrest on a dinky wheelworld in the Bibi Ah-whachamacallit System."

Pen nodded, and added more free liquor to the man's glass.

Propaganda, his for the taking. Good agitprop was better if it could be gotten before the public media started chewing it. It made a would-be revolutionary feel like he or she was one up on the enemy to know things in advance.

So far, his revolutionaries had only printed radical pamphlets and pulse-painted graffiti on a few Confed walls. A gnat flitting around a dinosaur, to be sure, but a start. A message to the dissident students on the wheelworld—he'd have to pry the name out of the drunken soldier carefully—from their brothers and sisters on Hadiya would create a sense of solidarity. He hoped. Whether it would help those about to be flattened by the Confed military machine was doubtful, but it would make his small group feel as if it had struck some kind of blow for freedom. Sometimes one had to nurse a tiny spark for a while before it burst into a major conflagration.

Pen also knew that inflammatory holograms and defaced walls were not going to be enough. In order to damage the beast, direct action had to be taken. Revolutionaries needed rallying points, events to which they could point and count as moral victories. Enough straws could break the back of the largest beast.

The three men and two women leaders used pseudonyms, at Pen's insistence. He had organized his radicals under the old cell concept, keeping each group to a maximum of five, using phony names, and never telling any one cell any more about the others than was necessary. In truth, he had only thirty-five people enlisted all total, but he allowed them to think the "Movement" was much larger. An old trick, but one these children did not know.

Children they were, too. Most of them were students, still young and idealistic, full of fire and rage against Confed oppression. There were a few older people, mostly with their own knives to sharpen over some wrong done them.

Talk was cheap, holograms denouncing Confed atrocities not much more expensive, and Pen had little trouble fanning his radicals into enough of a heat for a direct strike. The plan was simple: they would topple a power substation, the one that fed the local garrison. Put out the lights, and let the army know they weren't safe even at home. It was, Pen knew, no more than a psychological strike—the Confed had its own generators and they would be online within minutes of the power failure. Still, the point would be made, and it would be made cheaply and without much danger.

Every text he'd read on revolution made that very clear: don't stand facing a stronger opponent unless you need a martyr; better to sneak in and prick his unprotected ass and then run. Even a big man can bleed to death from pinpricks, if there are enough of them. Pinpricks and straws were what made a revolution. Those, and information.

The main problem with the plan lay in coming up with sufficient high-powered explosives to do the job properly. Sure, there were ways to use readily available chemicals, making one's own bombs, but Pen did not want to appear to be some half-baked radical group. That was true enough, but he wanted his troops to seem much more dangerous. What he wanted was state-of-the-art weaponry, something that would make the Confed worry. Sure, a couple of kilos of homemade dynamite or nitroflex would do the job, but anybody could come up with those. A few grams of L-40 MicroGel or a cable of slapfuse would make the military engineers studying the explosion sit up and take notice: nobody but the Confed was supposed to *have* shit like that! What are we dealing with here? Precisely the kind of question Pen wanted them asking.

Of course, that was a problem. One did not walk into the local chemstore and buy such items. They were available only on the black market, and the price was high.

Pen explained none of this to his five cell leaders. Instead, he said, "I will secure explosives from our supply depot offworld. You five have been chosen out of the hundreds of cells because of your abilities. You are the best."

Pen paused, to let that sink in, knowing it would give them a warm ego-glow.

"Return to your cells, but say nothing of this. I will contact you with further plans in a week."

The five filed out of the cheap room. Pen had rented the place under a pseudonym, wearing his skinmask. It would be used only this once. The owner had been led to believe it was for a sexual encounter.

After they had gone, Pen left, and took a public transport in the form of a wheeled bus. After ten minutes, he alighted, caught another bus going the opposite way, and rode for another fifteen minutes. Finally, certain he was not being watched, he switched to a port shuttle, got off at the port, and walked the klick back to the pub.

If his five cell leaders talked to their members, so much the better. He had given the impression they were part of a large organization. Such a feeling would help the troops. And, in the unlikely event one of them should be picked up for Confed questioning, any kind of electronic or chemical truthscan would reveal the same information. The Confed would be a lot more worried about some shadowy organization purported to be thousands strong, with easy access to military-only explosives, than it would about a local group of students.

Pen felt a small pang as he thought about one of his people being caught by the Confed, but he pushed it into a corner of his mind. There were risks in disobeying the law. He had known of them as a thief.

But not when you were young and running with Gworn, said the voice in his head. *The young cannot really believe anything bad will happen to them.*

He pushed that voice away, too. The path he'd chosen had its dangers. He was prepared to risk the consequences personally, but he did not know how ruthless he could be when using others, and that worried him. All the texts pointed out the obvious: one could not make an omelette without breaking eggs. In this case, however, the eggs would be starry-eyed young radicals. Could he send them out to be injured or killed? He didn't know. Did the end justify the means, as so many of the revolutionary heroes of the past had asserted? Sometimes it did, certainly. Sometimes, maybe not. Pen did not know if it was possible to be a humanist revolutionary. The term might be oxymoronic. But he was going to find out.

The man Pen was looking for sat in a corner of the pub, sipping ale. Pen didn't know his name, but he knew what the man was. You didn't spend years running the lanes and then as a full-time thief without learning to recognize one of your own. Without being obvious the man watched the inside of the pub, quickly shifting his gaze back and forth, looking for trouble. He was young, early twenties, Pen figured, but he had the look of somebody experienced in the biz. A couple of days had passed since Pen's meeting with the cell leaders, and he needed somebody. This might be the one.

The place was fairly crowded, and three servers worked the floor. Pen pulled one of them aside and asked him to watch the bar for a few minutes. Then he put a glass of icy ale on a tray and moved toward the young man in the corner.

The man looked up. "I didn't order this," he said.

"A man at the bar sent it to you," Pen said. "Along with a message."

The young man searched the stools at the bar, flicking his gaze back and forth. His body language was good; from a few meters away, you wouldn't be able to tell what he was doing.

"What man? Which one?"

Pen turned and pretended to look at the line of customers seated and standing by the bar. He turned back. "Funny, he's gone."

"What did he look like?"

Pen was glad his face was hidden behind the shroud. This one would be hard to lie to if he could see your face. "Medium height, about my size. Wore a cargo handler's coverall, maybe thirty-five T.S. Short hair, kind of gray."

"That's all?"

Pen shrugged. "I get a lot of customers. He gave me a five-stad coin to deliver the ale and the message."

"What's the message?"

" 'Maybe you and I can do some biz. Meet me at the port sleeper, stall #363, two hundred, if you're interested.' "

The man sipped at the fresh ale. "That's it?"

"What he said."

The young man's stare was direct. "You been a tender here long?"

"A few months."

"You some kinda priest, aren't you?"

"Priests have to eat."

"Yeah. You know the local cools?"

Pen glanced around, then back at the man. Here was where he made the sale. He rubbed his thumb over his fingertips, the ancient sign for money.

The young man smiled, a hard-edged expression. He produced a five-stad coin and flipped it at Pen. Pen caught the coin and shook his head. "Guy at the bar wasn't a cool."

"You sound sure. You ever done biz?"

"Some. It's been awhile."

"Thanks for the message."

"Thanks for the stads." The conversation finished, Pen turned and walked back to the bar.

The young man showed up at the sleeper stall fifteen minutes early. Pen, sans robe, now wearing a new skinmask and a hidden throat inducer, had arrived fifteen minutes before that. He opened the door. The sleeper had a chair next to a bed, and enough floor space to stand. Pen lay sprawled on the bed, hands in the open and away from his coverall.

The other man remained standing.

"I don't know you," the man said.

"Mwili Kalamu," Pen said, "from Cibule." True enough.

"I hear you are looking for something." He kept his hand near the pocket of his synlin jacket. Probably had a small gun there, Pen figured.

"You got a name?" Interesting how fast the flow of biz came back to him. It wouldn't do just to blurt out what he wanted. There was a kind of protocol, and a certain amount of tough that had to be put forth. Not fugue, exactly, but enough of an undercurrent to let someone know you weren't a cool or a Confed or if you were, you were a hell of a fake.

The young man thought about it. In biz, you trusted your gut more than your ears. Good instincts were worth more than brains. "Maro. Dain Maro."

Pen grinned. He'd passed the first test. "After the planet," Pen said.

"My parents liked it there."

"Hypothetically speaking, suppose I knew somebody who wanted something only the Confed military was likely to have on hand?"

Maro grinned. Biz-talk. It wouldn't keep somebody listening from being suspicious, but it might keep a conspiracy charge off your back. "Hypothetically speaking, I might know somebody who might be able to get ahold of something like that. Depending on what it was. But I probably wouldn't want to talk about it here."

Pen sat up straighter on the bed, and said, "In my right coverall pocket I've got a confounder. I'll take it out, real slow."

Maro nodded. His right hand slipped into his jacket pocket.

Pen came out with the electronic jammer. It was the size of

a deck of cards, with a pair of LEDs on the back, next to an off-on button. Green light pulsed from one of the LEDs. He put the device on the bed.

Maro moved his empty hand from his jacket pocket. He reached for the confounder, picked it up, and looked at it. "Nicholson Five," he said. "Nice machine."

"Hard to rascal," Pen said.

"What I understand. And I just happen to have a line scanner." From his left jacket pocket, he pulled a small, flat disc and pressed his thumb against the center. It beeped once, and flashed a thin line of LED red. "So, your confounder is running."

"I don't want anybody listening."

"I like a careful man."

"So do I."

The two men grinned at each other. They could do biz.

Maro was a smuggler, mostly, but he had connections. He never said, but Pen figured the young man was dancing with Black Sun as a sometimes partner. The crime syndicate did serious biz, and they could get anything they wanted. Three hundred grams of slapfuse? Sure, Maro had said, I can get that. No problem. He named a price. Pen halved it, and they bargained for a few minutes before settling. Maro didn't ask why Pen wanted the explosive, and Pen didn't say. In biz, you kept things as simple as possible.

It took three days for the delivery.

"Pleasure," Maro said, counting the hard curry Pen gave him. "You ever need anything else, leave a message with that tender, the one in the blankets."

"I will," Pen said.

He watched Maro leave, and smiled at the retreating figure. Maro reminded him of a time that seemed long past.

The run at the power substation was anticlimactic. It was a one-man job, but Pen included the five cell leaders. A moonless night under an overcast sky gave them a thick darkness in which to work. Rain began sprinkling down as they cut through the fence and made their way into the unmanned station. No guards, no security, save the tall mesh fence topped with razor wire, but Pen made his group think a Confed quad might arrive at any second, Parker carbines blasting. Adventure and risk would buy more troops, once the story got out. The story would get out—he'd make sure of that.

He laid the explosive cord against the main rebroadcast unit and triggered the timer.

When the station blew and shattered, Pen was tending bar. The rain damped the sound somewhat and swallowed the ensuing fire, but the effect was immediate. Some of the Confed troops had seen combat, they knew a cord explosion when they heard one. The soldiers streamed out of their barracks, armed ants, looking for an enemy. They didn't think for a moment that the cause was serving drinks in a port pub less than a klick away. In five minutes, the back-up generators had the garrison lit up again, but the damage had been done. Somewhere in the city, a handful of radicals must be grinning like fools.

The gnat had bitten the dinosaur.

The revolution had begun!

Pen knew he couldn't stay. One small group on one world could not begin to do the job needed. He brought the brightest of the cell leaders into a rented room and passed the mantle of command to her. He, he told her, was being called offplanet to another post. She knew the goals, and was being given command of seven cells, as a beginning. If she handled them well, and recruited others, she would be promoted. Somebody might check on them, from time to time, but she must consider that she would be on her own, maybe for a long period.

The young woman nodded. She understood. She would prove herself. The Movement could trust her.

Pen smiled through the tightness of his skinmask. Of course it could. Long live the revolution.

She echoed his words.

As he left, Pen reflected on his first year as a radical rouser. He had teachers spreading the radical word, trying to recruit others. He had a symbolic victory to which they could point: See? They aren't invulnerable. It was a start. A year was not so long. Many men working together could do much in a short time. One man working alone would have to take longer to do the same job. It was a start.

Long live the revolution.

THIRTY-FOUR

FIVE YEARS PASSED.

Pen moved across the faces of four worlds, in four different systems, working toward his goal.

From the bustling civilization of Mason, in Centauri, where another patch of laserglass helped his cause; to Rim, the Darkworld, in the Beta System; to the backrocket Fox, in Pigme; and Aqua, in Sto; four worlds, nine cities, twelve pubs.

On his workshift, he was Pen, Sibling of the Shroud, who mixed a fine Sinclo Suicide and was always sympathetic toward a man or woman with a problem; or he was the oddball character who danced in the park, practicing something called the Ninety-seven Steps, dances with names like Bamboo Pond, Arc of Air, and Cold Fire Burns Bright.

When he wasn't working, he was Mwili, or Ferret, or sometimes Stoll. The names didn't matter. Only the cause mattered.

He had given up looking very hard for God, but he found the disaffected; he grew polished at his presentations; he became very persuasive. His personal fire lit up others.

To a group of would-be radicals on Rim, he preached:

"There is no one man upon which we can focus," the skin-masked man known as Stoll told them. "The villain is the system. Ten million bureaucrats work at their jobs, unaware that they are evil. They must be shown! They must know that the will of the people is to be free! It is up to you to demonstrate it to the galaxy.''

The would-be radicals cheered.

On a moonless night at a wooded site on Fox, the man called Ferret spoke to a small gathering around a campfire:

''The Confed seems invulnerable only because it is so large. A group our size can do little more than sting it, but we can spread the word! United, we can stand and make the monster take notice of us! If each of you can convince five people of the rightness of our cause, and each of those can convince five more, we will ripple through the galaxy!''

The small gathering roared its approval. His words inflamed with the idea, but even as he spoke, Pen was less than certain of it himself. You bring in five, and they bring in five and so on and so on, he thought. At that rate, we'll be in a position to stand toe-to-toe with the Confed in about a thousand years.

There were times when he looked at his chosen task as not only impossible, but as downright funny. Still, he kept at it. One could not expect success on such an undertaking overnight. A year, five years—these were short times in the life of a galaxy, after all. Not even particularly long in the life of a single man.

The tropical heat of the bush around the group of tree cutters simmered even after the bright sun had set. Insects buzzed the gathering, as Pen said:

''Nothing worth so much can be achieved without hard work and danger! No one gives up any power willingly, and certainly no one gives up the complete power that the Confed has without a fierce struggle! The price of freedom is high, but the goal is worth it!''

The tree cutters buzzed, louder versions of the insects.

And while the cold winds of winter laid a white coat over the roof of the prefab shed, a dozen miners hunched together for warmth listened to the man called Mwili Dain as his voice seemed to thunder in the small space:

''United, you can stand! You have nothing to lose but your

shackles! Is a slow but certain death in the mines better than learning how to fight back?''

The miners rumbled their approval.

On it went. Pen learned to move into a territory, find the local troublemakers, get them organized, and leave. Never such a small town that he would stand out. Always taking care to screen each potential member. There were Confed agents, he had run into some of them, but he was lucky as well as careful. On the rare occasions that the Confed made a sweep to gather in treasoners, Pen was never among those collected. He moved, he ate, he slept, he sometimes found partners for sex, but he stayed a loner. He slept lightly, part of him always listening. He checked his clothing for electronic taps, and knew within a few seconds the position of everyone in any room he entered. It was not paranoia, it was caution.

Somewhere along the way, he realized that his undertaking was much vaster than he had thought at first. A simple goal, certainly, but never easy. Well. He had time.

Sometimes, though, he thought about Moon and the peaceful life he had enjoyed on Earth. Ah, if he could but see her again, even for an hour. . . .

No. He damped that thought when it came up. Moon was no longer his goal. He was not enough for her. When the Confed went to hell, sent there by him, then, *then* he would return to Earth in triumph. Then he would be enough. That kind of accomplishment would impress anybody.

Although he was not much of a writer, he sent Moon letters. He tried to keep them dispassionate, a generalized chronicle of his mundane life—how he'd collected a special curved knife from a miner on Rim, what kind of thing they liked to drink on Mason—and he never mentioned anything about his revolutionary activities. She knew, if she had spoken to Von, and Pen was certain that she had done that.

Now and again, when he was still long enough, a letter would arrive from Moon. Her words were much like his, superficial, filled with everyday happenings at the compound on Earth. Anyone who might chance to read their correspondence would see nothing seditious in it. Beneath the chatty tone, Pen could feel more depth, a between-the-lines thing, indicating that

Moon had not forgotten what they had shared. He felt from her what he felt for her. The light-years between them could not take that away.

So he continued his work. So it would take longer than he had thought. All right. Whatever it took, he was prepared. Whatever it took.

THIRTY-FIVE _____

FIFTEEN MORE YEARS passed.

Nine planets, six systems, thirteen cities, twenty pubs. He spoke millions of words, roused thousands to his cry for freedom from the Confed yoke, met dozens of would-be saviors like himself. He no longer worried about the end. Not after fifteen years. It was enough to survive each day, growing a little more tired of it all with each new cell of shiny faces looking at him for direction. He was like an actor who had exhausted his roles, to-the-bone weary of giving the same speech over and over again. True, he spoke to a passing parade, it was new to them. Of course it was new, most of his listeners were little more than children, some of them barely born when he had started his crusade.

What had he to show for it? He could mix drinks or dispense chem as well as anyone. He was fit for a man approaching his middle years. He had begun hundreds of small groups around the galaxy, but—

Nothing was happening. He had spent more than twenty years running around, beating a horse that, if not dead, certainly seemed immune to his whip. He was a good speaker, he knew that, but something was lacking. He could pump up a group and keep them inflated to near bursting, but when he left, they deflated. He did not seem to have the power to keep them volatile once he departed. He was not charismatic enough to be a symbol, once he was out of sight. Oh, they meant well, but something seemed to go out of them without him there goading them. It was not that his revolution was dying so much as that it had never really gotten born. His fire-breathing children. Left alone, they wandered away, lost their focus. Or maybe just grew up: Bring down the Confed? Are you crazy?

He did not doubt that it was largely his fault. The thing he had worried about, his lack of ruthless drive, that was part of it. A real revolutionary would not worry if he had to harvest lives like wheat. Martyrs, soldiers, innocent civilians, whatever it took. He had usually found a way to avoid that. Sometimes his children went out on their own, but always after he was gone, or without his knowledge. Now and again, he would firm his resolve, decide he was going to lay waste to a target and too bad about anybody that got hurt; it never happened. At the last moment, something would stop it. Always.

Often, he wondered about what his life would have been like had he found what he'd been looking for when he'd left Moon. He still dreamed of returning to Earth, to the headquarters of the order, seeing Moon again. He wrote, he felt the connection, though time had dimmed the brightness of it. At times, he thought he would simply walk away from it, climb on a ship for Earth and to hell with it all.

No. His path was hard, but he had expected no less. Had he truly thought to bring down the Confed with a few words to a few people? Had he been that naive?

Yes, he supposed he had. All right. It didn't matter. He was committed. You didn't just throw out more than two decades of effort. He'd keep going. He'd figure out something. His life was not going to be wasted.

His life was going to mean something.

Pen lay in bed next to a naked young woman who slept the sleep of one sated, if not exhausted. Idly, he stroked her hair, raising a dream-smile from her that quickly faded. She was one of the idealistic ones, mesmerized by the words of the man who spoke revolution. She wanted to warm herself with Pen's fire, and he was not averse to the idea. Each had something for the other, and it was a fair exchange. Under him, she was passionate and practiced for one so young. He had worked hard to stay with her. It had been satisfactory to them both. She slept, but he lay there awake.

There had been other lovers, Pen was not immune to that call. Lovers, but not friends. He was too deep inside his shell to permit anyone to peer in, much less join him. Sometimes he felt sparks when he lay next to a compliant woman, the desire to share his vision and himself with her. He never did. Some tried to touch him other than physically, but his defenses were too sound. There was no room for love, for a partner, for family. He took what he needed and gave what he could. The machine worked on that level, piston and receptacle, but there was only physical release without joy. He got no complaints on his technique, he was adept at knowing what went where, but he got no compliments on anything other than his technique. Sex without love, he discovered, was hollow.

As his life seemed to be hollow. The fire that had burned within him so long ago smoldered low, only a few dusty coals barely glimmering under mounds of ash. It was a worthwhile goal, he still believed that, but he was also beginning to wonder if he would ever accomplish it.

The young woman rolled toward him, still asleep, and draped one leg over his groin. She pressed against his hip, humping gently for a minute before she drifted deeper into slumber.

Pen looked at her face in the dim light of his bedroom, and for a moment, did not recall her name, nor the name of the city in which he lay. So many towns, so many worlds. He truly was tired. What if he were to wake the woman next to him and tell her of his past? Of who he had been, where he had gone, what he had done? Would she understand?

Unlikely. She was enthusiastic with her youthful body, but only time gave one experiences like his. How would she relate to Mwili or Ferret or the Pen of twenty years past? She might enjoy any one of them, but she would not be able to understand that one man could be all of them. He didn't understand it himself.

What he had given her was idealism and excitement. A cause. And she had given him her youth and sex. A fair exchange, but an empty trade, in the end.

He felt old. He had lived so many lives: a farm boy, a criminal, a drifter, a would-be priest and a revolutionary. He felt as ancient as a pharaoh's tomb, weathered by storms this—this *child* could not begin to understand. Why was he here, in this bed, in this city, on this world? Despite the woman pressed against him, he was alone, had been alone all of his life. He had always put his happiness on the back of another, he'd known that for years. Stoll. Shar Li. Moon. Von. Somebody else—or in the case of his quest to topple the Confed, some *thing* else— had always been a primary focus for him. He had always reached outside himself for approbation, for respect. For love. This had been his choice, but he wondered. Was it really for him? Or had he still been trying unconsciously to please someone else? How could a man ever know? What did it take to be sure? Even in a war, certainly there must be a way to feel some kind of inner peace?

The momentum of the thought kept it going. He remembered when Moon had told him he would have to leave. How she had said his vision was fogged, and that she was the cause. He had said then she was wrong. Now, he realized the truth of what he had said—even though his reasoning had been flawed. He had thought his eyes unscaled, when in fact he had been blind. Only it was not Moon's fault. It was his. Now that he saw it, it was so fucking simple that he couldn't understand how he had failed to see it before. Of course. He had been blind, all of his life. Even when he thought he could see, back with Von, so many years ago. Me. I'll save the galaxy, I will topple the Confed. Pen and his massive ego. He had thought himself so clear then, too.

All of his life, he had needed some one or some thing to be complete. Now as he lay in bed next to a stranger, still wrapped in the musk of their love-making, it clawed at him with cruel talons. What was it he was doing? How could he know the truth of it?

The young woman sighed in her sleep.

Pen looked at her again. There was no certainty. Not for him, not for her, not for anybody, save those few souls touched by the *Relampago*. And that might well be a delusion. No security.

He did not want to think about it. Why not, instead, wake the woman and fuck her again? That way, he wouldn't have to think. He could spend himself totally, consume the doubts with passion, and fall into an exhausted slumber. It had worked before.

He sighed. No. Not this time. Once you could see that the escape route was only a trick, you couldn't fool yourself. He needed something else. What was it? A sign from the cosmos? A chat with God?

Right, an assurance from somebody, *any*body, that what he was doing was right, was just, was a valid way to spend his years. Somebody else needed to say it.

It wasn't going to happen that way, he knew, but he also knew there was no other path for him at this point. He could only do what he had been doing for so long. He was trapped in the ship with a thick web of inertia, and there was no way to escape.

"—cannot stand by and allow the Confed's evil—"

"—up to you to resist the tyranny—"

"—future of the galaxy rests upon you—"

"—nothing to lose but your chains—"

The group on Tomadachi was more militant than many he'd worked with, and they were all hot to blow the Confed installations on the planet into plastic and metal confetti. Preferably with the troopers inside. Pen had always counseled destruction of property and not lives. Even if he was not going to be the one pulling the trigger, human life had meaning. He trotted out his trained rationalizations for them.

"A lot of troops are impress," he said to the small group of cell leaders. "They didn't ask to be dragged into the military, and they are only doing what they have to do."

That didn't fuse much reaction material with this group. Was Pen talking about war or diaper school?

"It may come to killing," he said. "But a good general picks his targets very carefully. Wipe out a few quads of draftees and you get bad publicity all around. You don't want that— you have to get the media and the public on your side." He was smooth in his argument. He'd done it before. Maybe you couldn't start a revolution without soldiers dying. Maybe it had to come to that. But not yet.

Well, they conceded, maybe he had something there.

"Of course," he continued. "Kill a few wet-faced troops and the Confed might come rolling in here with a Military Interdict, Army law, you don't want that. We are strong, but not ready to slug it out with even a ten-kay just now."

They grumbled, but agreed. But they wanted to do something dramatic. They wanted to *show* the bastards!

"All right. I have an idea . . ."

It was a variation on the first target he'd hit, one of a hundred such similar themes he had played over the years. There was a Confed storage depot on the edge of town, no weapons, just uniforms, dried foodstuffs, computers, like that. Pen convinced his cell leaders that the best way to sting the military was to hit them in the credit cube. After all, they could always replace men, but some of the supplies came from half a galaxy away. Better to have 'em running round naked, eh?

The cell leaders all laughed, save for a stone-faced boy of eighteen who used the war-name Blade. Blade wanted to blood himself, and Pen had seen enough of his like to know he'd better keep an eye on him.

Still, the plan was simple. There were guards, a quad assigned to cover the warehouse, but those four stayed near the building's entrances, mostly, and the idea was not to get inside and steal, but to destroy. A fast shuffle to the darkest wall and back, and the job would be done. He already had the necessary explosives, and all they needed was a rainy night, something easily gotten in the local semitropical region. A good electrical storm would be effective cover, and *blam!* the depot would be history.

Pen chose three leaders to accompany him. The first was pseudonymed Fire, a small, dark and intense young woman who was a college gymnast. The second, Snake, was a rotund young man of twenty who wore a full beard. The last was Blade, whippet thin and edgy. Pen wanted Blade where he could be watched, and the closer the better. He'd be leaving this world soon, and after that, Blade could get into all the trouble he wanted. Not before. Pen had not survived more than twenty years on the underside of the Confed by being careless.

The weathercast called for the needed storm the next night. In a rented room two klicks from the target, Pen went over the plan for the fourth and final time.

He dialed the holoprojic image to full brightness and gestured at the three-dimensional overhead image of the warehouse.

"All right, here we go again. Snake, where is your watch position?"

The fat man pointed to a clump of bushes a hundred meters away from the south wall of the building.

"Right. You have your transceiver?"

"Here." He waved the coin-sized earpiece.

"Fire, you and Blade are where?"

The woman stuck her finger into the image next to the east wall.

"Fine. And I'll lay the charge here." Pen pointed. "We retreat, and wait for the bang, half an hour later. Any questions?"

There were none.

"Good. The rain is supposed to start in about twenty minutes. Get dressed."

The four of them slipped one-way osmotic coveralls over their clothes. The dead-black cloth made no sound as they dressed. Each of them blackened his or her face with waterproof makeup. Around his waist, Pen strapped the pouch containing the blasting putty. He felt a little nervous, but not much. The guards would huddle under the porch roof away from the rain on the opposite end of the building from the blast. The explosion itself would wreck half the building and the rain would ruin a good part of the contents. Nobody would get hurt, and the local group would feel the sense of power that came from an active strike against the Confederation. Grist for the revolutionary mill.

Another gnat bite, another pinprick. For a second, Pen considered calling it off. The stabs of the last twenty years had all healed before leaking enough blood to cause any real damage. But this group couldn't appreciate that. They were the first to discover the wheel, the first to feel the heat of homemade fire. At least that's what they thought. They wanted their chance.

"All right. Soon as the storm starts, we move out."

The warm rain was punctuated by occasional flashes of lightning and rumbles of thunder.

Pen counted seconds. The main force of the storm's pod was several kilometers away, but it was coming down hard enough here. He lay prone under what looked like an azalea bush, feeling the water run down his neck between his cap and coverall.

Snake's voice erupted in his ear. "Okay, I'm set."

Pen adjusted the transceiver's volume downward—it wouldn't do to go deaf—and said, "Right. We're going."

A yellow cone of light pooled under the porch overhang thirty meters away, on the end of the building. Four troopers, wearing issue raingear, stood under the shelter laughing and talking. He didn't need to worry about them venturing out into the weather.

Pen waved, and Fire scrambled across the dark and muddy ground, reaching her position in a few seconds. After a beat Blade followed.

So far, so good.

Pen crawled toward his target. It was slushy going, but relatively flat ground. Whenever lightning strobed, he froze, until he was around the corner and out of the line-of-sight of the guard quad. Then he rose into a half crouch and hurried to the prefab plastic wall. He pulled the putty from his pouch and pressed it against the line of rivets that indicated a bracing beam on the other side of the wall. The water didn't affect its adhesion. Quickly, he found the timer, clicked it on, and stuck it into the putty. Thirty minutes, and . . . mark.

He grinned. There was enough adrenaline circulating so he felt a little wired. Things were moving along like a fine electronic atom separator—

The blast of a .177 Parker on full auto killed that thought. Right behind it came Snake's scream, audible without the ear transceiver Pen wore: "Oh, *shit*!"

Pen shoved away from the wall, ran to the corner, and dived, coming up in a roll, slinging mud.

Lightning flashed, and in the second of brightness, Pen took in the scene. Two of the troopers lay sprawled in the mud, half out of the light; the third and fourth members of the quad were firing into the rainy night. Facing the soldiers, his back to Pen, stood Blade. He held some kind of handgun—the weapon coughed, and Pen knew it to be a steel pellet high-pop air pistol, deadly at close range.

The lightning blinked out, and Pen ran toward Blade, who in turn was running toward the troopers. Was he fucking crazy?

Those were explosive slugs they were shooting! A single hit
would turn half the boy into mush!

Another strobe flashed. Pen saw that the third trooper was
down, and the fourth was still waving his carbine back and
forth. Blade continued sprinting straight at the last trooper.
And Fire? She was down, fallen in that rubbery boneless posture that means no muscle tone remains. Dead.

Pen ran faster as the light died. He slipped and skidded in
the mire, but kept his footing, calling on his years of movement
training. He was very nearly skiing over the mud.

The next lightning flash happened just in time to show Blade
taking the impact of several explosive bullets. The boy spun,
the air pistol flying toward Pen, not three meters back. Without
thinking, Pen caught the weapon, shifted his grip, and raised
it. His weapon instinct took him and the gun centered on the
last soldier, just as the man's carbine ran dry. The action
whined against the empty magazine.

Pen hurdled Blade's body—no doubt that he was dead, too—
and slid to a halt two meters away from the trooper. The man
crouched in the gleam of the porch light, scrabbling at his belt
for another magazine. He looked up and saw Pen within the
cone of light, the air pistol aimed at his heart.

As in a dream, Pen saw the man's face. No. Not a man. No
more than a boy, like Blade had been. Fear held the young
soldier in an icy grip, his eyes were wide, his mouth open in
a wordless scream.

Shoot him! yelled Pen's inner voice. *Kill him!*

"Please, sir!" the soldier said. He dropped the carbine and
spread his arms.

*He killed Blade and Fire! Shoot! You can't miss! Kill him!
He's the enemy! He's the fucking Confed!*

Pen's finger tightened on the trigger. Another two grams of
pressure was all it would take, a hair more—

"Oh, God, sir, please, please don't!"

It's a war, isn't it? Revolutions demand sacrifices. There were
already three like him down and dead. What would one more
matter?

*Do it! Do it! Shoot! Shoot! Hurry! Help will be coming! Kill
him kill him, killkillkillkillkill—!*

The soldier dropped to his knees, hands clasped as if in
prayer. A boy, knowing he was about to die.

Yes!

No.

Pen snapped his hand to one side, the action enough to fire the pistol. The pellet flew half a meter wide. The soldier looked up.

"No, son. Not today. Not by my hand.'"

The soldier was hyperventilating, tears streaming down his face. He tried to speak, couldn't, then fainted.

Pen tossed the pistol away, into the rainy darkness. It hit a puddle, splashing. He turned away from the terrified soldier and walked into the night. He couldn't do it. This was no faceless enemy, it was a boy who didn't want to die. He had his answer then, about how ruthless he could be.

Pen's revolution was over.

THIRTY-SIX

ODD HOW A man's life changed.

In the dark and rain of last night, Pen had been a revolutionary. Tired but still playing the game, he had gone to destroy a building. Instead he had destroyed an illusion. Another piece of one, anyway.

Ahead, the line of people moved into the orbital shuttle. A pair of Confed troopers stood behind a quad leader, watching the passengers. Occasionally, they stopped a man or woman and had words with them. The quad leader, a Sub-Lojt, kept nervously touching the butt of his holstered sidearm as he scanned the incoming line. The trooper was afraid, Pen realized. The beast had felt the sting, only for Pen, at least, it was too late.

Pen glanced at the man's gun. Until last night, he had kept his feelings about guns suppressed. He had told himself he was not attracted to them, that he did not feel the call, but he had been fooling himself. No more. Last night, the gun had sung to him again, a siren calling him to a doom no less certain than the boy Blade had brought upon himself. In the heat of the moment, he could have easily killed the soldier, it was no more than a single contraction of a finger. The gun had called, but its price was too high. He would have won the battle, but lost his soul. The truth was, he *was* in control of himself, and that was the most important thing of all. He had a choice, and he had *chosen* to override the compulsion. What had Von told him, so long ago? He might not be able to control what he felt or thought, but he could control what he *did*. That was the important thing, that was the crux of free will. Last night, he had *done* the right thing, and it didn't matter what he had *felt*—

"Your pardon, citizen."

Pen realized he was facing the quad leader. "Yes?"

"When did you book your flight offworld?"

"Early last month. Why?"

"Your name?"

"Pen."

The quad leader nodded at one of the men behind him, who punched something into a modem. After a few seconds, the soldier glanced up from the device's screen. "Three weeks ago, yesterday," the man said. "A religious discount. He's some kind of holy man."

The quad leader flashed a nervous, almost relieved smile. "Thank you for your time, citizen. You may move on."

He should be curious, Pen knew. "What's the problem, officer?"

The quad leader had already dismissed the robed figure from his attention, it seemed, and was busy scanning the next passengers. To Pen, he said, "Confederation business, reverend. Nothing to concern yourself over."

Pen moved on. Anyone who had booked a flight immediately before or after the shooting of three troopers last night would be answering harder questions, especially if they had somehow gotten past the prescreening in the main port complex. Fortunately, Pen always had a flight booked to somewhere a month in advance, just in case. It was easy to cancel or simply not show and pay the fare. Besides, the Confed had a witness—and the face the soldier would remember until his dying day was not the one Pen wore under the shroud. They weren't looking for a Sibling.

He boarded the shuttle, and found his way to his seat. The adjacent seats were empty, and Pen settled into his form-chair and looked at the seat's holoproj. The exterior pickups showed the three soldiers, watching the last of the passengers enter the craft.

Last night, seeing the soldier afraid, hearing him beg for his life, it had come to Pen with the force of a boot in the gut.

With the bodies of five humans dead in the rain and mud around him, Pen had known. This was not his path.

This was not his path.

He had been on it more than two decades, and it was an expensive lesson to find it out after that long, but it was undeniable. He was not the man to face the Confed and wage war. It was not in him to kill another man, ever again.

It had been a soul-thumping jolt. More than twenty years of his life had been spent moving in the wrong direction. The cause might be just, but he was not the man to preach it. He lacked the charisma to keep the fires burning. Yes, the Confed was intrinsically evil, but it was not so apparently so that people would risk imprisonment or death to topple it—at least not at Pen's urgings. It would take someone with more zeal than his, someone who could do whatever was necessary, no matter what the cost.

Somebody who could break eggs while smiling.

There was more. Standing there in the downpour, Pen had also understood that in making the mistakes he had made, he had learned a major thing about himself. What Moon had tried to tell him. What Von had tried to teach him. What had been there all along: he did *not* need anyone else to be whole. He didn't need a cause. He really *was* okay alone. More, until he realized that, he would never have anything to offer anybody else. Until he knew who he was, how could he give of himself to another person or some monumental effort? Knowing that he did not know was the first step. Not being attached to the desire to know was the second step.

There it was, simple and yet glorious. Not the cosmic lightning, but maybe a close enough passage of it for him to feel a static electric harmonic. He did not have to have all the answers. Hell, he didn't have to have any of them. All he could do was the best he could. Nothing else much mattered worth a damn.

So there it was. Whatever skill or luck or magic was needed to topple the Confed, he did not have it. Surprisingly, the thought did not bring with it disappointment; to the contrary, it freed him. So, he had picked the wrong path. It had cost him twenty years, and was an expensive mistake, but that was better than wasting his entire life on it. Better to learn slow than not at all.

It had given him knowledge. Maybe it had been by the process of elimination—he'd had to learn all kinds of things he was not—but some people never understood. In that tiny fraction of time, holding life and death in his hand over that soldier, having that power, something came through, and for the first time in his life, he felt complete within himself. The words he had first heard so many years past came to him:

"When you know who you are, you know what to do."

My, my. Aren't we being philosophical?

Yes. Tomorrow, he might be a different man, beset with different feelings and thoughts. That was to be expected. People changed, constantly, and certainty might well be the most ephemeral emotion of all, but there and then, in that moment, he had *known*.

He laughed softly to himself, remembering the picture that had hung on the wall of Von's zendo, on Koji. The leaping man. He knew now why the man had done it. Because he had to or he needed to or he *wanted* to. That was reason enough. Whether he had made the jump successfully, how he had gotten down, those things weren't important. There was a way the man must have known who he was, to take that risk. Even if he had been a fool, he had known. Just as Pen now knew. Damn. He felt good, as good as he had ever felt. He knew who he was, for now, at least, and so he knew what to do.

He was going back to Earth. To Manus Island. To Moon.

He had not found God, but he had found something much more important.

He had found himself.

THIRTY-SEVEN _____

COMING IN FROM orbit, the clouds were broken up enough so that he could actually see Manus Island. It looked like he remembered: a fish with a hooked nose, small turds dribbling from its rear.

Had it really been more than twenty years? How fast the time had gone. It seemed quick, but it also seemed a lifetime; he could hold both views easily.

When he stepped off the local shuttle into the tropical summer at the port on Manus, a shrouded figure stood there waiting for him. She could just as easily have been naked, for he would have recognized her through a mound of *kawa*.

"Hello, Pen."

"Hello, Moon."

He couldn't say who moved first, but a moment later, they were hugging each other tightly.

"Welcome home," she said. Her voice broke, and he very nearly started crying. The years dropped away, and she felt the same in his arms as she had the last time they had embraced.

Eons later, he pulled back and smiled at her. Arms around each other's waists, they walked slowly toward a waiting ground car.

"I don't have to walk this time?"

"Well, it's not every day a legend returns. Some of the

younger sibs wanted to stage a welcome at the port, no doubt carrying you back to the compound on their shoulders.''

''They must be thinking of somebody else.''

''You know students. They're impressed by almost anything. No one has ever walked more of the pattern on their first try than you did.''

''A bunch of slow learners.''

She hugged him to her tighter. ''I'm glad to see you,'' she said. ''You can't know how glad.''

''Yes, I can. I was afraid you might have found someone else.''

''There have been others. I have had lovers, made friends, I haven't been sitting around pining or anything. But I think we each only get one soulmate.''

He nodded. ''I think you're right.'' He smiled through his shroud, seeing her do the same beneath her own covering. ''I think I found what I was looking for.''

''I know you did.''

They reached the car. ''Oh?'' he asked. ''How so?''

''I knew you wouldn't come back until you had.''

''You always were sure of yourself.''

''Not really. I've missed you.''

''And I have missed you, Moon.''

Moon talked as she drove. ''Not much has changed. We've put a new coat of everlast on here and there. Some of the buildings have recent additions. I told you a lot of it in my letters.''

''The bonsai still growing?''

''Still are. And the wine cellar has been expanded.''

''I'm still not sure I've learned the lesson of patience you tried to teach me doing those chores.''

''You've learned something. There's a solidity in you that wasn't there before.''

He laughed. ''It only took a score of years for me to figure it out. I wonder what the new students would think about that, speaking of slow learners.''

''Better late than never.''

He reached over and put his hand on her leg just above the knee and massaged her gently. When he spoke, the essence of twenty years was in his voice. All of them boiled down into one simple statement: "That's what I found out—better late than never."

The place hadn't changed all that much. Some of the shrubbery was taller and thicker, some of the buildings a different hue than he recalled, and there were some additions. The feel of the compound was the same. Except for the lack of insects. He said something about it to Moon.

"A project from the biolab," she said. "A few years ago, one of the more creative students got the idea to breed mules for most of the bug pests native to the island. Souped-up their pheromones so the local females would breed with them exclusively. He left the bees and beetles and ants alone. A year later, we shut down the repellors, except for the weather. Every now and then, somebody cranks out a new lot of sterile bugs and turns 'em loose. It seems to be working."

Thunder rumbled in the distance as they pulled into the fenced compound. Moon waved at the gate guard.

"Hear from Von?" Pen said.

"Now and again. He's still on Koji, helping to keep the Confed interference there to a minimum. He's come back to visit a few times."

Pen turned that thought over in his mind. Nope. It didn't bother him. What he'd felt for Moon before had not been real love. Being "in love," having a romantic fixation that was more an addiction than anything else was not the same as truly loving somebody. You had to be standing on fairly solid ground to think that way. For the moment, at least, the earth felt firm enough beneath his boots, physically and spiritually.

"Glad to hear it."

Moon pulled the car to a halt. The two of them alighted. Moon walked toward the barracks, and Pen followed her.

She went to her room.

Inside, she said, "There are a lot of things we need to talk about. We've had a breakthrough in integratic science. There are things happening, big things."

As she spoke, she began to disrobe. "But we can talk later."

Pen grinned, and began to remove his own shroud. He pulled his hood off, so she could see his smile. "Yes," he said. "Talking later is a good idea."

The years had been kind to her, he saw. Her hair was gray,

but her muscles still remained firm; her skin was wrinkled some but still clear and ghostly pale. Protection from the sun and weather had its benefits. Her nose was still slightly crooked, her mouth a hair too wide, and she was still beautiful. Older, yes, but still Moon.

When he touched her, it was as if he had never been away. At the same time, it was like the first time he had ever felt her body next to his.

They stood pressed nakedly against each other for a moment. Then, in a move he never expected, she picked him up in her arms and carried him to the bed, dropped him, and then fell on top of him. Talk would come later, but right now, laughter was fine.

It was all just fine.

He could not keep from touching her, even after he was completely drained sexually. He leaned his hip against hers, raised himself onto one elbow and draped his leg over her, twining with her legs. Gods, how good she felt!

For her part, Moon seemed as glad to be with him.

"We have some catching up to do," he said. He bent and kissed her hair. It looked terrific gray.

"Yes. We'll have awhile before . . ." She stopped, letting the last word trail off.

"Before what?"

"Nothing. Are you hungry?"

"Not in the least."

"We should go out. The others will want to see you."

"They can wait."

"Well, aside from the new students, there's Agate."

"Still tending the bonsai?"

"Yes." She paused for a beat, then smiled at him. "And Spiral."

"Spiral is here? I thought sure he'd be off taming some frontier planet somewhere."

"He's about ready to become Elder Brother."

Pen blinked at her. "Spiral? Are you planning on retiring?"

"In a manner of speaking. He's better qualified than any of us, Pen. He's been touched by the *Relampago*, has been burning with the cosmic fire for years."

"Good old Spiral." Pause. "Where are you going?"

"There are a lot of things that need to be done. I'll show you later."

He smiled at her. "Look, I know there are people out there, but do you suppose we could just lie here and hold hands for a little while longer?"

She returned his smile with a grin of her own. "I guess we could manage that."

"Hey?"

"Um?"

"I love you, Moon. For the right reasons, this time."

"I know. I love you, too. I always have."

Later, Pen and Moon went out, and he was introduced to new siblings and reintroduced to those he'd known before. He hadn't realized how good it would feel to actually be here again.

He sensed Spiral approaching before he saw him. He caught Moon watching him carefully as he turned to see the source of the energy he felt warming the already hot afternoon air. His HSP was stronger than ever before. It wasn't just Moon, he knew. It was him.

"Ah, Pen."

"Spiral!"

The two men embraced, and Pen felt the warmth grow hotter. It was not a physical sensation so much as an awareness on a psychic level. Spiral did indeed burn with some kind of spiritual glow. Hard to say exactly what it was, he didn't shine like a candle or anything, but there it was, for certain.

Spiral pulled back and smiled beneath his shroud. "You've changed, Pen. For the better."

"Looks like you have too, friend. Ever learn how to do Flower Unfolding properly?"

Spiral shook his head. "Your memory is as bad as ever."

"Your foot was crooked."

"I confess that it was," Spiral said, laughing. "The least of my many errors."

Spiral had changed, all right. Pen felt the lack of ego about the man, the same energy he had noticed about Babaji and other holy souls he'd met over the years. A childlike bearing and innocence, a high optimism.

"Moon tells me you are about to become Elder Brother."

"Well, for a short while, at least."

"Already grooming a replacement? You aren't *that* old."

"I confess also that worldly matters are concerning me less and less. I'll be a caretaker for a year or two for the next Elder Brother."

"Anybody I know?"

"You, of course."

Pen stared at him. "Me? That's a good one."

"No less than the truth."

Pen turned to look at Moon. She said, "I told you big things were happening."

Pen thought about it. All right. He could live with that. He did not have to hide behind his ego to know he was qualified, and probably better than most. Sure. No problem. He *was* learning.

"Come on. You've been wandering in the wilderness a long time, my love. It's time you learned what we've been up to while you were gone."

One of the additions to the auditorium was a full-scan holoproj room. It was, Moon told him as they entered the dimly lit space, tied into a superframe viral matrix computer complex orbiting Earth near L-5 prime. A very bright computer, she said, and very fast. For years, the Siblings had been programming integratic calculations into the complex. The programs were coded, of course, so that a Confederation check would show something vaguely consistent with the stated programs of history, business and what-not. But the electrochemviral brain was producing results. Crunching several billion bits of information every second, it had come up with some very interesting data.

"This is Moon," she said to the empty room. "Give us the latest scan on Project Savior. Visual graphics for climax point, please."

The air lit with a swirl of bright colors that snapped into sharp focus. A graph appeared, spiky peaks rising from a flat table, the tops increasing in height in a kind of inward spiral toward the center. The innermost peak jutted twice the height of the pointed fingers surrounding it.

A second projection flicked into life, smaller, but no less bright. It was a stellar system, three planets orbiting a G-class star. Even at this magnification, the detail was fine enough to show several moons and a blinking dot that must represent a wheelworld.

A third graphic flowered in the air. This was a two-dimensional chart that showed the first graph superimposed over the second.

"What are we looking at?" Pen said.

"Watch. Focus and fix," she said.

The third graphic expanded, showing a close-up of a single planet. The viewpoint pushed in, moved closer, and stopped.

"Give us geographics," Moon said.

The image flashed, and names of cities, roads, mountains and rivers appeared as a map grid lit up an area perhaps the size of Australia.

Moon turned to Pen. "This is the planet Maro," she said. "The major populated subcontinent. We have it this close. The image shifts minutely each day, but we haven't pinpointed the city yet."

"Excuse my ignorance, but just what are we talking about?"

"Project Savior. All our projections add up to this, Pen. On this planet, this continent, somewhere, in the next month—plus or minus seven days—the focal point in the galactic balance is going to appear."

"Really? You are that sure?"

"We're that sure, my love. Three to five weeks from today, somebody is going to be down there who could affect the course of the entire galaxy. We think it'll be the man you were trying to be for so long."

Pen stared at the projection. Had integratics come to this at last? It was a pretty specific prediction.

"Wait a second. You said 'could' affect things."

"Yes. What happens to that person will determine if 'could' turns into 'will.' It might be that the wave recedes. All we have is raw data, and there is no guarantee that the probabilities will become reality. There are a number of ways to interpolate them. In one, the Confed grows stronger, overwhelmingly so, and endures for at least another five hundred years."

"That's some crystal ball, Moon."

"In another scenario, whoever it is that appears at the apex of our integratic projection could possibly bring down the Confederation to a virtual halt within a quarter of a century."

"Jesu damn," Pen said softly. "I tried to do it for twenty years and never even scratched the paint."

"Exactly."

"I wasn't the man. You say somebody there will be?"

"If our calculations are correct. We could be wrong."

"You don't think so."

"No, my love."

Pen watched the projection. Magic, to be able to tell the future, or at least come up with a good guess.

"And what are we supposed to do about this person?"

Moon looked at him. "Find him or her. Teach them whatever they need to know. Guide them. Help them in any way we can."

"Do we know what will replace the Confed if it falls?"

"Not yet. We're working on that."

He laughed. "The impossible takes until lunch?"

"Something like that."

"So that's where you're going," Pen said. "That's why Spiral is taking over your job."

"No, Pen. My path lies elsewhere."

"Then who—" He stopped, understanding what she meant. Exactly what she meant. A year ago, even a week ago, he would not have known. He knew now.

"Me."

"You are figured into our calculations, Pen. You always have been."

"Seems as if you took a hell of a risk, planning on one man for this all these years. Especially given what you had to work with."

"Perhaps; but we took the risk and it paid off."

He nodded, not speaking. He had grown up some.

"Here you are. You have the tools. You know your path is not to oppose the Confed with a gun, but you have the teaching experience, the skills, the desire. And you aren't attached to it personally, as you once were. What we have done is to find you a worthy student.

"Think about it, Pen. To know your student might do more to help people than any one man in history. He or she might be the person who changes a galaxy."

"It's a big 'might.' "

"There aren't any guarantees. You must have learned that by now."

Pen looked at the projection. Yes. He had learned that, along with so much else.

"Well?"

"Well, what?"

"Are you going to do it? Go and find this person and teach them?"

Here was a question of some significance. Are you, Pen, formerly Ferret, formerly Mwili, the man to teach the would-be savior how to save the galaxy? How to bring the Confed down? Are you willing to shelve your ego and play second to this person, whoever he or she is? There will not be any personal glory attached to it, you know. No statues dedicated to Pen the savior. Likely as not, nobody will even know, save Moon and a few others. Can you do it? Do you *want* to do it? Is this your place, after all this time?

Well? Is it?

Pen grinned at the projection, then turned to face his soulmate.

Yeah. I think it is. That's good enough.

"Of course." He shook his head. "Did you ever really have any doubt?"

"It was always your choice, my love. That was always the point of it for you."

"You knew what I would choose."

"I had a suspicion. A hope."

"Isn't life strange," he said, extending one hand toward her.

Moon caught his hand in hers and laughed softly. "Isn't it just?"

THIRTY-EIGHT _____

ON THE STARLINER to Maro, Pen noticed a group of Confederation officials bending their way to an earlier stop in the same system. A factor and two senators from Earth, he gathered from their conversation, a trialog none of them bothered to keep private—or quiet. Each of the dignitaries was worth a quad of bodyguards, sharp-eyed men and women dressed in working black, gazes constantly roving the other passengers for any sign of trouble. Also traveling with the officials was a phalanx of crack-sharp troopers, resplendent in their full dress uniforms, sidearmed and all polished plastic and drill field snappiness, swaggering about the ship looking for mischief.

Pen mostly avoided them, nodding and greeting them politely when he could not. He did not want trouble, not at this point.

The men and women of the Confed contingent also wore an arrogance, as visible as their uniforms, as loud as their self-satisfied laughter. Perhaps one could not blame them. They were part of the most powerful machine in the known galaxy, the chosen who could not be touched by the lowly. They were like the ancient Ksatriya caste, the warriors, or perhaps the Brahmins, the priests, rulers of all they beheld. To them, everyone else was below—sudra or pariah, it did not matter. It had been that way for hundreds of years, and no reason why it shouldn't go on for hundreds more.

Pen wondered what they would think if they knew that a threat to their power was about to come into being. A focal point for the entire system to fear, should it come to pass as the Siblings thought it might.

The coarse laugh of one of the Confed officials reached Pen, as the man nudged his companion and pointed at an attractive woman passing them. The two men snickered like adolescents sharing a smutty joke. Little doubt they were doing just that.

As the woman came abreast of Pen, he could see her face was flushed with anger and embarrassment. Probably she was safe, if she just ignored them and kept on about her business. But she had to know that any—or all—of the Confed arrogants who smirked at her could drag her into a cabin or take her right here, and she would have little recourse. They had the power and there was little anyone would or could do to stop them, if it came to that.

The woman's voice was low when she spoke, so it did not carry far. Just loud enough for Pen to hear.

"I wish somebody would do something about those idiots."

Beneath his hood, Pen smiled. "Perhaps someone will," he said, also sotto voce.

The woman looked up, and managed a small smile. "Now there's a pleasant thought," she said.

Indeed, Pen thought.

Indeed.

THIRTY-NINE

ON-MARO:

Pulling at Pen was a feeling of impending something that made his path easy. A distant warmth called to him, and he had but to follow it to find that which he sought. Never had his higher perceptive aspect worked better.

He rented a ground craft and began driving it toward the energy he could feel.

There was also trouble brewing on Maro. Confed troopers were in evidence on nearly every major road. The rumor was that the local priesthood was about to spark a holy war. That must be part of it, Pen knew. Maro might not be a pleasant place to be in the near future, but that didn't matter to Pen. He had survived a long time without knowing why. Now, he had a reason.

He smiled to himself, and went to find his destiny.

About time, but, hey, better late than never.

FORTY

THE CITY WAS called Notzeerath, and there was a human cosmic furnace radiating within it somewhere.

To Pen, it was like a bonfire in the middle of a snowy plateau. Anyone with the slightest sensitivity to such energies could not fail to at least notice it.

Pen walked down a crowded street. This was a city of believers in the cycle of reincarnation, albeit some of the faithful were half-hearted. Otherwise, many of them would no longer be in their present incarnations—on the plains a few kilometers from here, three-quarters of a million people had died only days earlier, directed by a manic priest fueled with hatred of the Confed or some god-inspired madness driving him. Those had surely been believers, for they had marched smiling into the jaws of destruction, never wavering. Pen had not seen it, but he had seen the results. There were bodies piled two meters high in places on that bloody plain. So senseless. So much waste. And yet somehow, all those deaths had produced the final conversion in Pen's quarry.

It was an expensive price to pay.

He had paid his own price, of course, years of wasted effort but compared to dying, it was little enough. He had wandered as Moon had said, in the wilderness, looking for something. Now, here, the time had finally come to find it.

When you know who you are, you know what to do? his inner

voice asked, a voice now filled with laughter instead of dread. It had what *it* wanted, finally. Truth—and truth is the defense against fear. Pen had not known it for far too long, but finally, he did. Better late than never at all.

"Yes," Pen said aloud. "Absolutely."

Well, let's go and find this furnace who is going to heat up the galaxy, shall we?

"Yes. Let's go and do that."

Pen felt the glow of his pupil-to-be shining through the morning as he walked in the bright sunlight. Various alcohol- and electrically-powered vehicles rolled on hard plastic tires along the smooth streets, humming intermittent Oms that overlaid the constant thrum of the local broadcast generator he could feel under his boots; pedestrians and scooterists went about their business, walking and scooting along; most were unconscious of the God-touched one in their midst. Not all, for Pen could see people turn with a puzzled look now and then, in the direction of the energy flow most could not feel. They did not know what, but they knew *some*thing unusual was happening. Confed quads marched here and there as well, weapons slung for fast action, eyes and ears alert.

Pen rounded a corner and stopped, as if hitting an invisible wall. There. Just ahead. There he was.

A man, young, dressed in a thin and ragged coverall, his feet bare, stood on the street staring into infinity. He looked to be a soldier, from his issue clothing and his bearing. Some irony there, perhaps. A man roasting in the fire of cosmic consciousness, holy, but undirected, and one of the Confed's own. At least he *had* been one of them. But no more. Now, what he needed was a teacher.

He needed Pen.

Feeling almost overwhelmed by emotion, Pen approached the young man. His heart speeded up, and his breathing started to come faster. He slowed his walk and breathing. Easy, Pen. Still, it bubbled joyously in him, and it was all he could do to keep from dancing. Here was what he had been preparing for nearly all of his life. It no longer mattered that he, Pen, was not going to be the hinge upon which the fate of civilized man turned. He understood truly for the first time what his role was to be, and knowing one's place was more important than the place itself. Such a simple thing, and yet it had taken him a lifetime to learn. All great truths were simple, and that was both great and true itself.

He was not going to be mankind's savior. But he *was* going to be the savior's teacher. It was a fine place to be. For him, the only place to be.

Here was the moment: Pen remembered what Von had said to him, decades past. It would serve as well now as it had then:

"Lost, pilgrim?" Pen said.

The young man refocused himself back into the physical world with visible effort. It must be hard to come back to *Maya* when one was living in Paradise. He smiled at Pen. "Lost? No. I don't know where I am, but I'm not lost."

Under his concealing mask, Pen's smile was radiant, nearly matching that of the younger man. The proper response, of course. He laughed. "A zen answer, pilgrim, and perfect for a holy man. Have you been such long?"

"I'm not a holy man. Until a few days ago, I was a soldier. Something . . . happened. I . . . saw something, felt something, somehow. A vision."

Pen nodded. He would have to explain things to this man simply, for despite his new-found power, this soldier was a child. Well, it was time for his work to begin, finally. Pen said, "Ah. *Relampago*. You are blessed, pilgrim." He smiled at the man's blank look.

Blessed: You have felt the cosmic fire I wanted to feel for so long. It was only when I gave up trying so hard to get it that it finally became possible for me. I have not basked in its glow as you have, but now, I have a purpose. It's a start.

Blessed: Knowing your place is more important than the place itself, I finally understand that.

Blessed: Knowing who you are gives you a freedom. You have felt the cosmic allness, and so you know in a way that is not possible for me to know. Someday, perhaps, but that's not important, not really.

Yes, you are blessed, young soldier. And after all these years, finally, so am I.

The young man stared at him, uncomprehending, and Pen smiled beneath his shroud. Time to go to work, Pen.

Time to go to work at last.

APPENDIX _____

THERE ARE FIFTY-SIX inhabited worlds by the beginning of the *Declination* in 2295, in twenty-three stellar systems. There are also some eighty-seven wheelworlds either in planetary or stellar orbits throughout the systems, and a number under construction.

The stellar systems are:

1. Solar
2. Centauri
3. Beta
4. Mu
5. Nu
6. Tau
7. Ceti
8. Omicron
9. Delta
10. Pigme
11. CinqueKirli
12. Sto
13. Haradali
14. Shin
15. Heiwa
16. Faust
17. Orm
18. Kar
19. Bruna
20. Nazo
21. Bibi Arusi
22. Svare
23. Ndama

Inhabited planets, including terraformed and domed colonies, by system:

Sol
1. Earth/Luna
2. Mars
3. Titan
4. Venus
5. Pluto (ten-person grid station only)

Centauri
6. Alpha Point (Mason)
7. PrimeSat (Largest of three moons orbiting Mason)

Beta
8. Stub
9. Harlan
10. Kaplan
11. Golstein
12. Rim

Mu
13. Spandle

Nu
14. 313-C (Ohshit)

Tau
all moons of Shiva, the gas giant
15. Krishna
16. Brahma
17. Vishnu (the pleasure world)

Ceti
18. Baszel

Omicron
19. Raft

Delta
20. Thompson's Gazelle
21. Rift
22. Lee

Pigme
23. Fox

CinqueKirli
24. Tembo
25. Simba(.)Numa

Sto
26. Aqua

Haradali
27. Wu
28. Tatsu

Shin
29. San Yubi
30. Tomadachi
31. Shin
32. Hadiya
33. Renault
34. Gebay

Heiwa
35. Koji (the Holy World)

Faust
36. Bocca
37. Ago's Moon

Orm
38. Greaves

Kar
39. Makaroni

Bruna
40. Farbis
41. Pentr'ado
42. Lagomustardo
43. Muta Kato

Nazo
44. Nazo
45. Kontrau'lega (Omega)
46. Maro

Bibi Arusi
47. Mwanamamke
48. Mtu
49. Rangi ya majani Mwezi (the Green Moon)

Svare
50. Kalk ⎫
51. Jatra ⎪
52. Vul ⎬ Moons of Kalk
53. Cibule ⎪
54. Zena ⎭

Ndama
55. Dirisha
56. Mti

Most of the wheelworlds—a generic term for any self-contained space habitat in a permanent orbit around a star, planet or moon—are located in the nine major systems. (These are: Sol, Centauri, Beta, Shin, Bruna, Nazo, Bibi Arusi, Svare and Delta.) However, there are wheelworlds in most of the other stellar systems.

The ten most important of the artificial worlds and the stars, planets or moons around which they orbit are:

1. L-5 Segundo (Earth/Sol)
2. Robert E. Lee (Earth/Sol)
3. Alpha Sub (Mason/Centauri)
4. Golda (Rim/Beta)
5. Rift II (Rift/Delta)
6. Chiisai Tomadachi (Tomadachi/Shin)
7. Malgrand Luno (Farbis/Bruna)
8. Gardo (Kontrau'lega/ Nazo)
9. Jicha Mungo (Mtu/Bibi Arusi)
10. Volny (stellar orbit, Svare)

Of these, L-5 Segundo is the largest in population, housing some 685,000 men or mues. Robert E. Lee is the largest in actual size, with an external diameter of 51.2 kilometers, but a population of only 345,000. Gardo is the smallest, hardly larger than a starliner, but self-contained and able to support a population of 250.

The Ninety-Seven Steps _____

THE MAIN DANCE of Sumito, The Ninety-seven Steps, is composed of an interconnected series of nineteen shorter dances. These movements (sometimes called *kata*) range from a single step to as many as ten. While Diamond is credited with the creation of Sumito, it was in fact the original Pen who aligned and formalized the dances, and who gave them their somewhat colorful names.

In order, the dances are:

1. The Thousand Klick Journey
2. The Flower Unfolding
3. Dark Shroud
4. Twisted Star
5. Snake and Spider
6. Magician's Hands
7. Cold Fire Burns Bright
8. Helicopter
9. Laughing Stone
10. Fleur de Lance
11. Bamboo Pond
12. Arc of Air
13. The Braided Laser
14. Sword of the Sun
15. The Neon Chain
16. The Vacuum Cage
17. Steel Circle
18. Spiral
19. Mimosa Sleeps Softly